Faith and Ruin

The Dawn of Reckoning

Faith and Ruin
Book 1

Amanda and Rory Webb

Illustrated by
Amanda Webb

Faith and Ruin Book 1: The Dawn of Reckoning. Copyright © 2025 by Amanda and Rory Webb

All rights reserved.

This is a work of fiction. Names, characters, places, and incidents are products of the authors' imaginations or are used fictitiously and are not to be construed as real. Any resemblance to actual events, locales, organizations, or persons, living or dead, is entirely coincidental.

No part of this story may be reproduced, distributed, or transmitted in any form or by any means, including photocopying, recording, or other electronic or mechanical methods, without the prior written permission of the publisher, except in the case of brief quotations embodied in reviews and certain other noncommercial uses permitted by copyright law. For permission requests, write the author and publisher, subject "Attention: Permissions Requests" at mandapandarawks@gmail.com

NO AI TRAINING: Without in any way limiting the authors' exclusive rights under copyright, any use of this publication to "train" generative artificial intelligence (AI) technologies to generate text is expressly prohibited. The authors reserve all rights to license uses of this work for generative AI training and development of machine learning language models.

Book cover and interior illustrations by Amanda Webb

Calligraphy by Annie Moriondo

Decorative frames on Character Portraits, Pronunciation Guide, and Maps by Century Designs

Map designed by Rory Webb

Edited by Anna P

First edition Feb. 26 2026

Library of Congress Control Number: 2025927876

Copyright © 2025 by Amanda and Rory Webb

www.legendsofaukera.com

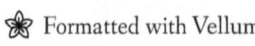 Formatted with Vellum

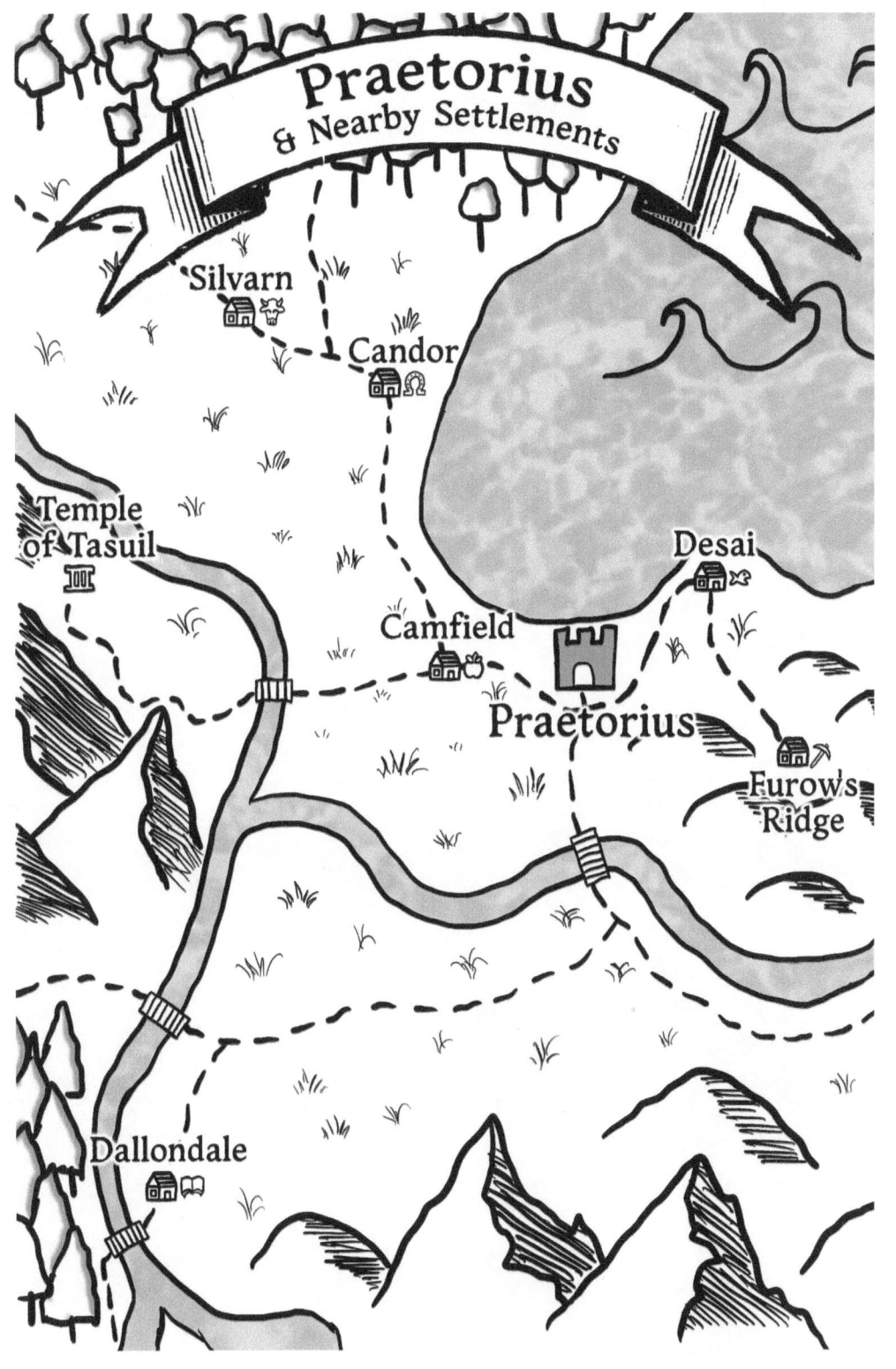

The Plenum of Praetorius

King Philemon Selderin
Monarch of Praetorius

Princess Alandria Selderin

Chancellor Tripp Eldivar

Lord Bashir Rendevas
Senior Diplomat

Captain Percival Riluk

Commander Rickard Rakeld

Lieutenant Sondrela Orvessa

The Plenum of Praetorius

Judge Jeremy Rodach

Constable Grenden Mald

Lady Uunar Urielle
Headmistress
of the Arcane Academy

Lady Avindea
Church of Vidamae

Lady Loresh Fontaine
Church of Velthunas

Lord Eglath Ver Trellior
Church of Thulkas

Pronunciation Guide

A note on pronunciations: this is a guideline for anyone who wants to know how we say these names. If you pronounce them differently due to cultural or language differences, that is perfectly fine! We wanted to provide a cheatsheet just in case any readers are curious.

Characters

Aisling: ASH-ling
Avindea: ay-vin-DEE-uh
Daryèr: dar-YAIR
Ghdion: GID-ee-un
Hypnocost: HIP-nuh-cost
Lucius: LOO-shus
Midori: mid-OHR-ee
Orvessa: or-VAY-suh
Quay: KWAY
Rakieos: ruh-KAY-ohs
Rakeld: ruh-KELD
Rendevas: REN-dah-vahs
Riluk: RYE-luk
Rodach: ROH-dak
Solange: suh-LONJ
Uunar: oo-NAR

Deities

Castor: KAS-tor
Demos: DEE-mohs
Dolgamar: DOAL-guh-mar
Ezraèal: ez-ray-AL
Galara: guh-LAR-uh
Jorah: JOR-uh
Kax: KAX
Nahal: nuh-HAWL
Thulkas: THUL-kiss
Velthunas: vel-THOO-niss
Vidamae: VEE-duh-may
Xandriasis: zan-dree-AY-sis

Locations

Arcaithos: ar-KAY-thohs
Aukera: AWK-er-uh
Desai: des-EYE
Khamris: KAHM-rees
Praetorius: pray-TOR-ee-us
Tasuil: TAHS-oo-eel
Uldinvelm: UL-din-velm
Vostrum: VAW-strum

Misc.

Theurgist: THEE-ur-jist

Chapter 1

Poor Edmund Brisby

"Well, shit." Ghdion scowled at the body at his feet.

It wasn't the first dead body he'd seen, nor was it likely to be the last. He did know, without a doubt, that it was definitely going to cause him no end of problems for the foreseeable future.

"Language!" Quay tittered behind him in a singsong voice. She picked her way delicately past the congealing pool of old blood beneath the body, clutching at the holy symbol around her neck as if it could offer her some kind of solace. She knelt beside the man's unmoving form, placing a light touch along his throat and chest. Checking for signs of life, he knew, which was very Quay. That was just her way. The man was obviously dead, and even the ministrations of a Priestess-in-training of Vidamae, Goddess of Life and Light, couldn't do anything about that.

He shifted aside, nearly overturning one of the pews that lined the tiny, one-room Chapel of Vidamae. Daylight filtered through the stained glass windows behind the altar, casting a rainbow of reflections across the empty nave. Joyous scenes of the beloved goddess were depicted in cut glass—Vidamae, portrayed as a pale nude woman with coiling red hair, her hands outstretched as beams of holy light spread from her fingers, the upturned faces of worshippers looking upon her visage in awe. The cut glass tableau clashed wildly with the bloody robed body lying still on the floor.

Quay pushed her long, dark hair out of her face and moved the dead man on his side to check if he was breathing. His head lolled into view. She let out a sharp gasp.

She's gonna start crying again, he thought with chagrin. Not only was she entirely too soft, *he* was always the one who had to comfort her. Not that he minded so much, but Ghdion—tall, broad-shouldered, covered in scars and tattoos—was anything but reassuring.

She glanced up at him with her soulful, shining gray eyes. "I know this man!" she said in a watery voice. "This is Edmund Brisby. We trained together back in Praetorius."

Ghdion opened his mouth to say—what? *"I'm sorry your friend was murdered?" I don't get paid enough to deal with this shit.* "Priestess, I'm—"

He was saved from responding by stomping footsteps and rough grumbling from the doorway. Two men—one tall and dark haired with a large burn scar covering half of his face, the other a willowy, pale half-elf with tattoos on his bald head—entered the dimly lit church. "You were right, Ghdion," Lucius, the scarred man, said in his somehow-always-cheerful voice. "Phyllis and Benj are both dead. Slit throats."

Lucius raked a shaking hand behind his neck, causing his shaggy black hair to stick up crazily in the back. "Gods, this is such a mess. Hypnocost and I found them both leaned against the wall outside, posed as if they were just sleeping on the job. Who the hells would do such a thing?"

Hypnocost, the half-elf, stepped up behind him. "Whoever these murderers are, they are professionals to be sure. We almost missed the fact that the two guards were dead in the first place."

Both Lucius and Hypnocost laid eyes upon the unfortunate priest's mangled body. Edmund Brisby's throat had been cut, too; the front of his golden priest robes was sheeted with dark blood, and the skin at his neck was so mutilated it barely looked human.

Quay let out a soft sob. They both had the decency to look at least somewhat uncomfortable.

"Gods dammit," Ghdion mumbled under his breath, kneeling beside her. He turned Edmund Brisby's bloody face aside so she wouldn't have to look at it any longer.

"Hey," he muttered quietly to the priestess, "it's gonna be okay."

"No, it's *not* gonna be okay!" Quay huffed, taking her hands from her tear-stained cheeks and gesturing wildly towards dearly departed Edmund. Her lower lip quivered. "He's *dead*! Edmund is *dead*! He was my friend! Who would do such a thing? Why? And to a Priest of Vidamae—!" She wiped at her eyes furiously and regarded Lucius and Hypnocost. "And now you tell me the town guards were murdered, too?"

Well, this wasn't going to plan. Not by a longshot.

This was *supposed* to be an easy gig. When Quay—in training to be the youngest Priestess of Vidamae in Praetorius because of her phenomenal skills with healing magic—hired Ghdion last year as her bodyguard, she had explained to him that his primary focus was to make sure she could travel the roads of Khamris unmolested. As the next step of her training, she was required to visit each of the Vidamae Churches in their sprawling country of fertile farmland, whether they be tiny, one-room steeples or sweeping, elegant shrines to her goddess. Her task was to provide whatever aid she could, whether it be in the form of food and supplies—courtesy of the very rich and very popular Church of Vidamae—or by using her impressive healing magic for any who needed it, free of charge.

Khamris was not a small country, and even though most people knew better than to mess with a priestess of the goddess whose sole purpose was to provide care to those less fortunate, it was still foolish for an innocent, fresh-faced, beautiful young woman to be traveling the roads alone. So she did what any woman fortunate enough to be backed by a wealthy and powerful church would do: hired a bodyguard.

That was him. Ghdion. *He* was the bodyguard, and more fool him for continuing to go along with what was rapidly becoming a capital S-Shitshow. Dealing with murdered priests was *not* supposed to be in his job description.

For the past year, Ghdion and Quay had been doing mind-numbingly boring runs back and forth from one backwoods town or another to Praetorius, capital city of Khamris. They were armed with a wagon full of food and blankets and churchy stuff, like candles and ... honestly, he had no idea what other religious things were in the care packages Quay assembled for each town. Mertha, Aukera's slowest ox, pulled their wagon, and his days were filled with wrangling the stubborn, shaggy white bovine and listening to Quay's relentlessly boundless optimism.

At first, he was alarmed by how *upbeat* she always was, constantly prattling away about whatever new topic struck her fancy, or writing her endless letters to all of the friends she made on their travels. But she didn't expect much from him; all he had to do was grunt and nod in the right places when she really got to talking.

Those days of lazy travel had been relatively quiet. Relaxing, even. He only had to scowl and rattle his sword to scare off any would-be brigands: his tall, muscular build, many, many battle scars, constantly glowering face, and huge two-handed sword were enough to make any criminal think twice about harassing them. The two of them worked well together, and they fell into an easy rhythm.

And then Quay went and hired *another* bodyguard. That bodyguard was Hypnocost, a very persnickety, bald-headed, eyebrows-always-up-on-his-forehead-because-he-looked-down-on-everyone mage who didn't cast spells like any Ghdion had ever seen before. (Seriously, they were creepy. Like shadowy tentacles and mind-reading kind of creepy.) Two became three, and Ghdion was stuck having to play nice with Aukera's most insufferable mage.

Hypnocost sniffed haughtily at the body of Edmund Brisby, may he rest in peace or travel with Vidamae's angels or some shit; Ghdion didn't exactly know how the Vidamae people prayed. (Which was somewhat troubling since he was literally employed by one of Her priestesses.)

"He has not been dead long," Hypnocost announced in a tone that evoked a professor lecturing to a room full of idiot students. "In theory, judging by the size and relative viscosity of the pool of blood, I would say he was terminated less than an hour ago."

Hypnocost was always saying things like, 'in theory' or 'terminated' or 'viscosity' instead of regular-people words like, "Hey, I think this guy has only been dead for a little while!"

"The killers might still be in town!" Lucius cried. Without waiting for an answer, he ran right back out of the church, pulling his longsword and shield out as he went.

Now Lucius was the kind of guy Ghdion could get behind. He was also a Sword Guy—rather, a Sword and Shield Guy, to be specific. He was friends with Priest Edmund Brisby, and had given them a tour of the town after they arrived yesterday. Lucius was tall and lean, dark haired and with a dark complexion, and had the athletic build typical of a soldier. He had an easy demeanor about him, always smiling and joking.

What really stood out about him was the huge burn scar that covered the entire left side of his face and body. It was hard not to gawk at something like that. Whatever hellish fire caused it made half of his face a wrinkled, angry shade of pink; the left eye was completely colorless, the matching eyebrow pure white. Ghdion and Quay had the decency not to mention it during their introductions, but he had been forced to nudge Hypnocost hard in the ribs to prevent him from blurting out, "What happened to your *face?*"

Which brought them to the here and now and the quickly unraveling debacle that was Ghdion's life.

"Godsdammit, Hypnocost," Ghdion growled. The half-elf merely stood there, eyeing the dead body with polite interest. Ghdion gestured towards Lucius's retreating form, exasperation apparent on his face."Go after him!"

Hypnocost gave him an annoyed look before half-heartedly jogging away. *What a useless fucking bodyguard*, he thought, helping Quay to her feet. She brushed the dirt from her pale lilac priestess robes and made to follow, but Ghdion, looming a full head and shoulders taller than the petite woman, stepped in her way.

"Oh, no." He crossed his muscular arms, the multicolored reflections of light from the windows playing across the dozens of tiny black dot tattoos that covered his left arm from shoulder to wrist. They were a relic from his admittedly tumultuous past; Hypnocost had asked him about them once, a few days after they'd met, but he only glared and told the half-elf to mind his own business. "We're not doing *that thing* again where you rush off into danger, Priestess."

Quay had a knack for finding the most dangerous and most *bizarre* situations and inserting herself—and by extension, *him*—into them. For instance, in one of the villages they visited—a backwoods hamlet near the coast called Little Rushford, implying there was a Big Rushford?—she somehow managed to stumble into an illegal demonic pig-fighting ring. Quay, naturally horrified by such inhumane treatment against the poor swine, stormed right into the thick of it, forcing him to have to rush after her to make sure she wasn't hurt in the process. They eventually set all the pigs free, except for Princess, the huge demon-touched sow who turned on them. Everyone in Little Rushford ate bacon for weeks afterwards.

It was remarkable how she could roll her eyes so sarcastically after sobbing uncontrollably only a few moments ago. "What else are we supposed to do? You want to let Lucius and Hypnocost rush off into danger instead?"

"Yes! That is literally what you pay Hypnocost to do for you."

She made a little *tchk*! noise.

"I'm your bodyguard." He grunted and crossed his arms. "It's my job to keep you safe. I take my job seriously."

She faltered, glancing down at Edmund Brisby, may his soul find peace in Vidamae's endless embrace. (That was the actual prayer. He winced in a moment of very familiar regret at remembering the words.) "I suppose you're right," she sighed, brushing her long brown hair out of her eyes. "I have to perform last rites and get Edmund buried. It's the least I can do for him."

Ghdion sensed a long day of digging up dirt for a fresh grave in his future. With a sigh, he went to look for a shovel.

Chapter 2

The Plenum

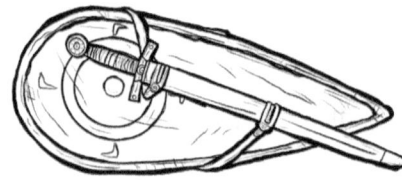

Avindea took a deep breath and, with more than a little bit of trepidation, stepped inside the plenum chamber.

The council chamber of the Plenum of Praetorius—governing body of the capital city of Khamris—was a lot smaller than Avindea had imagined. It was one of those stately rooms made of marble columns and gilt framing, the kind that made anyone who didn't have a fancy title in the front of their name feel insignificant. But she couldn't help thinking, *Shouldn't it be a bit ... larger?*

She ran her hands along the top of the rectangular wooden table at the center of the room, expertly smoothed and crafted from a fine strain of mahogany, probably. A throne-like chair, elaborately carved with the forms of griffins, dragons, unicorns, and other fanciful creatures, sat at the head of the table, with smaller, slightly less ostentatious chairs pushed in along either side. A colorful woven rug protected the polished marble floor, some of the threads glinting with golden stitches. Columns held up the high, vaulted ceiling, and gleaming sconces were spaced between each of the spotless glass windows.

What am I doing here? Avindea thought frantically. *The gods-*

damned carpet here alone costs more than twice my yearly salary as a Paladin of Vidamae!

She followed along the edge of the table, noticing small gilt placards placed before every seat. Each had the name of the plenum member who would be seated there shortly. Near the end of the table was the one she was looking for.

'Lady Avindea of the Church of Vidamae.'

If that doesn't prove how little I belong here, nothing does, she thought with a snort as she considered her lack of a surname. She'd denounced it after her father—also a paladin of the faith—had ruined it. That name no longer meant what it once had, not within the Church of Vidamae. Quay had offered her the use of her own last name, being the thoughtful, generous cousin she was, but Avindea Hallandor didn't have quite the paladinly ring to it. Besides, she was usually referred to as Avin anyways, which was good enough for her.

An older gentleman stepped into the room from a side chamber she hadn't initially noticed. "Ah, Lady Avindea!" The man beamed as he strode towards her. "I was hoping to catch you before the meeting began."

"Chancellor Eldivar," she greeted with a nervous smile, "it's a pleasure."

Second only to King Selderin, Chancellor Eldivar was the most powerful man in Praetorius. He was older, she guessed about seventy, but hardly a wrinkle marred his creamy pinkish complexion. He was dressed lavishly in a forest green velvet tunic trimmed in gold, with matching puffy breeches and a pair of shiny buckled leather shoes. He looked a bit, well, *foppish* was the only word that came to mind, but Avin supposed that's how all ultra-wealthy diplomats dressed. His pure white hair smoothed back from his high forehead in a delicate little pouf, and various bejeweled rings decorated his long fingers.

"I assure you, young paladin, the pleasure is all mine." He placed his hand upon the small of her back, leading her to her seat. Was he always so familiar with the other plenum members?

Perhaps he was being overly friendly to help her adjust to her new role. *The role I never even asked for.* High Priestess Lucina Balladoni, head of Praetorius's Cathedral of Vidamae, had specifically requested it, however, so how could she say no? She was now the interim official representative of the Church of Vidamae on the Plenum of Praetorius, whether she wanted it or not.

She smiled lamely. *I am so not ready for this.* Avin felt woefully out of place in her shining golden armor, emblazoned with the stylized sunburst symbol of the Goddess Vidamae. Normally, her sword would have hung from its scabbard at her waist, but weapons were not allowed during plenum meetings. Her black hair was pulled back into a ponytail, displaying her high brown cheekbones and thick black eyebrows. "Chancellor Eldivar," she repeated. "I want to thank you again for allowing me the opportunity to work with you."

The chancellor nodded and pulled out her seat. "Of course! The Church of Vidamae is highly regarded in Praetorius. When the king heard High Priestess Balladoni was called away so suddenly, we knew we simply *must* fill her spot on the council, even if only for a few sessions. The needs of the church must not be overlooked." He peered at her shrewdly. "I daresay, I was quite surprised that High Priestess Balladoni chose a humble paladin out of all of her clergy as her replacement. No offense to you, of course. I'm sure you'll do swimmingly."

"Of course." She wince-smiled back without showing any teeth. *Talk about a back-handed compliment.* "I hope to make the High Priestess proud."

"Well, we will certainly miss her presence," Chancellor Eldivar continued. "We are glad to have you serving in her stead, of course. I wanted to make sure you feel comfortable in your new role, and that you understand your responsibilities. Please, let me know if there is anything I can help you with."

Yes! Avindea thought, *I don't know what the hells I'm doing! Give me a sword and shield and a demon to fight, but politics? Vidamae, please don't let me fuck this up!* But she just shook her head and tried to look confident. "Thank you, but I believe I am prepared."

If reading the entirety of the Plenum of Praetorius Handbook until she had every passage memorized couldn't prepare her, then nothing could.

The chancellor smiled and moved off to his spot at the right hand side of the king's throne-like chair. She couldn't help but notice that the chancellor's seat sat a little higher than the rest; what a silly bit of vanity. She supposed he'd earned it after serving as chancellor for so long. Almost fifteen years, if she remembered correctly.

Other people began filing into the room. They moved with confident ease, some chatting amicably, others arguing in heated whispers. All were dressed well, though not as extravagantly as the chancellor.

Avindea tried to smooth her hair out of her face as she sneaked glances at the distinguished people surrounding her. They were mostly strangers, though she recognized a few of them.

There was Captain Riluk, the stern and serious captain of the Praetorius City Guard. He wore his breastplate as easily as she wore hers, though he kept trying to rest his hands upon the pommel of a sword that wasn't there.

Near him glided the effortlessly elegant Lady Loresh Fontaine, who represented the Church of Velthunas, God of Luck. Her hair was short and stylish and as black as Avin's, but glossy and full where Avindea's was dull and plain.

Though unfamiliar with him personally, Avin recognized the very distinct profile of Lord Eglath ver Trellior, representative of the Church of Thulkas, God of Strength and Freedom. He was so tall, he stood head and shoulders above every other plenum member in the room. (Did he have giant's blood? It would certainly explain his towering stature.) Scars interspersed with tattoos scrawled all across his muscular arms and bare, barrel-shaped chest; apparently he wasn't required to wear a shirt while on official business. A huge, gaudy holy symbol of Thulkas—a giant warhammer—was tattooed across his back. Avin couldn't help but be impressed by how fervently the bear-like man stuck to the theme.

The others she only vaguely knew of. She surreptitiously glanced at their name placards as they took their seats, trying to connect the names with the faces before the meeting began.

Her nervousness must have been obvious, for a man's voice sounded behind her. "First time, eh?" He took the seat next to her, a slim, fit man with crinkly eyes that looked as if he was laughing inwardly at some joke. Silky salt and pepper hair hung just past his ears and flopped across his forehead in a rakish curl. A trim beard covered his chin, the ends of his mustache twirled ever-so-slightly at the tips. His clothes were simple but well tailored: a black brocade doublet and slim-fitting pants that highlighted his well-shaped thighs.

"I, ah … yeah," Avindea admitted, eyeing him up and down approvingly. Just because she was a paladin didn't mean she had to ignore the sight of a well-built man's body; she hadn't taken any vows of chastity like some of her brothers and sisters in arms. She cleared her throat and felt her face flush. "Is it that obvious?"

The man smiled warmly. "Especially as I haven't seen you

around the plenum before. Allow me to introduce myself. I am Lord Bashir Rendevas, senior diplomat and representative of imports and exports. You must be High Priestess Lucina's replacement." He gestured towards the symbol of Vidamae on her armor.

Avindea nodded. "Yes, I am filling in for the high priestess temporarily. My name's Avindea. A pleasure." She shook his hand firmly, then glanced all around her as the empty seats began to fill. Throwing caution to the winds, she whispered, "And I have no idea what I'm doing here!"

Rendevas grinned. "Don't worry," he replied cheerfully. "Neither does anyone else!"

A hush fell as the final two people entered from the gilt door at the back of the room: King Selderin, ruler of Praetorius, and his teenage daughter, Princess Alandria. The monarch walked towards the head of the table, a slim golden circlet upon his head of brown curls. Solemn-faced Alandria was only a step or two behind him. Strangely, they both wore clothes that were plain and chosen obviously for comfort; Avin had expected the royal family to dress more ostentatiously. They almost looked out of place amidst the gathered counselors in their gemstone-studded belts and heavily embroidered tunics.

The king paused for a moment as the entire council stood up respectfully and bowed their heads; Avin had to scramble to her feet and just barely managed to follow suit.

"Good afternoon," King Selderin began. He had a tired face and looked much older than his forty-seven years. Ruling the capital of an upstart new country constantly on the edge of war aged a man. "Please, be seated. Chancellor Eldivar, shall we begin?"

Everyone sat back down. The chancellor smiled, steepling his fingers as he spoke. "Thank you, Your Majesty. Before we begin, I'd like to introduce the newest member of the plenum." He gestured towards Avindea with a little flourish. "Please welcome Lady Avindea, Paladin of the Church of Vidamae. She is replacing High Priestess Lucina Balladoni as the plenum's Vidamae Church representative for a few sessions while the high priestess is away on temple matters."

Avindea blushed furiously as all eyes turned upon her. She gave them a jaunty little wave. "Pleased to, uh, meet you all," she said. She winced as she realized she hadn't actually met anyone at all yet.

The chancellor clapped his hands, either unaware or uncaring of her discomfort. "Shall we formally begin?" He looked from face to face, warming to his audience.

Avindea's stomach did a few somersaults. *No, let's NOT formally begin! I'm not ready!*

"Our first order of business involves the Cathedral of Vidamae. I believe Lady Avindea has a matter she wishes to bring up to the plenum?" He looked towards her expectantly.

Her blood ran cold. "I do?" she blurted. She could feel her face heat up even as her fingers drained of blood, leaving them icy and clutching to the arms of her chair.

The chancellor blinked. "Yes, you do. The expansion of the Cathedral of Vidamae, correct?"

She would have laughed wildly in relief if she wasn't so *gods-damned nervous*. She caught herself just as the laugh was coming up her throat, causing her to sputter and cough uncontrollably. The other plenum counselors eyed her with varying degrees of concern. It took her a few agonizing seconds to get enough air in her lungs to respond. "Yes! The cathedral, of course! I was so ... I mean, I couldn't ..."

She stopped, took a breath. "I have a report here if anyone would like to see it."

There was no report. She had forgotten it back at the temple.

"I mean, not *here* here, but somewhere. At the Church, I mean." *Shitshitshitfuckfuck!*

There was an awful moment of silence as all eyes stared at her. *Vidamae strike me down*, the paladin thought, *before I die here of pure embarrassment.*

"Oh, I don't believe we'll need to see the whole report," Lord

Rendevas cheerfully broke the awkward silence. "Just summarize it for us. What does the temple need, and does the plenum need to assist with funding the project?"

She smiled at the diplomat and tried to convey without words just how grateful she was for his interference. "Oh, the plenum won't have to pay for any of it, actually." Leaning forward, she felt more confident. High Priestess Balladoni, before she left on her mysterious church business, made her rehearse this part endlessly until it was committed to memory. "The cathedral has more than enough money to pay for the expansion, but the law forbidding it is what stands in our way. We're almost always at capacity, dealing with the sick and the injured as well as our usual parishioners, and we'd hate to turn away someone in need just because we don't have room for them. We need the restrictions on church expansions lifted, but only the plenum can vote on something like that."

She looked around her hopefully. Nobody really seemed to be listening, except for Lord Rendevas, who regarded her thoughtfully, and King Selderin, who was obviously used to pretending to be interested. That was practically his job, right? Pretending to care about the common folk?

"What do the other religious leaders think about this?" a cranky, sour-faced elderly man barked from the other end of the table. He didn't even bother looking her in the eye when he spoke, instead directing his squinty gaze at his thick yellow fingernails.

Avin squinted at his name placard, which read Judge Jeremy Rodach. She'd heard rumors of him and his stringent sentences; if she ever found herself on the wrong side of the law, she would hate to have to face someone like him in the courtroom.

"I haven't spoken with them yet, actually," the paladin answered, eyeing Lady Loresh and Lord Eglath. "I assumed the council meeting was the appropriate place to bring such matters up."

"You haven't spoken with them at all?" Judge Rodach snapped, his voice sharp and thin like a whipcrack.

"Well, no, I mean, I just started, and—"

"Well, why should we change the laws just for you?" Judge Rodach picked at his nails lazily. "This could open up all sorts of unexpected issues. The law states that no other churches are to be built within the city limits. It ever and always has been only Vidamae, Velthunas, and Thulkas. If we let Vidamae's church expand, it stands to reason that the law could be interpreted to allow *other* churches to set up here. Remember when there was a Church of Kax inside the city?"

Avindea sputtered, trying to form the words for a response. "Of course I remember!" Kax, Goddess of Chaos and Anarchy, was the antithesis to Avindea's chosen goddess, Vidamae. Kax had even tried to usurp Vidamae years ago by ordering Her devotees to massacre as many followers and clergy of Vidamae as they could. Even the mere mention of Kax to a devout follower of Vidamae was enough to cause the mildest-mannered of them to spit vehemently upon hearing Kax's name.

"Have you really thought this through?" the judge continued savagely. "Sure, the Cathedral of Vidamae may have the funds to expand, but what of the others? What if the Church of Thulkas wants to grow, and they don't have enough money for it? If we have to fund one church, then it logically follows that the others will expect the same."

"The Church of Thulkas is doing just fine," piped in Lord Eglath helpfully.

Avindea could feel her hot temper flaring, and it was all she could do to keep her voice calm. "I'm not asking for funds. I'm asking for a change in the church expansion laws so the cathedral can be better equipped to deal with our parishioners, as I believe I already mentioned."

"How will this expansion benefit the people of Praetorius?" the judge countered. "Is this simply a vanity project, or is it really for the good of *all* of our citizens?"

"I think you're being overly critical," Avindea snapped, her voice rising. "Of course this will benefit the city! Everyone knows that

Vidamae doesn't turn away anyone who comes to Her for aid. She's the Goddess of Life, for Aukera's sake!"

This wasn't going well at all. How could someone be *against* the remodeling of the Cathedral of Vidamae? It was like being against free food for the poor; it just wasn't done! (At least not out loud.) "We're literally just *running out of room*. All we need is the okay from the council to expand. It's that simple!"

King Selderin held up his hand for silence before Judge Rodach could snarl back a response. "Before this gets carried away, I say we take this to a vote. All in favor of rewriting the church expansion law so the Cathedral of Vidamae may legally expand their premises?"

It managed to pass, just barely; Judge Rodach and Constable Mald, the head of the Praetorius Jail, voted against it. Since nine people sat upon the plenum, five had to vote yes for any motions to pass. Neither King Selderin nor Princess Alandria had the ability to vote, though the standing monarch could veto a vote entirely, should the need arise. It didn't happen often.

Next, a craggy-faced, dark-skinned man with a wide forehead and the look of a seasoned veteran stood up. Avindea glanced at his name placard and balked a little when she read his name: Commander Rickard Rakeld, head of the Army of Praetorius. He eyed the assembly silently for a moment, his stare intense to the point of being invasive. She had the feeling that he didn't do it on purpose. It was just how his face looked. "I want to talk about Athessa."

The atmosphere changed immediately. Everyone sat up straighter in their seats, instantly on alert. Athessa? Why hadn't she been warned they would be discussing Athessa, the country to the north that had once been sovereign of all the lands of Khamris?

Around one hundred years ago, the people of Khamris fought, and won, their independence, a fact that filled the average Khamrian with patriotic pride. The way the Athessians told it, however, Khamris was still just an upstart collection of unruly villages that the Ternian Czars, the trio of siblings who currently ruled Athessa, had yet to bring to heel.

The chancellor tittered nervously, looking a bit put out that he hadn't been given a chance to announce the next order of business. "Yes, yes, the security issues are next. Please, Rakeld, continue."

"I want to lay this out as simply and as quickly as possible." Rakeld's lined face was grim. "We have seven spies installed inside the walls of Uldinvelm. Each spy reports back to me in different ways and on different days of the week, in a code only Orvessa and I know." He gestured towards the woman sitting next to him, her placard revealing her to be Lieutenant Sondrela Orvessa. She was black-haired, thick in the chest, and sporting a look of contempt made all the more apparent by the jagged scar that bisected her top lip.

The commander paused for effect. "I haven't heard from any of the spies in over two weeks."

A brief murmur ran through the assembly. Avindea leaned forward in her seat. That certainly sounded bad.

"A party of five of my scouts was found dead in Feywynn," he continued. The country of Feywynn, though only loosely allied with Khamris, had the unfortunate geographical position of being right between the borders of Khamris and Athessa.

"We have reason to suspect they were murdered by Athessian soldiers. The rulers of Feywynn assure us the culprits were simply bandits and claim to have them incarcerated there. Their leaders refuse to meet with us or release the bandits into our custody, but they are still willing to work with us, at least for now."

The other counselors shifted nervously in their seats and murmured amongst each other darkly. Before anyone had a chance to interrupt, King Selderin held up his hand for silence.

The commander inclined his head towards the king. "The recall of the soldiers from the surrounding villages back to Praetorius is moving along nicely," he continued in his gravelly voice. "Most from the closest cities have already returned, with only a small percentage still on route to reconvene with the troops stationed here."

Avindea wasn't aware that such a proclamation had been made; it must have been voted on previously. It seemed a bit short-sighted to her—why pull back *all* the troops, leaving the smaller villages unprotected? Khamris wasn't an especially dangerous land, but bandits and wandering monsters were still a common problem. Most of the villages relied on the guards to keep their people safe from both, so if there were no longer any guards ...

"Mercenary groups have begun camping outside some of the bigger cities in the hopes of getting hired by the local mayors, but there's not much we can do to stop that," Rakeld said. "They aren't breaking any laws, and as long as they stay peaceful, we can't really tell them to leave. They are more of a nuisance than anything."

He continued, "We've also instated stricter measures regarding who and what can pass through the city gates." The other counselors murmured in concern at this; pulling back necessary soldiers from protecting the smaller villages? Not a problem. That didn't affect *them* in any way. But making it harder for goods to come into the city, thus negatively impacting the tax monies that went directly into the plenum members' pockets? *That* was simply not done!

"We've installed extra guards at the gate to try to help mitigate the effects this will have on the flow of traffic into the city, but be forewarned there will be delays on some of the things that we have all come to rely upon." He fixed his steely gaze upon the plenum at large. "In times of conflict, sacrifices must be made."

Everyone began speaking all at once and over one another. "What does this mean about our exports?" "Our constituents will need some of those luxuries!" "I heard that the Athessian Army was training more than usual. Now it makes sense why!" "War? Is it really going to be war again?"

Avindea sat back in her chair, dumbfounded. The countries of Athessa and Khamris were historically bitter enemies, constantly sniping at one another, making empty threats or sending scouting missions too close to the other's borders to loosely threaten without actually causing any damage. Avindea had no idea things had escalated so quickly.

Athessa's capital of Uldinvelm housed the Ternian Czars, dictators who governed Athessa with ruthless cunning and iron fists. Rumors abounded about just how tightly the czars controlled their people, and how little personal freedoms the Athessians enjoyed. If there was one thing Khamrians took pride in, it was their fierce sense of freedom. That was the heart of the conflict between the two countries: Khamris valued freedom above all else, while in Athessa, loyalty to their country was most important.

"Enough!" Chancellor Eldivar cried, bringing the tumult to an uneasy silence. "We won't get anything accomplished until we have some order. Now," he regarded Commander Rakeld, "what is it you wish for the council to do with all of these military reports?"

"I want us to formally declare war on Athessa."

A tense silence followed, leaving all of the plenum members, both known and unfamiliar to Avindea, frozen at the theoretical edges of their seats. All eyes turned onto the commander, who stood firm, the steely glint in his eyes daring anyone to contradict him. A formal declaration of war? Sure, Khamris and Athessa hated each other, but to send the whole country headlong into war could prove ruinous for both countries. Avindea could hardly contain her bursting emotions. *Of course my first day on the plenum—as a temporary member, even—would have something as serious as a fucking war against Athessa on the agenda!*

"I will not allow that," King Selderin stated emphatically. "We have remained at peace with Athessa for many years. I will not pledge the entire country to war over a few rumors and what-ifs."

He fixed Commander Rakeld with a stern eye. "Get me proof that Athessa is, indeed, behind these ... these attacks and subterfuge, and then—*and only then*—will I entertain a declaration of war."

The commander glowered at the king, and Orvessa beside him looked outright murderous. Her hands clutched her chair so tightly her knuckles turned white. "You're making a mistake, Your Majesty," she growled. The scar on her top lip looked especially intimidating when she snarled. "War is inevitable. We never *truly* won the last one against Athessa, and you know it! We need an official declaration to secure our alliances. Delaying will only cause more problems for the future."

"If keeping Praetorius out of a costly, unnecessary, and, frankly, *dangerous* war with Athessa is a mistake, then I will gladly accept any punishments that occur because of it. Now," he glanced towards Chancellor Eldivar, who nodded briskly, "I consider the motion shelved while we await further information."

"I believe that concludes the council meeting," the chancellor declared immediately. He bowed deferentially while the king and the princess both stood up, nodded to the assembly, and left.

Well, that was certainly exciting, Avindea thought as she followed the rest of the council out of the chambers. *First day on the job and we're already talking war with our most hated enemy?*

She felt anxious at the thought. *I've certainly got my work cut out for me.*

Chapter 3

The Voice

"Why do you struggle to see where the killers went?" the voice inside Hypnocost's head said.

It wasn't like he was *hearing voices*. He wasn't *insane*. It was an *actual* voice speaking inside his mind that only *he* happened to be able to hear. The difference between those two things was vast. Besides, would an imaginary voice sound so ragged, whispery and gruff, like sandpaper brushed ever-so-lightly against his skull?

"How do you know this?" He had to focus his considerable mental energies to respond. He assumed the voice couldn't hear his idle thoughts.

"Their tracks are clear. You cannot see them?"

Hypnocost and Lucius stood just outside Furow's Ridge, near the edge of the forest that served as the village's northernmost border. He squinted in the rapidly descending gloom of evening, trying to see the tracks the voice spoke of. It just looked like a whole lot of dirt and grass to him. Lucius, hovering beside him with sword and shield in hand, frantically searched the ground, the bushes, the path leading out of Furow's Ridge, anywhere that could give him a clue as to the murderer's (or murderers' plural?) whereabouts.

"Shit," the scar-faced man swore. "I can't see anything in this darkness."

Hypnocost sniffed, raised his hands, and produced a ghostly pale light that emanated from his fingers. A small globe of magic hovered at his fingertips, illuminating the area directly in front of it.

Lucius's eyes widened. "Why didn't you tell me you were a mage?!" he hissed. "C'mon, now we can keep looking!"

"Actually," Hypnocost corrected punctiliously, "I am not a mage. I am *more* than a mage. I am—"

His words didn't reach Lucius. The man was already long gone, loping on his long legs into the trees.

"—gifted."

Hypnocost ran a hand over his freshly shaven, heavily tattooed head. He let out a long-suffering sigh. *That simpleton will not understand the difference anyways,* he thought smugly. *Those sword types never do. He is no better than Ghdion, shaking his sword at anything that so much as looks at him sideways. Hmph.*

Hypnocost knew for a fact that mages and the gifted were as different as night and day. Mages—with their ridiculous spellcasting words, spellbooks, and official papers espousing their credentials that they shoved under your nose every chance they could—had to rely upon *stealing* their magic from the other realms that lay just outside Aukera. They relied upon elemental powers from the realm of fire or the realm of air, and tended to favor flashy, pyrotechnic spells like explosive fire or arcane blasts, magics that were loud and damaging and caused the most amount of destruction. Spells that were just smoke and mirrors. Spells that lacked a certain *artistry*.

But not the gifted. Not the *theurgists*. Theurgists had *finesse*.

Hypnocost was proud to count himself as one among their lofty ranks. Theurgists didn't steal their powers, they were *gifted* them, usually by a friendly demon or some other sort of otherworldly creature. (He wasn't exactly sure of all the details. Why should it matter as long as the power was provided?) Hypnocost had been gifted his magical talents many years after first hearing the voice inside his head. He'd been a child, so the details were a bit fuzzy. He didn't know with certainty that the voice belonged to his elusive theurgist patron, though coincidences that large were usually unheard of.

Regardless, his magic didn't come from an outside source. It came from *inside his own mind*. If he concentrated hard enough, he could even read peoples' thoughts, a fact he kept, by necessity, close to the vest.

"You will lose them,"

the voice chastised.

"Hypnocost!" Lucius yelled from just outside the sphere of light. "I think I might have something!"

He hustled over, holding the flaps of his yellow silken coat closed to keep out the chill night air. *Some* people (namely Ghdion) thought him ridiculous for refusing to wear a shirt beneath his expertly tailored jackets, but Hypnocost believed that one must sometimes suffer on the altar of fashion, even if that meant constantly shivering to allow his sleek, pale bare chest to be visible.

Holding his glowing hand aloft, his eyes followed where Lucius pointed down at a scuff in the dirt. It was barely visible amongst all the grass and weeds. "I do not see anything."

"It's a boot mark, see?" Lucius pointed with his own booted toe.

"He is right,"

the voice told him.

"This one has some small talent for tracking, it seems."

"You are right," Hypnocost grunted begrudgingly. "You have some small talent for tracking, it seems."

Lucius gave him an odd look. "I've lived here a long time. This might be the clue we're looking for!"

"Look at the direction the boot mark is going. The killers headed to the north,"

the voice said.

Hypnocost knelt down and pretended to more thoroughly investigate what was supposedly the boot mark. He got right down onto the ground and sniffed, ran his finger across the dirt, licked the finger, then stood back up, dusting off his jacket. "I believe they are heading north," he announced.

Lucius gaped at him. "Wha—? How do you know that? Could you ... could you *taste* it or something?" He eyed Hypnocost with a look of begrudging and puzzled admiration.

Hypnocost waggled his glowing fingers. "Mysterious are the ways of us gifted!"

"And you think *I'm* the skilled tracker?" Lucius shook his head in disbelief. "Let's head back to the church. It's getting too dark now to see much else out here anyways. We should tell Ghdion and Quay what we found out."

Ah, right. *Those* two. "Of course." He held out his arm to allow Lucius to lead the way; the man rushed along much faster than he was prepared for, and he had to hustle breathlessly to keep up.

"None of this makes any sense," Lucius muttered as he strode towards the church. It was the only building with any lights twinkling in its windows; every other home in Furow's Ridge was dark and firmly locked up. Such was the way of tiny hamlets; as soon as full dark hit, everything shut down for the night. "Why would anyone want to kill Priest Edmund? He was immensely popular in the village. He knew everyone!"

"It is a question for the ages, is it not?" Hypnocost huffed and puffed, having to take two paces for every one of Lucius's. "Why snuff the life of another person? What good does such a foul deed do? Philosophers throughout history have argued this very conundrum."

Lucius glanced back at him. "Do you always talk like that?" he asked.

"Like what? Like an intelligent half-elf?"

Lucius sighed. "Yeah, I guess so."

"Naturally." If Hypnocost had any hair, he would've flung it back vaingloriously. As it was, the only decorations upon his bald pate were the thick black tattoo lines that twirled in mysterious patterns from the crown of his head, as well as a few ill-considered piercings on the tips of his pointed ears. He'd gotten those as a youth. Elder Hulthorpe *hated* them.

As they reached the chapel, thumping and scratching sounds came from out back. They could see Ghdion laboring at a fresh grave, his face grim as he shoveled. Quay knelt at the foot of the shallow hole he'd managed to dig out, her head bowed and her lips moving in a silent prayer, her holy symbol pressed tightly between her hands. The body of poor Edmund Brisby was only a dimly lit bulge beside her.

"We found tracks," Lucius announced with a directness that Hypnocost felt was quickly growing stale. "Hypnocost here thinks the killers have moved on to the north."

Ghdion paused and leaned heavily upon the shovel. "Does he now?"

Lucius missed the sarcastic undertone in Ghdion's voice. "Desai, maybe? It's the closest city north. I think it's worth checking out."

Quay scrambled to her feet, her elegant robes stained at the knees. Honestly, the woman had no panache when it came to clothes; who wore filmy, lilac-hued, ankle-length *gowns* while traveling the countryside? Her ample chest was partially exposed! He supposed she had to wear what all Priestesses of Vidamae favored, which seemed to be nigh-translucent, light colored, high-waisted gowns with gaudily beaded trimmings and no sleeves. It was all rather *gauche*. At least *he* wasn't expected to dress so atrociously.

"We've got to follow them!" she cried. Her face was tear-stained and red, her brown hair in a flyaway tangle around her head.

"Not so fast, Priestess," Ghdion warned, jabbing a finger in her direction. "It's the middle of the night and we've been awake the last *twenty hours*. We're not in any shape to be traveling."

"As much as I hate to admit it, he's right," Lucius replied reluctantly. "It would be suicide to travel in this darkness. There's hardly a sliver of moon to guide us."

"*Us?*" Hypnocost questioned.

"I'm going with you." Lucius gazed evenly at each of them, daring them to contradict him. He looked particularly menacing, the scarred half of his face all jagged shadows in the gloomy darkness.

"You are?" Ghdion quirked an eyebrow.

"Why?" Quay cut in.

"I'm as much a part of this as you three now," Lucius countered firmly. "Edmund was my friend, too, and I would see his killer come to justice."

"Interesting. There is more that Lucius is not telling you. Why else would he pledge his troth to someone he only just met?"

the voice said.

"Hmm," Hypnocost pondered aloud. "There is more that you are not telling us, methinks."

Lucius rolled his eyes. "Now, just a m—"

"He makes a good point," Ghdion interrupted. "Why would you suddenly be willing to upend your entire life here, in Furow's Ridge, to travel with three strangers who you only just met yesterday?" He scowled, but since he was always scowling, it didn't really change his face all that much. "You're a nice enough guy, Lucius, but we know next to nothing about you."

Lucius threw his hands up in disgust. "I'm just trying to do the right thing here, alright? Is that so hard to understand?"

"Press him,"

demanded the voice.

"Why?" Hypnocost thought back.

"I am ... curious. Humor me."

"We are all friends here," Hypnocost spoke unctuously. "And thus, there are no secrets between us." He raised his eyebrows expectantly.

"Fine, I lost my job at the mines," Lucius grumbled, crossing his arms. "I was their hired guard. The mine recently ran dry, so the company pulled up stakes and all the miners moved on a few days ago. I don't have enough money to pay for next month's rent, so ... I've been pondering a change of scenery since then anyways. And now, with this whole murderers-in-the-night thing that I've been helping you three out with ..." He shrugged and glanced away, face visibly reddening even in the dim light of the moon. "Makes sense to go along with you. There, that's my big secret: I lost my job and ran out of money. Happy?"

"Immensely." Hypnocost gave him an oily smile.

"I suppose I could use a third bodyguard," Quay pondered aloud. "Are you any good with that sword you carry, Lucius?"

He grinned boyishly. The puckered scars pulled up his skin and made bizarre shapes around his mouth and eyes when he smiled. It was extremely disconcerting. "I've been known to swing a sword a time or two, yeah. I have some experience fighting, though I much prefer the non-violent route if I can help it."

She beamed and clasped her hands. She really was very pretty, in a wholesome, sunshiney sort of way, if one was into that. Personally, Hypnocost wasn't into any type of person, at least not that he had yet to meet. "Me too," she said. "I wish Ghdion here would take a page out of your book. He's usually a 'damage first, ask questions later' kind of guy. It's gotten us into a whole heap of trouble before." She eyed her first bodyguard with a fondness that the half-elf just could not understand.

Ghdion rolled his eyes. "Fine, Pretty Boy, if you wanna help, go find a shovel and help me finish this grave so I can finally get some sleep."

"Do I have to take orders from this guy?" Lucius laughed.

"Nope, just me." Quay held out her hand. "As long as you're okay with that, and with me hashing out the details later, consider this a formal job offer. Lucius, ah ... I realize I don't know your full name?"

"Just Lucius is fine."

"Lies,"

said the voice.

"Alright, Just Lucius Is Fine." Hypnocost could see Quay's delight at the play on words. He rolled his eyes. Puns. So adolescent. "Do you accept the job as my bodyguard and by extension, protector for the Church of Vidamae, for the sum of five gold pieces a day, to be paid directly from the Church's coffers each time we resupply in Praetorius?"

Lucius took her hand and shook it vigorously. "I accept," he answered with mock solemnity.

"And thus, three becomes four," Hypnocost declared with a flourish. "Welcome to the party, my good ex-guard. I hope you like discovering the bodies of dead Vidamae worshippers."

He had meant it as a joke, but clearly, due to the looks of horror upon their faces, it flew right over their heads.

Chapter 4

The Annals of Briselius: A Brief History of the War Between Athessa and Khamris

As far as Rendevas was concerned, the Library of Praetorius was, to put it mildly, the single most important building in the city.

He strode up its stone staircase, the impressively huge, intricately carved double doors open ahead of him. Mythological beasts and twining floral reliefs, interspersed with depictions of heroes of legend, were carved into the doors themselves. Even the trim around the doorway was decorated with matching designs. Large rectangular windows let in the sunlight, illuminating bookshelves inside stacked all the way to the ceiling. The place smelled of ink, fresh parchment, and old books; Rendevas, smiling contentedly, inhaled the heady scent as he stepped through the doors.

Aside from its beauty, Praetorius was known throughout Khamris for having the largest, most well-stocked library in the region. The Library of Praetorius boasted four floors and a basement filled almost to overflowing with books on all subjects. *This place never ceases to amaze me*, he thought with fondness. *All that knowledge at one's fingertips. And one need only ask for it!*

The librarians all knew him by sight, and not just because of his status as a high-ranking diplomat. "Lord Rendevas!" his favorite, a pretty young lady named Panya, greeted him with genuine warmth in her voice. "I was starting to wonder if you'd ever come back!"

He gave her an elegant bow and took her hand across the counter, laying a light kiss upon her fingertips. "I apologize. My duties kept me away far longer than I would have liked. I simply could not stay away from you any longer, dear Panya!"

She tittered, equal parts embarrassed and pleased. "I trust you're returning those books you borrowed? You know they are all overdue." She fixed him with a stern look that was somewhat nullified by the cheeky grin that played around her lips. "There was a young woman in here just yesterday looking for one of the books you still have checked out: *The Annals of Briselius: A Brief History of the War Between Athessa and Khamris.*"

Rendevas quickly hid the shock from his face by plastering on a fake grin. *Well, well, well, who could be looking for that dusty old tome? Interesting...*

He'd been pouring over the old text to further understand the hatred between the countries of Khamris and Athessa. Though written in a dry, scholarly voice, the book was full of interesting accounts of the past, detailing the diplomacies employed and the skirmishes fought for Khamris to gain its shaky independence. He was particularly interested in any allies Khamris once had; could he perhaps use his diplomatic privileges to call on those same allies, should the need arise?

How could he use the histories to better prepare Praetorius for what was doomed to be yet another war?

"I have it safely tucked away at home, but alas! I regret to inform you that I will have to return the book later. Do you happen to know the woman who was requesting it?" He knew the chances were slim that she would, but he figured he may as well ask. "Perhaps I can give it directly to her and save her a trip."

Panya shook her head. "You know I cannot divulge that information, my lord," she scolded him lightly. "But I will say that she came here three times just yesterday. She obviously wants that book badly. If I see her, perhaps I can send her your way?"

"Delightful." He winked. "Now, if you could direct me to the books about past military conscriptions in Praetorius, that would be most appreciated!"

Truly he hoped it wouldn't come to such a thing, but rumors about involuntary conscriptions abounded. Part of his job was to keep an ear out on the regular folk; it was too easy to lose sight of who he actually worked for, surrounded by nobles and powerful government types as he was. He made it a point to listen to the word on the street as much as possible; if the draft really was reinstated, he knew the general populace would *not* be pleased. The average Praetorian was patriotic and proud of their city, but that only went so far.

Panya stepped from behind the desk and led him to the section of the library labeled 'Military History.' She didn't even have to consult with the card catalog to know just where the books on conscriptions were located, she just gestured towards a neatly stacked shelf. "Here you are. Books on military conscription. Can I help you find anything else?"

Rendevas shook his head. "Thank you, my dear. This will do just nicely." He waited until she stepped away before perusing the spines of the books, searching for anything helpful.

He was so preoccupied that he didn't realize someone stepped right behind him. They cleared their throat and said in a familiar trilling, breathy voice, "Lord Rendevas! I'm so glad I found you."

It was Chancellor Eldivar, smiling obsequiously. His white hair was slicked back on the sides, leaving his telltale little pouf at the front. He wore a fetching outfit of pale lavender and cream. Truly, the man had impeccable fashion sense, though he tended to favor more traditional styles and cuts, whereas Rendevas himself preferred his garments to be bolder and more fashion-forward.

Rendevas smiled. "Greetings, Chancellor. I'm surprised you were able to get away from all of your pressing duties at the capitol."

The chancellor's warm eyes sparkled. "There never is any rest for us, is there?" He gave a long-suffering sigh. "But now that I have you, I wanted to speak with you about something that concerns me. One diplomat to another."

Chancellor Eldivar used to serve as a diplomat like Rendevas, before he was raised to the title of chancellor almost fifteen years ago. "I hesitate to say it, but I have ... reservations about Judge Rodach."

Rendevas raised his eyebrows. "The judge?" That was a surprise. He was under the impression that Chancellor Eldivar and Judge Rodach went way back. They were not necessarily friends, but long-time colleagues at the very least, which had to count for something. "May I ask why?"

The chancellor guided him by the arm until they were out of

earshot of a few patrons nearby. "It's a ... delicate situation," he disclosed. "I am loath to speak of it outside of the plenum, but..." He drew out the last syllable. "I will be frank. Based on information I have recently obtained, I don't believe Judge Rodach has Praetorius's best interests in mind."

He was intrigued. Though technically illegal, these little backroom dealings were bread and butter for diplomats such as himself. No one would ever admit to such subterfuge, of course; should they be called out for it, any diplomat worth their salt would vehemently deny any wrongdoing. The chancellor was excellent at playing at propriety, toeing the line between what was legal and what was right. Rendevas could always count upon him to provide the juiciest, most up to date intel.

"What have you heard?" he asked, trying to hide his interest.

The chancellor frowned. "He ... well, he has a conflict of interest. He likes to tout his patriotism and claim he wants only what is best for Praetorius, but in reality, there are rumors he's been selling his plenum votes."

Rendevas let out a low whistle. "That is certainly something to worry about. How do you know for sure?"

Chancellor Eldivar pursed his lips. "I've heard from a few independent sources."

That usually meant informants. If he didn't miss his guess, he was almost certain Chancellor Eldivar employed The Maelstrom. Every self-respecting government official did.

"What are you going to do about it?"

The older man sighed. "Nothing for now. I don't have any hard evidence that proves it." He eyed Rendevas pointedly, raising his bushy white eyebrows.

Rendevas opened his mouth once, closed it, then let out a little sigh. "I ... may or may not already have some inquiries out." He ran his finger absently over the spine of a thin leather book on the shelf in front of them. "This information will definitely be helpful should my inquiries bear fruit."

He was prevented from saying anything more on the topic by the arrival of Avindea, the dark-haired Paladin of Vidamae and newest (if only temporary) member of the plenum. She strode confidently through the stacks, her eyes widening as she came across the two of them alone together between two shelves. "Lord Rendevas, Chancellor Eldivar." She nodded her greeting to them. She looked extremely out of place in her intimidating golden armor—did the woman wear it everywhere? Did she not own any regular clothes? "Are you also looking up books about military drafts?"

She had the kind of open, readily transparent face that was too easy for people like Rendevas to take advantage of. When he first met her yesterday, he wanted to warn her that her obvious naivety would only hinder her efforts in the plenum. He read interest, nervousness, and a tiny bit of self-righteousness in her that all paladin types had. She was simply too easy to lead astray.

"Yes, actually." He smiled, gesturing towards the book in his hand. "Mostly that, and histories about the Khamris/Athessa conflict. You?"

"I've been trying to find *The Annals of Briselius: A Brief History of the War Between Athessa and Khamris*, but its been checked out for weeks now. The librarian keeps giving me excuses about why it hasn't been returned yet."

"That was you?" Rendevas blurted, his mouth working much faster than his mind. It wasn't often he was caught off guard, and by a *paladin,* no less. "Oh goodness, *I'm* the one who has that book!"

"Really? Would it be possible for me to borrow it from you?" She laughed self-deprecatingly. "And would it be terribly gauche of me to admit that I'm studying up on all this stuff for the next plenum meeting? I fear my first impression yesterday didn't go so well."

The chancellor looked pleased. "Why, of course not! There is nothing wrong with wanting to be well-informed. I applaud your initiative. Young people these days are always too busy to take time for a little quiet study."

Avindea snorted. "I'm thirty years old, chancellor. I'm not so young myself." She let out a deep sigh. "That makes me feel so much better, though. I'm afraid I'm in over my head." Peering more closely at the two of them, she asked, "Did I interrupt something? I apologize if so."

"Oh, we were just discussing how we thought the votes went yesterday," Rendevas answered breezily. "What do you think? Are we on a crash course towards war?"

Her lips thinned and her dark eyebrows furrowed. "Forgive me if I'm wrong, but according to clause nineteen: section forty-two of the plenum handbook, councilors are to refrain from discussing any and all plenum business outside of the council chambers."

Has ... has she memorized *the plenum handbook?* he thought, bewildered.

They both merely blinked at her.

"Not that I am accusing you of doing such a thing," she was quick to add. She held her hands up in a warding off gesture. "Far be it from me to tell you how to do your own jobs!" She laughed, a bit too loudly to be genuine. Coupled with the fact they were in a library, it made the whole situation that much more awkward.

"When it comes to discussions outside of official plenum meetings," the chancellor answered after a beat, "it's more of a 'spirit of the law' as opposed to 'letter of the law' kind of rule, if you take my meaning."

"Of course! Of course," she repeated. "Forgive my ignorance." She shuffled her feet, looking the very picture of a chastised child. "Well, I ... it's been nice chatting with you both. Chancellor Eldivar. Lord Rendevas." She inclined her head before walking out of the aisle, a bit too quickly to be casual. She hadn't even looked through the stacks for any books.

Chancellor Eldivar shook his head with a grimace of mild distaste. "Paladins, hmph. Why High Priestess Balladoni chose a *paladin* to replace her ..."

"Mmm, I find her ... *endearing*," Rendevas admitted. "Though paladin types are known to meddle when they find out rules are being broken." He raised his eyebrows knowingly.

"You'll talk with her, won't you?" said the chancellor. "I would hate it if she had the wrong idea about our little chats."

"Naturally. I have a library book she needs, so I can do so sooner as opposed to later."

The chancellor clapped his hands, signaling his imminent departure. "Excellent! Well, I've taken enough of your time, Lord Rendevas. Please, let me know if you find out anything about *our mutual friend*." He winked. "I would hate for his misplaced motivations to put Praetorius in any danger. And if you happen to find any proof ..." He shrugged, leaving the sentence unfinished. "Let's just say it would be *greatly appreciated*."

Rendevas nodded in agreement. "Of course, Chancellor, I will." He had a lot to ponder.

And a certain judge to keep an eye on.

Chapter 5
Desai

"What the fuck is up with all these mercenaries?" Ghdion grumbled to no one in particular.

"Language!" came Quay's immediate reply. It didn't matter how quietly or under his breath he swore, she somehow always heard him. Ears of a bat, that one. "But yes, I was wondering the same thing."

The town was completely overrun with people in various armor styles, sporting tabards or armbands that loudly proclaimed their mercenary companies. They loitered around just outside the city proper, trying to look menacing with their big weapons and flashy armor. There must have been four or five different companies, based on the huge, colorful tents staked on the outskirts of the city.

The group had reached Desai, a mid-sized fishing town near the ocean, earlier that afternoon. Lucius, newest member of 'Quay's Bodyguard Club,' had graciously offered to let them sleep at his place in Furow's Ridge after they finished burying Edmund Brisby the previous night. He assured Quay, who fretted about leaving the tiny church empty, that he would make sure some of the locals would keep the church safe. She insisted upon sending a letter to Praetorius requesting a replacement priest before allowing them to leave Furow's Ridge that morning.

Lucius's house had been small and cozy, sparsely furnished and hardly decorated; Ghdion had to sleep on the floor because the couch was too short for his long legs, and he must've slept funny because his upper back and neck *ached*. It also could've been the fact that he had spent hours digging an entire *grave* all by himself last night. Of course, 'Prince' Hypnocost got the spare bed, making Lucius sleep on his own couch; His Highness would never *deign* to sleep upon anything less than the softest of mattresses and pillows! The half-elf originally wanted to take Lucius's room, with the adjoining private bathroom, for himself, but Ghdion shut that down right away, insisting that Quay, as the only woman present, be the one to spend the night there. She shot him a sweet, grateful smile that made his chest feel all fluttery, but he quickly blamed that on exhaustion.

It was because it had been such a long, weird night. For sure. Definitely. It didn't mean anything.

And now, after traveling most of the morning, they were surrounded by mercenaries, the most obnoxious type of fighter Ghdion ever had the misfortune to work with. They constantly strutted around, proudly flashing their colors, picking fights as a way to show off their prowess. He should know—he'd been one once.

"Hey, mercenary!" Ghdion called out.

Three different people, all armed to the teeth and sporting different colored armbands, turned around to look at them.

He paused, then picked one out randomly. "You. Yeah, you with the spiked hair." A man with a truly impressive half bald, half-spiked head of flaming red hair stepped towards them. A nasty looking spiked mace hung at his belt, and metal spikes protruded from his black leather boots and gauntlets. "Spike. Can I call you Spike?"

The mercenary shrugged, looking bored. "It's actually Ebrath. You lookin' to hire the elite members of The Claws of Kharon?"

Ghdion couldn't help but snort derisively. The Claws of Kharon, elite? Bunch of jumped-up amateurs, more like it.

"Ah, no, unfortunately," Lucius piped up from beside him. "Just had a quick question for you, Spike. Why are there so many of you guys in Desai? Is there some sort of mercenary convention happening?"

Ebrath/Spike snorted and rolled his eyes. "Nah. We're waiting to see if the mayor's gonna hire one of our companies. Y'know, for protection." He paused a beat, then eyed the two of them in annoyance. "And it's Ebrath."

"Protection from what?" Hypnocost butted in. "Or from whom?"

Spike shot His Highness Hypnocost a puzzled look, then turned back towards Lucius, apparently preferring to talk to the guy with a sword instead of the guy who used fancy words like 'whom.' He didn't even bother trying to hide that he openly stared at Lucius's conspicuous facial scars. "For the city's protection, of course."

"Aren't there guards for that?" Quay mused aloud.

Spike did a double take. When he caught sight of Quay, his gaze zeroed in right onto her prominent chest. Ghdion glowered and moved a little closer. "Not anymore," the mercenary answered. "Didn't you hear? The king called back all the guards and soldiers to go back to Praetorius. Some official proclamation, mustering the troops or whatever it's called. Lookin' like there's gonna be a war soon."

Lucius, lazily watching a couple other mercenaries across the way, snapped his gaze onto Spike's face. "A war? With Athessa?" His voice sounded higher than normal, enough that it made his concern evident to Ghdion.

Spike shrugged. "Yeah, I guess so." He shifted a bit closer to the group, so his shoulder very nearly brushed against Quay's.

"How exceedingly foolish of the king!" Hypnocost tutted. "That is a bit short-sighted to leave all these villages unprotected and open for any nearby brigands or monsters to come attack!"

"That's why we're here." Spike grinned. He turned back towards Quay, eyeing her up and down lasciviously. "Hey, listen, you're a Priestess of Vidamae, right?" He gestured towards the holy symbol resting against her chest. His hand came dangerously close to brushing her there 'accidentally.' "You staying in town for a while? I've got my own tent over there and—"

"She's not interested," Ghdion growled, placing a light touch upon her lower back to lead her away from the man's hungry gaze.

"Hey, you sure, man?" Spike called after their retreating forms. "I've heard some interesting *rumors* about the Priestesses of Vidamae! Just so you know, I'm known all over Khamris as 'Ebrath the Eleven Inch Erec—'"

"Not! Interested!" Ghdion bellowed over him.

It wasn't the first time something like that had happened. The Priestesses of Vidamae were known the world over for being exceedingly easy on the eyes, which led to rumors of them being promiscuous. The rumors were just that, rumors—at least for Quay, not that it was any of his business—but people tended to make up salacious falsehoods about beautiful women simply because they were good-looking. In Ghdion's experience, all the priestesses, pretty or not, were actually rather stuck-up. They flaunted their looks and the fact that they were universally beloved by the general populace.

Well, all save Quay. She was usually too busy rescuing kittens or healing orphans or whatever to pay attention to such things.

"That was rude!" She scowled once they were out of earshot. "What if I was interested in that man?"

"You're not."

"I'm pretty sure I know my own mind, Ghdion. I don't need you to babysit me." Her face flushed a pretty dark pink and she lifted her chin haughtily. "Maybe I was going to hire him as my fourth bodyguard!"

"I do not believe that mercenary had the best intentions for you, Quay," Hypnocost, ever oblivious, interjected. "If I were to guess, I do believe he was propositioning you."

Lucius snorted.

Quay rolled her eyes. "I was being facetious, Hypnocost," she explained gently. How she was so patient with the guy, Ghdion couldn't fathom. At least Hypnocost didn't spend all his time staring at her chest or ass like most men did.

But not *him*, oh no. His eyes never wandered while she bent down to pick something up, causing her already low-cut bodice to fall open even farther, or when she stood on tiptoes to try to reach something that he would eventually have to retrieve for her, revealing her very shapely ... ankles.

"Ah, I see," was all Hypnocost said.

"We should ask around, see if anyone knows anything about the killer," Lucius suggested, snapping Ghdion's thoughts out of the gutter and back into the present. "Though, with this influx of mercenaries, I'm not sure how easy it will be to get any information. This whole town's been inundated with newcomers, and we don't even know who we're looking for!"

"It's worth a try," she replied in a soothing tone. "We have to start somewhere, don't we? Let's try the tavern, see if any of the locals have any insights."

Desai wasn't a large enough city to host more than one tavern, so it was easy to find. They only had to walk a few minutes into the city to find The Feisty Angler Inn, one of the largest buildings in the main square. It sported a rickety front porch with a thatched roof overhang, a large glass front window that was in dire need of a cleaning, and garlands that festooned the doorway.

Inside was packed with people, mostly locals enjoying a pint or three before returning home from their jobs at the nearby lumber yard or the docks as part of the fishing crews. There were even a few mercenaries there.

The barkeep was a wrinkled old biddy, the type of woman who could sling mugs of ale like there was no tomorrow and wouldn't take shit from anyone, no matter how big or scary they were. Ghdion could even see the outline of a 'hidden' knife in her shirt, right between her breasts. He chuckled to himself, impressed; now *this* was the type of person he could gather information from.

"I'll be at the bar," he announced, and, without awaiting their responses, proceeded to plop down right in the middle seat at the counter, shifting his two-handed greatsword out of the way so he could sit more comfortably.

"What'll ya have?" the gray-haired barkeep asked in a rough voice, pulling a large pewter mug from beneath the counter.

"Whatever's cheapest."

"Not the picky type, eh?" She chuckled, turning around to fill the mug at the tap.

"Nope."

He had to play this right. Barkeeps like her didn't like it when a patron started yapping too quickly. They'd heard it all, from the sorriest sob stories to the most boastful retellings, and they were constantly getting asked, "What news, barkeep?" or "Any sightings of monsters that need slaying?" by the wayward adventuring types. If he wanted any information, he had to ease his way into it.

She turned back around and handed him the mug. He slid a silver piece across the counter, gave her a little nod as a salute, and drank deeply. The beer wasn't half bad, a little hoppy, not too watered down. It was ... acceptable.

She left him to it, wiping down cups and filling other customers' mugs, chatting easily with the regulars. Ghdion amused himself by appreciating the giant fish head that was mounted on the wall in pride of place above the bar. He'd been in plenty of taverns across all of Khamris, but never before had he seen one decorated with a stuffed fish head. He shook his own head and finished off his ale, slamming it down in a signal for more.

She was before him in moments, slipping his second proffered coin deftly into her apron pocket before refilling his mug. Only then did she really take the time to eye him up and down, appraising him. "You're pretty big," she said bluntly.

"Yep."

"Big enough and noticeable enough that I would have recognized you if you'd been in here before." She didn't let his terseness dissuade her. "You one of those mercenaries, come to seek your fortune off Desai's *mis*fortune?"

"Nope."

"Didn't think so. You don't have the right ... what's the word? ... *demeanor* for it." She fixed him with a gimlet gaze. "Lemme guess: you're gonna ask me if I've seen anything strange or heard any disturbing news lately."

Ghdion took a long swallow of the beer. "Yep," he replied honestly, wiping the foam from his lips.

"As a matter of fact..." She leaned in closer, lowering her voice to a carrying whisper. "I heard about a coupla' murders. Happened just this morning, around sunrise."

Ghdion raised a single eyebrow, careful to conceal his growing interest.

She took that as encouragement to continue. "Yeah, it was really terrible. Some guy's wife and kid were slaughtered in cold blood. No motive, nothin' was stolen, just—" She ran her hand across her throat in a slicing motion. "Dead. Mayor's tryin' to keep it hush hush 'cuz it makes him look bad, not havin' hired any mercenaries for protection yet, but you know how it goes." She shrugged. "That poor man. What an awful thing, losin' yer family like that."

Ghdion knew a thing or two about 'losin' yer family like that.' He swallowed thickly, then rolled a gold piece back and forth across the tabletop, pretending to play with it. He slid it across the counter surreptitiously; she yanked it up much quicker than his last coin. "Any idea who this man is or where he lives?"

She bit into the coin, nodded to herself, and tucked it down the front of her blouse. "Leon. Lives four houses down, on the left. Between the fishmonger's house—you'll know it by the smell—and the stables. Green door and shutters, cute little flower wreath on the front door." She smiled, revealing a mouth full of crooked teeth. "But you didn't hear it from me."

"Nope." He finished his ale, dropped a couple copper pieces next to the empty mug, and stood. All in all, his tactics were fruitful. At least it was something they could start with. And it hadn't cost nearly as much as he anticipated. He'd make sure to have Quay reimburse him from the church's overflowing coffers.

"Those yer friends over there?" she asked him, indicating Hypnocost, Quay, and Lucius, who sat glumly around one of the rectangular tables. When he nodded, she continued, "That bald fella with the tattoos on his head. Is he available? I like me a fancy lad like that." She licked her lips. "They don't make 'em like that here in Desai."

Ghdion grunted noncommittally, eyeing Hypnocost. He sat primly at the table, his pointed ears and delicate bone structure out of place in the tavern full of rough, dirty humans. He was receiving just as many, if not more, open looks of interest from the locals as Quay was. "I'm not really sure if he's interested in women," he answered slowly. "Or men, really. In fact, I don't think he's interested in anyone but himself."

"Shame. It's always the pretty ones." She shook her head sadly, then moved on to her other customers.

He made his way towards their table in an unhurried fashion, unable to hide the smugness from his face. He could overhear the others muttering to each other, disappointment evident on their faces.

"Just more propositions," Quay hissed indignantly. "Can't they see I'm from the *Church*?"

"No luck for me, either," Lucius sighed.

"I did have a gentleman offer me a drink," Hypnocost said. "But that is not really relevant to our investigations."

Ghdion slid into the seat beside Quay, who glanced over at him with an affronted little pout. "Why do you look so satisfied?" she demanded, holding an almost full cup of ale between her hands.

He plucked it from her fingers, took a long, languorous gulp, set it back down empty, and smacked his lips. "Oh, just got us a lead," he told her airily.

She gawped. "What? How?"

"What's the lead?" Lucius leaned forward eagerly.

"Some bloke named Leon. His wife and kid were murdered early this morning, and nobody knows why." He tipped his chair onto its back two legs, stretching his long legs beneath the table. "I even know where he lives. Shall we pay him a visit?"

Quay looked stricken, torn between feeling remorse for Leon's awful circumstances and excitement at having a lead. "I don't know ... the man is grieving!"

"And what better person to comfort a grieving man in his hour of need than a Priestess of Vidamae?" Hypnocost supplied, smiling fulsomely. "Honestly, Quay, you will be doing this man a service. He needs you!"

Lucius nodded earnestly. "Kill two birds with one stone!" He winced at his poor choice of words. "I mean—I didn't, er ... You know what I mean."

"I'm not a priestess yet, but ... You're right. You're right!" Quay brightened. "Poor Leon needs me, and we need his information. It's a win-win all around." She stood up, her chair scraping loudly against the wooden floorboards. "Ghdion, lead the way."

He saluted her lazily with two fingers. "Aye, aye, Priestess."

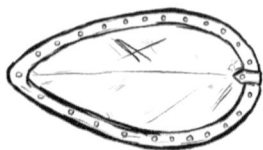

Lucius pounded on Leon's front door for a solid five minutes.

The first minute, he felt bad; they were disturbing a man who had lost it all and probably wanted nothing more than to be left alone. The second and third minutes he started to get annoyed, and his pounding increased in tempo and volume.

By minute five, he was fuming. "I can see your watery eyeball on the other side of that slider there!" he growled, thumping relentlessly upon the wood. It was a supreme effort of will not to bellow like an enraged bull.

Hypnocost wrangled his hands in distress. "Perhaps we should—"

"What do you want from me?" came a muffled voice from the other side of the door. "Just leave me alone!"

"Leon," Lucius said with strained calm. "We simply want to ask you a few questions about ... about what happened to your wife and child."

A heavy, pregnant silence.

"We're here to help," Quay spoke up. She held her holy symbol aloft so Leon could see it from behind the sliding-peephole on his door. "We're part of the Church of Vidamae. We're investigating the murders and want to help bring your family to justice!"

They heard a loud sob, then the slider on the peephole opened all the way. "You're from the church?! Why didn't you say so?"

Lucius groaned. "We tried to! We ... y'know what, nevermind. May we please come inside?"

Leon looked from one person to the next, eyeing them up and down distrustfully. It was painfully evident he did *not* like the looks of either Ghdion, Hypnocost, or Lucius himself; honestly, how could he blame the guy? Lucius's extensive scars always made people uncomfortable. Ghdion was, well, Ghdion: tall and *looming* and glowering at everyone and everything. And Hypnocost? He just looked *otherworldly*.

But when Leon laid eyes upon Quay and her very obvious symbol of Vidamae, he relaxed visibly. "Priestess! I would be honored to receive you. Are these three, ah ... men ... with you?"

Quay gave him her most dazzling, most trusting smile. Her Priestess Smile, her I'm Here To Help Smile. The one that was enough to make any impressionable person fall half in love with her. He hadn't known her for very long, but he'd seen her use it to remarkable effect multiple times already. "These are my bodyguards. As you well know, the roads are no longer safe to travel alone, even though I'm an Acolyte of Vidamae."

"Of course." Leon nodded sagely. "Please, come in."

He finally opened the door. His little house was in quite the disarray. It looked as if someone had come crashing inside—the furniture was at odd angles, the rug pulled up in the middle, some shattered glass spilled all over the floor. Leon, middle-aged and slightly stooped, winced as he stepped around it. "I ... I haven't been up to cleaning this mess yet. I just can't seem to ... can't seem to ..." He burst into tears.

Quay was upon him in an instant, wrapping her arms around him and shushing him softly. "Let those tears fall," she soothed. "Release your anguish to Vidamae, and She will shore you up against these heavy burdens."

The others watched the display with varying faces of discomfort. Hypnocost pursed his lips and looked away; Ghdion just looked bored, like he'd been through similar situations many times before. Lucius was in awe; how could Quay *talk like that* and still be so sincere?

"Why don't you tell us what happened?" he asked when nobody else spoke up.

Leon pulled out of the embrace and wiped his leaking eyes. "Well, where do I even start? My wife Eleanor and I went to bed last night, like we usually do, a while after sunset. Our son, Jeffrey—he's seventeen—was out late and didn't come in until after full dark, which is normal for young people, of course, so I woke up when he got home. I heard him go up to his room, so I fell back asleep and then ..."

His voice trailed off, his eyes haunted. "Something must've registered in my mind that all was not as it should be. I woke up a second time. I'm usually such a heavy sleeper! I don't know what woke me up but I ... but I rolled over and I saw ..."

He took a shuddering breath. "My wife was lying dead beside me. Someone slit her throat. Her side of the bed was just covered in blood! My dumb brain couldn't comprehend it, and all I could think about was how much of a mess there was ..."

Quay rubbed his back as he covered his face in his hands. Lucius listened intently, feeling for the poor man. He couldn't imagine dealing with such a tragedy. "I jumped out of bed and couldn't even scream, I was so overwhelmed! Then I heard a noise in Jeffrey's room, and I just ran in there without thinking. I just ran in! The killer was standing over my son's body, holding a bloody knife. I was too late! I couldn't save him ... couldn't save poor Jeffrey ..."

Sobs overtook his frail body. Quay continued to rub Leon's back while Hypnocost looked on sadly. Ghdion and Lucius exchanged knowing looks. "You *saw* the killer?" Lucius asked, unable to contain the excited note in his voice. Maybe this was the lead they needed!

"Well, it was very dark, but yes." Leon wiped at his nose and sniffled.

"Can you tell us what they looked like? What they were wearing? Anything, please."

"I told all of this to the mayor's men already!" Leon whined. "They came here this morning to take away the bodies. They *assured* me they would take care of it ..."

He could have screamed in frustration. Instead, he clenched his fists at his sides, took a calming breath, and replied, "I understand, and I am very sorry to make you relive what is probably the worst event in your life."

"But we want to help," Quay assured him softly. She had a faint cultured accent that really helped with her whole gentle priestess persona. "Any information you can give us, no matter how insignificant it seems, could be the key to us finding your wife and son's killer." Her eyes lit up as she had a sudden thought. "And of course, the Church would compensate you for your losses. Whatever you need, the Church of Vidamae is here to help."

Leon's face brightened. "Bless you, priestess," he blabbered. "Let me see ... like I said, it was very dark, but I am almost positive the killer was a man. He was cloaked and masked and had his hood pulled up, and was probably, oh, maybe the same height as this young man." He indicated Hypnocost. The half-elf scowled as they all looked over at him, the annoyance at being referred to as a 'young man' obvious on his face. "When I got in there, he looked right at me.

Right into my eyes! His skin was so pale that it almost glowed a little in the darkness." He shuddered. "I could've sworn he was going to kill me right then. But he didn't, he just sort of leapt over the bed and jumped right out the open window. He was so fast! Jeffrey must've opened it to let in the breeze ..."

"Did you see where he went?" Ghdion pressed.

Leon sobbed before answering. "Towards the woods outside of town." He gestured vaguely in the direction behind his house. "There might even be tracks still, if you go out there and look. I told the mayor's men, but I didn't see them go out back and check. Do you think they will finish their investigation soon?"

Quay's face turned stony, and she pursed her lips. "A moment, please, Leon, while I consult with my associates." She stepped into the alcove near the front door, gesturing to the others to follow.

"I don't like this," she said right away. "The mayor sent his 'men' to investigate, but they left without actually investigating? And took the bodies with them?"

"He's trying to cover his tracks," Lucius guessed. "Since he hasn't actually hired any of the mercenaries as guardsmen, there weren't any guards on duty when the murders happened. He's banking on Leon forgetting about that fact and just accepting that this is the normal way of things when a fucking *murder* happens inside of his town." He clenched his fists. Certain types of people, when given even an ounce of power, couldn't help but abuse it. He had a feeling the mayor of Desai was one of those types.

"What are we gonna do about it?" asked Ghdion. He crossed his arms and looked as menacing as ever.

"See if there are any tracks," Quay instructed. "If you find any, I want all three of you to follow them, see if it leads anywhere. Doesn't it seem odd that there have been murders in both Furow's Ridge and Desai, both within a day of each other?" She tapped her chin in agitation. "Something weird is going on, and I have a feeling these murders are connected. It's too big of a coincidence for them not to be."

"And what about you, Priestess?" Ghdion asked.

"Not a priestess yet. I'll stay here with Leon, help him clean up and offer him what comfort and prayers I can. Maybe we can even go to the mayor, see about performing last rites on the bodies." She sighed and crossed her arms. "The Church of Vidamae will provide any necessary monetary compensation."

Ghdion seemed hesitant to leave her. "Are you sure you'll be safe? I can't be much of a bodyguard if I'm not actually near your, err... body to guard."

She laid a hand upon his forearm and smiled. "I'll be fine! It's broad daylight, I'm perfectly safe in this house with Leon, and besides, I have Vidamae to protect me."

"Well, all of the riches of Vidamae's church, anyways," Lucius added.

"That too," she answered seriously. "Now go, before whatever trail is left grows cold."

Chapter 6

The Murky Bard

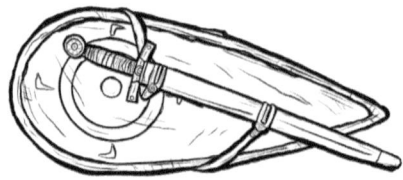

Avindea needed a drink.

Praetorius boasted not one, not two, but *five* different bars for its thirsty citizens. The Scarlet Harlot was closest to her house, but the crowd there was much rowdier than she preferred, and their beer tasted average at best. Two Pearls One Chalice was the fanciest, catering to the most affluent and influential clientele; their signature cocktail was named after the establishment, featuring a heady mixture of whisky and vermouth, garnished with a thin slice of clementine. There were even actual *pearls* plunked into the bottom of the glass. She'd overheard some of the plenum members talk about patronizing the place, which made her even less likely to visit; she already felt inadequate enough during the meetings. No sense bringing that outside work hours.

But if one just wanted a good atmosphere, local musician performances, a really great mug of beer that didn't cost an arm and a leg, and—most importantly of all, to be left alone—The Murky Bard was the only choice. This was where her feet led her after a long and frustrating day: first, with endless meetings at the Cathedral of Vidamae discussing the Church expansion, followed by a much-needed bout of sword practice with her fellow paladins. It had been *weeks* since she'd had time to hone those particular skills, so she got her ass handed to her three times in a row. It ended with another long and argumentative plenum meeting where the only topic of discussion was the escalating hostilities with Athessa. Commander Rakeld kept insisting on reopening involuntary conscriptions; his reasoning was that the army needed to be ready in case a war really was declared. King Selderin refused him at every turn.

She shook her head to try to clear it of those sobering thoughts. There wasn't much she could do to stop what was quickly becoming an inevitable declaration of war; she knew the king was trying his hardest to stall the council from simply rolling over his objections and forcing a vote themselves. The disagreements were almost always between Commander Rakeld (and Lieutenant Orvessa, by extension) and the king, with a supportive Chancellor Eldivar by his side, leaving the rest of the plenum on their own to pick sides.

More disturbing was the fact that Avindea kept seeing some of the counselors whispering together outside of the council chambers, not even trying to hide that they were illegally discussing plenum business outside of the meetings. She was stuck feeling righteous indignation at their flagrant disregard for the law and extreme nervousness about speaking up about it, especially since she was the 'newbie' and didn't want to rock the boat. It didn't help that Chancellor Eldivar himself seemed to ignore that particular rule, since she'd basically caught him and Lord Rendevas doing just that in the library only yesterday.

That's enough dwelling on stuff you cannot change, she told herself firmly. *Now, it's time for that drink!*

The moment she stepped inside The Murky Bard, she was immediately soothed by the familiar scents of malty brews and roast beef, their specialty. The place was crowded with patrons, some happily slugging down mugs of ale, others clapping and singing along with the quartet of musicians who played upon the little wooden stage in the back room. An ostentatious bard with a lute and a truly horrendous feathered cap sang and played energetically with a fiddler and two drummers; their performance of the ribald tune, "Molly's Lips," a favorite amongst the regulars because of its risqué, tongue-in-cheek lyrics, actually sounded quite good.

The barkeep, a jolly middle-aged man named Jerald, knew her by name and by face, and hailed her with a grin as soon as she stepped up to the bar.

"Ah, Lady Avin!" He beamed, already sliding her a mug of her favorite stout. "Haven't seen you in a while. Busy with paladinly duties?"

"Worse, plenum business," she grumbled, taking a hearty swig of the beer. It went down smooth, just like it always did. "I know I say this every time, but damn, your ale is the best, Jerald."

He blushed. "And I never tire of hearing it!"

Avindea scanned the tavern leisurely, taking note of any patrons who looked a bit too drunk or like they might cause trouble. She felt fiercely protective of The Murky Bard and took it upon herself to act as a freelance bouncer any time she visited. She eyed the shadowy back corner, where the less savory patrons tended to commingle. Her eyes landed upon Lord Rendevas, sitting alone at a table. He watched the doorway as if waiting for someone.

She did a double-take, surprised. She couldn't remember ever seeing any other plenum members at The Murky Bard before, so his presence unmoored her. What was he doing there? Should she go speak with him? She always hated it when people tried to talk with her while she was at the bar, but they were strangers and usually only interested in drunkenly propositioning her. Would Lord Rendevas appreciate her stopping over to say hello?

The point was moot, as Rendevas caught her staring and gave her a friendly little wave. *Well, shit, now I have to go over there to say hello.* She grabbed her half-finished beer and sidled over.

"I didn't know you frequented The Murky Bard." Rendevas smiled by way of a greeting. He gestured towards an empty seat at his table. "Please, join me for a drink."

"I was about to say the same to you," she countered. Reluctantly she sat, sipping at her beer to allow herself a moment to think. "What brings you here tonight?"

"Same as you, I would venture to guess." He raised his mug in a mock salute. "I always find I need a drink after plenum meetings like the one we just had."

"I'll drink to that." She eyed him, curious about his motivations. "I'm surprised you didn't head to Two Pearls One Chalice with the other counselors."

He waved the comment away breezily. "That overpriced establishment? Psh! Too pretentious for me." He grinned, aware of how much finer his garb was compared to what the other patrons wore. "Their drinks are sub-par, at best, and only snobs go there. Besides, I'm meeting someone here."

Avindea blanched. "Oh! Don't let me interrupt, I'll—"

"No, no, don't leave! That was not my intention," he assured her. "I think you might actually find my companion to be quite ... illuminating. You could benefit from making their acquaintance."

She was intrigued despite herself. "Alright," was her drawn out response. "So ... who is this mystery person?"

"Hello, dearie!" came a high-pitched old man's voice from behind her. Avindea whirled around and saw a hunched over elderly man, clutching a cane and wearing a fringed shawl over his shock of white hair. How in all of Aukera had this harmless little old man appeared like magic right behind her, without making a sound? Sure, the tavern was loud and crowded and Avin was more than a little distracted, but she hadn't sensed his presence behind her at all. That fact alone put her immediately on edge—as a paladin, she relied on her finely honed situational awareness to keep her safe in both battle and in everyday circumstances.

"Oh! Hello, uh ...?"

"Milford, please sit!" Rendevas drawled. One corner of his mouth turned up into a half smile, his eyes twinkling at some hidden joke. "I was just telling Lady Avindea here about how she should meet you."

"Oh yes, Lady Avindea!" Milford cooed, resting his cane against the side of the table. He settled himself wearily into the chair opposite her, his wrinkly face both pleased and assessing at once. "How are you finding your duties on the plenum, my dear? It must be so overwhelming, what with High Priestess Lucina Balladoni out of the city."

Just as she was getting over the shock of how silently he showed up, she was right back on high alert. "How do you know about the high priestess?" she demanded. High Priestess Lucina Balladoni had quietly left Praetorius, along with most of the higher-ranking clerics and priests, weeks ago. Avin wasn't privy to all the insider knowledge within the church, but she was an important enough paladin of the faith that she had been told that there was a serious liturgical matter that required the high priestess's attention.

"Don't be silly! Why else would you be serving her plenum role?" Milford tittered.

She immediately relaxed. Of course! Of course, that made sense. It wasn't exactly a secret that she was the high priestess's replacement. She wasn't sure *why* she was so rattled by this old man. "Temporarily, thank the gods. Hopefully only for a few more weeks."

"Oh, I'm not so sure about that," Milford replied in his creaky voice. "The meeting with all the higher-ups of your church is happening outside of Khamris, isn't it? She's traveling away from the region, last I heard."

Avindea, suffering from emotional whiplash, sputtered, "Wha—how?" *She* hadn't even been aware of Lucina's destination, so how did this Milford know?

He leaned across the table and patted her arm sympathetically. The old man's hands were wrinkled and rough. "What's wrong, dearie? Cat got your tongue?"

Rendevas took pity on her and spoke up. "Milford hears all kinds of things inside the city." He watched her, his eyebrows raised conspiratorially. "He's been invaluable to any research I need to conduct, especially regarding the histories of both Praetorius and the region. For the benefit of the plenum and the people of Praetorius, of course."

She frowned, looking from Milford to Rendevas and back. "Are you... are you some sort of *informant*? Or a *spy*?" She spat the last word out as if it was a curse. She *hated* spies. They were anathema to all she stood for. Give her an opponent with a sword and a shield that she could see to attack any day, but *spies*? They were almost as bad as *assassins*!

"Oh, ho, nothing so exciting as that." Milford chuckled, waving away the words lightheartedly. "I'm just a harmless old man who notices things without being noticed."

Avindea stood up, the sound of the chair scraping loud even in the din of the tavern. Her ears burned hotly, and her face flushed. Suddenly she regretted coming to The Murky Bard that night. "I want no part of this," she stated.

"Oh, sit down," Rendevas chided. "There's nothing illegal or *untoward* happening here, Avindea, so push those worries right out of your head." He waited until she sat back down, still looking unconvinced, before continuing. "I am actually meeting with Milford tonight because he has some information about the previous wars with Athessa. His knowledge may be invaluable to figuring out any weaknesses Uldinvelm, or the Ternian Czars themselves, may have."

"What about those library books you've had checked out forever?"

"Not everything can be found within the pages of library books," Rendevas answered gently. "I understand that sentiment, being a lover of libraries as well, really, I do ... but sometimes, firsthand knowledge is superior."

"You're telling me *Milford* has firsthand knowledge of the Ternian Czars?" Avindea asked doubtfully.

"Of course not!" Milford chortled. "But perhaps I know someone, who knows someone else, who does." The smile he gave her was both mischievous and mysterious at the same time. He suddenly didn't look like a silly old man anymore. He looked like a force to be reckoned with.

"I don't know ..." Avin hedged. "Still seems a little too close to spying than I am comfortable with."

"Spies are a way of life, my lady," Rendevas remarked. "If you're to survive your time on the plenum unscathed, you'll have to get used to that."

She had come to that realization already, much to her extreme discomfort. "I'm not built for this," she murmured, swigging the last of her beer. It had gone warm from sitting out for too long. Just one more disappointment to top off an already terrible day. "All of this politicking ... I hate it."

"There, there, dearie." Milford patted her arm again. "That's what I'm here for! You can let little old Milford do the digging for you, for a small fee, of course. Then you don't have to get your hands dirty, and you can stay in the loop, just like the rest of the council."

"I would never do such a thing," she spat vehemently. She turned towards Rendevas, giving him a look of such supreme disappointment he glanced away in embarrassment. "Lord Rendevas, shame on you. Now I see you're no better than the rest of the plenum."

"Now, I wouldn't go that far!" Rendevas exclaimed, a note of dismay lacing his smooth voice.

She wasn't interested in hearing more. It was bad enough that she could be implicated in ... whatever this was ... simply by being present. She stood up, gave them each a curt nod, and stalked off, more annoyed than she was when she first arrived.

"You'll be back, dearie," came Milford's high-pitched voice from behind her. "Just you wait and see!"

"Well, that could've gone better."

Rendevas lifted his mug to his lips, realized there was no beer left, sighed, then slumped in his seat.

Milford patted him on the shoulder in sympathy. "Like I said, she'll be back. It's only a matter of time. Hey, when you go get another drink, grab one for me too, will ya?"

Rendevas scowled but stood up and did as asked. When he returned with two overflowing cups of beer, he saw the old man had brought out a neat sheaf of papers. He pushed them across the table. "Oh ho!" Rendevas exclaimed cheerfully. "This is what I asked about?"

"Yep." Milford nodded. He grabbed his proffered mug and brought it to his lips, chugging it down in one fell swoop. Rendevas cocked an eyebrow, impressed. He'd never known a man of Milford's advanced age to drink quite so heartily.

He wiped the foam from his upper lip. "That's only the first bit of it," Milford expressed, eyes twinkling merrily. "Judge Rodach is fairly easy to get information on. He doesn't deal with The Maelstrom; thinks he's too good for the likes of us." He made a look of disgust. "That'll come back to bite him in the ass, it will! I tried to warn him, but the stubborn man wouldn't listen."

Rendevas nodded along, only half paying attention. He scanned the contents of the documents with interest. "So the judge has been giving members of the Claws of Kharon lighter sentences ... I wonder why?"

"Keep reading," Milford suggested. "It gets even better!"

Rendevas placed the first page face down on the tabletop and began reading through the second. "He splits the profits with the members themselves ... oh, you sneaky bastard!" He smiled darkly and shook his head.

The Maelstrom had come through for him once again—Brakten, the shadowy and mysterious leader of the 'information guild,' and by extension, his wide network of informants like Milford, provided sensitive information at wildly exorbitant but very-much-worth-it costs. Rendevas had been a customer of the guild for years, ever since he was appointed senior diplomat. He knew a majority of the other plenum members partook of The Maelstrom's unique services, but none of them ever spoke of it, as that would be considered highly impolite. Why speak aloud about such back-stabbing dealings when you could pretend nothing of the sort ever happened?

He considered the consequences of this newest bit of knowledge. "This is amazing stuff, Milford, but it's not enough," he pondered aloud. "I cannot bring this to the chancellor. I need more. See if you can find proof of the judge selling his plenum votes."

Milford raised his eyebrows and let out a low whistle. "That's certainly something. What makes you think he would do a thing like that?"

"I may have heard a rumor from someone. It seemed just plausible enough for me to bring it up to you."

He grinned. "Well, we'll certainly look into that." He held out his wrinkled old hand, palm up. "And as for the agreed-upon payment?"

Rendevas pulled out a heavy coin purse and placed it upon his waiting palm. "Give Brakten my regards," he said, and with one last swig of beer, he stood up. "Same time next week?"

"Of course." Milford settled back in his chair and eyed him with an assessing stare. "Be careful, Rendevas," he warned. "The judge may not pay The Maelstrom for our protections from prying eyes like yours, but he is still a very powerful man. He may be involved in some things that even *we* aren't aware of, if you catch my drift. Besides, it was way too easy for us to uncover this information. Doesn't that seem strange to you, especially considering how powerful he is?" He lifted his eyebrows meaningfully. "Just keep that in mind if you want to continue down this line of inquiry."

Rendevas gave him a little mock salute. "Duly noted. Until next time."

His mind was awhirl with possibilities. He didn't see Milford shake his head in disappointment behind him as he left.

Chapter 7
Campsite

"I think we are lost."

Hypnocost sighed heavily, placing his hands on his hips. He watched as Lucius rubbed the back of his neck and Ghdion, restless, shifted from one foot to the other. They stood beneath a small copse of trees just outside of Desai; they had followed what little trail they could find from Leon's house, not quite to the forest proper, but not entirely within the outskirts where the thickness of the forest took over.

The 'trail' consisted of one slightly smudged boot print that had been pressed into the mud, and another, less visible print near the edge of the woods. They charged headlong into the undergrowth, Lucius calling out when he would see broken twigs or branches that could theoretically be where someone had recently passed. The mad rush led them into a tiny clearing devoid of any other clues, tracks or otherwise.

The setting sun's warm light dappled the leaf-covered ground. "I thought you were some sort of tracking phenom." Ghdion grunted, eyeing Hypnocost expectantly.

Hypnocost huffed. *"Help me,"* he pleaded with the voice in his head.

There was no answer.

Sometimes the voice did that. Hypnocost had a hard time determining when he could count on receiving an answer, and when he would get nothing but empty silence. Was the voice uninterested in helping him? Why now, when it had helped earlier? *"Why will you not answer me? I look like an idiot right now!"*

There was nothing but silence inside his vast brain.

He sighed, pretending to look this way and that. "I cannot track what is not there. Like I said, I think we are lost. Let us just give it up as hopeless and go b—"

"What's that?" Lucius cried out, pointing into the shadowy section of deeper woods in front of them. "I think I see something."

Hypnocost and Ghdion both squinted, leaning forward to get a better look. Ghdion grunted, impressed. "You're right. Looks like ... a camp of some sort?"

Irritatingly, Hypnocost could still not see it. He moved forward, pushed past some claw-like branches and bushes, frowned, silently cursed the voice for not being there when he needed it, and finally spotted something in the gloom. It was a roughly squarish shape, humped solidly as a slightly lighter shadow amongst the deeper darkness of the forest. "Hmm, I think you are right," he determined. "Could be a tent, perhaps?"

"Let's check it out." Lucius didn't wait for them to agree; he just pushed past them. He blundered through the undergrowth, constantly ducking his head for fear of whacking it onto the low-hanging branches. He cursed under his breath, managing to snap every twig he stepped on. Lucius sounded like an entire army marching loudly through the woods.

Ghdion shot Hypnocost a long-suffering look that seemed to say, *This guy, am I right?* before he followed. His steps were eerily quiet as he made his way through the heavy undergrowth.

Hypnocost picked his way carefully around the fallen logs and waist-high weeds that cluttered the area. The closer they came to the tent-like shape, the more apparent it was that they had stumbled upon a campsite, complete with a medium sized tent, an unlit campfire, and various metal jugs, food detritus, and utensils scattered all around. It looked like the site had been in recent use—some of the logs stacked in the firepit were charred—but something, or someone, had rumbled right through it. There were deep scuffs in the dirt, the tent flaps were torn, and scattered camping paraphernalia was strewn all over the ground. Whatever catastrophe happened there left the place in chaotic disarray.

Lucius whispered from ahead, "I don't see anyone." He held his sword, his free hand twitching nervously. He didn't carry his shield; he must have left it back in the wagon.

"We should check the tent," Ghdion murmured, surveying the place with suspicion. "See if we can figure out who's staying here and why."

"*I could* really *use your help right now*," Hypnocost spoke to the voice.

No answer.

Lucius crept silently up to the tent. He used the tip of his sword to peel open the flap, which had been slashed and ripped across the front. Hypnocost held his breath, waiting for an attack ...

... that never came. Lucius peered inside for a moment, then beckoned them forward. "It's empty," he whispered, stepping inside.

The inside of the tent was dark, filled with the vague shapes of bedrolls and a few cots. It smelled very lived in, like cooked beef, grass, and sweat. It was very off-putting. "Can you give us some of that mage light?" Lucius asked in a low voice as he peered around the edges.

"It is not—oh, fine." Hypnocost willed the ghostly light to emanate from his hand and held it aloft.

The tent was most certainly *not* empty. Slumped in the far corner was a huddled, beaten and bloody young woman. Her hands were bound together and tied tightly to one of the tent posts, and, judging by the drastic bruises across her bare arms, she had been in a fight for her life recently.

"Shit!" Lucius whisper-screamed, jumping back in surprise at the same time Ghdion muttered, "What the fuck?"

"Language?" Hypnocost jibed, earning him an exasperated look from the blond bodyguard.

The two swordsmen knelt down beside the wounded woman. She had short black hair that framed her pointed, pale face, and wore exotic dark leather clothes that were in a style Hypnocost had not seen before. She breathed shallowly, dried blood caking her bottom lip. There was a nasty gash across her collarbone. Her throat was heavily bruised; it looked like someone had tried to strangle her.

"What the fuck are we supposed to do with her?" Ghdion asked Lucius.

"We can't leave her tied up in here," he replied. "She might be in trouble."

"She might also be a *part* of the trouble," Ghdion reminded him. "What if *she's* the one who killed Leon's family?"

While the two of them quietly argued, Hypnocost took it upon himself to investigate the rest of the tent. He held out his glowing hand as he peered closely at the rumpled bedrolls, the piles of candles and blank papers and quills that littered the ground next to them. There were at least five sets of blankets inside, which meant there could be five angry strangers about to come across them pilfering their campsite ...

A glint of light shone out of the corner of his eye; when he turned, he spotted an elaborately decorated mirror propped against the canvas wall. It was about an arm's length tall and slightly smaller in width and painted in blacks and reds along the ornate frame. Hypnocost picked it up—it was a lot lighter than he anticipated—and turned it around in his hands. It certainly felt significant, somehow, like some small bit of magic was trapped inside. He focused upon it, trying to determine what, if any, enchantments lay upon the glass. He brought it closer to his face.

That was when he spotted the fiery triple-clawed symbol of Kax, Goddess of Chaos, imprinted in multiple places around the frame.

"Oh, dear," he breathed, nearly dropping the glass in his astonishment. He noticed other symbols of Kax, carved onto the tent posts, painted across the inside fabric of the tent opening, emblazoned as a pendant style holy symbol in the piles of belongings at each bedroll ...

Kax and Her adherents were not known to be particularly friendly. The goddess had a reputation for choosing some of the most insane, unhinged followers who would blindly follow Her edicts, no matter the danger to the public. They vehemently abhorred governments of all kinds, whether they be democratic in nature or not, and considered it their goddess-demanded right to try to dismantle them at every turn. Hypnocost had even heard tales of a militant group of Kax cultists who, years ago, went around murdering people in some insane plot to bring more power to their church.

No, being alone in a tent in the woods, surrounded by Kax symbols which, theoretically, meant that Kax followers were most likely nearby, did not bode well for them.

"I believe we have a problem," he spoke up in a shaky voice.

His tone held enough alarm that both Ghdion and Lucius turned towards him immediately, hands upon their swords. Hypnocost held up the mirror, pointing at the larger Kax symbol at the top. "See this? I think we may have just stumbled into some sort of Kax worshipper's encampment."

The realization that they were in way over their heads hit them all at the same time. Lucius blanched and Ghdion groaned. "We gotta get out of here," Lucius announced. "Cut the woman down and we'll bring her back with us. Quay can do something about her wounds, and then we'll figure out what to do afterwards."

Ghdion began sawing through the tightly wrapped ropes that bound the unconscious woman. Hypnocost nervously held the mirror to his chest, eyes darting from the tent flap and back. "Do make haste!" he pleaded. "There are at least five bedrolls in here and it is getting dark outside. The Kax people could be back at any moment!"

"I'll keep watch," said Lucius, and he strode confidently out of the tent.

There came an immediate thump and the sound of Lucius letting out a forced rush of air. Then more thumping sounds, in quick succession.

Hypnocost's eyes widened and Ghdion cried, "Shit!" He ran towards the tent flap and yanked it open, revealing Lucius fighting for his life against a hooded, cloaked, swiftly striking opponent. Their eyes glinted fanatically in the gloaming. The hooded person held two wicked looking daggers in a reverse grip and sliced with skillful ease towards the scarred man's throat. He barely had room to parry with his longsword. The move sent him off balance and he stumbled out of sight.

"Get her out of here!" Ghdion roared as he leapt into the fray. He nearly tore down the entire tent's structure with a powerful two-handed strike of his greatsword, but the agile opponent jumped out of the way with ease.

Hypnocost ran over to the wounded woman, patting his sides frantically as he looked for something, anything, to cut the rope with. "I do not have a knife!" he hissed in desperation, trying unsuccessfully to pry the rope apart with his bare fingers.

"There are two knives near that bedroll,"

the voice told him.

"Do you not see them?"

"NOW *you speak to me?*" Hypnocost thought indignantly. He searched the nearest bedroll and, sure enough, found a pair of slim daggers, half hidden by a dark blanket.

Outside, he could hear the hooded person laughing in a frenzy, followed by a loud curse from Ghdion, and the sound of a sword slashing through the air.

"I can't get this guy pinned down!" Ghdion roared. Someone slammed against the tent, shaking it wildly.

Hypnocost sawed through the thick ropes, muttering aloud at the voice darkly. "All I ask is for a little help and you do not show up until the literal last second ..."

"Your friends are not doing so well,"

the voice said.

"You may want to think about assisting them."

"I'm trying!" he cried, much louder than he intended. Nobody seemed to notice, as they were all either fighting for their lives or, in the woman's case, knocked out cold.

The ropes finally unraveled, the woman's arms falling heavily into her lap. She fell over, no longer held up by her bindings.

With that task completed, Hypnocost stood tall and walked with purpose towards the tent entrance, where he assessed the battle coolly.

Lucius and Ghdion were overmatched, even two against one. The light, deft movements of the much faster hooded attacker kept both of them on the defensive, and their opponent had already managed to land two nasty hits upon Ghdion's arm. Lucius couldn't strike for fear of accidentally hitting the blond man, so they were both in a standoff, with the jumpy attacker laughing crazily between them.

The theurgist took a deep breath and focused all of his considerable will upon the stranger. He opened his mind to the hooded person, imagining a thin tunnel that stretched from his brain to theirs. That imaginary tunnel burrowed deep inside of the opponent's mind; the stranger stopped bouncing on the balls of their feet and blinked, shaking their head to try to clear the weird feelings of *cobwebs* and *intrusion* sent their way. He could lightly sense the attacker's thoughts behind what looked, to his mind's eye, like a solitary door; the attacker was delighted at finally having a couple of foes they could play with. Hypnocost opened the mind door, revealing deeper thoughts—an intense, fanatical devotion to almighty Kax, Lady of Chaos! *The bloodline of The Whore Goddess Vidamae shall be cleansed in Kax's HOLY FIRE!*

Hypnocost firmly re-centered his thoughts—it was all too easy to get caught up in the cultist's fanaticism—and burrowed deeper, deeper, opening more and more doors until he hit what he saw as a wall at the base of the person's mind. There, the burrowing stopped, and he focused on widening his tunnel until it encompassed all of the attacker's front brain and forward thoughts.

STAND STILL, he demanded of the Kax devotee's mind. **STAND STILL AND ACCEPT YOUR FATE.**

All of this happened in mere moments. The power of Hypnocost's thoughts, the significant force of his will, were much stronger than that of the hooded stranger's.

The cloaked person stood still, their eyes blank and staring out at nothing. It happened so quickly and came as such a surprise to Hypnocost that he almost let go of the connection. Almost.

Ghdion, seeing the attacker suddenly standing there stupidly, took the opportunity to slice across their neck, separating their head from their body with one fell swoop.

The head fell with a sickening thump and rolled across the ground, trailing hot, gushing blood. The rest of the body fell in a heap. Weak moonlight caught on the glint of a golden symbol of Kax from a chain necklace as it tumbled free of the bloody neck stump.

The three men stared incomprehensibly at the gruesome spectacle, breathing hard from their exertions. Ghdion, panting, glanced over at Hypnocost, a question in his eyes. "Was that—was that *you*? Did you make them stop like that?"

Hypnocost nodded, both stunned and thoroughly impressed with himself. The contact with the person's brain had severed as abruptly as Ghdion had lopped the head from their shoulders.

He was left with a curious feeling of ... regret? at the lost contact. It had been both heady and terrifying to be so intertwined with another's mind! "Thank me later. Let us grab the woman and get out of here before the rest of these cultists or ... or whatever they are—return."

And then he promptly collapsed to the ground.

Chapter 8

Rabble-Rouser

Milford heard the commotion before he saw it.

"*The city guard is not here for your protection, citizens of Praetorius! They are nothing but a bunch of bullies and brutes whose only job is to keep the populace ill-informed and poverty-stricken! The government does not care about you!*"

Milford sighed and pulled his shawl tighter around his neck. *Keegan's back at it with his protests again, eh?* he thought. His nose itched like crazy, but he couldn't scratch it. Not with the prosthetic on. The glue he used to tamp it down onto his actual nose was the problem; in warmer weather it was always so much worse because it would start to *melt* onto his skin.

The day was unseasonably hot for autumn in Praetorius. Milford, his long gray and purple robes trailing on the cobblestones behind him, followed the sound of the speaking trumpet until he reached the square in the middle of the Merchant District.

Sure enough, there, right in front of the stone fountain and trim green bushes and wrought-iron benches stood Keegan, Praetorius's top rabble-rouser. He held a rolled-up piece of parchment to his mouth and used his free arm to wave maniacally at passersby, taking turns screaming at them as they walked past.

"Do not be fooled by the plenum's false promises! They take and they take, but they never give back! Your taxes are being hoarded for their own interests and are being wasted on this useless war with Athessa!"

Milford stuck to the shadows cast by a nearby candlemaker's shop. *You're not exactly wrong, Keegan.* Given everything Milford knew about the leaders of the city, Keegan's heated exclamations were mostly true. *Just ... why do you have to go about it like this? Who are you doing this for? You, or the citizens of Praetorius like you claim?*

He watched the shaggy-haired young man for a while, careful to keep up the appearance as a stooped over old man. He used the wall as a support, his hood kept low over his wrinkled face; the makeup that gave him the appearance of an elderly gentleman felt stiff and caked onto his skin. Keegan's anti-government shenanigans had been escalating for months now; Milford had been pleased, and not surprised at all, when Captain Riluk approached him for help in keeping an eye on the malcontent. The pay wasn't the greatest, but when the captain of the city guard asked The Maelstrom for help, it wasn't something he could refuse.

Besides, it was always nice to be owed a favor (or two) by someone so highly placed in the government.

It was hard to tell just how old Keegan actually was. He was lanky and tall, with shaggy brown hair that reached his shoulders. His clothes were always well-worn and heavily mended, but clean. His large nose and droopy eyes gave him the appearance of a man constantly wallowing in sorrow; perhaps he was. Milford knew little of the man's circumstances. What he had managed to dig up was that Keegan had tried, and failed, to join the Arcane Academy; his magical abilities must not have been enough to impress Lady Uunar, the headmistress of the elite school of mages. Afterwards, he joined the city guard but was kicked out—unsurprisingly—due to issues with disobedience. Since then, he'd made it a point to be a thorn in the side of the city guard, or really anyone with any sort of authority, spending most of his days traveling across the city, yelling about the injustices of the guard, the plenum, the king, anything to stir up the anger of the general populace.

The thing about Keegan was that he was quite well-informed. Milford was impressed, despite himself, at Keegan's awareness of the issues; he was well-spoken and direct while addressing the public. He would've made an excellent informant for The Maelstrom, had the organization been larger than just one man with many different disguises.

That one man being him. Milford—well, Brakten, really, Milford was one of his many personas—was the leader and sole member of The Maelstrom, elite information guild of Praetorius. If anyone found out that closely guarded secret, The Maelstrom would lose all credibility.

Which was why Brakten, dressed as Milford, had to be careful not to blow his cover.

Keegan continued his verbal assault on the unsuspecting citizens of the Merchant District. *He must be using magic to make his voice louder,* Brakten thought, squinting his eyes as if that would make it easier to see the spell floating around or something. *It's the only explanation; that rolled up parchment wouldn't make his voice travel as far as it is.*

The apparent spell and the speaking trumpet sent his words crashing through the streets. A few people glanced at him with interest, nodding their agreement or holding out their fists in solidarity. *"The war only serves to line their already overflowing pockets! They take your money in the form of taxes, they take your children in the form of conscriptions, they send them off to die for their country! The city guard will come for you soon!"*

A crowd started to gather. Brakten moved closer, blending in with the rest of the people listening to Keegan's fiery diatribe. The activist pointed ominously at a middle-aged woman with her teenage son. The woman's eyes widened, and she clutched at her son fearfully. *"That's right! You are good to fear these words, for they are naught by the **truth**! Do not fear the messenger, fear those who will take everything away from you! Fear the city guard! **Down with the plenum**!"*

Brakten could see a younger woman trawling the rapt crowd, observing the pockets of those surrounding her. It was obvious she was looking for an easy mark. *Pickpockets*, he thought, rolling his eyes. He watched as she loosened the purse strings at one woman's belt, then loped casually to the other side of the crowd, towards where Brakten, as old man Milford, watched on the fringes.

The pickpocket sidled up beside him and reached a hand towards his voluminous robes; he snatched at her wrist with a speed that obviously threw her off guard. "Keep your hands to yourself, missy," he hissed in Milford's airy, wheezy voice.

The pickpocket met his eyes and gasped at the dangerous look she was met with. Her mouth dropped open and she took a step backward, holding up her free hand in surrender.

It would've been so easy to simply gut her right there in the middle of the crowd. He'd done it before. Many times. But that was before. He wasn't that man anymore. So instead, he shoved her ungently aside and growled, "Mind your manners, young lady."

She nodded fearfully and scampered off, away from the crowd entirely. Maybe she sensed just how close she'd been to trouble.

The crowd started to grow. Brakten didn't expect Keegan's words to have as big of an effect on the people of the Merchant District; apparently, they were just as frustrated by the plenum as Keegan was. *Might be time to find Captain Riluk*, he thought, but just as he turned away, the flash of sunlight on plate armor caught his eye.

Captain Riluk himself, as well as three other city guards, marched up from behind Keegan. They took up positions on either side, where he stood upon the lip of the stone fountain.

"That's enough, Keegan," Captain Riluk called out in a mild voice.

The crowd, wary of the appearance of the authorities, immediately started to disperse. Brakten slowly moved along with them, but instead of leaving entirely, he made his way back to his hiding spot in the candle shop's shadows.

"Riluk." Keegan spat at the ground right next to Riluk's leather boots. "Come to silence my rights to free speech again?"

The captain sighed wearily. "You know the rules, Keegan," he replied evenly. "You can spout off as much nonsense as you'd like, but once you start causing a public disturbance, the city guard must step in." He eyed his former colleague, taking in the unevenly sewn patches on Keegan's tunic, the ragged, frayed edges of his sleeves and trousers. "I understand your frustration, and I even agree with some of what you are saying. But please stop, or I'll have to throw you back in jail."

Brakten was constantly amazed at the depths of patience Captain Riluk possessed. If he'd been in charge, he would've executed the rabble-rouser months ago. *That's why I'm The Maelstrom instead of a soldier,* he thought to himself in amusement. *I'd make a terrible city guard.*

"Never!" Keegan cried, pumping his closed fist into the air. His stringy brown hair flopped into his face. "You'll never silence me!"

He raised the speaking trumpet to his lips. He took a deep breath and bellowed, *"See how the guard targets me? They fear the truths I speak! They seek to silence me, to keep you all in the dark!"*

Unfortunately, he was yelling at no one. The crowd had completely disappeared as soon as the authorities arrived. The only one left to witness Keegan's distress was Brakten himself, hidden within the shadows.

Captain Riluk sighed, reaching for Keegan's arm. "Alright, have it your way." He gestured to the side, and the three guards with him moved in.

Riluk was too close for Keegan to make a run for it, but he tried anyway.

And failed.

Brakten winced as the three guards tackled Keegan to the ground before he made it two paces. They slammed his head into the cobblestones. His nose gushed blood, dripping freely as they hauled him to his feet.

"That's enough," Captain Riluk said to them. "There's no need to hurt him."

Keegan scowled. "You can never silence me for long, Riluk!" he screeched, struggling as the guards bound his hands behind his back. "I'll be back out here tomorrow after you release me, and the next day, and the next! Your oppression will not stop me!"

"I've no doubt about that," the captain answered. He waved towards the three guards holding Keegan. "Take him to jail. Perhaps one night behind bars will cool his temper."

The guards hauled Keegan away. The courtyard was soon empty of people save Captain Riluk himself, who gazed off in the distance thoughtfully.

Brakten stepped up beside him, as silent as the night. "Trouble, Captain Riluk?" he asked in his Milford voice.

Riluk jumped, his hand going immediately to the pommel of his sword. When he saw it was only Milford's hunched, robed form, he visibly relaxed. "Milford," he greeted gruffly. "I don't know how you manage to sneak up on me like that every time." He eyed Milford sidelong. "One would almost suspect you'd been a thief in your younger years. Or something worse."

"Something worse." Brakten smiled mysteriously and shrugged. "I was just coming to alert you about Keegan, but you beat me to it. I'm impressed. It's not often the guard reacts to trouble faster than The Maelstrom does."

Riluk frowned but didn't otherwise react to the dig. "I just so happened to be on patrol in the neighborhood. Good thing, too. The situation could have gotten out of hand." He peered down at the old man. "What am I paying you for, Milford? You assured me you'd keep an eye on Keegan."

"And I was." Brakten didn't meet Riluk's discerning dark eyes. He gestured towards the empty square. "I do have other clients, you know."

"Mmm." The captain crossed his arms over his breastplate. Golden epaulettes decorated the shoulders, displaying his high rank. "I'd appreciate it if you kept a closer eye on that one for me. I fear he's up to something. He draws larger and larger crowds lately, and his mental state is ... well, let's just say he is *unwell*."

He sighed and rubbed at his forehead. "I cannot be everywhere at once. Today's situation just proves it." The captain reached down towards his belt, where a leather coin purse was strapped. "Here, I have your payment. I expect a speedier response next time."

Brakten pushed away the proffered payment. "Not in public, if you please, Captain," he whispered, eyeing the empty square suspiciously. "I have a reputation to uphold!"

Riluk scowled but did not argue. He reattached the coin pouch to his belt. "Until next time, Milford."

"Until next time." He nodded politely and turned away, not before brushing lightly against the captain.

He grinned when he saw, as he stepped back into the shadows of a nearby alley, Riluk pat at his sides as he realized the coin purse was missing. Brakten tossed it lightly into the air before securing it deep within one of his many pockets. *Still got it*, he mused. *The poor sod never stood a chance.*

Chapter 9

Mystery Woman

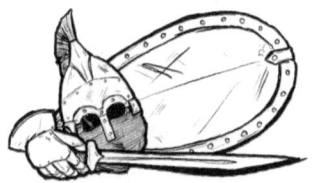

Lucius was the only one of the trio of bodyguards who both remained conscious and unwounded after the campsite attack. Hypnocost had immediately passed out after doing whatever bizarre mind spell to the now headless Kax cultist. Ghdion's arm was pretty badly mangled from two dagger hits, and he was bleeding all over the place. By necessity, that made the ex-guard the one who had to rush back into Desai to search for Quay.

In an insane stroke of luck, Lucius spotted her just as she was returning from the Desai City Hall with Leon. When he ran over, he must have looked a little crazed, based on the matching looks of alarm on their faces.

"Lucius!" she called out, her cheerfulness a little too forced to be natural. "Whaaaaat are you doing?"

He feigned laughter, loud and violently boisterous. It made poor Quay jump in shock. "I'm so glad I found you, Quay!" he nearly shouted. "Could I please have a word with you?"

She muttered some weak excuse to Leon, the bereaved widower. Leon merely nodded, shot Lucius a confused look, and, after some whispered assurances from the priestess, headed off back to his home.

"There was an ... altercation," Lucius told her hurriedly. "We, ah ... ended up having to kill someone who attacked us."

"You did *what*?" Quay hissed.

"Shhhhhh!" He waved frantically in the air and grabbed her hand to pull her away. "Sorry, Quay, just be quiet a sec and come with me. I'll show you."

"Where are Ghdion and Hypnocost?" she demanded. "How bad are their wounds?"

"Ummmm ... not great!" he admitted. "C'mon, you'll just have to see for yourself. We're nearly there."

The sun was almost below the horizon. The dimness of the light made it hard to find where the other two hid with the unconscious woman. Lucius and Ghdion had managed to drag both Hypnocost and the mystery woman out of the campsite and through the woods, where Ghdion waited with them on the outskirts, hidden among some sparse weeds and underbrush.

The trees cast menacing shadows in the lengthening gloom. Each one seemed to jump out like a dagger wielding cultist bent on revenge.

"Ghdion!" Lucius whisper-screamed at a likely clump of bushes. "Psssst! Are you in there?"

"I'm right here, you idiot!" came Ghdion's raspy reply.

Lucius was looking in the completely wrong spot. Ghdion peeked out of a lumpy bush about five feet away. He waved his good arm to get their attention.

Quay rushed over, hiking up her long skirts, the translucent fabric of her headband crown thing—Lucius had no idea what it was called, but it was something all Vidamae Priestesses seemed to wear—floating in her wake. "Are you okay? Let me see your wounds," she commanded. Ghdion obediently held out his bloody arm, but then she pulled up short.

"Wha—? Who is *that*?"

The unconscious woman sat propped up against a tree, her many bruises and cuts looking much worse even in the gloomy light.

She shoved Ghdion's arm aside; he let out a grunt of pain. "What did you *do* to this poor woman!?"

"*We* didn't do anything." Ghdion reacted defensively. "We found her like that, tied up inside of a tent. A tent, I might add," he sneered, "that was *full of Kax shit!*"

"Language!" Quay muttered, focusing all her attention on the unconscious woman. She held her hands together briefly, murmuring a silent prayer to Vidamae, and then her fingers began to glow with a soft golden light. Delicately she placed her hands upon the woman's chest, right above her heart; the golden luminescence spread like glowing tendrils across the woman's arms and legs, up her neck, around her face.

Quay, eyes closed, frowned. "Hmmm. She's been very badly injured for quite a while," she diagnosed. "These are wounds that are too old for me to heal effectively. They could be infected. I'll do what I can, but it's actually better for her to remain unconscious while her body does the hard work of healing itself." She turned towards the others. "She needs a physician, not a healer."

"Okayyyy... but will she live?" Lucius asked breathlessly. He wanted to know more about this mystery woman. Who was she? Why was she beaten up so badly? Did she have something to do with the string of murders they were investigating? And most importantly, why on all of Aukera was she tied up inside a Kax cultist's tent?

"She should," Quay told him. "She seems young and healthy, despite the fact that she was beaten up so badly." She narrowed her eyes, looking more closely at the girl. "I wonder who she is?"

Ghdion cleared his throat loudly. "Priestess, a little help here, please?" He thrust his bloody arm towards her once again.

"Oh! Sorry, Ghdion, I forgot about you. You're always getting sliced up." She made her hands glow again and placed them upon the deep cuts in his bicep, where his torn flesh and muscle tissue began to knit together rapidly, aided by the magical golden light. He winced; magical healing was fast and effective in a pinch, but that didn't mean it didn't hurt like hells. Lucius had been on the receiving end of many a healing spell in his past, so he sympathized.

"Always getting ... *tch*! I almost died, Priestess."

"I've told you before, Ghdion, you cannot call me 'Priestess' like that, with a capital 'P.' I'm not a full priestess, not yet."

Lucius eyed them with interest; he could actually hear the capital 'P' whenever Ghdion called her that. Secretly, he suspected he did it just to exasperate her. They had an interesting dynamic, like a pair long used to being comfortable with one another, while at the same time dancing around what was an obvious mutual attraction. Well, it was obvious to Lucius, anyways. He had a feeling neither realized the other felt the same.

"Whatever." Ghdion scowled and glanced away. He looked a bit squeamish after seeing his own flesh knit itself back together. Lucius knew the feeling. "You may as well be."

"Were there any other survivors?" she asked, ignoring Ghdion and looking to Lucius instead. "At the camp?"

He shook his head. "Not that we saw. Looked like there were maybe five or more people staying there, but we didn't see anyone else other than this woman and the person who attacked us."

Quay was so focused on her healing that she hadn't even noticed Hypnocost, senseless and leaned haphazardly against the other side of the tree. She did a double take, then asked, "When were you going to tell me that Hypnocost is knocked out, as well?"

"Oh, he did that to himself." Lucius grinned. "Happened after he did some sorta mind ... magic ... spell thing. I've never seen anything like it before."

She huffed out a breath, looking somewhat worse for the wear after two major healings in a row. Lucius had seen some healers work themselves so hard on a battlefield they fell right over from pure exhaustion onto the very people they were meant to help. Quay seemed to be just like those medics from his past, willing to compromise their own health and safety in exchange for saving others. He couldn't help but admire their commitment.

Ghdion's arm finished stitching itself up, so she shuffled towards Hypnocost and placed a hand upon his forehead. "He seems stable. Must have overworked himself from casting spells."

"Spell, you mean. Spell *singular*," Ghdion corrected as he rubbed his freshly healed arm. Lucius knew, also from experience, that in a few hours, that arm was going to itch like all *hells*. "Some bodyguard. Baldy can't handle casting more than *one spell* at a time without passing out afterwards."

"Oh, hush! He's trying his best."

"Well, his best isn't good enough. What if he drops when you need his help, huh? What if—"

"Alright, can you two stop bickering like an old married couple?!" Lucius groaned, annoyed. "Ghdion, we'd both be dead if 'Baldy' hadn't cast his *one* spell, so maybe you should be a little more grateful and a little less judgy next time he saves your ass."

He turned towards the not-yet-a-priestess. "And Quay? We need to know what to do. What's the plan? Where do we go from here?"

She sat back on her heels, looking bewildered. "You said the tent was full of Kax paraphernalia?" When they both nodded, she shuddered. "This sounds awfully similar to what the Kax cult did to Vidamae's followers fifteen years ago." She paused, frowning. "Eerily similar, actually."

"I'm afraid to ask," Lucius said, though he was secretly intrigued. He loved a good tale of high drama.

Quay clasped her hands in her lap, her face taking a faraway cast. "You don't know about it? Oh, it was awful. A big group of Kax followers—cultists, really—decided that the best way to end Vidamae's reign as the most powerful deity was to kill as many of Her followers, clerics, and priestesses as they possibly could. There were even rumors they had some magical device that allowed them to find, and subsequently kill, anyone who shared a bloodline with the goddess! Vidamae has been known to frequent Aukera, you know, spreading Her blessings among Her people."

Lucius snorted derisively. "Spreading Her blessings, eh?"

She shot him an annoyed look—he slammed his mouth shut, preventing any further comments on the matter.

"Anyways, it was a bloodbath. No church was safe, and they killed unchecked for many months before High Priestess Lucina Balladoni—well, she wasn't the High Priestess then, not yet—led a mass prayer at the Altar of Tasuil, begging for Vidamae's aid."

"What did that accomplish?" Lucius, genuinely interested, asked. He wasn't a religious man by any stretch of the imagination, which was probably why he was so ignorant of this obviously traumatic piece of Vidamae Church history.

"Vidamae made Her presence known. Her avatar descended from on high and cast a divine spell of heavenly brightness that affected only the Kax cultists that had murdered Her followers. They were all blinded, and some were actually smote right where they stood! They've been weakened and in hiding ever since then."

"Huh." Lucius wasn't really sure what else to say. "So you think this might be happening again?"

"It's possible. Are you sure the person who attacked you was a Kax cultist? And were they the one who killed Leon's family?"

"Well, we aren't entirely sure," he confessed. "But it seems an awfully big coincidence that the tracks we followed from Leon's house led us right to that Kax encampment, and that a cloaked, seriously skilled *knife-fighter* attacked us as soon as we left the tent." He shrugged. "It seems likely. I'd be willing to put money on it. Not my life or anything, but money? Sure."

Ghdion nodded along with him. "How many campsites have tents full of Kax holy symbols and women tied up inside of them? Not many, I'd hope. And the fact that two small villages this close to that Kax campsite both suffered mysterious murders? One of which was a Vidamae Priest? Seems pretty clear cut, if you ask me."

Slowly she nodded her agreement. "This is way above my pay grade."

"You're the boss," Lucius said. "We do what you want us to do. Go where you go."

She slumped back. "We should return to Praetorius," she decided after a pause. "We need to bring this news to the high priestess. She will know what to do."

"Are you sure we should leave so soon?" he asked. "Maybe we stay in Desai, see what else we can find out here." He didn't mention the real reason why he was so hesitant to go to Praetorius. That was the *last* place he wanted to be.

"All of my resources are in Praetorius," she answered. "It's honestly the best place we can go."

Lucius was disappointed. "And our wounded mystery woman?"

Quay glanced over at the strangely dressed woman. "We can't just leave her here." She got to her feet, brushing the leaves and twigs from her gown, face thoughtful. "She'll have to come with us."

Ghdion stood with a groan of pain and rubbed his lower back. "Whatever you say, Priestess."

She ignored him and turned towards Lucius. "We'd better grab Mertha and the wagon. We've got a long road to Praetorius ahead of us."

Chapter 10

The Other Diplomat

Rendevas had the most amazing news.

It was the next morning, and the latest plenum meeting was about to begin. He was so excited he could not sit still. His leg bounced rapidly, and he kept clasping and unclasping his hands, over and over. It was better than the alternative; he had been a ferocious nail-biter in his youth, and only after years of mentally training himself was he able to stop the nasty habit.

It took the other counselors *ages* to settle in. They seemed chattier than usual, pausing to trade gossip or laugh lightly at each other's jokes. It was *maddening*! Didn't they see how anxious he was to get this meeting started?

Finally, King Selderin and his daughter, Princess Alandria, glided gracefully into the meeting chambers. The princess looked poised and polite, her floor length gown of royal blue velvet trailing behind her. Rendevas pondered her thoughtfully; she really was growing into a remarkable young woman. He was proud of her.

The king, however, looked somewhat worse for the wear, with dark circles under his eyes and his crown slightly askew atop his brown curls. He knew the job would be rough on his old friend;

when he'd been announced king almost fifteen years ago, it had opened the senior diplomat position for Rendevas. He was grateful for the rise in status, especially as it allowed him to work more closely with his childhood friend Philemon Selderin, known as Phil to his tight-knit inner circle.

Chancellor Eldivar, today wearing a golden and white trimmed doublet with matching trousers, stood up graciously as soon as the king sat, allowing the proceedings to begin. "Shall we begin with the security updates today?" he announced, and it was all Rendevas could do to not groan outwardly at the delay.

Commander Rakeld, in his typical dulcet tones, informed them that one of his spies, firmly entrenched deep inside Uldinvelm, had finally managed to get a report out. The news was dire: Uldinvelm was openly mustering their troops.

"'The other spies have disappeared one by one,'" the commander read aloud from the spy's last communication. "'This may very well be my last report.'"

Rendevas brought his fingers to his mouth to start nibbling at his nails before he realized fully what he was about to do. Damn the nervous habit! This news about the missing spies was dire—the looks of concern upon the faces of his fellow counselors showed just how much they worried. They asked thoughtful questions of the commander while Rendevas sat there, quietly fuming. Their anxiety could negatively affect the reaction he expected from his grand announcement.

"We need to reinstate conscriptions," Lieutenant Orvessa blurted in her usual direct manner. She looked like a snarling bulldog with that scar on her lip. "We can't keep delaying the inevitable, Your Highness. This latest report should be enough to convince you. We need to start training anyone who could be listed on the draft if we are to be ready for whatever Athessa throws our way."

King Selderin shook his head. "Let us hold off on that vote for now," he cautioned. "Besides, I believe Lord Rendevas has an exciting development to announce that may change your mind."

"It does have some relevance to what we are discussing," Chancellor Eldivar added. "Lord Rendevas, if you would?"

He shot to his feet. Finally! "Thank you, Chancellor Eldivar." He bowed towards the head of the table, then took a deep, steadying breath. "I received an interesting missive this morning, all the way from Uldinvelm itself. They are requesting we allow one of their diplomats safe passage into the city to discuss the heightened aggressions between our two countries. They are willing to open peaceful negotiations."

Murmurs of approval spread around the table, though Commander Rakeld and Lieutenant Orvessa both scowled. Judge Rodach, his long face always sneering, shot Rendevas a pointed look. "Let me guess," he spat, "you're hoping to force a vote to allow the Athessian diplomat safe passage into the city."

Judge Rodach took the wind right out of his sails. Deflated, he plastered a cheery grin upon his face anyways. "That is exactly what I was going to suggest. Thank you, Judge Rodach, for your succinct observations." He turned towards the assembly. "This is huge, unprecedented, even. When was the last time Athessa wished to discuss peace with Khamris?"

"This seems awfully suspicious," Commander Rakeld added. "How sure are you of their intentions? They could be looking for a way to exploit Praetorius, or worse, confront us about our spies!"

"And how do we know you're giving us the whole story?" the judge continued. "Was there anyone else involved in your 'dealings' with the Uldinvelm diplomat?"

Rendevas scoffed. "Why would there be? I am, after all, Praetorius's highest-ranking diplomat. Who else would they have contacted?" He chuckled mirthlessly. "I sent them a letter weeks ago, not expecting anything to come of it. The fact that they actually responded, and so quickly, is a good sign!"

Scattering mutterings and dark looks abounded. Judge Rodach, seizing the moment, pressed on. "It just seems suspect. Something as momentous as this should require more than one plenum member to verify its authenticity."

"Would you like to see the correspondence?" Rendevas spat, unable to contain his annoyance. This was not going at all how he planned! This was insanely good news. He may have just single-handedly started the path to nonviolence between the two rival countries, and the judge dared to question his motives ...?

The notes he had obtained from Milford and The Maelstrom suddenly came rushing into his mind. *Of course!* he thought in excitement. *It's just like the chancellor warned me, Rodach doesn't have Praetorius' best interests in mind. I'm not sure how this may benefit him, but he must have a personal stake in making sure war is actually declared ...*

"Actually, I would," Judge Rodach told him haughtily. "I'd like to independently verify its legality, as is my right as a judge."

I'm sure you would, Rendevas thought darkly. *You just want to exploit this situation somehow. Or make my correspondence 'accidentally disappear,' more like it.*

Faith and Ruin

"Is that really necessary?" Avindea asked from her end of the table. She watched the two men argue with interest, her chin resting on her hand. "Seems like a waste of time. Lord Rendevas hasn't given any of us a reason to doubt him before, so why would he lie about something as important as this? Besides, isn't this *good* news? Shouldn't we be actively *trying* to prevent a war? Seems like meeting with one of their diplomats is the best avenue towards peace."

Rendevas shot her a grateful look. Chancellor Eldivar hummed thoughtfully, hands on his hips as he stood at his spot near the head of the table. "What do we think? Shall we vote on it?"

Most of the plenum nodded from around the table. The chancellor called out, "Those in favor of Lord Rendevas providing the correspondence from his contact in Uldinvelm to Judge Rodach so he can independently verify it?"

Judge Rodach and Constable Mald, the dull-eyed head of the Praetorius Jail, both raised their hands.

"Those against?"

The rest of the plenum raised their hands. Rendevas shot the judge a look of triumph.

"The no's have it," Chancellor Eldivar announced, unable to hide the glint of delight in his eyes. He smiled at Rendevas. "Now, can you please give us some more details regarding this Athessian diplomat?"

He stopped from rubbing his hands gleefully, but only just barely. "I would be honored," he stated. "The diplomat, one Lord Tullie Mason of Uldinvelm, has humbly petitioned for an audience with the plenum in about four weeks' time. He seeks an open dialogue with the leaders of Praetorius regarding the escalating tensions between our two countries and assures me that a peaceful resolution is foremost on his agenda. He has on his list of requests that he be allowed a small cadre of soldiers—for his protection both on his travels and here within the city—and he assures me he speaks as the voice of the Ternian Czars. Whatever agreements we come to will have the full support of their leadership."

The king looked impressed. "However did you manage to secure such a dialogue with one of Uldinvelm's diplomats?"

"I simply wrote to him." Rendevas shrugged, unable to suppress the floaty feeling of pride the king's words gave him. And in front of the plenum! "I figured it was worth a try. Instead of jumping immediately into violence, why not try diplomacy instead? Besides, there is no harm in hearing them out, is there? This is just the beginning of a dialogue, nothing more. We don't need to agree to anything if we suspect foul intentions."

"It's something some of us on the plenum could learn from," King Selderin replied, pointedly not looking towards Commander Rakeld and Lieutenant Orvessa. "Chancellor, let us bring this motion to a vote. I have a feeling there will be much work to be done behind the scenes depending on the outcome. I'd rather we get started now than find ourselves delayed."

The chancellor nodded sharply. "Of course, Your Majesty. All in favor of allowing the Athessian diplomat, Lord Tullie Mason of Uldinvelm, free and safe passage into Praetorius in four weeks' time?"

All raised their hands except Judge Rodach, Constable Mald, Commander Rakeld, and Lieutenant Orvessa.

"All those against?"

Those four, of course, raised their hands. "This is a bad idea," Lieutenant Orvessa murmured darkly. "You're okay with allowing an Athessian diplomat—and *Athessian soldiers*—unfettered access into the city? This won't end well!"

"Nobody said anything about unfettered access." Rendevas scowled, clenching his fists in his lap. "You act as if I am asking to throw open the city gates and allow the entire Athessian Army to march right on through!"

Chancellor Eldivar ignored both of them, raising his voice to cut over their jibes. "The ayes have it."

Rendevas was unable to contain a triumphant smile from cracking across his face. "Thank you, Chancellor. And thank you,

Your Majesty." He bowed towards the head of the table. "You won't be disappointed!"

"I should certainly hope not," the king drawled. "We're all counting on you. Do not let us down."

Chapter 11
A Complication

Mertha had to be Aukera's slowest ox.

Ghdion tipped his head back with a groan, not even bothering to flick the switch to get the damn beast to move faster. Firstly, Quay would have him out for it as she hated to hurt any creatures, great or small. Second, the whip wouldn't work anyways. In fact, Mertha would probably trudge along even slower, if that was possible.

"C'mon, you sluggish cow," he groaned aloud. "Don't you know we're in a hurry here?"

"Are you talking to Mertha again?" Quay asked from beside him. They sat side by side on the narrow bench at the front of the wagon. Ghdion held the reins in one hand and a block of wood he was attempting to carve in the other, and Quay was quietly writing a letter. Lucius lounged in the back amongst all of their supplies, and Hypnocost, still recovering from what he called his 'mind blast,' slept fitfully beside the still unconscious mystery woman.

"No," Ghdion grumbled, flicking a sliver of wood onto the road as he carved at the chunk of it with his tiny knife. "Even if I was, Mertha hates me. I'm convinced she moves even slower when I've got the reins."

"It's because you're so mean to her," she answered primly, not looking up from her writing. "Isn't he, Mertha?" Her voice was high and singsong as she spoke to the shaggy white ox. "Ghdion's just a mean ole' grump, isn't he? You'll move faster if I ask nicely, won't you?"

Damned if Mertha didn't turn her head back to look worshipfully at Quay when she spoke. She even *wagged her tail!* And sure enough, she started to trot a little faster, holding her thick bovine head high in the air.

Quay gave Ghdion a pointed, victorious smile. He just rolled his eyes and scowled even deeper.

"It wouldn't kill you to be nice at least *sometimes*," she said after a slight pause. "I know that deep down, *way* deep deep down, you're secretly a soft old man."

He quirked an eyebrow. "I'm not *that* old. Is thirty-eight old?"

"Ancient. I'm surprised you're still able to walk. Shall I procure you a cane?"

"Don't tempt me." He held the reins loosely in his lap and leaned back, eyeing his chunk of wood critically. It was only just starting to take shape. A few more cuts along the sides should do it. "If my limp gets any worse, I'll actually need one." He stretched out his bad leg; an old injury from his days spent in the fighting pits of Gilden now caused him daily irritations. He gave her a sidelong glance. "What're you, like eighteen? Fresh out of Priestess School and ready to smite all the evil in the land?"

"I'll be twenty-nine next month, actually."

Gods, not even thirty! She's way too young, he thought. He didn't allow himself to finish the thought with, *for me*. What in the hells was he thinking?! He decided a change of subject was needed. "Who are you writing to anyway?"

"Leon," she answered evenly. "I just want to make sure he's getting taken care of after losing his family, the poor man. I'm also writing a report to the Church to make sure they actually send someone to Furow's Ridge to replace poor Edmund Brisby."

How this woman had the capacity to care so much for everyone was a subject of constant admiration on his part. His way of showing it, however, was to just grunt in reply.

"Is that the 'approving grunt' or the, 'I don't understand you at all' grunt?"

"There's a difference?"

"Oh, yes," she told him, grinning mischievously. It showed off that absolutely *adorable* dimple in her left cheek. He caught himself staring. "After all these months of traveling with you, I am fluent in Ghdion Grunt-ese."

He just grunted again and looked away, blushing.

"What are you carving there?" She indicated the block of wood with a nod of her head.

He lowered the small knife to his lap. "Not sure yet," he lied with ease. He was planning on carving stupid Mertha as a stupid gift for Quay. Damn him for having a soft heart just like she said. "It'll come to me eventually."

She opened her mouth for another sassy retort, but he was spared by Lucius yelling from behind them, "Hey! Our mystery woman is coming to!"

Faith and Ruin

Immediately Quay shoved her writing things into Ghdion's lap and scrambled over the bench into the wagon bed in her haste to tend to her new patient. Lucius shifted to the side to make room; the mystery woman, propped against rolled up blankets and a couple pillows, started to stir. Quay placed her hand upon the woman's neck, trying to avoid the worst of the bruises there, and checked her pulse.

The woman's eyelids fluttered, and she moved her mouth as if she was groaning in pain, but no sounds came out. "Her pulse is stronger than it was back in Desai," Quay murmured, then pressed her head against her chest. "Her heartbeat is stronger, too."

"I think she's trying to speak," Lucius said, his eyes shining with concern.

The woman's eyes finally opened, and she stared uncomprehendingly at the two of them. She tried to move away from them, but Quay stopped her by placing a gentle hand upon her shoulder. "Don't try to move! You've been gravely injured."

Her eyes darted frantically from their faces, to the wagon, to her surroundings. She gasped and tried to speak, but only pitiful mewls came out. Stricken, she resumed her efforts at escape, but she was so weak from whatever ordeal she had endured that she collapsed back, gasping, within seconds.

"It's okay," Quay soothed. "I'm a priestess-in-training from the Church of Vidamae." She smiled, expecting that to ease the poor woman's worries.

For some reason, that made her even more desperate to get away. Lucius and Quay exchanged puzzled glances.

"I don't think she likes Vidamae," Ghdion suggested mildly from up front.

"May I try to heal you?" Quay asked her patiently. "I just need to lay my hands upon your wounds and I—"

The woman shook her head vigorously. Quay, perturbed, held up her hands in surrender. What in all of Aukera ...? That was an unexpected response!

"Well, at least we know she understands us," Lucius muttered. "Though I have no idea how we're supposed to communicate with her if she can't talk and she won't accept any more healing from you."

Quay's eyes lit up and she leaned across the front bench, reaching for her stack of half-finished letters. Ghdion, seeming to read her mind, was already handing them back to her. "She can write out her answers!" she crowed, brandishing a blank sheet of parchment and an inked quill. She thrust them towards the woman. "Can you write?" she inquired.

The woman nodded reluctantly.

"Prop her up," Quay instructed. "Let's make her as comfortable as possible. Do you think you can manage to answer a few basic questions for us?"

Lucius helped the woman sit up against the wall of the wagon, packing a few softer bags and some more blankets all around her to help keep her comfortable. "Do you want some water?" he asked her softly; she watched him suspiciously for a moment before nodding.

He turned to grab a waterskin while Quay once again offered the paper and quill. The woman took them with obvious reluctance, then looked to Quay expectantly.

"First of all, what is your name?"

The woman tried to speak, was only able to make more pitiful gasping noises, shook her head angrily, and began to write. The wagon ran over a particularly rough spot in the road, jerking her hand. A black splot of ink smudged the paper; the woman frowned and tried again. She turned the paper over to display the words when she finished.

MIDORI <u>WHO ARE YOU?</u>

She underlined her question for emphasis.

"My name is Quay," she smiled. "These are my bodyguards, Lucius, Ghdion, and the one still asleep is Hypnocost."

She peered more closely at Midori, who stared defiantly back. Even with all of her various bruises and lacerations, she was a strikingly beautiful woman. Her skin was a creamy shade of pale that contrasted sharply with her blue-black cropped hair. High cheekbones, elegantly arched eyebrows, and lush lips only served to accentuate her looks. Obvious distrust blazed from her eyes; Quay was confused as to why she was so adamant in her refusal to be healed.

Lucius reappeared, holding a waterskin sloshing full of cool water. He offered it to Midori; she struggled to heft it to her lips, so he held it for her. Greedily she drank from it, her eyes never leaving his, almost like she expected him to yank it away.

"See? We're here to help," Quay assured her. "What happened to you?" She gestured towards Midori's many wounds.

She didn't bother taking up the pen; she shook her head, unable or unwilling to answer.

"Okay, hmm." Quay tapped her chin, pondering her next inquiry.

"Ask her if she's with the Kax cultists," Ghdion offered without turning around to look at them.

Quay was just about to scoff, but Midori's eyes widened. She pushed the paper and quill pen back towards Quay, shaking her head vehemently.

That's an odd way to react to that question, Quay thought, narrowing her eyes.

"Are you?"

Midori shook her head even harder, squeezing her eyes shut.

Why was she being so weird about that particular question?

"Maybe we should give it a rest for now," Lucius urged. "She's still pretty beat up, and it's gonna be hard to understand much with her not able to speak yet."

Midori glared at Lucius, her face a mask of sudden fury. She began patting her sides determinedly, looking for something in her pockets; a moment later, she produced a small metallic object, about the size of a gold coin, and thrust it in their faces.

It was a holy symbol of Kax, lovingly etched into a silver medallion. She shoved it into the air with emphasis, as if to ensure they both saw that it was hers and knew what it meant: she was a follower of Kax. Her dark eyes blazed with pride.

"Well, that answers that question," Lucius sighed in resignation.

Things just got a lot more complicated.

Chapter 12

Happy Birthday, Midori!

Fifteen Years Ago

It was Midori's twelfth birthday.

She sat at the kitchen table, wearing her new pink skirt with the frilly lace ruffles at the bottom. She kept smoothing her hands over the silky fabric, admiring the way it perfectly matched the embroidered flowers along the front of her lace-up vest; she loudly proclaimed this fact four or five times to her older brother, Kang. (He was fifteen, and never played dolls with her like he used to.) He just rolled his eyes and tossed his shiny black hair out of his eyes. He was growing it out long, trying to make himself look more like their neighbor Magnus, who, Midori would *never* admit out loud, *was* very handsome with his long brown ponytail. When Kang's back was turned, she stuck her tongue out at him. It wasn't very 'I'm-a-twelve-year-old-girl-so-I'm-older-and-wiser' behavior, but since it was just Kang, it didn't count.

Father came into the tiny kitchen with a bundle of candles in his hands. "Where's the flint and steel?" he asked nobody in particular. "I was able to scrounge up exactly twelve candles for Midori's cake."

Beaming at her, he scanned the countertops to no avail; only the crumpled remnants of brown wrapping paper from her gift remained, as well as a few smudges of pink frosting smeared across the battered wooden countertop.

Mother had baked her a cake, a frothy pink confection with the words, 'Happy 12th Birthday!' written across the top in red icing. She set it directly across from Midori; Kang, a mischievous grin on his face, leaned across her and swiped a finger through the frosting.

"*Hey!*" Midori howled in righteous anger. "Kang, that's *my* cake! *Mom!* Kang just stuck his finger in my cake!"

Mother glanced behind her absently, wiping her hands on her apron. "Kang, knock it off," she muttered without much vitriol; Midori glared at him and slid the cake farther from him so he couldn't reach it.

He snickered, licking his frosting-coated finger. "Tattling still?" he said with distaste. "I thought you were supposed to be *grown-up* now?"

He was always talking to her in that nasty-sarcastic voice lately. He never had time for her anymore, was always too busy either running around with his older friends or brooding melodramatically in his room. He used to push her on the swing in the backyard, take walks with her in the woods to point out all the different birds that lived there, show her some of the cool knife tricks he'd been practicing—he made her promise not to tell their parents about that. But lately, he was colder and distant. Was this what getting older did to a person?

Midori opened her mouth for a sharp retort when suddenly, the front door was kicked open from the outside. The sounds of splintering wood erupted in their little hovel of a house. The family, shocked into motionlessness, gaped as a knight in shining golden armor appeared, and Midori had a split second to wonder, *Why is there a knight here on my birthday?*

Faith and Ruin

Then she saw the bloody sword in his hand.

Father dropped the candles, blurting, "Wha—", and her brother stood up so quickly from the table his chair clattered loudly to the floor. Father stepped in front of Mother and opened his mouth to speak, but the knight slid his sword straight into Father's belly before he could so much as utter a single word. Just like that, indifferent, as if he went around sticking his sword into random bellies all the time.

Father's eyes widened in confused-yet-polite surprise. The knight yanked the sword from his limp body and whipped the blood off the blade with a vicious snapping motion of his wrist. A bunch of blood splattered all across Midori's cake.

"NO!" Mother screamed. She lunged at the swordsman with the cake-cutting knife still in her hand. She stabbed towards the knight's neck savagely, her teeth clenched in barely contained rage. The knight just laughed—*he laughed*—and batted the knife out of her hand with the back of his gauntleted fist.

"Get out of here!" Mother screamed, turning towards her two children. Her eyes fixed upon Midori's. She had always been told she had her mother's eyes, wide and dark brown and slightly pointed at the ends. She'd never seen a look of such pained horror in those eyes before. Did her eyes match her mother's just then? What look did Mother see in the moment before the knight grabbed her throat and began to squeeze?

"Midori!" Kang's strangled cries ripped her attention. He rushed around the kitchen table, nearly tripping over their father's slumped form in his haste. The table shook wildly. Her cake slid off the top and landed with a soft splat onto the floor, right in the spreading pool of her father's blood. That same blood splattered across Kang's white shirt front and all over the lower part of his face. He looked like a wild creature, unrecognizable. He grabbed Midori's arm—it *hurt* how painfully he held her—and began to drag her towards the back door.

"Run!" Mother called out. Her voice was hoarse and weak. "Don't look back, children! RUN!"

Midori looked back. The knight's face was covered by a golden helm with a yellow sunburst symbol etched across the top, so she couldn't see his face as he choked the life out of her. She could hear him laughing, though.

Then another knight appeared in the broken front doorway, a wicked mace held in one hand and a large metal shield in the other. The shield glowed a soft yellow and featured the same sunburst symbol as the first knight's helm. Neither one of them spoke; if they communicated, it was silent, or so quiet that Midori could not hear.

She struggled weakly against her brother's pulling. Weren't knights supposed to be *good*? Wasn't their whole *deal* that they eradicated evil doers? Why were these ones killing her parents? Her parents were *good*! "Mother!" she shrieked, reaching back as if she could *will* the insane swordsman to release her.

The second knight, the one with the mace, glanced up at the sound of her cries. Kang yanked her along with him forcefully, hissing, "Come on!" as he shoved the back door open with his shoulder.

Outside was chaos. The dirt road was kicked up with dust from armored horses and stampeding knights as they chased after some of the other villagers. Midori watched in disbelief as one of the knights, a woman, judging by the narrowness of her shoulders and waist, cut down Bennett's elderly mother as she ran towards the woods. Bennett, only a few feet behind her, screamed and almost lost his head as the knight's sword swung towards his neck; he ducked beneath the swing in a truly impressive slide on his knees right beneath the blade.

"Bennett!" Kang screamed. He waved his arms towards his friend. Bennett—he was the same age as Kang, and the two of them had been good friends their whole lives—glanced up, his brown hair flopping in his face. He scrambled on all fours towards the two of them, narrowly avoiding getting trampled by an armored horse and rider that galloped past.

"What's going on?!" Bennett rasped. His cheeks were dirt streaked and stained with tears. "These paladins came outta nowhere and started killing everyone in town! Why?"

"There's no time!" Kang interrupted. He pulled Midori roughly behind him as he crossed the empty dirt road towards the woods. "We gotta get into the woods. We gotta hide!"

Bennett glanced behind him at his mother, who lay bleeding out on the road. Her neck was bent at a weird angle. Hesitating, his decision was swiftly made for him as the mace-wielding knight burst out the back door of Midori's house and stalked right towards them.

"RUN!" The three of them burst for the trees.

Behind them, the knight cackled. "There is nowhere for you to hide, Kax trash!"

Tears streamed unchecked down her face as Kang pulled her along. Tree branches whipped at her cheeks, her neck, her bare arms, her new pink skirt; she couldn't see where they were going. The forest, once comfortable and beloved and familiar, seemed menacing and dangerous as they tore through it, their breaths sharp and jagged. A thick branch tore a jagged hole right at the knee of her new skirt; she let out a strangled cry of indignation. Bennett huffed along beside her, his longer stride making it easier for him to keep up. Kang's stubby black ponytail flipped wildly from side to side ahead of them both.

Kax trash? What was that supposed to mean? Did these knights hate her and her family because they worshipped Kax, the Lady of Chaos? Was that really all it took to send an armored knight on a rampage like this?

They were well and truly in the thick of the woods now, so far from their home that Midori lost all sense of direction. Still Kang ran, his grip upon her arm unrelenting. They crashed through the undergrowth, not bothering with stealth; the knight could be upon them at any moment!

She risked a glance behind her. The golden armored man strode purposely, unrelentingly forward.

"Kang!" she cried, her voice cracking. They couldn't keep this up. They couldn't hide. The knight was almost upon them.

She could see a vicious smile from beneath the shadow of his helm.

A flash of green light shot suddenly from somewhere amidst the trees. It knocked the knight off course, sending him careening to his knees. He howled in pain, his head swiveling this way and that as he sought out the source of the magic. Before he could stand back up, another green blast hit him from behind. He fell face first onto the ground, his mace falling from suddenly nerveless fingers. His body stopped moving.

A robed figure appeared out of the trees, cloaked and unrecognizable in the gloom. Kang swiftly positioned himself in front of Midori, his fists clenched. Bennett crouched at the ready beside him, both of them tense and expectant.

"Midori, when I tell you to, I want you to run as far and fast into the woods as you can, do you understand me?" Kang muttered. His voice cracked on the last word.

"I'm not leaving you!" Midori whispered back. She squeezed Kang's arm and shuffled closer.

The robed figure took three steps forward until they stood in a thin beam of sunlight that shone through the trees. Immediately their postures relaxed; the sunshine revealed the figure to be Kang and Midori's Aunt Solange.

"Kang?" Solange called out in hesitation. "Is that you?"

"Aunt Solange!" Kang rushed forward, dragging Midori behind him. The two of them ran into her arms. She embraced them both tightly.

"What's happening?" Kang asked in anguished tones. "These ... these golden knights just came into our house and ... and ..."

"Where are your parents?" Solange asked, her dark eyes flashing. She glanced at the ground where the fallen knight still lay motionless; she kicked at his head viciously with her booted foot.

"They are—they were—"

"The knight killed them," Midori cut in, her voice sounding small to her ears. She was *twelve* now, so why did she still sound like a baby?

Solange let out a heavy sigh. "Damn it. That means I'm the last vicar left ..." Her eyes took on a faraway cast, and she stared into the trees for a long while before Bennett, stepping closer, cleared his throat to get her attention.

Solange shook her head and refocused upon the three children. "You three are the only ones I've seen still alive," she told them bluntly. "The paladins swarmed the whole village. They went to the temple first—trashed the whole place, naturally—then came here. I was lucky to get out alive, and that was only because of my magic." She looked down at her hands, held in loose fists at her sides. Blood speckled her knuckles and fingernails. She ran a shaking hand through her cropped black hair and said, "We gotta get out of here before more of them find us."

"Where can we go?" Bennett asked.

Solange's lips pursed into a thin line. "The temple," she answered. "Hopefully they won't double back to it since they've been there already. Even so, there's bound to be hiding places inside. It's not far. We can hide out there until the paladins leave." She started to walk into the woods, and when the three of them didn't immediately follow, she turned around and asked, "Are you coming?"

Kang glanced towards Bennett, who shrugged. What else could they do? They had nowhere else to go.

"Yeah, we're coming," Kang replied softly. He grabbed Midori's hand. Bennett followed, walking on her other side.

The Temple of Kax, Our Lady of Chaos, was the only safe haven that remained to them.

Chapter 13
The Mirror

Hypnocost woke up with the worst headache in his life.

Light stabbed his eyes. The muffled sounds of people talking blared like alarms to his ears. The bumping, choppy motions beneath his body made him nauseous. He covered his eyes with the back of his hand; even that small movement made him feel faint and dizzy.

"Whu—?" was all he managed before he retched violently at his side.

"You're alive,"

the voice said with absolutely no inflection in its tone, as always.

"Whoa, whoa, settle down, Hypnocost!" said Lucius, instantly at his side. "Take it easy, man, I've got you."

He squinted his eyes open just a sliver so he could see what in the hells was happening. He was in the back of the wagon—that would explain the sporadic bumps and jitters—surrounded by lumpy canvas sacks of supplies. The sun was high in the sky, though that didn't tell him much. He still had no idea what day it was or how long he had been out.

"You've been unconscious for a full day,"

the voice answered his unspoken question.

Lucius appeared in his field of view, looking down on him with concern. He placed a cool wet cloth upon his forehead, using another one to clean up the mess he'd made next to his head. "You still with us?"

Hypnocost started to nod but thought better of it when the world started to spin again. "Yes," he croaked, then cleared his throat, starting again. "Yes, I am with you now. Where are we? What happened?"

Lucius glanced away, then spoke to someone out of his field of view. "Yeah, he's awake finally," he said, then turned back towards him. "We're on the road to Praetorius. Should arrive sometime this afternoon. You've been out cold since last night. What do you remember?"

Gingerly, Hypnocost pulled himself up into a sitting position, shielding his eyes from the glare of the sun. Had it always been that blasted *bright*? "I ... remember the battle ... in the tent. And the tied-up woman. Ghdion was hurt, I believe? ... That is it."

Lucius handed him a waterskin, which he drank from gratefully. "That's what I figured," he told him slowly, watching him with concern. "You did something with your mind, Hypnocost. To that Kax cultist who attacked us. You called it a mind blast, I think?" He shrugged. "Whatever it was, it was pretty damn potent, and it knocked you flat on your ass pretty much immediately."

Hypnocost sighed and closed his eyes. "Yes, that can happen sometimes if I overdo it. Are we—"

"Where is the mirror?"

demanded the voice.

Hypnocost's eyes flew open. "The mirror!" he gasped, sitting up quickly. Blackness edged his vision, so he squeezed his eyes shut and took a deep, steadying breath to stay conscious. "I had a mirror. I found it inside the tent. Where is it?"

Lucius rummaged around behind him. "This mirror?" he asked, pulling it from Hypnocost's pack.

He breathed a sigh of relief. "Yes! The very one. Give it to me, please."

"What is it?" The scarred man asked, quirking an eyebrow.

"I am not sure," Hypnocost answered honestly. "Although it most definitely is magical in nature. What kind of magic it contains is something I intend to discover." He took it from the swordsman's hands a bit too eagerly, his eyes snagging on the weird symbols etched all around its frame.

"Maybe she can help you with that." He jerked a thumb at the mystery woman. She was awake, propped up like he was against a bunch of blankets and sacks.

Hypnocost blanched. He had been so absorbed in his own private musings that he hadn't even realized she was with them. "You brought her *with us*?" he cried, aghast. "She could be one of the Kax cultists!"

"Oh, she is," came Ghdion's gruff voice from the front bench of the wagon. "And our boss here thinks it's a good idea to bring her with us to Praetorius for some reason."

The mystery woman glared at them both but said nothing.

Quay, indignant, retorted, "We can't just leave her out here in the wilderness by herself, Kax cultist or not!"

"Her name's Midori," Lucius exhaled, "and yeah, that's about the gist of what you missed." He met Hypnocost's light-colored eyes. "Maybe don't use those mind blasts for a while, yeah? I'd hate to see what kinda excitement happens next time you're knocked unconscious for this long."

The theurgist groaned in despair, tipping his head back against the wooden slat wall of the wagon. "What have you all gotten us into?" he bemoaned.

Silence settled around the wagon, each of them quiet in their own thoughts as they trundled along towards Praetorius. The sky was a cheerful blue and the sun was shining. The mild autumn weather didn't match his foul mood.

Hypnocost shifted his position to get more comfortable. He asked the voice, *"Why are you so interested in this mirror?"*

"Observe it,"

the voice told him.

"See if you can discover its secrets."

Intrigued despite himself, he turned the mirror over in his hands. For all of its elaborate markings, it was not heavy. It fit easily into his pack, and it seemed to operate just like a regular mirror, reflecting its surroundings. The only thing remotely interesting about it was the frame, with its fantastical creatures and Kax symbolism heavily worked into the metal.

"*I do not see what is so interesting about—*"

A loud snapping noise broke his concentration. He looked over to see Midori trying to get his attention, snapping her fingers loudly towards him.

He raised his eyebrows, gesturing towards the mirror. "You know about this?"

She hesitated, then nodded. Then she immediately shook her head, her face relaying deep concern. Her expressive dark eyebrows furrowed as she pointed at the mirror, then shook her head emphatically once again.

"What does this do?"

More head shaking.

Hypnocost, frustrated, asked, "It is magical, though, yes?"

A nod, somewhat stilted, but a nod nonetheless.

"Do you know how it works?"

She pursed her lips and refused to answer either way.

Scowling, he turned his gaze back to the mirror. It was even more fascinating than before, now that his hypothesis had been proven true. It was magical. But in what way? How did it work? Obviously this Midori was not willing to assist him. "I will just have to figure it out myself," he muttered.

Out of the corner of his eye, he could see her shaking her head, a pitying look on her face.

Chapter 14

At The Gate

Rendevas groaned when he saw the long line of merchants waiting outside the city gates.

"This is an absolute nightmare!" he muttered aloud, clipboard in hand, loaded with fresh sheafs of paper listing the incoming deliveries still waiting to be checked in. There were three full pages, and that was just for *today!*

Ever since the plenum had voted to restrict access to Praetorius due to the escalating tensions with Athessa, the steady flow of goods and supplies had dwindled—not for lack of items or interest, but because Praetorius did not have the manpower to efficiently go through each and every vehicle seeking entrance to the city. Harvest season was upon them, as well, further complicating matters, as more wagons full of produce from nearby farms lined up at the gates.

Captain Riluk, as head of the city guard, was the one responsible for the gate inspections. He'd basically begged Rendevas and his team to take a more active role in dealing with the merchants specifically, and now he could see why.

A long line of impatient travelers snaked from the city gates all the way along the high stone wall that surrounded Praetorius. The wall was the pride and joy of the capital; shortly after they won their independence from Athessa a century ago, the leaders of Praetorius erected the wall to deter Athessa from attacking again. They used most of their resources at the time to get the wall built as quickly and solidly as possible; to this day, it stood as an effective defense from any would-be attackers. With the ocean on one side and the wall on the other, Praetorius was considered the safest city in Khamris.

Today, however, the wall only served as a useful resting place for the grumpy merchants to rest against. The guardsmen working the gate tried their hardest to get through as many people as they could, but it was obvious they were overwhelmed and understaffed.

Rendevas, briskly walking towards the line, saw one of the guards arguing with a short, scowling borean standing in front of an overloaded wagon; as soon as he realized who it was, he cursed under his breath and ran to intercept.

"Tobias Wiltwater!" Rendevas exclaimed in the most upbeat, charming voice he could muster, interrupting the borean as he opened his mouth to berate the poor city guard. "I wasn't aware you were returning to Praetorius so soon!"

The borean turned his hard, fierce dark eyes upon Rendevas and snarled, "I have been waiting in this godsforsaken line for two days, Lord Rendevas! *Two! Days!* I should have been back at my shop and doing business *days* ago!"

Tobias Wiltwater was infamous in Praetorius, known for his uncanny ability to procure goods, mostly of a less than legal nature, that other merchants were unable to. He was more known for his terrible personality, however. Rendevas was very familiar with the short-statured borean trader, with his extravagant clothes, excessive jewelry—he wore rings with huge gemstones on each finger—and explosive temper. If one needed anything rare or hard to find, including false mage papers, a new identity, or a way to slip past the guards into and out of the city, Tobias was the best. He was good at his job, quick and moderately affordable, but the tradeoff was having to deal with his spectacularly hostile attitude.

Most boreans, the short, pointed eared folk who hailed from Northern Aukera, weren't as volatile in nature as Tobias Wiltwater, and weren't known to travel so far from their wintry mountain homes. Tobias was obviously an outlier in more ways than one.

"I'll get this straightened out," Rendevas assured Tobias as he flipped through his paperwork. The guard who had been dealing with him hovered awkwardly nearby. "Please, allow Master Wiltwater through the gates. You have my word as plenum diplomat that he is who he says he is, and I will personally vouch for him."

The guardsman shot Rendevas a grateful look. "If you could just sign off for him here," he said as he thrust his own clipboard and quill his way. The diplomat signed his name with a flourish.

The guardsman retrieved his clipboard and jogged off down the line, leaving Rendevas to deal with the angry merchant alone. Tobias glared at him, apparently uncaring that he had basically put his own name on the line for him. "What's going to happen the next time I leave Praetorius, hmm?" Tobias spat. "Are you going to be waiting here for me personally so I won't have to wait in line with all these commoners? I hope you know I have important business to attend to outside the capital that cannot be delayed."

"I assure you, we will have it all taken care of." Rendevas smiled around gritted teeth. "You know how these things can go; the plenum votes in a new rule and it takes a little while before the wrinkles are all ironed out." He held out his hands as if to say, 'what can you do?'

Tobias spat off to the side, narrowly missing Rendevas's fine leather buckle shoes. "We shall see!" he screeched, climbing into his wagon and slapping his horse's reins sharply. The wagon rumbled off beneath the gate, trailing a plume of dust in its wake.

Rendevas thought about shooting a rude gesture at Tobias's retreating wagon but decided against it. There were far too many witnesses around, and that kind of behavior was unbecoming of a city official. Instead, he sniffed in distaste and turned towards the next group in line.

The following hour was spent at the grueling task of questioning each and every merchant waiting their turn to be let into the city. As he suspected, they were all legitimate; no Athessian spies were sent that day in the guise of Praetorian merchants. Logically, he knew Commander Rakeld's security measures were needed—with tensions as high as they were between Khamris and Athessa, it only made sense to make Praetorius less accessible. But did they really expect Uldinvelm to send spies so blatantly to the city? He scribbled on his clipboard, chatted amiably with some of the traders he knew personally, and tried to ease the short tempers of those he didn't. The job wasn't flashy or even appreciated, but he was good at it.

Later, as he pondered a way to make the queue more efficient, his eyes snagged on a familiar profile. There stood Quay, the lovely young Priestess of Vidamae. Quay was well known in the religious circles of Praetorius as a rising star in the Vidamae Church. It was rumored she had been hand-picked by High Priestess Lucina Balladoni to be her replacement someday. He didn't know Quay very well—a diplomat and religious type didn't cross paths often, Lady Avindea notwithstanding—but he recognized her exceptional beauty (and the well-known floor-length robes of a priestess-in-training) nonetheless.

He cocked an eyebrow, curious; she stood beside a wagon emblazoned with the stylized sunburst symbol of Vidamae, meaning she was on church business. But who were those three rough looking men with her?

An exceedingly tall, tattooed, and scarred blond man stood nearest to her, his arms crossed to showcase his bulging muscles to full effect. An intimidatingly large greatsword was strapped across his back. He stood a full head above everyone around him, all broad-shoulders and gruff demeanor, judging by the scowl on his face. Beside him, talking animatedly with one of the guards, was a slightly younger man with shaggy black hair. The entire left side of his face and neck was covered in what looked to be a large burn scar. The third gentleman was completely bald, with strange black tattoos upon his pate, his pale bare chest exposed from his open jacket, a bored expression upon his face. He leaned against the wagon, arms crossed, trying to look insouciant but failing miserably; he was either an elf or a half-elf, judging by his delicately pointed ears.

Rendevas watched them speak with Constable Mald, who must've been roped into helping at the gate, as well. Mald shook his head angrily and jabbed his finger at his clipboard. Quay said something back, gesturing towards the wagon, but the stubborn constable just crossed his arms and planted his feet more firmly in front of her.

His curiosity fully piqued, he made his way towards them. As he got closer, he heard some of what they were saying.

"—a priestess-in-training!" Quay beseeched Constable Mald.

"You only need to send word to High Priestess Lucina Balladoni, and she will vouch for me."

"That's not gonna work." Mald shook his head. "She hasn't been in the city for days now. If you don't have the proper paperwork, you aren't going inside."

"C'mon, man," the blond man grumbled, looming above the armored constable like a thundercloud. "I know you've seen us traveling to and from Praetorius multiple times. Hells, even *I* recognize you. Aren't you the constable or something? Malt?"

Mald crossed his beefy arms. "It's Mald. And it doesn't matter. The rules have changed, and I can't let you inside without proper aufor—arthur—proper papers. Get me those papers, and you'll be free to enter. Until then, you'll have to wait outside the city gates."

"We just need to go to the church to resupply," the scarred, dark-haired man added. "But we can set up camp out here. We'll figure something else out."

Both Quay and the tall blond man looked at him as if he were crazy. "What?" the priestess cried. "No, we are definitely getting back inside! I *live* here!"

Mald, his jaw clamped shut, eyed the scar-faced man darkly. "And who are *you* anyways?" He circled around the dark-haired man with suspicion. "Blondie and Baldy and Quay over here I recognize, but you? I've never seen you before. You have any identifying papers?"

The scarred man's face paled. "No. I-I'm from Furow's Ridge. I've lived there the past couple of years."

"Lucius is helping me with church business," Quay supplied helpfully. "He's my newest bodyguard. We've got to get him to the cathedral to sign his contract and make it official. Another reason we desperately need to get inside!"

"As far as I know he could be a spy from Uldinvelm!" Constable Mald glared at Lucius.

The man named Lucius took a step back, hands in the air. His eyes widened. "I'm no spy."

"Then let me see what's in the wagon," Mald demanded, walking around to the back and reaching a hand out to remove the canvas cover.

"That will not be necessary!" the bald half-elf cried, a bit too forcefully. "We only have meager supplies back there, hence our impatience to get inside the city. Surely that is reason enough to let us pass?"

Rendevas, gliding closer, thought, *O-ho! Are they hiding something in the back of that wagon? Things just got more interesting ...*

Mald eyed the bald half-elf distrustfully. "I remember you," he stated, jabbing a finger in his chest. "You're Hypnocost! I had trouble with you a few weeks back, didn't I?" He paused, thinking hard. "Yeah! You're that mage traveling with no mage papers. The one who was showing off with that illusion spell. Remember? The one of me sleeping at my post and scratching myself?" Constable Mald brought his face right up to Hypnocost's and grinned darkly. "Bet you thought that was pretty funny, huh?"

Hypnocost groaned, his face flushing bright red. "Ahhh yes, a silly little joke on my part, ha ha! But I must correct your assumptions about me. I am *not* a mage. Like I told you before, I am a *theurgist*, thus I *require* no magical identification, and—"

"What the hells is a theurgist?" Mald shook his head. "You cast spells? You're a mage." Mald held out his open palm. "No mage papers, no entry. Those are the rules. I let it slide once before, because Lady Quay here assured me she would take care of it for you. So?" He raised his eyebrows expectantly. "You have the papers now?"

"What seems to be the problem?" Rendevas called out, brandishing his quill and clipboard as he stepped up to the group.

The constable met his eyes, a look of surprise and disappointment mingling on his face. "Lord Rendevas. I didn't know you were helping at the gate." He eyed the diplomat up and down distrustfully.

Rendevas shrugged, trying to broadcast humbleness. "I aid wherever I am needed." He turned towards Quay. "Lady Quay! I did not expect to see you traveling with such ... unique company." He smiled charmingly and gave her a little bow.

Quay looked up in confusion, unable to hide the shock from her face. "Oh! Lord Rendevas? How very nice to see you." She curtsied back, puzzled at his attention.

Mald looked between them, his dark eyebrows furrowing. "Lady Quay is trying to enter the city without any papers," he explained. "As you know, we can't let them in because of the threat from Athessa and—"

"I know all about the laws, constable," Rendevas interrupted. "I helped write them, after all. But surely, we are not so rude as to stand out here in the open, arguing with a much beloved Priestess of Vidamae about something so silly as *papers*."

"But Lord Rendevas—"

"It simply will not stand!" He meandered around to the back of the wagon, hands on his hips. "I will vouch for them."

"But they haven't let me search their wagon!"

"Then I will do it for you." Before anyone could react, he flipped open a corner of the canvas fabric, just wide enough so only he could see what was inside.

A dark-haired woman laid there amidst various burlap sacks and crates, looking much the worse for wear with dark bruises around her neck and cuts on her hands and arms. Her terror-stricken eyes met his.

He willed his face into a mask of impassivity, only raising a single eyebrow in his shock. "All seems to be in order," he called out, then cleared his throat. He laid the canvas cover back closed. "It is as they said. A small quantity of burlap sacks and crates."

"You're willing to sign off on them then?" Mald asked with no small amount of reluctance.

"Of course." Once again, he scrawled his signature in looping, elegant script upon the constable's clipboard. "There. Now that that is all settled, I believe I'll accompany Lady Quay and her entourage into the city."

Quay's stricken face met his; she scrambled her features into a weak smile to better hide her shock and fear. "Of course! That would be most appreciated."

He didn't leave her any room for argument. With a gentlemanly bow, he helped her up onto the bench. The other three hopped onto the wagon, and then they were off, rumbling their way through the city gates. Whatever schemes were afoot, whoever that wounded woman was inside the wagon, Rendevas had every intention of finding out.

Chapter 15

The Cathedral of Vidamae

The short wagon ride from the Praetorius city gates to the Cathedral of Vidamae was fraught with tension, not to mention extremely awkward.

Rendevas—who was he and why was he helping them? Ghdion had no idea!—sat on the front bench, squeezed right between him and Quay, looking for all the world as if he hadn't just accidentally discovered the wounded, mute woman they had successfully smuggled into the city. Quay had a rigid smile fixed upon her face, trying desperately to gauge what the man would do next. And Ghdion? Well, he just leaned back, reins in hand, wondering if he would be required to harm a *fucking city official* in the name of protecting her. He should ask for a raise.

Quay, unable to keep her pretty mouth shut, spoke up, "What you saw back there—"

"Lovely weather we are having, don't you think?" Rendevas cut her off loudly. "The summer heat's finally over, but it's not yet cool enough to require a person to wear much more than a light jacket. Autumn is my favorite season."

Quay huffed out an artificial laugh, eyeing the diplomat with uncertainty. Ghdion closed his eyes, took a deep breath through his nose, and shook his head at her curtly. *Don't do it!* he thought desperately. *Just stop talking!*

She either didn't see or didn't understand his body language, for she continued doggedly, "But my lord, I need to explain—"

"Oh look!" Rendevas cried, pointing. "We're nearly to the cathedral. Perhaps we will be lucky enough to meet up with Lady Avindea there, eh? She is your cousin, is she not?"

Ghdion slapped a hand over his face.

Quay continued, "Yes, she is, but I—"

"Good sir, could you assist the lady in departing the vessel while I seek out the Lady Avindea?" Rendevas pointedly looked away from Quay and towards Ghdion, raising his eyebrows. "I have a feeling Lady Quay has *important news* to impart upon her cousin."

Rendevas hopped from the wagon before Mertha had fully come to a stop. Straightening his black velvet doublet, the man strode purposely into the cathedral. Strong masculine perfume wafted in his wake. Just what in the hells was this guy's deal?

The Cathedral of Vidamae was one of the largest and most beautiful buildings in all of Praetorius. Sweeping parapets, stained glass windows, and decorative angelic creatures made of soft white marble graced the circular steps and at the tops of each of the crenellations. The heavy double front doors always stood open as a way to show how welcoming Vidamae was, and candles were lit at each window to further prove how Her light was a beacon to all who needed Her.

A small group of workers, dressed in thick aprons and floppy hats, took measurements outside—the church must have hired them for one of their many vanity projects, Ghdion assumed. They were always throwing their money around on things like that. Probably one of their higher-up priestesses needed a third bathroom or something equally as frivolous.

Ghdion watched Rendevas disappear inside the cathedral, ostensibly to fetch Lady Avindea. "Well, that was certainly ... something," he stated flatly.

"That was a disaster!" Quay cried, as soon as Rendevas was out of earshot. "Gods help me, he *saw Midori in the wagon*. Who knows what he's going to do with that information?!" She covered her face in despair. "Avin's gonna kill me when she finds out."

Ghdion offered his hand to help her out of the wagon, which she took gratefully. "I dunno, actually. He could've ratted us out to Constable Mald, but he didn't. What I don't understand is *why*."

Hypnocost hopped gracefully from the back of the wagon. "He is a politician, that is why," he answered easily. "Any secret discovered is another weapon in his arsenal. We should be wary of that one."

"As much as it pains me to admit, Hypnocost is right," Lucius said. "Never trust a politician. They only have their own best interests in mind." He pulled up the canvas cloth covering the back of the wagon to check on Midori. "Doing okay in there?" he whispered. She must have nodded, for he closed it back up. "So what are we supposed to do with her?"

"We'll have to smuggle her inside somehow," Quay answered, looking nervous. "I'll lead Mertha around to the back entrance. There are less people back there."

She didn't get very far before a tall, striking young woman with a long back ponytail and dark skin marched down the circular steps of the cathedral, a pleased looking Rendevas right behind her. It was Avindea, Quay's intimidating paladin cousin. She wore a set of scale mail beneath a golden breastplate, a longsword swinging in its scabbard at her belt. She looked like she had been born wearing armor and wielding a sword.

"Oh, no," Quay murmured under her breath. "She's already *here*?"

Ghdion watched the woman stalk towards them. He'd had his fair share of run-ins with the paladin. She was the one who interviewed him for the bodyguard job, after all. That hadn't been one of his finer moments. Ever since then, Avindea had treated him with a cool politeness that only barely concealed the fact that she did not approve of him.

She was *frightening*.

"Avindea!" Quay beamed, rushing towards her much taller cousin. She wrapped her arms around her in a tight hug, which the armored woman returned only slightly less fervently. Quay was always hugging people. She was one of the touchiest people he'd ever met, though, if he was honest, he didn't mind all that much when he was on the receiving end. Had it been anyone but her, he would feel *much* differently. "It's been too long, cousin!"

Avindea pulled back to eye Quay with a dubious look. "Quay, I didn't realize you would be back from your pilgrimage so soon. Have you already finished tending to all of the congregations?"

"Ah ... no, not exactly," Quay answered with a breezy little laugh.

"If we could take the wagon to the back entrance so I can unload my, erm, cargo, I will tell you all that has transpired."

"We can unload it just fine right here," said Avindea, oblivious to Quay's nervousness. "Your bodyguards look strong enough to help." She cast her eyes over Ghdion, Hypnocost, and Lucius, with a look that screamed, 'unimpressed.' He was *very* familiar with that look from her.

"Actually, I—"

"There are some items of a delicate nature in the back of that wagon," Rendevas offered helpfully. "Perhaps Lady Quay is right to operate with discretion?"

Avindea's eyebrows raised so high up on her forehead they almost collided with her dark hairline. "Is that so?" she responded, forced politeness in her voice. "I believe my *beloved* cousin has some explaining to do."

"What in the actual hells, Quay?!" Avindea whisper-screamed as soon as she saw Midori in the back of the wagon.

Thank the gods it was in the middle of the afternoon, and the foot traffic behind the cathedral was slow. They parked the wagon between two ornamental trees right next to the back door of the church, out of sight of any prying eyes. Luckily, most of the clerics, priestesses, and other clergy members in residence were already inside, tending to various church duties.

It had been a quiet, lazy afternoon until Quay showed up.

"What was I supposed to do?" Quay hissed back. "Leave her out there in the wilderness at the mercy of ... of *beasts* or *brigands* or worse, *Kax cultists*?"

"Yes!" Avin derided hotly. "From what you've told me, she *is* a Kax cultist herself!" She began to pace fretfully, running a hand through her hair. "She literally hates *anything to do with our goddess!* The Kax religion's *whole reason for existence* is to cause as much trouble for Vidamae as possible!"

"That's a bit of an exaggeration, and besides, it doesn't matter! She was in trouble, and it is my calling to help!"

Quay had always been impetuous and full of misplaced good intentions. Ever since they were youths growing up together in the church, Quay was the one bringing home stray kittens that turned out to be wild animals—more specifically, a baby manticore that hadn't yet grown its stinging tail or leathery wings—or giving away all of her coins to the beggars on the streets, only to be chased by pickpockets for being so foolish as to reveal her meager fortune. Avindea was the one who did the saving, bandaging the painful claw wounds from the wild felines and running off the pickpockets with hurled insults and threats.

As they grew into adulthood, Quay's eagerness to help only strengthened; she channeled her innate goodness into becoming the youngest priestess at the Church, while Avindea's restless sense of adventure lent itself towards a calling as a Paladin of Vidamae. She hoped that Quay's training, and, in turn, her traveling Khamris to visit the smaller congregations—both as a way to further her skills as a healer and help her see more of the world outside Praetorius—would impart upon her more of a sense of responsibility. She had, apparently, hoped in vain.

Once again, she took on the role of the levelheaded adult. *And I'm only a few months older than her!* Hands on hips, she regarded her cousin with a mixture of exasperation and fondness. "Quay. I know you're only trying to help, but think of the consequences. You said your bodyguards were attacked when you found this ... this *Midori*, right?"

Quay nodded, chewing on her thumbnail. "They, uh ... dispatched their attacker. Oh gods, should we have done something with that person's body?"

Avin shook her head. "That's not the point, but ... wait, what would you have done with the body?!"

"Buried it, of course!"

"Quay, that was a *Kax cultist!*" She couldn't help raising her voice; a couple of robed clerics passing by gave her odd looks. Scowling, she continued in a lower voice, "Listen to me. Your bodyguards were defending themselves, so don't worry about that part. What we really need to focus on is what in the hells are we going to do with Midori. What if the other cultists turn up looking for her?"

"I thought we could keep her here," Quay told her in a quiet voice. "She needs medical attention, Avin. Her wounds are too old for healing. Infection could be setting in! She needs rest and a quiet place to recover."

The paladin couldn't remember a time when she had last felt so supremely vexed. "We absolutely *cannot* keep her here. What if someone ..." Avindea's voice trailed off as she realized Lord Rendevas was still about, lounging ever-so-casually against the back wall of the cathedral. He was trying to look as if he wasn't listening intently to their every word.

"Fuck," she muttered under her breath.

Quay gasped. "Language!"

Avindea ignored her and strode right up to Rendevas. She took a deep breath before speaking. "You realize my ... ah ... *predicament*, don't you, Lord Rendevas?"

He looked at his fingernails nonchalantly. "I do, Lady Avindea. Honestly, I am surprised you're even speaking to me. I thought you were still upset regarding my *dealings* with Milford and The Maelstrom."

She shook her head in frustration. "That's neither here nor there. But I admit, it would be less than ideal if anyone were to find out about the ... *circumstances* I suddenly find myself in."

"Understood!" he answered brightly. "I've no wish to earn the ire of a Paladin of the Church of Vidamae. Your secret is safe with me." He mimed buttoning his mouth closed.

Avindea eyed him coldly, her dark eyes full of suspicion. "I have a feeling this comes with strings attached."

Rendevas shrugged, standing up to his full height and brushing off his spotless velvet breeches. "Perhaps. It is never a bad thing to be owed a favor from a paladin." He smiled at her unctuously and with a little wave and a bow, ambled away, whistling a jaunty tune as he left.

Avindea scowled, watching him pass. "This will not end well," she muttered to herself.

Quay bounced on the balls of her feet anxiously. "So can we keep her here? I'm sure there's a discreet doctor on the church's payroll we can bribe to treat her, and once she's well, we can question her about the murders!"

"Murders?!" Avindea spat.

Ghdion spoke up. "Yep. Murders. Plural."

Gods, he looked like a criminal with all those scars and weird dot tattoos. Why Quay kept collecting these strays was a constant source of bewilderment.

"Everyone inside. Now." Avindea pointed at the back door, eyes aflame, looking every inch the authoritative, righteous paladin. "You three," she jabbed her finger at the loitering bodyguards, "grab Midori and we'll bring her into the basement. Quay, you come with me. You have a lot of explaining to do."

Chapter 16

Mind Reading

Hypnocost watched the others try to interrogate Midori. He was bored out of his mind.

For one thing, they questioned a woman who literally could not talk. What did they think they would glean from more questions? Midori, though she was more fully awake after seeing a doctor employed by the church—and bribed a hefty sum to keep quiet—flat out refused to so much as look at them when they spoke. She lay enveloped in soft blankets and pillows, upon a nicer bed than Hypnocost had ever had the pleasure of sleeping on, deep within the bowels of the cathedral. Unbeknownst to the common folk of Praetorius, the Cathedral of Vidamae had an extensive basement beneath its main floor. It was mostly used for storage.

The paladin, Avindea, had helped them arrange a small empty room down there into a makeshift infirmary, complete with the lavish bed, a chamber pot, large storage chest, and a few mismatched stools for seating. The door had a lock with only one copy of the key; it was given to Quay for safekeeping. The doctor they summoned had assured them he would check in frequently, and that all Midori needed now was time to rest up and heal. Lady Avindea left shortly after, claiming pressing plenum business, but not before finishing her heated, whispered conversation with her cousin.

Quay was attempting to speak with Midori now, perched on the edge of a stool she had pulled up to the side of the bed. "Now you can see how serious we are about wanting to help," she said gently. "We've got a doctor coming to tend to your many wounds, and you are welcome to stay here as long as you'd like. Why won't you help us by answering our questions?"

Midori, eyes ablaze, thrust her finger towards the locked door, then to the key hanging from Quay's neck next to her holy symbol. She raised her eyebrows questioningly.

Quay sighed. "I know it seems cruel, but really, it's for your own protection, Midori. We can't have any random person stumbling upon you in here."

Midori shook her head and crossed her arms.

Unbothered, Quay held out a sheet of paper and a quill. "What if you answer a question from me, and then I will answer one from you? Would that help?"

Midori took the paper and quill, held it above her lap for a moment, then threw it violently to the ground.

"Well, that answers that," Ghdion, leaning (more like *looming*) against the wall behind Quay, mused aloud.

Hypnocost, who had been studying the magical mirror while the rest of them continued this fool's errand, set the glass gently against the wall, finally taking pity on the poor souls. "I believe I may have a way to help." He stepped forward, straightening the lapels of his silk jacket. He had changed into one that was a pale shade of lilac, with tiny flowers embroidered along the trim. It was one of his favorites.

"And you only just now thought it prudent to let us know?" Lucius queried in an annoyed tone.

"I thought it wise to see if more ... *classical* means of questioning would give us positive results." He gazed upon each of their confused faces, reveling in the dramatic moment. "My methods are much more *unorthodox*."

"What, like you can read her mind?" Lucius said skeptically.

"Precisely."

Midori's eyes widened. She pushed back on the bed, trying to distance herself from him as he strode to her bedside.

"Do not worry. It will not hurt a bit," he promised in a soothing tone. The woman still struggled weakly, her face a mask of fear mingled with horrified loathing. As he stood above her, she cringed back as if expecting a strike.

"Hypnocost, I don't think you sh—"

Too late. He was already burrowing inside of her mind, erecting the invisible tunnel between his brain and hers. Instead of a wide-open door like the previous time he tried this, her consciousness slammed against his, sending him staggering backwards from the shock. She struggled to keep him out, but his will was stronger. The tunnel thinned, but he was still able to traverse across his consciousness straight into hers.

Memories and fragmented thoughts flashed through his mind, merely hinting at Midori's troubled past and what she believed to be her uncertain future. He saw her arguing with a man who looked like a masculine version of herself—her brother? Her twin? He had her same dark hair and eyes, though his were filled with a zealous fervor. Then he saw her fleeing somewhere with a small group of people. They traveled, facing many hardships, hunger, lack of supplies, and doubt that what they did was prudent. There was a small campsite, shadowed with fears of survival, fears of being chased. A mountain featured largely in her thoughts, towering above all others, an ominous presence behind it that Hypnocost could not explain. The mountain felt dangerous, like it was waiting and watching, like it would devour her. The mountain changed into the face of a weary old man, his eyes covered with a black cloth. And above it all, blazing fiercely with an unholy aura, was the three-pronged claw symbol of Kax, proving how devoted, how loyal to the goddess Midori really was.

"Tread carefully with these powers,"

the voice suddenly warned him.

"You are still new to these abilities. Go farther. See what else she hides."

Hypnocost hesitated, but in the end tried to delve deeper, to gauge her motivations, to see if she was an active threat. His curiosity got the better of him. Spurred on by the voice, he channeled his will forcefully, pushing further, harder, faster ... He began to convulse, his entire body shivering with effort.

"**No!**" Midori's mind screamed at the same time the voice called out,

"You are faltering!"

For the first time since the voice started speaking to him, he heard fear in its flat tones. Fear of what? Fear that Hypnocost was going too far? Didn't the voice *want* that?

Midori screamed an ear-shattering shriek and pushed him out of her mind by the sheer force of her own will. He slammed back against the wall then slid right onto his rump. A single stream of blood slowly trickled from his nose.

"Hypnocost!" Quay cried out while Lucius howled, "What did you *do*?" Quay and Ghdion rushed towards him; Lucius hovered over Midori's bedside, gently lifting her closed eyelids and checking her pulse.

Groaning, Hypnocost struggled upright. Ghdion grabbed his arm and helped him to stand. "What in the hells was that?" he murmured, and though he wasn't speaking any louder than normal, Ghdion's voice sounded as if he was screaming directly into his ears.

He clapped his hands over his ears, but it didn't stop the loud noises or the shaky feeling that threatened to send him toppling right back over. Quay supported him on his other side. "Are you okay?"

"I am well," he panted. "I just need a moment of quiet." Everything was muffled and blurry; he closed his eyes and focused on taking deep, steadying breaths.

"You certainly did a number on Midori," Lucius growled in anger. "She's knocked out cold. What were you thinking?"

"You lost your focus,"

the voice chastised.

"You cannot take such risks."

He winced and held his head in his hands. "I know!" he cried aloud.

The others looked at him with concern. "You know what?" Ghdion asked.

"Nothing! I-I thought I could read her thoughts, but she was able to block me. It ... caught me off guard."

"What does that mean?" asked Lucius, frowning.

"No one has ever been able to block me before," Hypnocost explained slowly. He rested his weight against the wall for fear of another dizzying attack. "Her will is strong."

Quay shuddered in horror. Ghdion, more practical, asked, "Did you manage to see anything that will help us?"

"I saw ... I saw her arguing with someone, her brother, I believe. Then she was running from something with a small group of people. There was a mountain and an old blind man. And above all, the symbol of Kax, which is ever present at the front of her thoughts."

"Nothing about the murders?" Quay asked in a small voice.

Hypnocost shook his head. "Everything moved too rapidly for me to track, but ... no. I saw no murders in her memories."

They were quiet for a beat, contemplating what it could mean. Ghdion was the first to break the silence, asking, "Do you think you could try again, see if you can get more information?"

"No!" Hypnocost and Lucius yelled simultaneously.

"I would not dare risk that again!" he voiced in a panic as he wiped clammy sweat from his forehead.

"You stay the hells away from her!" Lucius admonished. He held a glass of water to Midori's lips and helped her to drink it as she slowly came to. "We'll find another way to glean what she knows. This mind-reading business is ... unnatural. I don't like it."

Hypnocost held up his hands. "You do not have to tell me twice, Lucius. I have no desire to repeat that experience."

"Stay the hell away from *my* mind, while you're at it!" Lucius continued, jabbing a finger at him.

"Why don't we all settle in for the night?" Quay cut in before things got more heated. "It won't be a problem for you all to stay here. There are plenty of beds in the clerics quarters you can use. We could all use some sleep, and we can try again in the morning, when we're fresh."

Even though it was still early evening, they all agreed. It had been a long and arduous day, with the next promising to be even more so if they couldn't figure out what was going on with Midori, the Kax cultists, and the murders. Hypnocost, Ghdion, and Quay trudged upstairs to find empty rooms; Lucius offered to stay with Midori for a while, promising to come up later that night to sleep.

When Hypnocost had settled into a small, plain bedchamber in the middle of the cleric's quarters, he closed his door, looked over the room briefly, then asked the voice, *"How did I do what I did earlier? How can I do more?"*

No response. He could feel the voice there, hovering at the edges of his mind. It was like it was hiding ... but from what?

"What caused me to lose my focus?"

Silence. Though the wrenching, overwhelming sense of his failure was, thankfully, dulled, it still lingered like a bad taste at the fringes of his mind.

"Please! Why will you not answer me?"

No answer.

Hypnocost sighed, wishing for Quay's healing to rid him of the dull headache that was slowly building in pressure. He would just have to cure it the old-fashioned way: with lots of rest. More troubled than he had felt in a while, he laid back onto the cot and fell into a fitful, dream-filled sleep.

Chapter 17

The Augur

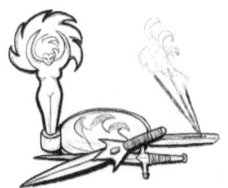

Fifteen Years Ago

It had been one month since Midori's life had changed for the worst.

One month since the decimation of her village—they called it Solace because it was supposed to be a safe place, nestled in the woods near the Camfield Temple of Kax. One month since all of her friends were murdered. Since Mother and Father were killed. On her birthday.

Midori sighed as she rummaged through their rapidly thinning pile of supplies. Only dusty old hardtack and a handful of tart blueberries scrounged from the surrounding woods were left of the little food they'd managed to gather after the paladins left Solace. They were thorough, those paladins; every house was burnt to the ground, some even with people still inside. They stole or trashed any valuables they found. They even killed beloved family pets; Midori overheard Bennett telling Kang that he found his cat's corpse just outside the burnt husk of his home.

She popped a couple blueberries into her mouth and chewed them thoughtfully, wincing slightly at the sourness. She'd figured out who those paladins were, and why they killed all of her loved ones. Since she was twelve now, she knew the best hiding places to listen in while the adults talked. She'd overheard Solange say they were paladins of the Goddess Vidamae, She of the sunburst sigil and false love of life and happiness. If She loved life so much, why had She allowed Her paladins to kill so many? Midori couldn't make sense of that.

Apparently, Vidamae and Kax hated each other. Aunt Solange had explained it all to Kang and Bennett—being fifteen meant they were adults, because Aunt Solange told them *everything*—but Midori had fallen asleep in the middle of her explanation, so she wasn't clear on some of the finer points of the story.

Anyways, it didn't matter. Her family was dead, she had nowhere to go and no house to live in anymore, she had only her older brother, aunt, and Bennett left, and they were running out of food.

Her stomach rumbled loudly. Bennett, sitting near the askew front door of the temple, glanced backwards at her as he struggled to string a bow he'd fashioned out of a thick hunk of wood. It didn't look much like a bow to Midori—she was pretty sure they were supposed to be slightly curved outward in the middle, not perfectly straight like his was—but it was all Bennett could talk about lately.

"I've almost got this figured out," he told her. His cheeks had hollowed out and whenever he took his shirt off to wash each morning, she could see each of his ribs; it wouldn't be long before they all starved to death. After only one month? It didn't seem fair. "Once I get this bow strung up, I can go into the woods and hunt some squirrels. Maybe even rabbits."

Her mouth watered. She could almost taste the roasted rabbit, juicy and tender, flavored with pepper and salt and spices and ...

Kang rushed into the temple. He'd been patrolling outside; it was his turn to keep watch. One of them was always posted outside to keep an eye out in case the Vidamae Paladins returned to finish what they started. Even Midori had to sometimes, though they never made her do it at night. Kang pushed the broken door aside; almost everything inside the church had been broken by the paladins during their rampage. "Someone's coming!" he breathed, his face a mask of terror. "They're heading right for the temple!"

Aunt Solange hurried into the nave from the corridor off to the side, where she'd made her own private little bedroom. Bennett, Kang, and Midori were still too nervous to sleep alone, and slept each night in a big nest together right there in the center of the nave. "Did you see them?" she demanded. "Are they paladins?"

Kang shook his head, his long black hair flopping around his ears. "I don't know, I couldn't tell from where I was hiding. It's a pretty big group, though."

"What do we do?" asked Bennett, abandoning his homemade bow.

Solange frowned, showing deep divots around her nose and mouth. She looked much older than her twenty-six years. Going days without food didn't help. "You three hide. Don't come out unless I tell you to, do you understand?" She pulled her robe tighter across her small chest and strode towards the doorway.

"We can help!" Kang hissed.

"You'll just get in my way," Solange replied, ushering the two boys back towards Midori. "Now hide! I'll go deal with them." And she walked confidently out of the temple.

Midori, eyes wide with fear, grabbed Kang's hand. "Follow me," she whispered. "I know a good hiding spot."

Bennett and Kang allowed her to lead them farther back into the nave, where a couple of smashed up pieces of wood were all that held up a section of the back wall. She pushed one plank out of the way and crawled inside, glancing over her shoulder. "C'mon!" she entreated, beckoning them to follow. "It's a lot bigger back here than it looks, I promise."

Bennett hunched down onto his hands and knees; he had a much harder time fitting beneath the broken wood than Midori due to his height. Kang followed, and with all three of them squeezed inside, it was a tight fit. Midori peered out through a crack in the wood; the space was perfect for eavesdropping because she could see outside, but nobody could see her inside.

Kang and Bennett took up spots on either side and copied her, pushing their faces against the boards so they, too, could see through the cracks. The temple interior was quiet, and Aunt Solange was too far from the entrance for them to see what she was doing.

Then they heard voices from outside. Solange said something, and an unfamiliar woman's voice replied. It didn't sound violent or strained—in fact, based on the tenor of their conversation, it sounded as if Solange maybe knew the person.

"Can you see anything?" Bennett whispered.

"Shh!" was Kang's sharp reply.

Midori's eyes fixed on the open doorway. She started to see shadows of people approaching ... were they friend or foe? Her whole body began to shake uncontrollably.

Kang wrapped a comforting arm around her shoulders.

Solange appeared in the doorway, leading a group of about a dozen or so people. They all looked as bedraggled and exhausted and starved as Midori felt. She then noticed that the woman at the front, a tall, severe faced middle-aged lady with bluntly cropped graying hair, wore a small symbol of Kax around her neck. "They're Kax followers!" she breathed, feeling a relief so deep she could have fallen right over.

"What? How do you know?" Bennett hissed, pushing closer to the gap in the wood.

Solange and the group of strangers walked into the nave. They were close enough that the three could hear some of what they said. "—been about a month," Solange said. She gestured towards the destroyed pews and disrepair of the place. "As you can see, the paladins did a number on the temple. I think they were searching for any information on other Kax followers, church logs, holy relics, things like that."

"I see that," the gray-haired lady replied. She had a snooty sounding voice, as if she belonged in some rich castle instead of a broken-down Temple of Kax. It sounded as if she blamed *them* for the temple's state of disrepair! Midori bristled in indignation.

Solange continued hurriedly, as if eager to explain herself. "The church logs were hidden in a secret compartment behind the altar. The paladins didn't manage to find them, thank Kax. I've been keeping them safe."

The old lady was obviously a vicar, a leader in the Kax church, like her Aunt Solange. She sniffed. "You've had no other visitors since the attack? It's safe here?"

"No one else has come, no," Solange answered. "You're welcome to stay and rest for as long as you need." Midori heard a note of barely suppressed panic in her aunt's voice; how in the hells would they be able to provide for this huge group of people? They barely had enough food for just the four of them!

The gray-haired woman turned towards her group and conversed quietly with an older man who, for some reason, had a black cloth wrapped over his eyes. Midori, curious, watched as the two spoke quietly; was the old man blind? Why wear the fabric over his eyes like that?

They watched as Solange waited awkwardly off to the side. More people filed in; all in all, Midori counted nineteen travelers, most wearing some small piece of jewelry or embroidered patch on their clothes that denoted their faith in Kax. She felt heartened to see it; it had been so long since she'd been around more people like her! But where did these newcomers come from?

The gray-haired woman turned back to Solange. "We will stay," she announced. "We thank you for your hospitality, such as it is. You are the only vicar from Solace left? Are you here alone?"

Solange hesitated before replying. "... No, actually, I'm not. My niece, nephew, and a family friend escaped Solace with me." She squinted into the darkness of the nave. "I told them to hide in case you were a group of Vidamae Paladins. Kang, Midori, Bennett? You can come out now."

Midori scrambled through the broken boards before Kang or

Bennett could stop her. The group of newcomers watched as she appeared; she self-consciously brushed the dirt from her skirt. It was the same one she'd gotten as a birthday gift from Mother a month ago, though the once bright pink fabric was now faded and torn.

"Hi!" She waved, offering the guests her best, most welcoming smile. "I'm Midori. Pleased to meet you." She gave them a little curtsy. A chunk of lace that had come unstitched from the hem of her skirt flopped with the movement.

Kang and Bennett crawled out from behind her, neither one of them offering their names. They eyed the new people distrustfully; Midori elbowed her brother in the ribs and said out of the corner of her mouth, "Kang!? Manners!"

"Who are you people?" he demanded instead, his voice hot with some strong emotion she couldn't place.

Solange opened her mouth to apologize, but the gray-haired woman spoke before she had a chance. "We are not your enemy, child," she spoke in what Midori assumed she thought was a soothing tone, but she knew it would irk Kang more than anything. The woman even held out her hands in a placating manner. She obviously didn't know how to speak with teenagers. "We are Kax worshippers, just like you, from near Praetorius."

The blindfolded old man stepped forward. He held out his hand until he touched the gray-haired woman's shoulder, which he used as support. "Vicar, hush now. I don't believe this child appreciates being patronized." He spoke in a wispy, scratchy sort of voice and wore ragged robes that looked two sizes too big for his gaunt frame. His hair was a forgettable shade of brown, all scraggly and hanging past his shoulders. Midori couldn't tell what his face looked like in the gloom. That black cloth over his eyes didn't help.

"We thank you for allowing us to spend some time within the safety of your temple," the old man continued. "I am called The Augur. It is a pleasure to meet you." He bowed towards them formally.

Faith and Ruin

Midori didn't miss the surprised little sneer that crossed the gray-haired woman's face.

The new people ended up staying with them for several days. It was both a blessing and a curse—more people meant more mouths to feed, but it also meant more people to go out and actively hunt and gather food and supplies. The newcomers freely shared what little they had; the first night was a veritable feast of different foods Midori hadn't eaten since well before Solace's destruction. For the first time in a month, she'd gone to sleep with a full belly.

The Augur, she found out the next day, wore the dark cloth over his eyes to cover the fact that they had been burned out of his head. It was some sort of spell the Vidamae Priestesses cast only a few days before the paladins had attacked her home. "A mass prayer in the form of divine retribution," he informed her after she asked him about it—Aunt Solange had gasped and shooed her away as if she'd done something wrong, but The Augur only smiled sadly and assured her he was not offended. "The Vidamae High Priestesses all gathered at the Altar of Tasuil and entreated their Goddess to punish Kax's followers. Vidamae heard their pleas and responded in kind."

He then unwound the black fabric from his head; Midori watched, fascinated, as the covering slid from his face. Two blackened, burnt-out pits were all that remained of his eyes. He didn't even have *eyebrows*. It was like the top half of his face was a skeleton, and the rest was a regular old man's face.

She stared raptly, her mind unable to comprehend how painful that must have felt. "But *why*?" she asked. "Why would She wanna burn your eyes out like that? What did you do?"

"Midori, that's enough," Solange scolded and ushered her out of the room, making up some excuse that Midori had chores to do.

So she asked Kang about it. He sat by himself outside, absently peeling bark off of a stick and throwing it out into the weeds. He was *brooding*. He did that a lot lately.

"Why'd Vidamae burn out his eyes?" he repeated, his dark eyebrows furrowed. "She did more than just that! Her spell killed *hundreds* of Kax's devotees, Midori. Those who didn't die from the spell immediately ended up like The Augur, with their eyes blasted from their heads just like that." He snapped his fingers loudly. "She shot out a light so bright it literally *melted peoples' eyeballs*."

Midori shivered. "Gross! Why would She do that?!"

"Because anyone who loves Vidamae *hates* us," he answered vehemently. "All because we love Kax." He flung the peeled stick into the grass. "Do you know why The Augur got such a potent dose of Vidamae's wrath?" he asked her then, gazing moodily towards the woods.

"No, why?"

"Because he was the one who created the blood fonts."

She frowned. "What's a blood font?"

Kang scoffed and flung his hair out of his face. It was like he was *trying* to draw attention to how long it had gotten. He did that *a lot*. "You don't know about the blood fonts?" He laughed mirthlessly. "Maybe I shouldn't tell you," he said in a singsong, sneering tone. "You're probably too young."

"I am not!" she cried indignantly. "Kang, c'mon, tell me!"

He eyed her sidelong and didn't speak for some moments. Finally, he sighed as if exasperated, but she knew he actually loved imparting secret, forbidden knowledge to her. He liked to lord it over her that he knew so much more than she did. Little did he know, she'd been eavesdropping on the new adults ever since they showed up. She'd heard them mention the blood fonts often, but she had no idea what they were.

"Fine, I guess I can tell you. The blood fonts are what the Kax Warriors use to find who has the bloodline of Vidamae flowing in their veins. The Augur designed the fonts based on a holy vision Kax sent him in his dreams, and then he crafted a whole bunch of them." His eyes took on a faraway cast. "The Warriors used them to find people descended from the Whore Goddess, then they killed them!"

Midori gasped. She didn't know what a whore was, but it sounded bad. Kang used the word like it was a curse. "Why would they kill them though? Is that why all the paladins came to Solace and killed everyone there? Because they were mad our people killed their people?"

Kang scowled. "Because they hate us, Midori! It was kill them first or they would kill *us*, don't you understand?"

She nodded, but she didn't understand. Not really. Why did

anyone have to kill in the first place? Why couldn't they just leave each other alone?

It went on like that for a few days. Midori listened intently whenever the adults spoke, particularly the new vicar and The Augur. She didn't like the gray-haired vicar—she never actually caught her name, so in her head she just called her 'Cranky.' She was bossy and persnickety and never had nice things to say to Aunt Solange, who was just doing her best. Aunt Solange acted as if everything Cranky said was the law, or part of some holy Kax text, or something. Midori didn't understand why Solange seemed to admire Cranky so much. She was nothing but a know-it-all.

So it was especially irritating when Aunt Solange announced, four days after The Augur's group arrived, that they would be leaving with them. "The Augur has a plan," she told Kang, Midori, and Bennett after they had gotten ready for the day. "They've found somewhere safe we can live, and they've invited us to come with them." What few possessions she still had were already tucked away in her backpack, which was slung across her shoulder.

"Where are we going?" Bennett asked.

"The Augur told us about an old abandoned mine up in the mountains near Feywynn," she replied. "It's a bit of a journey, but from what I was told, the Vidamae Church doesn't know anything about it, so we will be much safer there than if we stay here in the temple. It's only a matter of time before the paladins return. I don't want us here when they do."

Kang and Midori eyed each other. The temple wasn't exactly home, but it was at least familiar. Now they were expected to just up and leave with this group of strangers? Midori opened her mouth to argue, but Aunt Solange cut her off before she had a chance.

"Pack up your things. We have a long journey ahead of us."

Chapter 18

Not A Cultist

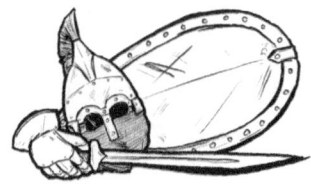

Lucius was determined to talk with Midori.

He couldn't explain why, but he felt a strange connection with the mysterious woman, her devotion to Kax notwithstanding. He felt sure he could get through to her, if only she would give him a chance. So he decided, after the others had left, he would stay with her a bit longer to see if he couldn't get her to open up a bit.

"Do you need anything? Water? Food?" Hunched over to tidy up the mess of papers she had thrown on the floor, he glanced up at her questioningly.

She shook her head, watching him distrustfully. Shrugging, he straightened the papers and placed them neatly upon the bedside table, laying the quill atop the stack. He placed a small jar of ink right next to it, in case she changed her mind and wanted to communicate after all.

Taking a seat on one of the taller stools, he rested his head against the wall and closed his eyes. He couldn't remember the last time he felt so bone-tired and world-weary. Everything in his life was upended and in chaos—losing his job as a guard for the miners in Furow's Ridge, discovering poor Edmund Brisby's dead body, and now this whole business with the murdering Kax cultists. He thought he'd finally found the peaceful life that had always eluded him when he settled in Furow's Ridge. The little village was as far from his home as possible, which was just how he liked it. The last place he wanted to be was back in the city of his birth.

Well, maybe not the *last* place. Praetorius was pretty high on the list. But he couldn't say that to the others.

As he was silently ruminating on his mess of a life, he felt something light hit the side of his head. Cracking an eye open, he saw that Midori had thrown a crumpled-up sheet of paper to get his attention. Puzzled, he noticed she held up a parchment that said:

WHAT ARE YOU DOING HERE?

He sat up and pondered how best to answer her. "I wanna help," he told her honestly. There was no sense in hiding his intentions from her; he had a feeling she was the type of person who would appreciate the truth above all else.

Scowling, she scribbled one word on the paper, then held it up for him to see again. It was underlined for emphasis.

WHY?

Lucius sighed and rubbed the back of his neck. "Honestly? I have no idea. You just ... remind me of someone I used to know. I don't even fully know why. You don't look anything like her! I think it's just more of a sense of ... I dunno, like you're both underdogs, I guess."

Marissa's face floated into his thoughts, her curly brown hair floating around her like a halo. It had been years since he'd seen her. Did she still think of him, even after everything? "We're the underdogs, Lucius," she had told him once, before everything had gone to shit. "And everyone likes to root for the underdog."

Midori cocked an eyebrow at him when he didn't elaborate. He sighed deeply, banishing Marissa from his mind. She was long gone, and likely glad to be rid of him. "Never mind, it's stupid."

She scribbled furiously.

WHAT MAKES YOU THINK I AM AN UNDERDOG?

Her script was harsh and jagged. He shrugged and said, "Just a hunch."

She furrowed her dark eyebrows and stared intently, looking like she struggled to come to a decision. After a few moments of silence, she wrote quickly.

DO YOU TRULY WANT TO HELP ME? EVEN THOUGH I FOLLOW KAX, YOUR MOST HATED GODDESS?

"I do," he told her simply. "And she's not *my* most hated goddess. I don't follow any of the gods."

WHY DO YOU SURROUND YOURSELF WITH THOSE WHO FOLLOW VIDAMAE?

She gestured around the room, as if to say, 'We're literally inside a Cathedral of Vidamae!'

"It's a job," he told her, shrugging. "At this point, it's better than the alternative. Poor and unemployed, I mean. I'm just as much of an outsider here as you are."

There was only the sound of quill scratching on parchment as she scribbled more words.

WHY IS YOUR FACE SCARRED LIKE THAT?

He knew that question was coming. It didn't bother him anymore; he'd had the scars nearly his whole life. And anyways, he had a sense her question was a test of some sort, and, depending on his answer, she might give him answers of her own.

So he told her the whole, awful truth. "My mother. She was a decently powerful mage but was disappointed when I was born without the talent. She used to make me stay up late every night as a kid, reading through spellbooks and practicing spells, but nothing ever stuck. For a year she did this, day in and day out, until she started looking into other alternatives. Apparently she found some ritual where she could separate the magical essence from some enchanted coin she had. A gift from Velthunas, supposedly, you know how He's known to hand out lucky coins to those who aid Him. Since she couldn't *fathom* having a child who was devoid of magic, she was just crazy and desperate enough to try the spell." He huffed out a humorless laugh. "Well, it didn't really work as intended and the damn thing blew up in my face instead. Literally. I don't remember all the details. I just remember the raging heat and how painful it was when it spread across my skin, and ... and, ah ... there you have it." He gestured theatrically to the left side of his face, where the burn scars left their lifelong mark.

He would never tell her about the bone-tingling fear he felt then, how the person he most trusted, the one who was supposed to keep him from harm at all costs, was the one who had hurt him so deeply. To this day, the smell of smoke made him shiver and retch uncontrollably.

Midori looked at him in horror and pity. He was so used to seeing those looks, they were like old friends. Everyone always looked at him that way, either shrinking away from his ugliness, or frowning with false concern that he suffered such a tragedy. He tried to pretend it didn't bother him, but how could it not? He was constantly reminded of his marks, always wondering what he would have looked like had his mother not been so cruel and foolish. People always told him that looks didn't matter, but those words rang hollow in his ears. It was easy for one to say such a thing when they weren't scarred themselves.

"It didn't work, by the way. In case you were wondering. No magical powers. Never been able to cast so much as a single cantrip."

Midori watched him carefully, then took a fresh sheet of paper and wrote some more.

WHAT HAPPENED AFTER SHE ABUSED YOU LIKE THAT?

He blinked, his stomach dropping at her bald question. He knew, deep down, that what his mother had done was, indeed, abuse, but to see it written out so plainly? He swallowed against his dry throat. "She left me at an orphanage. Said she couldn't live with the guilt of what she had done to me. So as soon as I was old enough, I signed up for the military, and I've been a soldier ever since." That was only half true: he had run away from the orphanage with Marissa when he was fourteen, lied to the military recruitment officer about his age, and signed up a full three years earlier than he should have been able to.

AND NOW? YOU ARE STILL A SOLDIER, BUT IN THE EMPLOY OF VIDAMAE?

"More or less. I'm Quay's bodyguard now." He had a sudden thought. "She's not that bad, either. I know Kax and Vidamae have some ancient grudge or something, but Quay isn't like most other Vidamae Priestesses I've known. Y'know, stuck up and arrogant." He grinned sheepishly. "I haven't known her that long, but I have a pretty good sense of these things. She's good people."

Midori regarded him skeptically but chose not to respond. She sat upon the bed, the stack of parchment in her lap and the quill poised in her fingers. She stared off into the middle distance, her dark eyes faraway as she struggled with some internal debate.

Lucius waited her out, not pushing, not threatening, just sitting there with her as she figured things out. He didn't talk about his past often, but for some reason, unloading it all on this woman—this stranger—made him feel ... lighter. Relieved. He had a feeling he was getting through to her after opening up, and at this stage in their slowly budding relationship, delicacy was key.

She bit her lip, put the quill to the paper, decided against it, then, with a huff, put it back down and began to write. She wrote for what felt like hours, filling the whole sheet with her words.

Finally, with a deep breath for courage, she handed him the paper to read.

I WILL HELP YOU WITH WHAT I CAN. YOU ALREADY KNOW I FOLLOW KAX, BUT I AM NOT A CULTIST LIKE YOU THINK. I AM NOT ONE OF THOSE FROM THE CAMPSITE OUTSIDE DESAI. THEY ARE THE CULTISTS, TRUE TYRANTS WHO

> SILENCE THOSE WHO WILL NOT FOLLOW THEM. THEY WERE THE ONES WHO ATTACKED ME AND TIED ME UP. MY FRIENDS WHO WERE WITH ME FLED, AND I DO NOT KNOW WHAT HAS BECOME OF THEM. IF YOU HAD NOT FOUND ME, THE PEOPLE FROM THAT CAMPSITE WOULD HAVE TAKEN ME BACK TO THEIR LEADER, WHO WOULD HAVE KILLED ME FOR CERTAIN.

He blanched at the words. They unwittingly saved her life, stumbling upon that campsite when they did. What luck was that? Glancing up, he saw she was already writing more on a new piece of paper.

> <u>NOT ALL KAX BELIEVERS ARE CULTISTS</u>. MY GROUP HAS BEEN FLEEING THOSE CULTISTS FOR MONTHS NOW. THE CULTISTS YOU SEEK ARE THE ONES TRYING TO ASSASSINATE ALL OF VIDAMAE'S BLOODLINE IN AN ATTEMPT TO FINISH WHAT THEY BEGAN 15 YEARS AGO. ME AND THE PEOPLE I TRAVEL WITH DO NOT AGREE WITH THEIR METHODS. WE ARE TRYING TO STOP THEM.

Lucius's eyes widened and his heart quickened in excitement. Finally! Now they were getting somewhere! "Do you know where the cultists are or where they might strike next?"

Furiously Midori wrote.

> GIVE ME A MAP. I CAN SHOW YOU WHERE THEY MAY GO NEXT, THOUGH I AM NOT WHOLLY CERTAIN. PLEASE DESTROY THESE NOTES. I DO NOT WISH FOR ANYONE ELSE TO SEE THEM.

"Noted," he replied gravely.

He knew the entire basement of the cathedral was one large storage library; surely there had to be a map of Khamris somewhere down there. "Give me a moment to look for a map," he said and stood up to leave.

She shook her head vehemently, making pitiful scratchy noises in her throat as she tried to speak. He froze, turning to look at her in concern.

Please don't leave,

she wrote.

I am reluctant to be alone anymore, especially when surrounded by enemies.

Touched, he smiled at her reassuringly. "Alright then. We can have someone bring a map tomorrow morning, if you're still willing to help."

She nodded, obviously relieved, then closed her eyes, exhausted from their long conversation.

Lucius sat against the wall, making himself as comfortable as he could. He watched her silently for a few moments, wondering about her and what circumstances led her to where she was, and how far he was willing to go to help her.

He had a feeling, based on their discussion and budding connection, that it would be quite far indeed.

Chapter 19

Camfield

"Camfield, huh?"

It was the next morning, and the group hovered over the large map of Khamris Quay found for them. They stared at the spot Midori indicated: a small village labeled Camfield.

While Midori jabbed her finger at the map emphatically, Ghdion blanched with a familiar, panic-inducing rush of emotions. He desperately pushed them back down where they belonged; now just seeing the *name* of his old hometown made him feel this way? What the fuck?

He was intimately familiar with Camfield: he used to live there with his wife and three daughters, after all.

Before they were killed.

He could still imagine the sweet, tangy aroma of the apples from his orchard, could see in his mind's eye Sari smiling as she hung the laundry on the line to dry in the cool breeze ...

"So you're pretty sure that's the next place the cultists are going to target," Lucius said, more as a statement of fact than as a question.

Lucius's voice snapped Ghdion back to attention. Midori, still convalescing in bed, nodded and scribbled an answer on a blank sheet of paper.

IT IS ONE OF THE LAST OF THE SMALLER VILLAGES LEFT THAT THEY HAVEN'T HIT YET. THEY WILL MOST LIKELY GO TO CAMFIELD'S CHURCH OF VIDAMAE FIRST.

"What do you think?" Lucius regarded the rest of the group with his hands on his hips. "Should we check it out?"

Ghdion frowned and crossed his arms. "I don't trust her," he stated bluntly. "She could be sending us right into a trap."

It seemed awfully convenient that Midori was suddenly bursting with answers for them after giving them all the cold shoulder for days. It didn't matter that she couldn't actually speak. He still didn't believe she was helping them out of the goodness of her heart. What reason did she have to do so? It didn't make sense. And in his experience, if it didn't make sense, it was probably dangerous.

Lucius scowled at him, causing his scars to wrinkle weirdly around his mouth and left eye. "She is also the only lead we have. We're going to have to take a risk at some point; why not now? Why not give her a chance to help like she says she wants to?"

"I'm inclined to agree with Lucius," Quay said softly. "If there's even a small chance we can save someone else from being murdered, we have to take it. Besides," she smiled encouragingly at Ghdion, "we should be safe enough with your two swords and Hypnocost's magic, right?"

"I'm not going," Lucius stated. The others looked at him, dumbfounded.

"What do you mean, you're not going? Didn't you literally *just* get hired as the new bodyguard?" Ghdion snapped.

"Someone's gotta stay back with Midori, make sure she isn't found or ... or harassed, y'know?" Lucius shrugged. "Why not me?"

Quay frowned. "I suppose that makes sense. You'll still have to be careful not to be seen if you can help it." She pulled off the necklace with the room key on it and handed it to him. "Just be careful."

"Are you seriously considering this, Priestess?" Ghdion growled, throwing out his arms in exasperation. "You're going to trust the word of an *open Kax follower*? Aren't you supposed to hate each other or something? From way back?"

Midori hissed, the sound weak and erratic in her wounded throat. She jabbed the quill onto her paper, writing furiously, then shoved the paper at Ghdion.

> **I HAD NOTHING TO DO WITH THAT TRAVESTY 15 YEARS AGO! I WAS A CHILD THEN! BESIDES, MY PEOPLE AND I DO NOT CONDONE WHAT THOSE CULTISTS ARE DOING. THEY SULLY KAX'S GOOD NAME WITH THEIR SENSELESS MURDERS.**

"How am I supposed to believe this?" Ghdion cried, slapping his hand on the paper. "You expect me to just up and travel to Camfield on the word of ... of some *woman* we don't even know?" He knew he was being unreasonable, but he couldn't help it. He couldn't risk them finding out. Camfield was small enough that, if any villager they passed got a good look at him, they'd recognize him for sure. Then they'd ask him all sorts of questions he wasn't ready to answer, and Quay would wonder what that was all about, and then he'd have to reveal everything that had happened ...

"Enough!" Quay cried, her face flushed. "Ghdion, I understand your concerns, but I'm the one in charge, and what I say is that you, Hypnocost, and I travel to Camfield. It cannot hurt to at least check it out, right? If nothing happens, we've only wasted a day or two, and we can come back and turn her over to the authorities. But if what she says is true? Then we've got a chance to save people who have no idea of the danger they are in."

Lucius nodded his agreement and Hypnocost stood from his stool, stretching his arms. "Shall we depart now?" he asked in his snooty voice. "I find myself eager to venture out." He seemed in much higher spirits after his disastrous attempt at mind-reading last night; his good mood was directly opposite Ghdion's grumpy one, and it only served to make him feel even more bad-tempered.

"I think that would be best," Quay answered, also standing. "Camfield is only a half day's travel by horseback, so if we leave now, we can make it before dinner."

They headed out of the room to prepare Mertha and the wagon for more traveling. Ghdion paused in the doorway, turning towards Lucius and Midori with hot resolve in his blue eyes.

"If her sending us on this fool's errand causes any harm to Quay," he warned darkly, pointing at Midori, "I'll kill you myself."

Lucius's jaw tightened, but he gave him a sharp nod in response. "We'll see," was all he said. "Isn't it *your* job to keep her safe, big guy?" He then turned away, effectively ending the conversation before Ghdion had a chance to retort.

Quay was already halfway done with hooking Mertha to the wagon when Ghdion stepped outside, carrying their bags of supplies. The ox chewed placidly at the grass around the cathedral's stables. The stablehand, Hooper, a boy of about sixteen who had dark skin and watery eyes, wrangled his hands nervously as he watched her buckle the straps that attached the reins to Mertha's bridle.

"My lady," he said in a quavery, not-yet deepened voice. "You only just got back last night. Surely you do not intend to take Mertha and the wagon back out? The poor ox needs her rest!"

"Nonsense!" Quay said brightly. "Mertha will do just fine. Besides, we'll only be gone for the day."

Ghdion highly doubted their task would be as quick as that, but he held his tongue. He loaded their bags into the back of the wagon, silently stewing in his bad temper.

"B-but Lady Avindea hasn't yet returned. Shouldn't you inform her of your journey?"

Quay's face paled, but she quickly covered it up with a forced smile. "Oh, she already knows I'm leaving. I'm certain I'll be back before she even realizes I'm gone!"

Ghdion cocked an eyebrow at that; when did the priestess take to *lying* to get her way? That wasn't very *righteous* of her. He finished throwing the packs into the wagon; Hypnocost, always too lazy and pretentious to help, was already lounging there with his ankle resting across his bent knee. "Good of you to be so helpful, *Your Highness*," Ghdion growled at him sarcastically, but the blasted half-elf didn't even deign to look at him.

"If I do happen to see Lady Avindea, shall I leave her a message for you?" Hooper blathered as Quay gracefully settled onto the wagon's front bench. Avindea must've warned the boy that she might try something like this, and Hooper was gamely trying to stop her. *Good luck with that*, Ghdion thought. *When Quay sets her mind to something, she's a force of nature. There's no stopping her.* He hopped up beside her and grabbed the reins, his bad knee twinging ever-so-slightly.

"Just tell her I'll explain everything when I get back," she called out with a little wave. "Goodbye, Hooper!"

"O-okay then, priestess. Safe travels!" Ghdion could see the boy mopping the nervous sweat from his brow as they rumbled away from the churchyard and down the cobbled street.

"I can't tell who's more nervous, him or you," Ghdion remarked flatly after a while, settling more comfortably against the wooden bench once they left Praetorius proper. He pulled out his carving knife and the hunk of vaguely ox shaped wood from his pocket.

"Whatever do you mean?" Quay asked, her voice slightly higher than normal.

"Why are you avoiding your cousin?" Ghdion asked his own question, giving her a sidelong glance.

"Oh, fine, I am avoiding her," she finally admitted, throwing her hands into the air in disgust. "She'd only tell me not to run off. She'd say I'm being too 'impetuous and hasty' and that I should 'think before I act.'" She scowled; Ghdion's heart did a little flutter at how adorable it looked on her naturally cheerful face. "She's not my mother. She thinks since she's a few years older than me that it gives her the right to boss me around."

"Well, are you?" he asked her, the corners of his mouth curling up into a smirk. "Being too hasty, I mean?"

"Just shut up and drive the wagon!"

He leaned back with a smug look on his face. "Whatever you say, Priestess."

They reached Camfield just before dusk. Quay was quiet most of the ride from Praetorius, her guilt simmering uncomfortably inside of her. She knew she shouldn't have left without telling Avindea; her cousin was one of the wisest, most level-headed people she knew, and she would only have given her sensible advice. But gods, Quay wanted to prove that she, too, could be decisive, that she had what it took to be a true leader, that their faith in her abilities to someday be a Priestess of Vidamae were not misplaced. She was tired of Avindea always being the one in charge, assuming a leadership position as if it was a foregone conclusion.

It didn't help that Ghdion kept giving her questioning glances as they rode along, as if waiting for her to blurt out that yes, she'd made a mistake, that running off to Camfield was foolish and they should turn right back around and think things through. Worse than that, he would have been right.

That only hardened her (maybe somewhat, slightly, teeny bit misplaced) resolve. She raised her chin and stared haughtily into the distance, deliberately ignoring Ghdion and choosing to instead converse with Hypnocost.

"I spoke with one of the Church's clerks about your mage papers yesterday," she began. "He assured me he would begin the process quickly, so you shouldn't run into any more problems at the city gate."

Hypnocost, who had been lolling languorously in the wagon bed with their packs as cushioning, glowered. "I do not need mage papers," he stated decisively. "I have told you this before, I am not a mage! I am a theurgist. There is a distinct difference."

She couldn't help but glance at Ghdion, who rolled his eyes so hard she feared the pupils would disappear into the back of his head. He kept paring away more slivers from that palm-sized piece of wood he was always fiddling with. What *was* he carving? She desperately wanted to ask him.

"I must admit I do not understand the difference between the two," she reluctantly continued. "They both cast spells, right?"

Hypnocost tutted his annoyance. "Well, yes, but it is so much more than just 'casting spells'!" He shook his bald head and snickered. "That is like comparing your healing spells to ... to simply placing a bandage upon a wound to try to stop the bleeding."

"I mean, that's kind of exactly what healing does, actually."

He scoffed. "No, it is not that simple! When I cast my spells, I am not *stealing* the power from the other realms like a common wizard." He curled his lip up in thinly veiled disgust. "I have been *given* my power. It resides *inside* of me. I can draw upon it whenever and however I wish."

"Who gave you your power then?" she asked, genuinely curious.

Hypnocost's face paled. "Ah, well that is ... I mean to say that I, um ..."

"Oh ho!" Ghdion blurted loudly, inserting himself into the conversation. "Suddenly at a loss for words, are you, Baldy?"

Hypnocost's face turned from pale white to a bright red. "Do not be ridiculous! Neither one of you would understand the nuance of how I came to my power!"

Ghdion grinned wolfishly. "You wanna know what *I* heard about theurgists? I heard they make deals with *Devils* for their unnatural powers. They sell their souls in exchange for a few paltry spells."

"That is categorically untrue!" Hypnocost wailed, aghast. His eyes widened in the telltale way that a liar's eyes grew large when called out for their dishonesty.

Quay regarded him quietly, lips pursed in disapproval. "Well, how do they actually get their spells, then?"

He sputtered, at a loss. "It is ... complicated. Truly. It is more akin to ... to how an artist has a patron, or how a king treats his Fool. The talent is already there, inborn and natural, but the patron simply ... helps it to grow."

"Who's your patron?"

He looked away nervously. "I do not know," he muttered.

Ghdion cleared his throat. "Hypnocost, I mean this in the nicest way, but you might wanna shut the fuck up about this theurgist shit."

Hypnocost and Quay both gasped. "Language!" she whispered under her breath.

"Why do you say that?" Hypnocost replied acidly.

Ghdion glanced over his shoulder. "Because I've seen people get dragged away for saying less. Especially in places like Camfield. Folks there don't much care for magic or anything they don't understand. You see what I'm saying?"

The theurgist swallowed audibly and nodded. "Yes, I understand your meaning."

The wagon rolled along quietly after that. The only one not moody was Mertha, who seemed happy enough to be back out on the road.

After a while, Ghdion thrust the hunk of wood into Quay's lap. "Here," he grunted, not looking at her. "It's for you."

She held it up, revealing an inexpertly carved version of what looked like an ox. The head was a bit blocky, and the legs a tad too long, but it certainly looked like he'd attempted to carve Mertha. "Is this ... Mertha?" she asked.

"It's stupid, I know, I've never carved an ox before, I—"

"I love it!" she beamed, holding it to her chest. She felt suddenly suffused with warmth, so much so that her face glowed red with it. And were those butterflies in her stomach?

She graced him with her sunniest, most heartfelt smile. "Ghdion, it's wonderful!" She reached her arm around his bulky shoulders in an awkward, one-armed hug.

He barely glanced her way, his cheeks flushing a deep red. "It's no big deal, Priestess. I was just practicing."

She elbowed him in the side. "Well, I'll treasure this for all my days." She leaned forward, holding the carved ox aloft as if Mertha could actually see it. "Look Mertha, Ghdion really does love you! See?"

Out of the corner of her eye, she thought she caught a small smile cracking Ghdion's taciturn features.

A few moments later, the village of Camfield finally came into view.

There wasn't much to it. Surrounded by fertile farmland, the village proper was nothing but a few gray buildings arranged around a community well that served as a town square. There was a general store, an inn, and the Church of Vidamae, with naught much else. Most of the villagers lived on their farmsteads on the outskirts of the town; on their way there, they'd glimpsed a couple barns and farmhouses dotting the fields near the edge of the forest.

The atmosphere of the town put her immediately on edge. What few townsfolk there were darted quick, nervous glances at them as they passed. Quay smiled at them reassuringly, used to being greeted graciously no matter where she went due to her status as a priestess-in-training. Villages were always happy to see a healer. But the folk in Camfield hurried away from their wagon as Mertha passed, ushering their children off the road and into their houses, whispering and casting dark looks in their direction.

"Good evening!" Quay called out in her best, 'I'm a priestess and I'm here to help' voice. "The Church of Vidamae sends me with good tidings and extra supplies to provide aid and succor to any in your village who may need them. Please don't be shy! We are here to help!"

No response. If it had been dark, there would only have been the sound of crickets chirping. But it was early afternoon, and sunny to boot. The villagers just watched her from round, worried faces, not daring to speak.

Quay cleared her throat. "Should any of you require supplies, please come find me at the Church. I would be glad to provide any assistance."

The wagon came to a stop right before the tiny Church of Vidamae, next to the community well. A lone washerwoman filled her bucket there and eyed them distrustfully.

Ghdion grunted as he jumped from the wagon seat, holding his hand out to help her down. "Guess they don't want our help."

She took his hand, her wide gray eyes scanning their surroundings.

"I cannot imagine why not," Hypnocost muttered as he came around from the back. "They look half-starved and frightened. I wonder why?"

"You here because of the murders?" the washerwoman asked, wandering over. Her accent was thick and uncultured, but she spoke boldly. At least she was willing to talk to them.

"Murders?" Quay gasped. "Has there been a murder here?"

The woman shook her head. She wore her hair wrapped up in a scarf, her dress tattered and threadbare. "No, not yet anyways," she replied. "We heard about 'em in Silvarn and Candor. 'S'only a matteratime before they hit us here. Doesn't help we ain't got no guards anymore." She spat off to the side in disgust. "Can thank the king for that."

Quay and Ghdion exchanged a wary glance. "What can you tell us about what you heard?" Quay questioned, her voice soothing and warm.

The woman shrugged, balancing the water bucket against her hip. "The Vidamae Churches were hit in both places," she said casually. "Dead priests or summat. People been gettin' scared. Even our own priest left, to the gods know where, not two days ago."

"Truly?" Quay cried in disbelief. "How craven! What is his name?! I will be sure to notify the Cathedral in Praetorius."

"You c'n notify 'em all ya want; it won't matter none. Praetorius never did much for us here out in the sticks." She looked Ghdion up and down, her eyes appraising him. "You look familiar, boy. Have I seen you around here before?"

Ghdion merely grunted, but Quay could see his ears reddening. Odd. She knew that only ever happened when he was embarrassed or hiding something. "Nope," he mumbled, turning away abruptly. "C'mon, Hypnocost, let's get this stuff unloaded and into the church."

It took them until it was almost dark to remove the sacks of supplies from the wagon and place them inside the empty church, tie Mertha up to the hitching post that served as Camfield's stables, then feed and water her. None of the other villagers spoke to them while they worked; in fact, they kept a very obvious distance from them, as if they were bad luck.

Quay surveyed the inside of the church, her heart sinking. From the looks of it, it had been much longer than two days since the local priest had fled from his duties: the pews were covered in dust, the candles in the window sills were burnt to nubs, and the pulpit was devoid of any of the written out sermons that should have been neatly stacked within.

"This is awful," she worried aloud, stepping gingerly over a pile of dirt and dried leaves on the floor. "How long have these people been without religious care?" She shook her head sadly. "I must write a letter to the cathedral at once, so they can send a replacement."

"Don't bother with the letter," Ghdion replied, stacking the last sack next to the open door. "We need to focus on the task at hand. If the priest already left Camfield, are the Kax cultists gonna bother showing up to kill him?"

Hypnocost brushed the dust from one of the pews, his lip curling in distaste. "Ghdion does bring up an excellent point. Do we bother staying here on the off chance that these cultists do, indeed, arrive?"

Quay crossed her arms, pondering her predicament. She could either stay the night in the hopes of catching the Kax killers in the act —how would *they* know that the priest had fled, anyways?—or she could leave the supplies and head back to Praetorius to formulate another plan. She hated the thought of leaving these poor villagers without any religious aid, but a secret part of her hated even more that, if she did leave, Avindea would chastise her for running off so recklessly in the first place, and all for nothing. She could feel her face flush at the thought. *I need to do something bold*, she told herself. *I need to prove that I can be brave and decisive.*

A sudden spark of inspiration hit. She stopped her pacing and whirled towards her bodyguards. "What if I'm bait?" she blurted. "What if I stay here tonight, 'alone' and 'defenseless' to try to lure out the cultists?"

Ghdion shook his head vigorously. "Absolutely not," was his immediate and expected answer.

"No, but listen! It's perfect. You two can pretend to leave with the wagon, and I'll stay here, inside the church. If the cultists are around and watching, they'd be fools not to sneak in here to try to kill me. I'm an easy target." She held out her hands as if to showcase just how simple it would be to take her down, with her curvy, short stature and lack of armor or weapons. "You two can double back and lie in wait in case they do attack. We can catch them in the act!"

"Your idea does have merit," Hypnocost conceded, tapping his pointy chin.

"No, we are not using you as *bait*, Quay," Ghdion growled angrily. "It's too dangerous."

She blinked. "Well, I'm sorry to say you don't have a choice in the matter, Ghdion," she replied evenly. "So you can either go along with the plan, or head back to Praetorius with the wagon and leave me in Hypnocost's care."

He clenched his fists at his sides and stepped right up to her. He

Faith and Ruin

loomed above her, and though he was obviously trying to be intimidating, his closeness only made her feel flushed all over. She couldn't suppress a little shiver ... of delight? Anxiety? Both? "You're not doing this," he growled under his breath so that only she could hear. "You know this is brash and wildly irresponsible. I'll not have you killed on my watch."

She pressed a single finger against his solid chest. "Then do as I say and make sure I'm not," she countered, unfazed by his threats. "That is your job, isn't it?" She quirked her eyebrow at him in a goading manner.

They matched fierce gazes, his blue eyes against her gray, both unwilling to bend. It was an inopportune time to notice just how icy blue his eyes actually were. They were beautiful. She could happily gaze into them forever.

After a moment he finally let out a breath through his nose and looked away, jaw clenched. "Fine," he spat, "only because nothing's gonna happen and even if it does, there's no way in all the hells I'm leaving your fate in *Hypnocost's* hands."

He was right, damn him. Nothing happened at all that night. She slept horribly. The only comfortable way to rest was to push two pews against each other as a makeshift bed, but the wood was old and splintery, and not even three piled up blankets laid across them helped. Every little noise caused her to jump, and the moon-cast shadows of the unfamiliar church looked menacing no matter the angle.

Her bodyguards had it even worse: Ghdion hid behind the huge barrels of ale outside the next door tavern, and Hypnocost was secured under a scratchy pile of brush and leaves near its back entrance. They left Mertha and the wagon hitched outside, just in case the cultist saw the church was occupied and thought it a good time to strike.

But the night was uneventful.

It wasn't until the following evening that things got really interesting.

Chapter 20

Errands

When Rendevas sauntered into The Murky Bard, Milford was already waiting for him at the bar.

Where Milford met him was a little code they had established after many long years of their dealings. If he had information that was only hearsay or lacked tangible evidence, he would wait for him at the table near the back of the tavern. If actual documents were obtained, he would sit at the bar. Therefore, it was with excitement and trepidation that Rendevas took the empty seat beside him.

Jerald, the jolly barkeep, slid his usual drink—called the Jolly Barkeep, strangely enough, as it was his speciality—in front of Rendevas, smiling at him warmly. "Back so soon, I see?" he said.

"Stresses of the plenum meetings, I fear," he answered with a shrug. He took a delicate sip of the brew, savoring the strong flavor. What *was* that hint of citrus? Orange? Clementine?

"Well, plenum stress equals good business for me," Jerald said cheerfully. "I just saw your paladin friend in here a bit ago, Lady Avindea. My, my, she can drink! I had no idea paladins were so, ah …"

"Thirsty?" Rendevas supplied with a twinkle in his eye.

"Just so!" He chuckled to himself and moved off to the other end of the bar.

"There's a dirty joke there somewhere," Milford said from beside him. He nursed his own mug of beer. "But alas, I am just an old man, and I know nothing of the ribald jestings of the youth."

Rendevas rolled his eyes. Milford, he knew, was not as he seemed, but out of loyalty to him—and by association, the guild he worked for, The Maelstrom—he kept his thoughts private. Just as he was about to ask what he had for him, the old man pulled out a roll of parchment from his voluminous robes.

"Brakten really came through this time," he said with a smile in his voice. "It's all here: signed and witnessed business deals, and a paper trail that proves Judge Rodach has been taking bribes from criminals for reduced sentences for *years*." He tapped the rolls smartly on the tabletop before handing them over. "I know this isn't what you asked for initially, but hopefully this will work out just as well."

"Excellent!" Rendevas grinned, pushing a heavy bag of coin his way. He wanted to rip off the ribbon binding the papers together and read all the damning proof right then, but he controlled that foolish notion. Instead, he tucked the roll safely within the breast of his blue brocade doublet. "I cannot *wait* to wipe the smug look from that coxcomb's ugly face."

Milford's bushy white eyebrows shot up. "Oooh, that's a good one. I woulda went with 'levereter' myself, but coxcomb works in a pinch, too." He took a healthy slurp of beer before continuing. "Mind who you show those to, Lord Rendevas. Remember my warning from before."

"Oh, how could I forget?"

They sat in companionable silence for a few moments, enjoying their drinks and the sounds of the lone violin player who was on the stage that night. She played a mournful tune that clashed with the wicked excitement Rendevas felt.

Milford slapped a coin on the bar top and stood up. "Welp, I suppose I should be going," he said. "Gotta get to Tobias's shop before he closes for the night."

Rendevas couldn't help but scowl at hearing the cranky merchant's name. "You do business with that scoundrel?" he asked with some surprise.

"Yep," he replied evenly. "He's the only one in the city who can get me my favorite kind of rum."

"I simply cannot *stand* working with him," he admitted. Tobias wasn't the only borean Rendevas had dealings with, but he was certainly the worst tempered. In his experience, they tended to be, at worst, *civil* towards the longer-limbed folks. He had heard a rumor that if a human wanted to purchase something from a borean town, they would charge twice as much because the human 'took up twice as much space.'

Milford shrugged. "He's not so bad if you can get past his piss-poor attitude. Besides, he's the only one left who manages to smuggle any of the good stuff into the city. He's charging even more for his services nowadays, what with the gate checkpoints and all that." He eyed him sideways. "That your doing, isn't it?"

"Well, not entirely mine, no, but yes, it was an issue the plenum voted on." He sighed, thinking of how stressful his job had become since the gate checkpoints had been set up. "It seemed like a good idea at the time, I'll admit, but the reality is proving to be far less ... efficient."

Thinking of the gates brought to mind the strange situation with the Vidamae Priestess Quay and the injured woman he'd helped smuggle into the city. "Oh, before you go, Milford," he spoke up, tapping the side of his mug thoughtfully. "I have an interesting bit of knowledge Brakten might find useful."

Milford paused, obvious interest flashing across his face. "Oh? And what is that?"

The diplomat considered him. "While working the gate, I came across something strange that may or may not be at the Cathedral of Vidamae right now."

The old man's eyebrows lifted. "What kind of strange are we talking about?

"The kind of strange that involves an injured young woman that a Priestess of Vidamae was attempting to sneak into the city."

"My, my, that is interesting." He straightened the shawl at his neck, eyes faraway. "I'll be sure to let Brakten know. You want The Maelstrom to look into it, or ...?"

Rendevas shook his head. "No, just a friendly tip. From one friend to another." He tilted his mug towards the elderly man and winked.

Milford patted his back fondly as he stepped away. "Well, thank you for that. And good luck with the gate checkpoints. I'd rather take my chances with Tobias Wiltwater any day." With one last cackle, he shuffled off in a whirl of silky, overly large robes and the smell of old mothballs.

That task attended to, Rendevas finished his drink, thanked Jerald with an exorbitant tip—he was feeling especially generous—and headed off to his next appointment, which would hopefully be a meeting with Captain Riluk. The man was extremely busy, what with all of the extra duties that came with the upcoming Athessian diplomat's arrival. The best way to speak with him was to corner him after his shift, basically *forcing* him to listen to his unorthodox request.

Just as he'd predicted, Captain Riluk was stepping away from the guard post at the top of the city wall just as he arrived. Night had well and truly fallen. The stars blinked serenely against their velvety dark backdrop. The view from atop the wall was breathtaking; Rendevas, stepping beside the haggard-looking captain, took a moment to appreciate just how beautiful the city was at night.

"Nice night," Riluk grunted by way of greeting. "I never get tired of this view."

"Nor I," Rendevas agreed, congenially enough. "It's a good reminder of what we are actually fighting for."

Faith and Ruin

"What are you doing here?" Riluk asked bluntly. He was a man of few words and forthright questions. Normally that would make him easy to take advantage of, but Riluk knew all the diplomat's tricks. They'd been serving on the plenum together for a long time.

He needed to be just as direct. "I'm worried about Lord Tullie Mason's visit." At Riluk's confused expression, he clarified, "The diplomat from Uldinvelm. I know you are pretty much well at capacity with your workload, but do you think you could provide even a few extra guards to help keep him safe during his stay here?"

Riluk frowned. "You really stopped me out here as I was heading home after a long day at work to ask about *that*?"

"Well, no, not exactly. There's maybe something more I was wondering about."

Riluk stared at him expectantly.

He let out a breath. "Okay, fine, I need to speak with the king. Alone."

Riluk shook his head. "You know I cannot do that."

"I only wish to speak with him about the princess."

"The princess? What about her?"

He struggled to form the words without making himself sound paranoid. "You have her guarded day and night, correct?"

"Of course. What's this about, Rendevas?" Riluk's impatience was growing more and more evident.

"I ... worry about her safety. Not for any specific reason, mind you, but I just fear she could be an easy target in the coming weeks." He wasn't about to spill the real reason he was concerned for her safety specifically, but how to make the stubborn man listen?

"She's young, not yet of age to take over as queen if something, gods forbid, should happen to her father. She's quite impressionable, from what I've gathered, and eager to learn all she can about politics and the business of the plenum. I simply worry about her, especially with everything that has been happening lately. Somebody needs to brief her on the gravity of the situation."

Riluk's eyebrows raised. "She has tutors for all of those things," he answered slowly. "She's learning all she can of leadership from the best teachers in the city. You know this, Rendevas. Why the sudden interest in the princess? And why speak with the king about it in private? You can easily ask him at the next plenum meeting."

"I was hoping to speak with him on a different, *private* matter," Rendevas replied, a hint of pleading in his voice. He needed to get the king by himself so he could show him the evidence Milford had provided. It was the only way the judge would finally receive the justice he deserved. He could give the documents to Chancellor Eldivar, but truth be told, Rendevas wanted to be the one to present them to Phil—the king—himself. Perhaps it was vanity, or simply foolishness on his part, but it was important to him that King Selderin knew how loyal he was and knew that it was *Rendevas himself* who acquired the proof of Judge Rodach's wrongdoings.

Besides, he knew his old friend Phil would appreciate the reminder of how things used to be, back before he'd been made king. It would be like the old days, when they would scheme and share gossip freely. Back when it was so much easier for them to be friends.

"That's not going to happen." The captain pursed his lips

together, shooting him a distrustful look. "I will relay your concerns to the king myself, but that is the best I can do. My hands are tied."

"Of course." Rendevas offered a weak smile, but he could tell that Riluk wasn't moved. "What of the extra guards for the Athessian diplomat—?"

"I can spare you two more, when the day comes."

"Thank you, Captain Riluk. I appreciate your time."

Riluk gave him a curt nod before stalking away silently. Rendevas, with a great sigh, leaned against the balustrade. *That was clumsily handled*, he thought with a wince. *Now Riluk probably thinks I'm a creep who's after the princess for entirely inappropriate reasons.* He snorted to himself. No, that was not even remotely close. The opposite, actually, but he couldn't tell Riluk that. He'd just have to live with the fact that the captain of the city guard most likely thought he was a lecher.

It wasn't an entirely unfruitful evening, at least. He patted his chest where the incriminating evidence against the judge was hidden. He just had to find another opportunity to share it with King Selderin.

Alone.

Chapter 21

One More Night

Quay, gods damn her, had successfully convinced Ghdion that they should stay in Camfield for one more night.

She did that thing with her eyes, making them large and shiny and pleading and just doleful enough that, as usual, he found himself lost in their smoky gray depths, unable to deny her anything. Which was funny, since she was the boss, as she so often liked to remind him, so why did it matter so much to her what *he* thought? He was just the hired muscle.

"These people need us!" she had argued after they all spent a terrible, sleepless night waiting anxiously for an attack that never came. Ghdion's backside ached like hells from crouching behind a barrel for most of the night. "They're too scared to talk to us, so if we stay one more day and night, show them we are only here to help, I bet we can get them to open up to us."

Hypnocost, the bloody idiot, nodded along sagely, as if the idea had been his all along. "She does make a good point," he said, looking well-rested and fresh-faced. Ghdion was convinced he hadn't actually been watching for assassins at all and had really just fallen asleep amidst the pile of leaves he'd been hiding in. "It will give us a chance to hand out these supplies, as well. It is a mutually beneficial arrangement."

Ghdion threw his hands in the air and stalked off, muttering angrily under his breath. Did no one listen to sense anymore?

They spent most of the day trying to convince the villagers to take the supplies they offered. Never before had they had such trouble *giving things away*. Ghdion could have told them the people of Camfield were too proud to take handouts—his late wife would have bent over backwards to avoid even *accidentally* asking for any aid—but he was feeling too resentful towards the pair to actively assist them. So instead, he passed the time lounging in the bed of their wagon, a fresh hunk of wood and his whittling knife in hand.

Quay was the one who figured out the trick to handling the Camfield locals, shortly after they ate a bland lunch of dumplings, boiled potatoes, and carrots—which Ghdion promptly gave to her because he *hated* carrots—that the local inn served them. The inn was subdued, with only a few patrons so early in the day; Ghdion insisted on taking his food with him back to the church. He didn't want any of the locals to recognize him. It was bad enough that the washerwoman yesterday thought she knew him from before.

Quay followed him reluctantly but only picked at her food half-heartedly. After a few restless moments, she finally set aside her plate and began poking around the exterior of the church. She started to fiddle with the front door; it didn't close properly and made a terrible squealing noise every time it was opened.

"I can't figure this out!" she scowled, hands on hips. She eyed the old hinges in annoyance. "I cleaned off all the rust. Why does it still squeal like that?"

Ghdion, paring at his piece of wood, just shrugged. "What does it matter?"

A few of the neighboring tavern's patrons watched her with interest from their post on the front step. One of the men, a farmer judging by his stained overalls and floppy straw hat, jogged over. "Excuse me, ma'am, but I think I can help." He looked over the church door, inspecting the hinges closely. "I see your problem. You cleaned up the rust, yes, but now the bolts are all too loose. It's making the door all wobbly and sticky like, causing that awful racket."

Quay frowned. "Oh! That makes sense. If I had some tools, I could—"

"Oh, don't you worry none!" The man smiled shyly. "I've got just the thing back at my place. Jus' gimme a mo'." He ran off back the way he came, ostensibly to retrieve his tools.

The other men hovered back, watching their friend run off. When he returned, they walked up to the church door right along with him to offer their helpful advice. The first man—he told her his name was Denn and was quite a bit chattier towards Quay as he worked—tightened the bolts in all three hinges. He moved the door back and forth to test it, and sure enough, it moved smoothly and quietly.

"There!" he proclaimed proudly, tucking his tool in his back pocket. "All fixed up."

Quay clapped in approval. "Oh, thank you so much! You've been such a help!" She beamed and clasped hands with Denn in a way that made Ghdion's stomach flip uncomfortably. Her face brightened as she conversed with the villagers. "Please, take some of the stuff we brought with us. It's all going to go to waste if nobody takes it, and it's the least I can do after all your help."

Denn blushed furiously but took the two sacks that she pushed into his arms. "Ah, well, if you say they'll go to waste ..." He peeked inside one of them, his eyes widening at the bounty of dry foods, candles, fabrics, blankets, and other useful goods packed inside of them. His two friends looked awestruck by his good fortune and tripped over themselves asking if there were any other small tasks that needed doing around the church.

Quay immediately set them to tidying the place up, fixing up broken pews or hammering loose nails; never let it be said she wasn't quick on the uptake. While those two were working, she hurried over to Hypnocost to whisper her discovery to him, sending him off into the village proper to see if he couldn't find anyone else who could assist them with odd jobs.

By the time the sun set, almost everyone from the village had procured their own Vidamae care package after helping Quay with such pivotal tasks as: beating the dirt off the rugs from the back of the wagon, feeding Mertha some extra treats of carrots and apples, sweeping the wooden floors of the church, washing the church windows, and scraping the candle drippings from the window sills so she could replace the old candles with new ones.

A few of the local girls even wove dandelion wreaths for both Quay and Mertha as a way for them to get in on the action. They presented these with all the solemnity of a page offering a golden, bejeweled crown to his king, and Quay, naturally, accepted the gifts with grace—and an appropriate amount of gleeful giggling after the ceremonial crowning was complete. This, in turn, gave Quay the idea to make matching wreaths for both Hypnocost and Ghdion; Hypnocost, the smarmy bastard, was overjoyed by the prospect.

"The yellow of the dandelions offset the violet of my robes in a most pleasing manner!" he exclaimed as she placed the wreath atop his bald, tattooed head.

Ghdion grumbled and scoffed, but in the end, he begrudgingly allowed Quay to place a small bouquet of the pretty weeds behind his ear. He blushed furiously the entire time.

Soon enough, all of the supplies had been claimed, and everyone who had helped treated them as if they had been friends all along. When asked, the villagers were more than eager to dispense what rumors they heard about the murders in Furow's Ridge and Silvarn. Most were salacious tales of mustache-twirling villains who poofed into the churches, stabbed the priests with their wicked, poisoned knives, laughed maniacally, and poofed right back out of there without a trace. Some of the stories held nuggets of truth, however; one of the farmers mentioned that his cousin in Desai had seen a cloaked, hooded figure racing out of the city late on the same night Leon's family had been murdered, matching up with what the group had already discovered.

Overall, it was a productive day. Regardless of how proud the townsfolk were, they desperately needed the help; none of the families they saw that day looked in particularly good health, nor were they exactly flush with funds. Quay did what she could to inform them of different ways they could stay healthy, such as good hygiene and keeping all of their meager medical supplies clean and dry.

A few of the villagers even remarked that they wished she would stay on as their priestess. "Ole' Pastor Burnip never spent an entire day cleanin' up the church like you are!" one of the locals informed them. "He was as lazy as they come!"

Ghdion sauntered over to her after the last villager finally left, holding a plate of dinner: a steaming mutton hand pie, some mashed potatoes, and a pile of cooked peas. "Here." He thrust it towards her; Quay took the offering gratefully. Her smile was soft and sweet and there were twin dimples along either side of her mouth that he found himself staring at in fascination.

He blushed and glanced away before he made a fool of himself. "The tavern keeper insisted on feeding us. Said the hand pies are their specialty."

"Oh, thank Vidamae, I'm starving." She took an enormous bite of the hand pie and chewed it slowly, savoring the flavor. It really was quite delicious—he'd already eaten three. He couldn't seem to take his eyes off of her, even though it was pretty rude to stare at her while she was eating.

"So," she said after swallowing the food, "how do you think we did?"

"I think *you* did amazingly." He met her eyes, then darted his gaze hastily away from her face. He had to clear his throat before he could continue. "You figured out Camfield's secret a lot faster than I thought."

"What do you mean?"

"Y'know, how they are too proud to take hand-outs. When I liv—" He stopped abruptly mid-sentence and turned away, lips pressed together tightly.

Quay gave him an odd look. "When you what?"

"Nothing. When I heard about Camfield, I mean," he corrected hastily. *Shit, that was close.* "I was told that about them. It didn't occur to me until just now, that's all."

She took another bite and eyed him suspiciously. "Alright." He could tell by her facial expression she didn't believe him, so he quickly changed the subject. "So are we gonna head back to Praetorius now that the supplies are all gone and our cultist never showed up?"

She shook her head. "I wanna try one more night of me as bait, see if we can't suss out the assassins. If nothing happens again, then we will leave first thing in the morning."

Ghdion sighed wearily. "I still don't think that's a good idea, Priestess."

Daintily wiping her mouth with a handkerchief, she stepped closer to him. Her head only came up to his collarbone, so she had to crane her neck to look him square in the eye. "If I didn't know any better, Ghdion, I'd say you were worried about me."

He rubbed the back of his neck. "I just don't want you to get hurt. It would look bad for me, as your bodyguard, if you came to any harm under my watch."

"Mmm-hmm." She smiled wickedly at him, causing his already pink cheeks to flush a deeper red.

She stayed right there next to him, so close he could feel her body heat emanating against his chest. He forgot to breathe, staring down into her playful, beautiful, and young! way too young! face. Clearing his throat, he took a tentative step backwards. "We should get ready for bed," he said hoarsely. All that did was bring to mind images of Quay laying in a bed and ... nope. *No way. Not going there.*

She patted his chest affectionately and turned away; he finally let out his breath, feeling relief mixed with disappointment.

Another night spent hiding behind a bunch of barrels. He sighed and took up his place against the wall of the tavern.

When the crickets stopped chirping, Quay knew something was wrong.

She'd been dozing off, the night sounds lulling her to sleep. Darkness descended deep and impenetrable on the little village; the sky was moonless, so Quay left a couple candles lit on the altar for light. She made another makeshift bed on one of the pews and was trying to make herself comfortable when all of a sudden, she realized there were no more noises.

I should've left the door hinges unfixed, she thought in a panic. *That way I'd be able to hear if it opens.* It was too late for that; she sat bolt upright, her heart beating quickly in her chest, her whole body thrumming with tension. She prayed to Vidamae silently that both Ghdion and Hypnocost were watching. *It could be nothing,* she thought. *Could just be a pause in the crickets' song. That's nothing to worry about.*

Just as she was about to lay back down, chastising herself for her misplaced worries, she heard a slight shuffle at the door. *Maybe it's Ghdion? Or Hypnocost?*

Her breath quickened and she stared with huge eyes at the door. She willed it to remain closed. But it started to open, so slowly and quietly—on newly smooth and soundless hinges!—she wasn't sure if she imagined it.

A man-shaped shadow filled the doorway. It was definitely not Ghdion or Hypnocost.

She opened her mouth to scream. Nothing came out but a pitiful little mewl.

The person didn't enter right away; all she could see was a hooded black silhouette. They raised an arm, a knife held in their hand, the candle's flickering glow glinting off of the sharpened edge.

Quay froze in her spot. *If I just sit here silent and still, they won't see me!* her fear-addled brain convinced her.

The person turned slightly and seemed to stare straight at her. They lunged forward, moving with an inhuman speed. She cried out her shock, scrambling backwards so forcefully she slammed her head against the pew and slipped halfway onto the floor.

The attacker swung the knife in a powerful downward lunge but missed; her accidental fall off of the pew sent the bench sliding forward with enough momentum that it knocked her just out of the knife's range.

The knife thudded dully against the wood right next to her head. She squeaked and pressed herself backwards against the askew bench.

The attacker growled and yanked out the blade.

She tried to scream, but a sharp bolt of pain through her head stopped her. Had she really hit her head that badly? She wobbled to the side, clutching her throbbing temples, trying desperately to think of something, anything, that would help her defend herself. *Get up!* her brain screamed, but her body refused to comply. *Run! Go for help!*

The attacker, already back on their feet after crashing into the bench, loomed over her crouching form menacingly. *I'm a healer, not a fighter!* she thought stupidly, frozen to the spot in fear.

"Down, Quay!" came Ghdion's raspy, deep voice from behind the would-be assassin; she obeyed immediately and dropped to the floor. He swung his two-handed sword in a powerful arc. The sword sliced with a squelch right across the assassin's shoulders. A spray of blood fountained from the wound.

The assassin howled in rage and pain, stumbling backwards, clutching at their shoulder to try to stop the rush of blood.

"There is another one!" Hypnocost called faintly from outside. They could hear his footsteps pounding as he raced after the second assassin. "They are heading into the village proper!"

"Fuck!" Ghdion cursed, flinging the blood from his blade. The attacker crumpled to the floor in a gory, senseless heap. They stopped moving.

Quay struggled upright and away from the wounded would-be-killer. She couldn't help but notice, pinned to the lapel of their cloak, a tiny metal symbol of Kax.

"Are you okay?" Ghdion offered her his hand; she took it and leaned against him for balance. Her legs felt wobbly and weak.

"Yes, just hit my head on the pew," she answered. "This one isn't a threat; go help Hypnocost before they get someone else!"

He offered her a sharp nod and ran off, his heavy boots thumping loudly against the floorboards.

"Follow that man,"

the voice demanded in Hypnocost's mind.

"*I am trying!*" he replied, huffing with the strain of trying to keep up. The assassin was fast! Hypnocost had never been known for his athleticism, but even so, there was no way on Aukera anyone could move that quickly without some sort of magical aid. They were so quiet, too! He had nearly missed seeing them as they crept through the darkness, as sure and silent as a shadow. If it hadn't been for the voice warning him of their presence, he wouldn't have spotted the assassin in the first place.

They wore a long, hooded cloak—not black, as that color would stand out in the nighttime gloom, but possibly a deep navy or a green so dark it could easily be mistaken for black—and they carried in their hands a curved knife and a small glowing orb. They tried to cover the soft light that emanated from the orb with their cloak, but it was too late; it caught Hypnocost's eye, and he immediately took up the chase, bursting from his hiding spot beneath a pile of leaves. He shot a bolt of spectral energy from his fingertips, but it narrowly missed the assassin as they zigzagged out of the way.

He followed them from the church into the village proper. The assassin leapt onto the low-hanging roof of a nearby house, pausing to pull the weird orb from under their cloak. Hypnocost was far enough away that any spell he sent would miss, but he could still see the hooded person look down at the orb and do something to it with their free hand. It flashed a hot red, and a small beam of light pointed from it to the house across the dirt path.

"*What is that thing?*" Hypnocost asked.

"I do not know,"

the voice said. As usual, its tone was inflectionless, but he had the feeling that it was begrudgingly admitting its lack of knowledge.

"You must get it. You must find out what it does."

Easier said than done! Hypnocost pumped his legs as fast as they would carry him. As soon as he reached the house where the assassin perched, they leaped across the wide chasm between buildings and landed gracefully atop a different house, the orb glowing a fierce, angry crimson in their hand.

Ghdion's thumping, uneven gait sounded from nearby as he ran towards Hypnocost; the theurgist pointed towards the assassin, hissing, "He is there! On that roof!"

Together, they rushed forward, Ghdion's sword held high and Hypnocost gathering his strength of will for a powerful mind blast.

The assassin rolled from the roof back onto the ground in front of the house, the whoosh of air from Ghdion's attack whipping right past their cloak. They laughed ghoulishly, the red light from the orb casting weird, underlit shadows onto their mask. Then they pushed the door open and darted inside. Ghdion's sword crashed through the wood right as the door slammed in his face.

They heard a faint cry of alarm from within; exchanging wide-eyed glances, they shoved inside.

The whole one-room hovel was lit with that sickly red orb's glow, casting the shadows and highlights of the scene in horrifying shades of blood. They were too late; the assassin stood over the crumpled form of what had once been a very alive, very frightened farmer. The killer held the glowing sphere aloft in one hand and a knife dripping the farmer's blood in the other.

The cloaked person shifted their head slightly towards them, their body faintly tensing for an attack.

Ghdion let out a feral roar and charged forward, his heavy sword swinging. The assassin laughed, then the orb went dark, casting the hovel into thick blackness.

Ghdion's sword slammed loudly into what sounded like the wooden bedside table. He grunted with strain as he yanked it from the wood. A puff of air and a swoosh of fabric flapped right past Hypnocost; he hurriedly called forth a light spell.

The ghostly light illuminated the room. The assassin was already gone.

"Fuck!" Ghdion's yell was strangled. He lunged back outside to give chase. Hypnocost followed, but he nearly ran into Ghdion's solid back as soon as the door shut behind him.

The assassin was nowhere to be seen, and Ghdion stood in the middle of the dirt road, heaving great breaths of anger and frustration.

"How did they get away so quickly?" Hypnocost asked, not really expecting an answer, but wanting to give voice to his vexation somehow. He scanned the shadowed edge of the trees in the distance, trying to pick up any sense of movement, but of course it was too dark for him to see much of anything that far away.

"I have no idea," Ghdion growled. "Maybe it was that weird glowing orb they had. Regardless, we're too late. That farmer's dead."

"What do we do?" Hypnocost asked, his voice shaky.

"We better get back to Quay. She'll wanna know what happened."

"I assume you took care of her would-be assassin?" They walked side by side along the gravel path, slumped postures and heavy panting giving away just how spent they both were.

Ghdion grunted in reply. "Got them in their shoulder. If we're lucky, they'll still be alive, and we can question them."

When they stepped back inside the dimly lit church, the assassin was, indeed, still very much alive: he sat upright, hood fallen off of his head to reveal his maniacally smiling face, his hand wrapped tightly around Quay's throat.

At a loss for what to do, Quay lit all of the candles inside the church, hoping the warm glow would chase off the chill that had taken over her body. She avoided the bleeding form of her would-be-killer, stepping gingerly around the pool of blood that spread from their cloaked body. Her head ached fiercely, causing her to stumble a bit as she made her way around the room.

She hoped fervently that Ghdion and Hypnocost had more success against the second attacker. How awful would it be for one of Camfield's own to be murdered in the dark in such a way? Shuddering, she blew out the match in her fingers and rubbed her bare arms.

I wish I knew why this keeps happening! she thought in despair. She began to pace, her thoughts whirling through her pounding head. If she just focused on the task at hand, she could keep away the despair of almost being killed. *Perhaps this Kax cultist—they definitely are of Kax, I saw the pin on their cloak—has something on their person that can help? Maybe some sort of evidence or a clue that will point to what they are planning next?*

She stopped, forcing herself to look fully at the assassin's limp body. The blood had finally stopped rushing from the shoulder wound, and the cloak's hood had fallen off their head, revealing short black hair and thick black eyebrows set in a masculine face of sharp cheekbones and protruding forehead.

Why did he want to kill her? Quay tried so hard not to cause harm to any creature, great or small—she wouldn't even swat at flies, a fact that Ghdion teased her endlessly about. But this man, whoever he was, didn't know any of that. He had been prepared to take her out based on her faith alone.

Pursing her lips, she took a step closer to the unconscious man, her eyes snagging on the three-clawed, flame-wreathed symbol of Kax pinned proudly to his cloak. "It's because of *you*," she murmured. "Why does Kax hate us so much? Why does She want all of Vidamae's people dead?"

She hovered over him, thinking hard about her next move. Should she rifle through his pockets and try to find incriminating evidence? Surely if she just removed the Kax symbol, that would be enough. She could show it to Avindea when they got back to Praetorius, proving that her ill-thought-out plan to travel to Camfield and to use herself as bait was a good one, that she really was onto something, and it was much bigger than any of them had anticipated.

She came to her decision, and honestly, it was the only thing she could do, right? She had to bring this news back to Praetorius. It was her duty as a priestess-in-training. With only a token bit of hesitation, she knelt beside the killer and reached for the pin.

His hand shot up so quickly her eyes didn't even track the movement. His fingers clamped tightly around her throat. The cultist's good arm, the one not slashed to shreds by Ghdion's sword thrust, tensed, locking her into place by his grip on her neck. She didn't even have time to gasp in shock, he moved so fast. With a strength he should not have had with as wounded as he was, he began to *squeeze*.

Her horror-struck eyes locked on his. They glinted with a mad fervor. Her fingers scrabbled uselessly against his taut knuckles. "I dedicate this murder of the Whore Goddess's devotee to My Lady Kax!" he gargled harshly, blood erupting from his open mouth and splattering all over her nightgown as he spoke.

She couldn't speak, she couldn't move, she couldn't breathe! Frantically she tried to pull away, her nails gouging into his fingers, her mouth opening and closing as she desperately sought air. She was unable to tear her eyes from his; she despaired at the thought that the last thing she would see was the pure hatred that set his dark eyes alight.

"Quay!" Ghdion roared, flying across the threshold.

Hypnocost burst through the doorway after him, sending a well-placed magical blast into the assassin's face. Just as the spell crackled through the Kax cultist, Ghdion swung down with all of his might, severing the man's arm from his body right at the elbow. The man and the bloody stump, spouting a fresh wave of blood, thumped lifelessly to the floor.

Quay slumped forward, clutching at her neck, her eyes bulging and her mouth gasping at air that would not go into her lungs. Ghdion threw down his sword and dropped to his knees before her, grasping her face in his hands.

"Breathe, dammit!" he demanded harshly. Her skin was turning a sickly blueish purple, her nails ragged and bleeding from how fiercely she had scratched at the killer's hands. Her neck was ringed with hand-shaped bruises that looked like some ghoulish necklace.

"Heal yourself!" he hissed, grabbing her hands and placing them upon her own neck. Her pulse was so weak in her wrists; *Gods, please don't be too late! Please!*

Quay's mouth closed and her eyes started to roll in the back of her head, but she had just enough presence of mind to draw forth the golden glow of her healing abilities. He pressed her glowing hands to her neck, where the divine light of Vidamae's Grace seeped into her skin, wiping away the bruises and repairing the damage to her crushed windpipe.

She drew forth a great, gasping breath and fell forward into his waiting arms.

He held her gently against his chest as she took in loud, whooping lungfuls of air. "Just breathe," he murmured. "Just keep breathing. It will get easier. You're okay." He wasn't even fully aware of what he was saying. He just kept muttering soothing words and petting her soft brown hair. Her body wracked with wretched sobs.

Hypnocost hovered behind them awkwardly, watching Quay's shuddering form with trepidation. "Is she well?" he asked softly. "Will she be okay?"

"She will be," Ghdion answered lowly. "Thank the gods she was able to heal herself, otherwise …" He let the rest of the sentence remain unsaid.

"What happened? I thought you said you had dispatched her attacker?"

"I did!" he cried. "I dunno what happened!"

Quay, her whole body shivering with shock, glanced up into his face. "It was my fault," she managed to croak. "I tried to take the Kax pin off of his cloak, y'know, as proof for when we go back to Praetorius, and he just …" She shuddered, wrapping her arms more tightly around his midsection. "He just grabbed me. I thought he was dead!"

"Gods, Quay, I thought *you* were dead!" His entire body shuddered at the thought of losing her. His arms tightened around her. He'd been *this close* to losing her for good, just like he'd lost Sari and the girls ...

Hypnocost cleared his throat. "Well, the plan worked at the very least. We should clean this up, and make sure we take care of the farmer's body in town, too. The villagers are bound to have questions."

Quay pulled out of his arms, and damn if Ghdion didn't regret the absence of her immediately. "Wait, you weren't able to stop the other attacker?" she asked hoarsely.

He shook his head. "They were too fast for us. They killed a farmer inside his house, then got away before we could even touch them." He scowled darkly at his failure. "They had some kind of glowing red orb thing. Maybe that's how they were able to escape so quickly."

Quay's pale face went stricken. "That poor farmer! We have to bury him, we have to make sure he is given all the proper arrangements, and that the village is compensated for his loss, and—"

"One thing at a time, Priestess," Ghdion gently admonished. He stood, his bad knee cracking loudly, then offered her his hand. "We'll take care of it all in the morning. For now, we need to get rid of this guy's body and try to get some rest. I have a feeling tomorrow's gonna be interesting."

Chapter 22

Hard Conversations

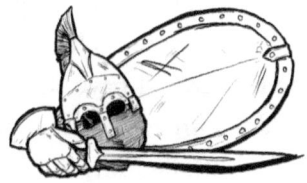

"Well, she looks to be healing up quite nicely," Leonidas, the squat little physician Quay hired, announced after completing his examination of Midori. "Her throat's looking much better than when I first saw her. The bruises have just about vanished. Must be from Quay's healing spells. I believe she should be able to speak again soon."

Lucius nodded, hovering anxiously at the foot of Midori's bed. Quay had assured him this doctor would be discreet, so his treatment of Midori would remain strictly confidential. He'd even used the secret knock pattern they had agreed upon, rapping smartly on the locked door to signal his arrival. Before they left for Camfield, she told Lucius she'd given Leonidas an astoundingly large sack of gold coins to further insure his silence. Thank the gods for rich churches and generous priestesses.

"Anything else I should know?" Lucius asked.

The doctor eyed him sideways. "Well, she really needs to be out and about, moving and stretching her legs. The fresh air will do her the most good now." He glanced around the small, windowless basement room with a frown. "But I have a feeling that won't be possible, so in the absence of that, just make sure she stays comfortable."

Lucius nodded. "Thank you, doc," he said gratefully.

The doctor pushed his spectacles up his nose, eyeing Lucius's ragged scars with professional interest. "Have you ever thought of having surgery on those scars?" he offered delicately. "There are all kinds of new procedures, particularly out of Thalconia, where they've been testing different healing poultices on the soldiers who fight at the rift there. You could really benefit from some of their experimenting, if you've a mind to be rid of your disfigurement."

Lucius winced. He reminded himself this man was a doctor, and that it was his job to be forward. "I have not really thought about it, no," he admitted. "But I'll be sure to keep that in mind."

"Well, if you do …" He trailed off, sensing that Lucius had no desire to further that particular avenue of conversation. With a nod, the doctor exited, carrying his little leather bag of tools.

Midori, on her bed and propped against the wall with mounds of blankets and pillows, arched an elegant eyebrow at him.

"You hush," he scolded playfully, crossing his arms. "You don't have to be able to speak for me to see what's written plain on your face."

She scribbled her reply on one of her rapidly dwindling pieces of blank parchment.

YOU DON'T NEED ANYTHING DONE TO YOUR SCAR,

she wrote.

IT GIVES YOU CHARACTER.

He snorted derisively, though his chest felt all warm and fuzzy at the compliment. "If you say so."

The past two days were spent inside the claustrophobic little room in the basement of the church. He left only to get their meals or to relieve himself in the privy. He'd managed to scrounge up a bedpan for Midori to use and only had to step out into the hallway whenever she needed privacy. When she complained about the filthiness of her old clothes, he headed upstairs to ask about getting her some clean outfits. Luckily, one of the younger priestesses—an acolyte or something, maybe fourteen or fifteen—took pity on him. She listened to his hastily made-up tale of woe about his poor sister who was staying there at the church, who had been attacked on the road and lost everything, including all her clothes and underthings, could she believe it? She showed him their communal closet and bade him take whatever he needed, no questions asked.

"These bandits are disturbed individuals!" she had exclaimed with a vehemence that took him aback. "Did you know that there is a black market for Vidamae Priestess *underwear*?" At his look of shock, she continued gleefully, "It's true! Isn't that *sick!*? I even heard they're worth more if they're *used!*"

The priestess was of a similar size to Midori: thin, lithe, and small-chested, so she stayed to help him pick out what was needed. She insisted on going with him to visit his poor sister, but he managed to fend her off by explaining his sister was "painfully shy, and she's suffering from her monthlies, you know, so she's very easily upset right now! Best not to disturb her just yet."

The priestess had nodded sympathetically and forced him to take an additional pack of clean rags specifically for that purpose. He was finally able to tear away from the helpful girl when she was called over to assist elsewhere, so, blushing furiously, Lucius presented a puzzled Midori with the armload of garments, underwear, and rags.

"Don't ask," he'd answered when she held up the menstruation cloths in polite puzzlement.

Midori eyed the various garments with a critical eye, scowling at the diaphanous, feminine robes and veils that were typical to the Vidamae Priestesshood. She held up a filmy, low-cut dress and cocked her eyebrow at Lucius, who blushed even harder. "I didn't pick these out! There was a priestess who helped me. Surely there's gotta be something less, ah … delicate in there?"

She ruffled through the pile of fabric and found a pair of loose, plain trousers and a dark linen shirt that was way too big for her. Lucius, an idea coming to him, dug through his pack and pulled out one of his extra belts. "Here," he offered it to her, "You can cinch that around your waist. Should help keep the shirt on."

She took the black leather belt and gave him a small smile. Suddenly bashful, he scratched at the scarred side of his face and backed out of the room so she could have some privacy to change.

Spending so much time together forced them to form a hesitant sort of alliance. On the second day, they chatted amiably enough, she with her quill and parchment, him answering each question or stray comment with equanimity. He found her to be fiercely intelligent and possessing a wicked sense of humor. He eagerly anticipated whatever interesting topic of conversation came next.

IF YOU DO NOT FOLLOW THE TENETS OF VIDAMAE, WHY DO YOU ALLOW YOURSELF TO BE LED BY A PRIESTESS OF THAT FAITH?

He knew she was asking not to judge, but because she was genuinely curious. Even given her questionable faith to the Goddess of Chaos Kax, she was extremely interested in the other religions of Aukera. They had touched upon the topic of religion before; in Aukera, there were twelve deities, all with varying degrees of popularity depending upon what the god was known for and the geographical region in question.

In Khamris, Vidamae was by far the most popular. Velthunas, God of Luck, was almost as beloved as Vidamae, followed by Xandriasis, Goddess of Intelligence—revered by mages and scholars—and Jorah, God of Tranquility and Dreams, who was beloved by poets and bards.

In Praetorius there was a small Temple of Thulkas, God of Strength and Freedom, and in nearby Feywynn, there was an ancient and beautiful Temple of Nahal, Goddess of Nature. Castor was the

God of Justice, Ezrael Goddess of Death, Kax—Midori's chosen—the Goddess of Chaos. Demos was the God of Control and Power, known the world over for his well-trained militaries, and Dolgamar the God of Wealth and Cunning—he was not super popular except with certain sects of thieves and assassin guilds and those ultra-wealthy types born with a silver spoon in their mouth. Lastly was Galara, Goddess of Sufferance and Sacrifice, who was also less than loved by most because of her proximity to plagues and sickness.

Lucius pondered Midori's question. "Well, aside from the fact that her church holds the purse strings?" He shrugged. "It just sort of ended up that way. Quay, Hypnocost and Ghdion happened to be in Furow's Ridge when Edmund Brisby was murdered—he was the Priest of the Church of Vidamae there, and also one of my friends. I wanted to find out who killed him, so I signed on as Quay's bodyguard when she asked me to help. I figured it would be the quickest way to find answers."

He glanced away self-consciously. "I also have a hard time telling people no, so here I am, wrapped up in all this stuff."

Midori nodded.

I AM SORRY ABOUT YOUR FRIEND. IF IT OFFERS ANY SOLACE, MY GROUP HAS BEEN TRYING TO STOP THOSE ATROCITIES FOR MANY MONTHS.

"Why?" he blurted. "Why do you choose to follow Kax, of all the deities on Aukera?" He hadn't meant it to sound so accusing, and his face flushed bright red when he realized his rudeness. "Sorry, I didn't mean—"

She shook her head and held up her hand to silence him. She spent a long time pondering her response, and when she finally put quill to parchment, it took her even longer to write out the words:

KAX ISN'T ALL ABOUT MURDERING AND HATING VIDAMAE.

THERE'S SO MUCH MORE TO HER. SHE'S A CHAMPION OF THE PEOPLE! HAVE YOU EVER LIVED IN A PLACE WHERE THE GOVERNMENT TREATS ITS PEOPLE UNFAIRLY? WHERE THE LAWS ONLY APPLY TO THOSE WHO DO NOT HAVE THE MEANS TO BRIBE THEIR WAY OUT OF CONSEQUENCES? KAX IS A GODDESS FOR THOSE PEOPLE, THE DOWNTRODDEN. THE UNDERDOGS.

Lucius met her eyes. He had, in fact, lived in a city of terrible corruption, with dictators as leaders, who kept their populace too oppressed to fight back. He could remember how some of the soldiers he had trained with, fresh with the newfound power being in the military granted them, would abuse their authority in the pettiest of ways. Harassing beggars on the streets just because they could, demanding bribes from foreign merchants because they looked and spoke differently from the locals ... It made him sick back then, and still to this day. It was the chief reason he had left the military back home, vowing never to go back to that life. It was just too easy to fall to corruption.

"I—yes, I have lived in a place like that," he admitted. "But it's like that pretty much everywhere. What does Kax promise to do about it?"

Midori leaned forward, her face brightening with religious fervor. She tried to speak, but only a harsh whisper escaped her lips. So, scowling, she turned back to writing.

IT DOESN'T HAVE TO BE LIKE THAT EVERYWHERE, DON'T YOU SEE? KAX WANTS TO END ALL GOVERNMENTS WHO ABUSE THEIR CITIZENS LIKE THAT. SHE PROMISES A GRAND RESHAPING OF HOW SOCIETY CAN WORK, A GIVING BACK OF POWER TO THE PEOPLE WHO RIGHTFULLY DESERVE IT!

He shook his head. "That sounds too good to be true, Midori. Tell me, how often has Kax delivered on these grand promises?"

SHE STRUGGLES BECAUSE OF HOW VEHEMENTLY THE REST OF THE DEITIES OPPOSE HER. YOU CANNOT EXPECT GREAT WORKS TO HAPPEN OVERNIGHT!

He wanted to believe her, he really did. Her confidence in her cause, her eagerness to believe, was admirable. "Honestly, I don't have much use for any of the gods. I wish I had your faith."

She pursed her lips tightly and looked away, laying the quill and parchment aside.

"Aw, c'mon, don't be like that," he pleaded.

She scribbled harshly,

I AM TIRED. LET ME REST.

Her pride was wounded, but her eyes looked troubled. He hadn't meant to upset her.

Guess that's the end of our conversations today, Lucius thought, with more than a little bit of regret.

Quay was uncharacteristically quiet on the ride back from Camfield.

Of course, she had almost been murdered, quite violently, by a religious nutjob who hated her goddess and sought to kill anyone who worshiped Her, so there was that. Ghdion chewed his bottom lip, trying to think of something, anything comforting to say, but all he could think of was, *I almost lost her. I almost lost her just like I lost Sari and the girls fifteen years ago.*

They'd spent most of the morning cleaning up the church, then speaking with the villagers about what had happened overnight. Ghdion and Hypnocost helped a few of the other farmers bury the dead man—his name was Chell—while Quay dealt with the churchy, funerary specifics. After all that was done, they packed up their things and left. It felt bad just leaving the villagers after such a traumatic murder happened on their doorstep, but they'd done all they could. It was time to go home.

Ghdion flicked Mertha's reins, not even able to bring himself to complain about how slowly she plodded along. He heard a sorrowful sniff, and when he glanced over, he saw a slow tear streak down Quay's cheek.

Immediately he panicked. "Oh, Priestess, don't … I mean, it's gonna be—"

"What I don't understand is *why*!" She gave a great, shuddering sob and covered her face with her hands.

At a loss, Ghdion merely gaped at her.

She continued unabated. "Why do they want me dead? He didn't even *know* me! Who is full of so much hate that they would just *do* that?" Her words were a garbled mess, but he understood the intent regardless. It was her first time getting almost murdered, of course she would have a hard time of it. His first was, well, less traumatic, but equally as disconcerting.

Ghdion sighed. He hated to be the one to break it to her, but it was time for Quay to hear some capital H Hard Truths. "Most everyone, I think, Priestess."

She turned to him, dumbstruck.

"I have a feeling you've lived a bit of a sheltered life, there in the Church," he rumbled, fiddling with the reins in his hands. "That's probably why you're so surprised by the depths a person can sink to in the name of what they think is righteous."

She wiped at her leaking eyes. "W-what's *that* supposed to mean?"

"It just means that not everyone is good, Priestess. You've lived your whole life believing that, and gods, I wish it were true, but it just isn't." He took a deep breath, staring straight ahead so as not to see the horrified look on her face. "To tell you the truth, most people aren't all the way good or all the way bad. They're just ... people. They do dumb shit all the time, including murdering people because they happen to believe in a different religious dogma."

There was a reason he didn't talk about it much. His jaded sense of things and general pessimism wasn't something people tended to regard highly. But, dammit, he'd *earned* it! His life had been nothing but a series of escalating atrocities; so what if it made him a little contemptuous?

Quay was silent for long moments, his words sinking in. "That's a very cynical way to view the world," she finally said.

"It's the only way to survive without getting badly hurt," he told her gruffly. "I used to be like you, all full of hopes and dreams and thinking the best of people. But then the gods saw fit to take that all away." He clamped his mouth shut, fearing he said too much.

Of course, Quay ran with it. "What happened to you?"

"I don't wanna talk about it."

She leaned forward to try to force him to look at her, but he didn't take the bait. He refused to speak more on the subject. "I am sorry that happened to you," he begrudged her. "And I am even sorrier that I wasn't there to prevent it from happening."

She laid a soft hand upon his forearm, right between three jagged scars. Remnants from his time spent in the Pits of Gilden. Those were *not* happy memories. "It's not your fault," she murmured. "You were there when it mattered."

Her touch was warm and inviting. He really hated being the cynical one, being the hardened old man who expected only darkness and despair. He never used to be! That was before, though. That Ghdion died a long time ago.

He glanced over and their eyes met. He saw nothing but trust reflected in her gray eyes. Fuck, how could she look at him like that? He didn't deserve her faith, not after all the terrible things he'd done in his life. He found himself reaching for her regardless; he wrapped his arm around her shoulders and pulled her close.

She rested her head on his shoulder with a heavy sigh. His body was so stiff, his back ramrod straight, he feared he would pull a muscle. *Gods, I never used to be this terrible with women,* he thought. *When did this all get so awkward?*

Quay didn't seem to notice his nervousness. He sat there, riding behind the world's slowest, grumpiest ox, with the lazy, know-it-all sleeping half-elf Hypnocost and a pretty priestess he was starting to think of way too fondly and way too often, stuck in the middle of some mysterious religious war of which he had no skin in the game other than because that same pretty priestess needed his help.

And, to add insult to injury, Quay looked to *him* as a source of comfort. The gods sure did have a sense of humor.

He patted her back awkwardly, his large hands heavy against the silken fabric of her gown. "It'll be alright," he spoke stiltedly.

She snorted. "You don't believe that. You may be many things, Ghdion, but you are not a liar. So don't lie to me, please."

"Alright, Priestess, if you say so." At least he managed to bring a half smile to her face. He would take that as a win.

Chapter 23

Friends Help Each Other Out

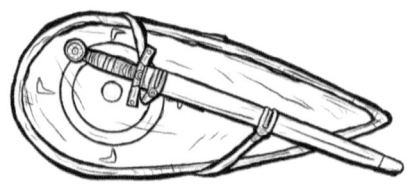

Avindea was already in a foul mood, mostly because of her growing list of plenum duties. A much younger paladin squire, a snot-nosed little thing named Bruce, managed to fully trounce her during weapons practice earlier, which didn't help. Her mood only got worse when Quay, Ghdion, and Hypnocost finally returned to Praetorius; they were extremely lucky she was nearby, for the guardsman at the gate almost didn't let them through again due to their lack of paperwork. She was growing to hate that new law in particular and would be glad when it was over—hopefully after the Athessian diplomat's visit. The paladin had spotted the bright Vidamae sigil upon the side of the wagon as they waited in line outside the walls and, after much arguing, was finally able to pull rank as a plenum member and sign off on allowing them entry.

Avin's dark eyes widened larger and larger as her cousin, Vidamae bless her soul, expounded in great detail why she simply *had* to use the church's wagon, ox, and supplies to travel clear out to the boondocks of Camfield and, while there, offer herself up as bait to draw out the assassins that were killing their way through the

Church's ranks. And oh, by the way, she was almost strangled to death as a result!

They huddled inside the Cathedral of Vidamae. "You always do this, Quay!" Avindea hissed after Quay finished narrating her tale. "You always run off without thinking fully of the consequences of your actions." She threw her arms up in frustration. "You could have been killed! And for what? To prove that yes, the Kax followers *hate us*? We already knew that!"

"That's not the reason why!" Quay cried back, her face glowing a shameful red. "I know what I did was maybe, possibly, just a little bit foolish and ill-thought out, but you cannot deny the results. There's a *group of Kax cultists still out there murdering our people*, Avin! We *must* do something to stop them!"

"Must we?" she spat, much more harshly than she intended. She drew a deep breath and pinched the bridge of her crooked nose. It had been broken and healed wrong long ago during some paladinly battle or other. They all sort of blurred together, she had fought in so many, so she couldn't even remember when it happened. "Quay, your heart is in the right place. But you don't fully grasp the whole picture. I can't run off on adventures with you, not anymore. I've got an important job serving on the plenum now. High Priestess Lucina tasked *me* to substitute for her while she is gone, and it's a job I take very seriously! I can't be there to pick up the pieces when you inevitably cause a mess with your ... with your *grand delusions* of saving everyone!"

Quay's entire demeanor immediately changed, her once outraged face shutting down into blankness. "I see," she simply stated, voice devoid of any emotion.

"Come on Quay, you know I don't mean it like that." She'd messed up. Her mind was so full of all her new political duties, her life so much more stressful and harried than she was used to, she hadn't been able to bite her tongue. She was usually so much better at keeping her temper in check. "I've been under a lot of pressure lately."

"It's fine." Quay turned away, the redness on her cheeks giving away just how upset she was. She bit her bottom lip to stop it from quivering. "I didn't mean to make such a mess of things. Forget I even said anything, okay? I'll take care of it all."

She moved to leave the room, but Avindea grabbed her by the wrist to stop her. "Quay, stop. I want to help you, I'm just not sure how much I can."

"Perhaps we should check in with Lucius and Midori," Hypnocost, standing awkwardly off to the side, offered.

"We'll go see what they've been up to while you and your cousin catch up," Ghdion said.

Her cousin's stricken face showed her just how little she liked that idea, but it was too late; Ghdion yanked Hypnocost by the arm and dragged him out of the room.

They regarded each other silently. It was just like when they were younger and would get into arguments; one would say something cruel, causing the other to clam up and give the silent treatment. Luckily, just as when they were kids, neither of them much liked fighting with each other for long.

They both spoke at the same time, talking over each other in their haste to make up. "I'm sorry, Avin—" Quay said just as Avindea blurted, "I didn't mean what I said, really. I want to help!"

"You first," Quay replied.

Avin took a deep, steadying breath. "I want to help, I really do. But you must *let* me help, and let me help *my* way, alright? No more running off without telling me!"

"That's fair." Quay nodded, chagrined. "To be honest, I could use some of your guidance on this. What should we do?"

Avindea rubbed her chin, pondering the situation. She owed her that much, regardless of how little she wanted to take more on her already overfilled plate. "Well, let's lay out the facts as we know them. First, there have been three murders in so many days, correct?"

Quay nodded. "Edmund Brisby in Furow's Ridge, Leon's wife and son in Desai, and now the farmer in Camfield, Chell." She frowned at that realization. "I still have to set up reparations for his family. Ugh, this is all such a mess!"

"That's a future problem." She quickly stopped that thought from running its course—Quay was always worried about details first, big picture second. "We're sure the murders were done by Kax cultists?"

"Pretty sure. Chell, at least, we know for sure because we witnessed it. The Desai murders are a sure bet, as well, given the attack at the campsite outside the city. Edmund Brisby is the one we are least sure of, though it would be a mighty large coincidence if his murderer wasn't of Kax."

"What do these people all have in common?"

"Well, aside from their likely killers? Nothing." Quay shrugged. "Edmund Brisby was a priest, which fits the whole Kax hating Vidamae narrative, same as for me being attacked last night. But Leon's family, as far as I know, didn't really attend church much, if at all. Same for the farmer in Camfield."

Avindea began to pace, her heavy leather boots thumping on the stone floor. "They all attack at night, leaving little to no trace of their presence after the fact. Maybe they're striking at both the clergy *and* the bloodline of Vidamae again? If this is, indeed, the same plot they are trying a second time, why else would they kill the random people, the farmers and family members?"

"Wouldn't that mean there is another blood font out there, then?" Quay asked, frowning. "I thought they were all destroyed."

Avindea shrugged. "That's what I was led to believe."

"We could see if Midori is willing to give us more answers," Quay suggested.

They headed towards the basement staircase. It was right in the middle of the lunch period, so most of the clergy were in the cafeteria. The younger acolytes all had to take turns in the kitchens, cooking and preparing the meals, as well as serving them to the higher-ranking priests and priestesses and any needy parishioners there for a free meal. Because of this, they didn't run into anyone on their way downstairs.

Avindea felt a little sick to her stomach at how grateful she was for this; she hated all the subterfuge, especially within the cathedral itself. Since High Priestess Balladoni left on her mysterious errand, Avindea held the loftiest title within the Vidamae Church at the moment. The paladins weren't usually involved in the day-to-day operations of the cathedral—that was a job for the clerics—but given the unique matriarchal nature of the Vidamae Priesthood, that meant that Avindea, who had been serving as a paladin the longest, was technically in charge.

She clung to that *technically* with all of her might, hoping fervently she wouldn't have to make any truly important decisions. Quay's latest bout of adventuring brought her dangerously close to having to do so.

They knocked at the door using their secret code, and Lucius cracked the door open. "We were just discussing Camfield," he told them, stepping aside so they could all fit inside the small room.

Midori was on the bed scribbling furiously at her notepad. Hypnocost sat near her, sketching something on a different sheet of paper.

"This is the best I can manage," the half-elf murmured, displaying his sketch. He drew what looked like a smallish orb, with lights protruding from all around it, like it was glowing. "It was small enough to fit in one of the assassin's hands, and it glowed a soft crimson. The glow intensified the closer the assassin got to Chell, the poor farmer they murdered."

Both Avindea and Midori's faces paled. "Let me see that," Avindea growled before snatching the drawing from Hypnocost's hands. She studied it closely, hoping, in vain, that it wasn't what she feared. "You're sure it glowed red?" she asked, touching the ink drawing as if doing so would make it miraculously disappear.

Hypnocost nodded. "Oh, yes. The light cast a garish glow inside the farmer's house. Like blood."

Ghdion spoke up. "What is it? Why did the assassin have it?"

She looked up and happened to catch Midori's eye. Midori's face was flushed, her lips downturned. "Did you know about this?" she asked her harshly, thrusting the drawing into her hands.

Midori nodded. She wrote,

I AM FAMILIAR WITH THE BLOOD FONTS, YES.

Was that excitement that made her write so quickly?

Avindea began to pace, her taut form moving as much as she could in the confined space. She felt claustrophobic, so overwhelmed that she wanted to scream. This could not be happening, not again! Everything was coming at her too fast: first the high priestess leaving without saying where, forcing the reins of plenum responsibility into her reluctant hands, then Quay's harebrained adventure through the countryside, leading to this, the return of the blood fonts and The Troubles?!

"Fuck!" she cried in strangled tones.

Quay's eyes widened. "Language, Avin!"

"What is a blood font?" Hypnocost asked the question everyone was thinking.

She scowled and ran a trembling hand through her silky black hair. "A bad omen is what it is. Godsdammit. They were all supposed to be destroyed! If they're using the blood fonts again ... fuck. Fuck!"

"Slow down, Paladin," rumbled Ghdion's deep voice. "Tell us what's happening here."

She turned towards the group, who all eyed her with looks of apprehension and puzzlement. "Settle in, everyone. You wanna know about the blood fonts? You gotta know Vidamae's history, particularly what happened fifteen years ago. You gotta know about The Troubles."

She frowned, unsure of her ability to relate the sordid history between the two churches. "Hang on a minute, I need to grab something," she said before leaving the room.

She headed down the hallway towards a storage room full of books and other written histories of the church. Hardly anyone came into this room. Scrolls were rolled up and shoved into every nook and cranny, chests overflowing with notes and scattered sermons and the detritus of an old cathedral making use of every available inch of space. She scanned the spines of the books along the shelves until she spotted the one she wanted. A cloud of dust poofed into her face when she pulled it from the shelf.

She hurried back to the room with the book tucked beneath her arm. When she re-entered, the group eyed the large tome with a mixture of trepidation and eagerness. "*The History of Vidamae in Khamris: A Treatise?*" Quay read the book's title aloud. "Did you really need to dig up that old thing to explain what's going on?"

"This book will explain it much better than I can," Avindea admitted. "Besides, it's not as old as you think. It's got a section on The Troubles near the back."

"The Troubles?" Lucius asked.

"Hush, and I'll read it to you." She felt like a schoolteacher as she cleared her throat and opened the musty old book. It smelled just as dry and crusty as she remembered the words written inside to be.

"Ah, here we go. The Troubles: Being an Account of the Culling of Vidamae's Bloodline by the Followers of Kax, circa 9648 in Praetorius and the surrounding Region of Khamris."

Ghdion groaned. "Please don't tell me this whole thing reads like that."

"Quiet!" she scolded. "It doesn't. Now, where was I? Okay, here we go." And she read aloud straight from the book.

"*After years of being constantly thwarted by Vidamae's superior number of followers, Kax devised an ingenious plan to weaken Her nemesis for good. If She could eliminate all of the people in Aukera who were blessed by even a small fraction of Vidamae's divine godhood, would that not, in theory, weaken the goddess herself? It was well known that Vidamae was a particularly promiscuous goddess, sharing the gifts of Her charms freely whenever She deigned to have*

Her avatar walk upon the land. As the Goddess of Life, it was Her divine right to do so. She has spread Her seed freely to Her people, using both a male and female form when She travels down to our realm, bearing children to those blessed mortals who are so lucky as to share in Her divine body."

"So you're saying Vidamae, ah... *got around a lot?*" Lucius asked, unable to hide the blush on his scarred face. "I had no idea the gods were so horny!"

Both Avindea and Quay glared at him. Midori, for her part, snorted derisively and shot him an approving look.

"If you're just gonna cast aspersions on our goddess, Lucius, you can leave." Avindea sniffed haughtily, though her cheeks burned bright red.

He threw his hands up in surrender. "Alright, alright, I couldn't help myself. Please, continue."

Avindea pulled her glaring eyes from him and read on. *"Because of Her generosity and goodwill in this way, there are thousands of souls* on Aukera who share a small piece of Her life force, carried through the ages in their bloodlines. Most are not even aware of their gifts, as they dilute significantly from generation to generation. It was this that spurred Kax to come up with Her plan: create a tool that would suss out the Vidamae-affected bloodlines in order to kill them, thus removing that small part of Vidamae's control of the populace from the world.

"Kax imparted Her schemes through visions sent to one of Her most trusted followers, a man known simply as The Augur. This man used his divine knowledge to create what we know of as blood fonts, magically crafted devices that glow a bloody red when a spawn of Vidamae is near. The brighter the flare, the stronger the tie to Vidamae's blood. The process by which he created these unholy apparatuses is a jealously guarded secret. All that is known about them is that untold numbers of some of Vidamae's highest priestesses and clerics were exsanguinated to cast the spell on the blood fonts to make them work so effectively."

Ghdion grunted. "Oof, exsanguinated? That's a terrible way to die," he muttered. "Messy, too. Not the way I'd wanna go."

"And how do you know this?" Hypnocost asked, his eyebrows raised on his forehead. "From experience, perhaps?"

Ghdion opened his mouth to reply but shut it immediately at the glare Avin shot at him.

She cleared her throat loudly and pointedly. "*Once the blood fonts were finished, Kax sent Her followers into the world to do their bloody work. They started in Khamris, specifically in Praetorius, where they could wreak the most havoc upon the Church, as it was by far the largest and most attended cathedral of the capital. No one was safe in that dark period of the Church's history; hundreds were hunted down by blood font-wielding Kax cultists and murdered viciously for simply existing. Not even the clergy was safe, whether or not they shared a bloodline with their beloved goddess. The Kax cult did not discriminate when it came to murdering anyone who was associated with Vidamae.*

"The religious leaders were shocked and dismayed by such evil acts and sought a way to end the annihilation of the innocent souls caught in the crossfire between the two feuding goddesses. Priestesses Baraz Segovia and Lucina Balladoni came up with a plan to entreat Vidamae directly for help by way of a ritual prayer, to be cast with all of the clergy at the Temple of Tasuil."

"Oh, I know about this!" Quay interrupted, her eyes shining. "They cast the spell that blinded their enemies, putting an end to The Troubles for good!"

Avindea quirked her eyebrow. "It certainly helped, but it didn't end The Troubles. Even with most of Kax's cultists blinded after the mass prayer, there were still pockets of resistance too stubborn to give up. It took a few years of clean up before they were rooted out of their hiding spots and forced to face justice for their crimes."

The room was silent as they pondered what they had just heard. Midori scribbled furiously; Avindea could only imagine what *she* would have to say about the whole thing. They all waited politely for her to finish writing before speaking.

Finally, Midori held up her paper. Avindea read it aloud for everyone's benefit.

I AM SURE YOUR HISTORIES DON'T INCLUDE THE VERY VICIOUS PUSHBACK VIDAMAE'S FINEST INFLICTED UPON ALL KAX FOLLOWERS, REGARDLESS IF THEY HAD ANYTHING TO DO WITH YOUR 'TROUBLES.'

"I don't see how you can claim the victim here," Avindea spat. "Besides, this was fifteen years ago. How old were you then, five? Six?"

I WAS 12!

Midori wrote back, eyes blazing.

I WAS THERE WHEN THE VIDAMAE PALADINS SWARMED MY HOME, KILLING WITH RECKLESS ABANDON! AND YOU CALL IT 'CLEANUP.' CLEANUP! THEY WERE HUMANS! MY FAMILY! YOU PALADINS WERE THE REASON MY PEOPLE SCATTERED AND HAD TO GO INTO HIDING IN THE FIRST PLACE!

Avindea was about to open her mouth for a retort when Ghdion barked, "Enough." He cut his hand through the air for emphasis. "We won't get anywhere by arguing back and forth. Let's focus on the here and now, and what we can do about it." He turned towards Avin and Quay. "So you think, since they've been using these blood fonts again somehow, that some group of Kax people are trying to start up The Troubles all over again?"

"It's definitely possible." Avin frowned, her eyes drawn to the one person in the room who could confirm or deny her hypothesis. "There's no way to know for sure unless Midori here decides she wants to *actually* help us."

Midori glowered at her. She held her tightly clenched fists at her side and visibly vibrated with rage.

"That's not fair," Lucius spoke up from where he sat at her bedside. Those two seemed awfully cozy. "Midori has been more than helpful. She told us about Camfield, and that turned out to be correct, didn't it?"

Quay nodded slowly. "Lucius is right. The assassins showed up two nights after she told us they might. If Midori hadn't told us …"

"The farmer would still be dead," Ghdion finished for her bluntly. "But at least we have confirmation."

"And we were able to eliminate one of the cultists," Hypnocost reminded them. "That is one less killer out in the world."

Avindea winced at the thought of the mess they had left in Camfield, one that, no doubt, the Church of Vidamae would have to clean up. *Add that to the never-ending list of tasks I have to complete today.* She could feel a headache forming right behind her eyes. "Alright, since I am technically in charge of the church while High

Priestess Balladoni is out, I'm the one who decides what happens next, yeah?"

They nodded their assent.

"So here's what's gonna happen: I give you all the authority to use the church funds and resources to get to the bottom of these ... these *incidents*." She paused, mind racing with the possibilities. "That doesn't mean you can gallivant across the countryside without alerting me!" She eyed Quay pointedly. "I need to be notified of any and all trips that you take so I can secure you the correct papers, make sure everything stays official and above-board. No more trying to talk your way past the city guards at the gate. Security's only gonna get tighter the closer we get to the—"

She stopped mid-sentence, horrified to realize she almost revealed a plenum secret so blatantly, that an Athessian diplomat was on his way at that very moment, and was scheduled to appear in four weeks. "The closer we get to the ... the problems we've been having with Athessa lately," she finished lamely.

Lucius looked at her, puzzled. "There's problems with Athessa?"

"There's always problems with Athessa." Quay waved it off breezily, and Avindea could have hugged her for her inadvertent aid. "Whatever it is will probably blow over in a couple days like it usually does. Anyways, don't worry, Avin. We won't let you down. I promise."

She stood up, placing the history book on the table next to Midori's bed. "Good, I'm counting on it. Keep me apprised of the situation. Quay knows how to get a hold of me. I'll get you your official papers, and then I've got to return to the capitol for some more plenum business." Heading to the door, she fixed Midori with a steely gaze. "And if you truly are trying to stop the cultists as you claim, then you'll be willing to help us no matter our history." Without waiting for a response, she stepped through the door.

I DON'T SEE WHY I SHOULD HELP HER.

Midori wrote as fast as she could, the sound of her quill scratching reminding Hypnocost of his time spent with Elder Hulthorpe so long ago. She had been a prolific scholar, and was constantly scribing some treatise or another, her fingertips permanently stained black from ink. He could remember Elder Hulthorpe's face, all gaunt planes and edges, as she banished Hypnocost from his home without giving him a reason why.

"Don't think of it as helping her," Lucius said.

Hypnocost was only half paying attention. He shook his head a bit to clear it of painful memories. He wanted his sole focus to be on the mirror that was still propped against the wall where he'd left it. What secrets did it hold? What magic powered it? What did it actually *do*?

"Think of it as ... as doing all you can, while you're recovering, to stop that cultist group from killing any more people," Lucius continued.

Hypnocost heard Midori scoff; her recovery was well underway if she was able to make that noise from her battered throat.

It was just the three of them in the room now; Ghdion left to get cleaned up and changed, and Quay ran off to do ... whatever priestesses did. Hypnocost glanced over so he could read Midori's response.

YOU'RE JUST USING ME TO GET WHAT YOU NEED. WHAT HAPPENS AFTER? WHAT WILL YOU DO WITH ME IF I REVEAL WHAT I KNOW?

She opened her mouth to try to speak. Nothing but pitiful rasping escaped her throat. She scowled in disappointment.

Hypnocost wondered that, himself. *Answer carefully*, he thought. *I have a feeling she is the only lead we have now. And she is the only one who can tell me the secret of this mirror.*

"Well, that's easy. Nothing. You're free to go whenever you'd like. Was that not already clear?"

Now *that* got his full attention. He turned on his heel, leaning his forearm against the wall to stay upright while he kneeled on the floor in front of the mirror.

Midori's face paled. She closed her mouth to keep from gaping.

"I mean, I don't know how far you'd get without our help," Lucius shrugged. "You don't have any official papers stating your business in the city, which is apparently a thing that's needed nowadays. If any of the city guards were to stop you, what would you tell them? That you're one of the *good* Kax people? That you had nothing to do with the murders in Desai, even though that's exactly where you were found?" He chuckled darkly. "I don't think they'd believe you for a second. Now if *I* were you," he continued, leaning forward, "I'd stay right here and help however I could until I was fully healed. Sure, you're stuck recovering in the church of your goddess's most hated enemy, but isn't there a sweet sort of irony about that? Forcing Vidamae's people to use up *their* resources to help *you*?"

Midori stared at him, her face painting a portrait of different emotions: anger, shock, confusion, and finally, calculation. Hypnocost couldn't help but admire how easily Lucius navigated this thorny back and forth. The man was a natural!

"I'll bet Kax thinks it's a great joke, you taking up the valuable time of Vidamae's people. And they're so foolish and good that they'll release you with a clean bill of health as soon as your convalescence is up. They'd have to! Vidamae is all about love and life and helping your fellow man, right? It'd literally be *against their religion* to hold you here."

His face brightened. "I'd even be willing to bet Avindea can get you whatever documents and things you need to secure your passage out of Praetorius and back to your people. She's a government employee, after all." His good eyebrow raised as if they were sharing some great secret. "But only if you help us."

Midori glared at Lucius. She really did have a truly impressive glare, with those expressive dark eyebrows and her intense eyes.

You planned this,

she wrote to him, her quill digging violently into the paper as she wrote.

This whole time I thought we were becoming friends, but I was wrong. You really are just using me!

Now that was interesting ... becoming *friends*? Hypnocost filed that away in his mind for later perusal.

Lucius, for his part, simply shrugged and said, "Friends help each other out, Midori. That's exactly what I'm doing right now."

Scowling, she pointedly looked away, as if the empty corner of the room held something immensely interesting. Hypnocost, pulled out of the spell Lucius cast with his crafty words, turned back towards the mirror. "Midori," he began, ignoring how upset the woman was, "can you tell me what exactly this mirror does?"

She crumpled up a piece of paper and chucked it at the back of his head, where it bounced off his bald pate and rolled into the corner. "Well, that was uncalled for," he murmured. "It was just an innocent question."

She wrote,

I suppose I better tell you before you report me to the city guard or something. It's a communication glass, but it only works with the other mirrors it

HAS BEEN PAIRED WITH. IT ALSO ONLY WORKS FOR A TRUE BELIEVER OF KAX, SO YOU WON'T BE ABLE TO DO ANYTHING WITH IT EVEN IF YOU TRIED. TRUST ME, YOU DO NOT WANT THE OTHERS WITH MIRRORS TO KNOW THAT YOU'VE STOLEN IT.

"Who else has one? How many are there?" He was intrigued despite the danger.

She threw another wadded paper, this one with her written answer.

KAX CULTISTS, ALL OF THEM, THOUGH I'M NOT SURE HOW MANY MIRRORS THERE ARE IN TOTAL. IF YOU TRY TO USE IT, WHOEVER ELSE HAS ONE WILL KNOW THAT THIS ONE IS NOT WHERE IT IS MEANT TO BE, AND THEY WILL COME SEARCHING FOR YOU. I ADVISE AGAINST DOING THAT.

"So you won't help us use this to find the other assassins?"

Midori didn't even bother writing anything. She just shook her head vehemently.

Hypnocost let out a long-suffering sigh. "Fine. I understand, I suppose. You are probably just too *frightened* to try using the mirror yourself." He gave her a devious sidelong look.

NICE TRY. THERE'S NO WAY IN ALL THE HELLS I WOULD USE THAT THING. JUST LEAVE IT ALONE. IT WILL ONLY CAUSE YOU SUFFERING.

The three of them spent an indeterminate amount of time stewing silently, Hypnocost still obsessing over the mirror, Lucius with his arms crossed and eyes closed as he leaned against the wall, feigning at sleep, Midori silently fuming on the bed. When Hypnocost heard the sounds of her writing again, he tried to hide his intense curiosity. He pivoted his body ever-so-slightly so he could catch her out of the corner of his eye and was rewarded when he saw her lean towards Lucius and poke him in the arm, a sheet filled with writing in her hand.

Lucius pried open his good eye and took the paper. He read through it silently, his face impassive.

"This is excellent, Midori," he finally breathed out.

"What does it say?" Hypnocost cried, unable to contain himself. Mirror forgotten, he scrambled to his feet so he could read what was written.

> **The cultists are using old Kax Temples as bases. They only travel at night, for obvious reasons. The closest one is near Camfield. It's been abandoned since its sacking 15 years ago. There's a well-hidden footpath through the woods that leads to the church. If you can find the path, you should be able to find at least one of the groups there.**
>
> **I expect whatever travel papers and supplies I need to leave Praetorius as payment for my help. I also want to make sure my people, who are still waiting for me to return, will be given all assistance possible to get them to safety. These are my demands, as soon as my recovery is over, for the help I have given the Church of Vidamae.**

"Brilliant!" Hypnocost beamed. "I suppose we will be heading right back to Camfield."

Chapter 24

The Troubles

They left the *priestess* to keep watch over Midori this time.

Lucius, Hypnocost, and Ghdion left that morning for Camfield. There had been some light arguing over who would stay behind to 'keep an eye' on Midori; she hated to admit it, but she wished Lucius had volunteered. She would never say it aloud, but she was starting to like the man. He was easy-going and frank, which was a refreshing change of pace. Her faith in Kax didn't seem to bother him; he didn't treat her as if she was a bomb about to explode like the others did.

Unfortunately for her, Quay volunteered immediately. "I'll stay," she announced with finality. She rubbed one hand absently along her throat; was there a faint bruise there? She tried to peer closer, but Quay turned away before she had a chance to spy. "I can use the time you're gone to research more about The Troubles and the blood fonts and maybe find out more about these other Kax Temples that are supposedly around."

Midori doubted any Vidamae literature would have information about Kax's hidden churches, but she kept her thoughts to herself. Why should she go out of her way to help a devotee of the Pretender Goddess Vidamae?

"You sure?" Lucius asked. "Aren't you supposed to be the leader or something? If you stay here, who's gonna boss these two around?" He thumbed at Hypnocost and Ghdion.

Quay smiled weakly. "I trust your collective judgment. Try to find the old temple, poke around, see if anyone is in there, but don't linger. I want you coming back safe and whole so we can figure out the next best course of action."

They got ready, gathering supplies and weapons for what they hoped would be a short trip. Midori watched as Ghdion pulled Quay aside. She strained her ears to hear what he said.

"Are you okay, Priestess?" he asked in a low voice. His eyes blazed with concern. More concern than a simple bodyguard should have for his charge, surely. It reminded her of a battered old copy of a romance novel she used to read and reread as a teenager, one about a knight, sworn to protect a princess, who had to hide his true feelings for her. She leaned in closer to listen.

Quay nodded. "I'm just a little jittery about heading back into the fray, is all. It'll be good for me to sit this one out." She smiled up at him softly. "I'm sure I'll be fine by the time you get back."

"Don't leave the cathedral while I'm gone," he ordered. As if he had some sort of say over her! Wasn't *Quay* the one in charge? Midori scoffed in outrage, but that didn't mean she actually *liked* the priestess. She just hated to see a bigger, meaner *man* bossing a woman around. Especially when the woman was his *actual boss*.

"I won't, don't worry." She pressed her hand to his cheek briefly before pulling away and leaving the room, probably off to wherever it was the church kept all of their books.

The three men finished their packing and hovered around until Quay returned, her arms full of books and rolled parchment. "Ready?" Lucius asked. "We've got all the supplies, the papers Avin got for us, weapons, everything?"

"Yes, mother," Ghdion replied mockingly. "Let's get this over with."

"Good luck!" Quay waved. "Be safe!"

Lucius looked right at Midori. "Don't be too hard on our priestess, Midori," he requested, a slight smile playing across his lips. "See you soon!" With a mock salute, he left.

That was hours ago. Quay hadn't left since then. Not even once. She just continued to read through her books, making little noises of interest as she looked through them all, almost as if she was trying to get Midori to engage with her.

The priestess had an annoying habit of talking to herself as she studied. "Oh, now *that* is interesting," she said, as if Midori was actually listening at all, or cared one whit about the Vidamae histories she was reading. "It says here that most of Vidamae's descendants are in Khamris, though nobody actually knows why. Huh! Maybe Vidamae just really likes it here?"

Midori shot her a sidelong glance. Was she expecting a comment? Did she forget Midori couldn't actually speak yet? She tried to clear her throat, but it was still too raw. It still *hurt*. She reached for the glass of water Lucius had thoughtfully left for her.

"You know, I may be able to speed up your recovery, if you'd only let me try to heal you," Quay remarked without looking away from her book.

Midori pursed her lips. The idea of a Chosen of Vidamae laying her hands upon her throat filled her with shuddering disgust. What if the priestess decided to *squeeze* with her hands instead of *heal*? *It wasn't a Vidamae follower who did this to me*, she thought with a wince. *It was one of my own.*

It really was getting annoying having to communicate via writing all the time. It was so slow and plodding, and her hand was constantly sore from clutching the quill so tightly.

"I promise I won't hurt you," Quay continued, as if she could read her hesitation. She placed her finger at the spot she left off in the book and looked right into her eyes. "I just want to help."

Midori let out a deep sigh. She twirled her fingers as if to say, 'fine, then, get on with it.' If the foolish priestess wanted to use her divine abilities to heal a follower of her goddess's bitter enemy, who was she to stop her? Besides, if for some reason Quay *did* decide to try to snap her neck, Midori knew she could stop her. She had years of training in specialized fighting techniques, after all.

Quay's face brightened, and she set aside the book to scooch closer to the bed. Her hands began to glow with a soft, inviting golden aura. "Lay your head back on the pillow," she instructed. Her fingers hovered over Midori's neck. "I'm not sure how much this will work since your injury is old, but it might be enough to speed up your healing so you can speak again."

She placed her fingertips gently upon Midori's throat, but even that small amount of contact made her jump. "I'm sorry, did I scare you?" Quay asked in hushed tones. "I have to touch the spot that is injured, you see. It's the only way this will work."

Midori closed her eyes, nodded sharply for her to continue, and tried to relax. It was hard, with Quay's face inches from hers, her fingers running soft circles over her tender neck. She could hear her soft breaths; she smelled like peppermint.

"I know how this feels, now," Quay murmured quietly, almost as a whisper. The healing warmth seeped beneath her skin everywhere Quay touched. "Being choked almost to death, I mean."

That caught her attention. She opened her eyes questioningly.

Quay winced. "Last night, in Camfield. One of the Kax assassins grabbed me by the throat when I got too close. I thought he was unconscious, but I was wrong." She shuddered at the memory. Midori could feel it through Quay's fingers as she poured more healing into her. "It was awful. I'm so sorry the same thing happened to you. I wouldn't wish that upon anyone, not even my mortal enemy."

That was funny, because Midori was as close to Quay's mortal enemy as she could be without being the assassin herself, and here she was, healing that same injury. The priestess pulled her hands from Midori's neck, the warmth dissipating slowly as the glow faded.

Midori tested her ability to speak, clearing her throat first in hesitation, then more forcefully, emboldened by the lack of pain that followed. "Th—" She coughed a bit, then tried again. "Thank you."

It was more of a croak than actual words, but she spoke. And even better, it no longer *hurt!*

Quay's eyes widened. "You're very welcome!" she blurted. "I ... honestly, I'm surprised that worked! How do you feel?"

"Hoarse," Midori replied, her voice jagged and rough. But she could *talk*. Quay's healing was just enough to give her back the ability to speak, and it was *wonderful*. She touched her throat in wonder, amazed at the lack of pain. "My voice is not normally this ... textured."

Quay laughed joyously. "That's one way of putting it. You sound like you have gravel stuck in your throat, but it should go away in the next few days. You should probably limit how much you actually talk, just in case."

The two women stared at each other, Quay in delight and Midori feeling immensely uncomfortable. Why was the priestess smiling at her like that? Why was she so happy to have helped someone she should actively disdain? Instead of asking these things, she hugged her arms and looked away, feeling weirdly embarrassed. She swallowed thickly; it made a loud clicking sound in the oppressive silence.

"We don't have to be enemies, you know," Quay murmured. "I believe everything you've told us. You've been nothing but helpful. We can be friends, if you'd like."

"I'm not interested in being your friend, *priestess*," she spat the last word like a curse. Midori had never had a friend in her life, and in fact spent the majority of her years running away from one atrocity after another, constantly weighed down with the responsibility of keeping her people safe. She knew more about fear and survival than joy. She was used to keeping people at arm's length. Just give it time, and Quay would leave her alone just like everyone else.

Or she would have to push her away, just like her brother had done to her.

Quay just shook her head and settled back more comfortably into her chair. "Fair enough. But you'll find I'm a lot more stubborn than I look. You won't be rid of me that easily." With a pointed look towards her, she picked up her book and got back to reading.

After hours of reading nothing but dry texts describing the different versions of Vidamae's Morning Scriptures—apparently Summaranian churches had a different Morning Scripture than the Khamrian branches, who knew?—or the specific instructions on how to best light a candle for a marriage ceremony performed during a full moon, (for some reason the full moon was supposed to signify a happier marriage) Quay finally slammed her latest book shut.

She closed her eyes wearily. This was not working, not at all like she thought it would. None of the information she'd poured over was helpful at all. Her stack of books was quickly shrinking; all she had left were the records of Vidamae worshippers' births and deaths from the last twenty years, and she highly doubted those would have any information about Kax.

With a lack of anything else to do, she flipped through the last few books anyway, skimming each page dutifully. A large part of her wished she had traveled back to Camfield, if only to confront her fear of coming so close to death. It was silly, she knew, to equate the village with her near-death experience, but for her the two were forever inextricably linked. She would have to get over it, and soon; if the abandoned Kax Church was, indeed, hidden near Camfield like Midori had said, she might be returning there sooner rather than later.

She glanced over at Midori. The taciturn woman refused to so much as look at her after her overtures of friendship a few hours ago. Quay wasn't concerned. In fact, she was more determined to make the Kax follower like her, no matter what it took. Everyone fell in love with Quay eventually—that was simply a fact she knew intrinsically. Life as a Vidamae priestess-in-training was a charmed one, and she wasn't ashamed to admit it. As long as she used her privilege for the greater good, of course.

She continued her one-sided chatting as she read through the books, making light-hearted comments while Midori sat in stormy silence beside her. "Now we're getting somewhere," she said, running her finger across the cover of the second to last book. "*Record of Vidamae's Parishioners During The Troubles, Praetorius and the Surrounding Region*, Years 9646 - 9648."

Midori ignored her. Unperturbed, Quay opened the book. It was another boring tome full of lists of alphabetical names, separated by towns and listed in chronological order by date of birth or death. "Where should we start? Furow's Ridge? Praetorius is gonna be the longest, let's skip that one for now. Or how about Camfield? That's appropriate." She flipped the pages until she reached one that read 'Camfield' in large letters at the top.

"I know you think this is a waste of time," she said as she perused the names listed under the column that read 'deceased.' "But I am nothing if not thorough."

A familiar name snagged her eye about halfway down the page.

Guilphrame, Sari.

Guilphrame ... that was not a common surname, but it tugged at her memory for some reason. She continued down the list, where three more names were listed:

Guilphrame, Aisling. Guilphrame, Bea. Guilphrame, Ronia.

She glanced at the column beside the names that listed age when deceased and reason for death, followed by any surviving family members:

Sari, age 24 at death. Three daughters, Aisling aged 5, Ronia aged 3, and Bea aged 2 at death. Survived by father, Guilphrame, Ghdion.

She let out an audible gasp. *That* was how she knew the name. It was *Ghdion's last name*. Frantically she read the last small bit of information:

Family was killed by Kax cultists in Camfield while in their home, most likely due to blood font involvement. The mother had a bloodline that traced back to Vidamae in her past, as only she and her three daughters were murdered, and the father was left unscathed. Full rites were performed for the deceased. Surviving husband and father to the deceased declined any aid from the church, monetary or otherwise.

That was it. That was all the book had to say about what most likely had been the worst day of Ghdion's life. Quay's mouth dropped open. She felt both hot and cold all over. All this time, Ghdion had had *a family*. He'd had an *entire life* before she met him, yet he never once spoke of it, never told her he had been married and with three daughters, all of whom were killed by Kax cultists because they shared a faint blood connection with Vidamae. And now it was all happening again, and she'd just *sent him to check out an abandoned Kax Temple.*

"Oh gods, I'm such a fool!" she moaned into her hands, covering her face.

Midori glanced over, unable to keep up her pretense of ambivalence. "What?" she croaked out in her raggedy voice.

"Ghdion, he ... I had no idea! His whole family was murdered fifteen years ago, during The Troubles." She stood up and began to pace. She couldn't just sit there and read books while he was out there, risking his life for the church his wife had loved and died for! If she was listed in their records, she had been a devout follower who tithed *a lot*, either monetarily or with acts of service. The average churchgoer wasn't listed in church records like these.

"Lots of people were murdered during that time," Midori reminded her sensibly. "If he did not tell you, there must be a reason for it."

"Yes, but ..." she sputtered, unable to frame her thoughts coherently. "Why didn't he tell me? We've been working closely together for over a year! Why keep something like that a secret?!"

Midori shrugged. "He's a man," she answered simply. "Don't ask for a reason for something that is inherently unreasonable. *Men* are inherently unreasonable."

Midori's words had a stark sort of logic about them. Ghdion had always been gruff and reticent; why would he feel the need to share his deepest, most painful memories with her? What would it matter if he had? It didn't change the fact that she was paying him to be her bodyguard. This was business, after all. But she thought maybe there was something more between them. She thought they were friends, growing even closer the more time they spent together. She even nursed a secret hope that their friendship could blossom into something maybe more akin to romance, though she hardly dared admit it, and never aloud. Had she misjudged their relationship so badly this whole time?

"Sit down!" Midori spat, her tattered voice bringing Quay up short. "You're making me nervous."

"I should go after him," Quay muttered. She finally sat on the stool, but she wrangled her hands in her lap.

"No, you should not," Midori snapped. "Do not be stupid. You wouldn't last one hour out there on your own."

Quay's head snapped towards Midori's in shock, her gray eyes wide and angry. "Excuse me, but what do you know?"

"I know enough!" she answered, slashing her hand through the air. "I do not know why I'm bothering to tell you this, but that church they are heading to? It could be very dangerous. You may be a Priestess of Vidamae, which automatically makes you, at best, an *idiot*, but at least be smart and listen to me about this one thing."

Quay was so taken aback she didn't have a response.

"Now, what happened to Ghdion's family is a tragedy, no doubt. I am sorry to hear they were murdered by those who shared my faith," she continued. Even though her voice still sounded rough, it made Quay strangely proud to know that she was the reason the woman could even speak at all. "Shall I tell you of the retaliation against all Kax followers perpetrated by the Church of Vidamae that followed your so-called 'Troubles?' Are you ready to hear *why* these recent Kax cultists are starting the murders again?"

Quay was about to argue, but instead, she slammed her mouth shut. Was Midori actually offering her information? She couldn't squander such a rare opportunity. "Tell me," she whispered in a shaky voice. "Please."

"Did your books tell of what happened after The Troubles, of how your church assembled all their paladins and sent them on a quest—no, a *hunt!*—to find and eliminate any and all Kax followers they came across? Does it tell of the many temples that were razed and defiled, in Vidamae's name, even if none of the members were a part of the killings, nor had any idea about the blood fonts? Or how anyone who was even *remotely* associated with Kax was shunned, kicked from their homes, sent from the cities with no place to call their own any longer?"

Of course those facts were not taught. Quay was only ever told that all people who believed in Kax were the enemy and would seek to destroy any Vidamae follower on principle. "Midori, I ... I had no idea."

"I lost my parents to the paladin cleansings. I lost my home! My brother and I had to flee when we were children. I was twelve years old when your Troubles happened. Do you know what we call what happened to us Kax worshippers afterward?"

Quay awaited the answer with bated breath.

"The Decimation."

Chapter 25

Eavesdropping

Nine Years Ago

Midori settled more comfortably in her hiding place as she eavesdropped on the vicars' meeting.

Aunt Solange held a rumpled sheet of parchment in one hand. "'—and I have successfully managed to reach the rank of Priestess within the Praetorius Cathedral of Vidamae,'" she read from a report below where Midori hid. "'I fully expect High Priestess Lucina Balladoni will bring me fully into her ranks within a fortnight.'"

Midori scowled as she peered through the crack in the rock that offered her the perfect view into the vicars' private meeting chambers. They called it that—a 'private chamber'—as if it was some grand room within a richly-appointed castle instead of a dank and dimly-lit hollowed out cave within a mountainside. She supposed it made the vicars feel better about being forced to live inside an abandoned mining facility.

Midori's hiding place, a hollow in the rock wall about ten feet above the floor of the 'chamber,' was a lot more cramped than it used to be when she discovered it nine years ago. When they first moved into the old mine shafts, she'd been able to lay spread-eagled comfortably with space to spare. Now eighteen and fully grown, she had to hunch on all fours just to be able to get inside the hidden cavity. It was worth it though. It was the only way for her to find out what the vicars were up to.

So Cranky infiltrated the Vidamae Church, she thought, frowning. *That cannot be good for them. Whatever the vicars are planning, it must be pretty big.*

Cranky—that wasn't her real name, of course, but Midori hated her so much she refused to think of her any other way—was the rising star of the vicar ranks. Even after eight years of living with the gray-haired, severe-faced woman, Midori still could not stand her. She could not understand why her aunt admired the woman so much. Sure, Cranky had volunteered to infiltrate the Vidamae Priestesshood in order to glean their secrets, and bravely traveled to Praetorius in order to do so years ago, but so what? They were all so obsessed with vengeance against Vidamae still. It was asinine.

"At least her part of the plan is coming along nicely," said another one of the vicars, a balding middle-aged man named Baylus. "I wish I could say the same about mine. Excavation of the mines further in the mountains has hit a bit of a snag." He sighed heavily and leaned against the same table Solange stood beside. His thinning brown hair, coupled with his dainty wire-rimmed spectacles and large dark eyes, gave him a distinctly owlish appearance. "I know we agreed not to use the dynamite we discovered, but—"

"Absolutely not." That was her brother Kang, of course. He stood at the head of the room, arms crossed, eyes stormy, mouth set in a frown. He possessed a self-assurance and a magnetism that drew all eyes towards him whenever he spoke. "It's too dangerous. I will not risk blowing up this entire mountain just to ensure we have a secret, safe passage out of it. The whole reason this mine was abandoned in the first place was because of how unstable it became after repeated explosions." He eyed Baylus darkly. "It's not worth it. Move on from those tunnels. Try a different area."

Baylus scowled but did not reply. Midori could tell what he was thinking just by the look on his face—what authority does this *boy* have amongst the group of vicars, the leaders of what was left of the Church of Kax? *I wonder the same thing*, Midori thought as she watched her brother shift on his feet down below. *How did Kang end up getting invited to these secret meetings and not me?*

Solange moved on. "There's more here," she broke the tense silence. "She's found a sympathetic party who is willing to transport supplies to us via his contacts. He's rather well-known in Praetorius, from what I can gather, though she didn't write his name for fear of her correspondence getting waylaid."

She glanced up from the parchment to regard everyone present: Kang, Baylus, the three other vicars, and The Augur, who sat near the back of the room with a peaceful expression on his face. His burnt-out eyes were ever covered with black fabric. Solange continued, "The plan is coming along nicely. We should be proud of our accomplishments."

"What of your project, Augur?" one of the other vicars asked, a woman not much younger than Solange named Jessica. She had long, straight brown hair that she always wore in a ponytail. Her dark robes swished quietly as she shifted to gaze expectantly at The Augur. "Are the written plans for crafting more blood fonts coming along?"

The Augur's covered face moved towards the sound of Jessica's voice. Midori could imagine him blinking slowly, if he had eyelids left to blink with. "It ... progresses," he finally answered, his voice scratchy and weak. His health had been failing for months, beginning with the constant tremor in his hands that he could no longer control. He wasn't as spry as he once was; he often required help traversing the many tunnels of the mining complex. He fell and broke his ankle two months ago after tripping on a loose stone, so he rarely left his private chambers anymore, other than to attend the vicar meetings. "I have dictated as much as I could to the scribes, but some of the finer aspects of engineering the blood fonts is ... hard to explain." He sighed. "I fear a written accounting of the crafting of the blood fonts will not suffice as well as we first anticipated."

The vicars exchanged nervous glances. It wasn't the first time The Augur had said as such. He was truly god-touched, a dedicated Chosen of Kax given the divinely mandated instructions on creating the blood fonts back before The Decimation. He claimed the instructions came to him in a dream, fully formed and blessed by Kax, and it was his life's work to craft as many of the magical objects as he possibly could.

The blood fonts, the magical glass globes that could track down even the weakest of Vidamae's bloodline, were truly a wonder of engineering melded with magic. They required an impressive amount of blood from descendants of Vidamae in order to work properly; only one font remained from the dozens The Augur had created years ago. The vicars were desperate to create more of them so they could continue their plan of vengeance against Vidamae's descendants.

"We brought you two new descendants," Kang spoke up, pushing his long black hair behind his ears. At twenty-one, he was exceedingly handsome, even Midori could see that. The rapidly growing darkness she glimpsed behind his eyes worried her. "We've already begun the exsanguination process on both of them."

The Augur shook his head sadly. "We will need much more blood than two descendants can provide." He rubbed at his forehead. "The last descendant perished much too quickly. We need a better way of keeping them whole and healthy so we can take smaller amounts of blood from them at a time, instead of bleeding them out all at once."

"How can we do that with only one blood font?" Kang interrupted savagely. He swiped at the air in a cutting motion with his hand, his frustration palpable. "The Warriors Bennett and I have been training are eager to go out into the field to test their mettle. They grow impatient with how long this is taking."

"Peace, Kang," Solange murmured. "We all knew this would take us years. Do not be so hasty as to jeopardize our carefully wrought plans." She folded the letter she had been reading from and tucked it safely into her pocket. "Crafting new blood fonts is our top priority. You know this. You have been told multiple times."

Kang scowled. "I still believe we should focus on toppling the church," he replied. "Would that not be a better use of our time and resources? We can begin the strikes within the year, and—"

"Enough!" Solange yelled. Her voice rang loudly in the cavern-like room. "You know your duty, Kang. Stop arguing and get to work."

His mouth slammed shut, but his eyes burned with a fury Midori hadn't seen before. She absently rubbed at her chest where a lump of apprehension formed.

Solange surveyed the other vicars. "Let us adjourn for now. We can gather again when we have more news."

The vicars got to their feet. Jessica strode over to The Augur to help him leave. Solange led the other two out of the meeting room, and soon it was only Kang left. He leaned against the rocky wall and stared off into the distance, until he lifted his eyes and met Midori's straight on through the crack in her hiding place.

"I know you're in there, Midori," he spoke softly.

She cursed under her breath. She hoped he had forgotten about her hiding place after so many years of him not joining her there to eavesdrop. They used to squeeze inside the small space to overhear Aunt Solange as she confided in the other vicars. Sometimes even Bennett would join them. That had been years ago.

She wiggled her way out backwards, careful to duck beneath a jagged piece of rock lest she scratch her cheek again, and hopped down to the floor gracefully. After checking to make sure all the vicars had cleared out, she stepped lightly around the curve in the tunnel and into the meeting chambers proper.

"Why do you still insist on eavesdropping?" Kang sighed as soon as she entered. "If the vicars wanted you to know what they spoke of, they would have invited you."

"Why didn't *you* invite me, then?" she countered hotly. "I'm sick of being left out of things, Kang. I have a right to know about the plan just as much as you do."

He crossed his arms again and regarded her thoughtfully. "Do you?" he asked after a slight pause.

She glared at him. "What's that supposed to mean?"

"Are you truly committed to the cause?" He flicked a nonexistent speck of dust from the front of his black leather tunic. "I've seen how hesitant you are when we speak of violence against the Church of Vidamae. The other Warriors have noticed it, too."

"What even is this almighty *plan* anyways?" she cried in embarrassed frustration. If the others noticed her hesitance, she hadn't been hiding it as well as she thought. "Just another scheme to get back at Vidamae's followers? Are we truly still holding onto that rage after all this time?"

"Of course we are!" he spat. "You saw what they did to us, Midori, you were there! The wanton, senseless killing. The destruction. They took everything from us!" He clenched his hands into tight fists at his sides. "I cannot let them escape unpunished. How can you *not* be consumed by righteous anger?!"

She had been, once upon a time. Shortly after they arrived at the mines, she'd gone through her angry phase where all she wanted to do was hurt somebody, anybody, for what the Paladins of Vidamae had taken from her. She'd been a lonely, scared little girl with no one to confide in. Solange was too busy trying to hold the group together; after they'd moved into the abandoned mining tunnels, other, smaller groups of Kax stragglers joined them, bringing the total number of refugees to around one hundred people. Bennett would listen to her whining sometimes, but eventually he started avoiding her, claiming he didn't have time for a little girl's problems. Even Kang hadn't been helpful back then, as consumed with his own dark thoughts as he had been. Still was.

She'd had a dark, lonely adolescence. Even surrounded by all her fellow Kax followers, Midori felt more and more like an outcast.

"What is the point?" she finally answered. She took a step towards him and grasped his hand in hers. "Why can't we just ... leave? Go someplace else, start over, start fresh." Her dark eyes flashed with hope. "Don't you ever just want to be *done* with revenge? Aren't you tired of being so *angry* all the time?"

He wrenched his hand from hers and turned away. "You sound like a coward," he huffed, without any real bite to his tone. "You should be ashamed of yourself."

Midori hesitated before admitting, "There are others who feel the same way as I do, Kang. It's not cowardice. It's ... something else. We just want to move on. We want peace. Is that such a bad thing?"

"Yes!" He shoved past her roughly towards the door. "I will hear no more of this, especially from *you*. No wonder Solange doesn't want you in these meetings."

Midori opened her mouth to respond, but Kang beat her to the punch. "Never speak of this again, with me or with anyone else, do you understand? We will continue with the vicars' plans, and you will do what is asked of you."

He left then, without waiting for her response.

Chapter 26

The Ruined Temple

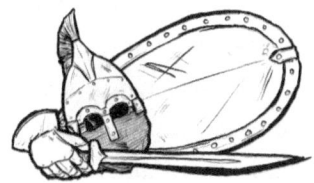

They passed the spot Midori had marked on their map four times before Hypnocost finally spotted it.

Lucius was already well past annoyed at that point: the sun was hot and beating on the back of his neck, Mertha the ox refused to walk any faster than a snail's pace, and Hypnocost, who sat beside him in the front of the wagon, had been mumbling to himself almost the entire journey. The half-elf was oblivious to the dark looks he shot at him periodically. He finally blurted, "Just who in the hells are you talking to, Hypnocost?"

He turned towards him with a look of surprise. "I am not talking with anyone," he answered, nonplussed.

"You were literally just muttering something not two seconds ago," Lucius replied, feeling argumentative.

"He does that sometimes," Ghdion called from the back of the wagon. The tall blond man was lounging comfortably, hands folded behind his head and ankle crossed on his knee. His huge greatsword lay next to him, within easy reach. "You'll learn to ignore it."

"I do *not* talk to myself," Hypnocost insisted. He turned away, scanning the treeline where the hidden path to the Kax Temple should have been. "It should be right around here somewhere," he mumbled. "Yes, I know, I already looked there, it was just more trees."

Lucius eyed him with some concern. *He's having a full-on conversation with someone I cannot see. Or with himself. Not sure which one is worse.*

They trundled along the stretch of road again, Ghdion only half-heartedly looking, Lucius holding the reins in too-tight fists and growing more frustrated by the minute, Hypnocost continuing his incessant one-sided chat. Just as Lucius opened his mouth to suggest they stop, Hypnocost pointed towards a shadowy portion of the trees and cried, "Wait, there it is! Beyond that tree there, the one with the crooked looking branch, you can just barely see a footpath."

"Well, I'll be damned." Ghdion, shading his eyes from the bright sun, sat up and leaned forward. "You're right. There is a path, just where Midori told us it would be."

Lucius yanked on the reins, silently thanking the gods that this leg of the journey was finally, blessedly, over. Mertha obediently came to a stop right in the middle of the dusty road; when he slapped the reins to try to get her to move off to the side, she ignored him and began eating grass. "What is wrong with this godsdamned ox?" he muttered.

"She only listens to Quay, that's what's wrong," came Ghdion's grunting answer. "I think she's convinced Mertha to not like men or something, because she sure hates me." He hopped off the wagon and stalked towards Mertha, approaching her as if she were an enraged bull about to charge.

Mertha eyed him distrustfully from the side, munching at the grass.

Hands in the air, Ghdion took a few tentative steps forward, cooing at the ox as soothingly as his deep voice could go. "C'mon, girl, we gotta get you off the road for a bit. The grass is better over there anyways." He reached out towards her bridle ... and she immediately turned her huge head away from him so she was just out of reach.

Lucius jumped from his seat and came around to the other side, effectively pinning her between the two of them. "Mertha, don't be difficult," he told her reasonably.

She flicked her tail at him as if he were as annoying to her as a fly. Giving him a savage look that contrasted with her round bovine eyes, she lowered her head and yanked another bite of grass from the ground, unbothered.

Lucius threw his arms up in exasperation. "Let's just leave her here," he suggested. "How busy can the road into Camfield be anyways?"

"There is a farmer traveling this way." Hypnocost pointed towards the distant village. Sure enough, there was a lone farmer atop a raggedy looking wagon, pulled by a single donkey, coming right towards them.

"Of fucking course there is," Ghdion grumbled. He looked at Lucius, grim determination on his face. "Alright, on the count of three, we each grab one of her horns and haul her off to the side of the road. Ready?"

Lucius nodded, getting into a crouching stance. *This is my life now*, he thought grimly. *Wrangling stubborn oxen and running errands for a Vidamae Priestess.*

"One, two, *three!*"

They each lunged, missing her horns by a wide margin as she took a few dainty steps off the road and away from them both just as they came for her. Ghdion nearly crashed into the yoke as she pulled the wagon behind her, and Lucius fell flat on his ass in the dust.

The wagon rattled loudly as she moved nearer to the trees, then paused, sniffing the ground for sweeter patches of grass. Apparently finding a better spot to feed, she lowered her head and, ignoring the buzzing humans around her, began to munch.

Hypnocost wiped the dirt from his silken jacket before he made his delicate way off the front bench. "Let us hurry," he called back as he walked purposefully into the trees towards the hidden path. "You should get Mertha tied up or she is liable to wander away."

Lucius and Ghdion exchanged stormy scowls from where they had fallen into the dirt. "I swear to the gods ..." Lucius muttered to himself.

"Yep, I know that feeling," Ghdion grunted, offering his hand, which Lucius took gratefully. "It's best to just ignore him when he gets like this. I know from experience."

"Duly noted." He grabbed the reins from Mertha's neck and tied them to a nearby tree before following Hypnocost through the woods.

"Keep going. You are close,"

the voice said.

Hypnocost, by some miracle staying well ahead of both Lucius and Ghdion's long-legged strides, panted as he rushed down the forest path. Even though it was nearly noon and the sky was bright with sunshine, the trees were so close, their branches so thick and leafy, it felt as if dusk had settled. It was no wonder they had missed the entrance to the hidden trail.

He'd been lucky that the voice told him where exactly to look. How did the voice *know that*? He pushed aside the sick nervousness that thought gave him; it was best to keep moving forward and not think about that too much. The fact that he had been muttering aloud to the voice, so much so that Lucius had heard him, was also cause for discomfort, but he ignored that, as well. That was a problem for future Hypnocost to deal with.

The trees grew closer and closer together the farther he traveled through the wood. The path was a barely perceptible trail of dirt that wound maze-like through the trees; was that on purpose? Had the

Kax cultists of the past been so paranoid as to make it this hard to find their temple?

"How far does this go?" Lucius grumbled behind him. Branches snapped and scratched at all three of them. Lucius lumbered loudly through the brush, causing such a racket with his taller frame and heavy tread that, if they had all been trying to be sneaky, they would've been spotted immediately.

"Just a bit farther in,"

the voice told him.

"Only a bit farther," Hypnocost puffed. His smaller frame provided some protection against the poking branches, but no amount of ducking and weaving could fully keep nature from pulling at his robes and tripping up his steps.

After a few more minutes, he was finally freed from the green darkness of the forest as he stepped into a small clearing. Beams of sunshine nearly blinded him after the shadows cast by the trees, and he had to squint to see what exactly lay beyond.

The ruins of what had once been an elegant, stone-carved cathedral lay in several tumbled-rock pieces. The dirt path changed from hardpack to gravel and then to flat stone as it led right to where the double front doors used to be. The doors no longer hung from the hinges; shards of broken wood, once painted red, scattered across the area in front of the church. The roof was caved in along the back half of the church, causing the main part of the building to cant drunkenly sideways. Pieces of what used to be marble pillars jutted in a circle around the structure; they were all knocked down, leaving only impressions of their past glory. A huge symbol of Kax was painted across the front: a three-pronged, wicked looking claw, with red flames at the tips. The paint was fresh.

Several horses, tied to the pillars, contentedly grazed upon the grass. They didn't seem to notice that three newcomers had just emerged from the woods.

Hypnocost drew up short, Lucius and Ghdion coming up right behind him. They took a moment to catch their breath, staring in open wonder at the hidden temple nestled amongst the trees.

"Well, shit," Ghdion breathed. "I was starting to think we were on a wild goose chase. But there it is, plain as day."

"Careful,"

the voice said.

"You must be silent. There are sure to be Kax followers within. Do not alert them to your presence."

"So what's the plan?" asked Lucius.

They exchanged glances, none of them speaking up right away.

"I would assume we would go inside," Hypnocost said blandly.

Lucius nodded, a look of determination on his face. "Okay, I'll go first to check the perimeter, make sure there aren't any scouts on watch. Since we don't have any idea how many people are inside, we should be as stealthy as possible. Once I give the signal, you two follow, as quietly as you can manage. Got it?"

Hypnocost and Ghdion both nodded. The half-elf was surprised by how easily Lucius assumed the leadership role; he spoke with confidence and moved with a lithe, easy grace, crouched over as he rushed across the clearing, using what scant shadows he could as cover. The clearing was a wide open, grassy area; if anyone was on watch, they would have seen him easily. He rushed towards one of the broken pillars near the entrance, pressed his back against it for an agonizing moment, then peeked his head around to scan the area.

After a nerve-wracking few minutes, Lucius turned towards them and pointed towards his eyes, then behind him at a portion of the caved-in roof. When Hypnocost looked where he'd indicated, he spotted a lone watchman posted behind what was probably the remains of a stone gargoyle. How in Aukera had the ex-guard managed to cross that open area without the scout seeing him? It had to have been pure luck! The scout was hidden expertly, wearing gray clothes that matched his surroundings; if Lucius hadn't pointed him out, Hypnocost doubted he nor Ghdion would have seen him.

They both watched from the relative cover of the underbrush as Lucius waited for the scout to turn his head in the opposite direction. As soon as he wasn't looking, Lucius scuttled silently from the pillar to the shadows near the doorless entryway. There he braced silently against the wall.

When he waved for them to follow, Hypnocost and Ghdion raced across the grass. The sun beat upon their exposed backs ... any minute now, and the scout would certainly spot them! They ran pell-mell right out in the open. Hypnocost was convinced that one of them would trip upon an unseen rock and make a loud noise as they fell, or that the horses would get spooked and start to whinny ... There was no way that scout couldn't hear Ghdion's harsh breathing or Hypnocost's panicked footsteps!

Before he knew it, they were both safe behind the same pillar Lucius had hid behind. They watched as Lucius glanced upwards towards the roof, trying to gauge the direction the scout was looking. Hypnocost and Ghdion froze, sweating, behind the pillar; Lucius finally waved them over, and they flew across the rock-strewn grass until they reached him.

Backs pressed against the coolness of the stone temple wall, they struggled to control their panting.

"That was lucky,"

the voice said, causing Hypnocost to start in surprise.

"The scout nearly spotted you at the end there."

"Please be quiet," Hypnocost pleaded. "I am already jumpy enough as it is!"

Lucius peered around the empty doorframe into the blackness inside. Slowly he pulled his sword from its sheath at his belt, the metal-on-metal sound muffled by his hand pressing against the flat of the blade. Ghdion followed suit, pulling his two-handed sword from his back and nearly knocking Hypnocost over in the process. Was it really necessary for the man to carry such a large, unwieldy blade?

He shot him a nasty look; Ghdion just scowled back. Lucius, pulling on Hypnocost's sleeve to get his attention, pointed towards the entrance and mouthed, "Follow me."

With Lucius in the lead, Hypnocost right on his heels and Ghdion taking up the rear, they headed into the darkness. The shadows were thick and oppressive without any light source to guide them; the sun's light only ventured so far into the building. A crumbling, frayed rug lined the front walkway, muffling the sounds of their boots; once their eyes adjusted to the darkness, they could see they stood in the nave.

Broken pieces of pews and other wooden furniture littered the floor. Iron candelabras were knocked over in places, one with a missing leg propped up against the far wall, near where the pulpit would have been if it hadn't been smashed into so much debris. Broken glass shards glittered through the stained glass windows, all of which were shattered, casting weird, colorful pools of light in bizarre patterns. Hanging on the far wall behind the ruined pulpit was a moth-eaten tapestry that depicted the claw symbol of Kax. In front of that stood a statue of Kax, carved into the artist's interpretation of what She looked like: stark white skin and long black hair that curled in bizarre tendrils around Her head like some unholy halo. She smiled knowingly out at Her missing congregation, Her fingers painted orange with red-tipped claws just like Her symbol.

There were dozens of sleeping people huddled amongst the debris. Nearly twenty Kax cultists rested on the floor, using their cloaks as pillows, their weapons at hand should anyone happen upon their hiding place.

Hypnocost let out a little gasp as he saw them; Lucius whirled around and covered his mouth with his hand, using his eyes to convey what his mouth couldn't right then: do not make a single sound!

The ex-guard turned back towards the minefield of sleeping cultists, taking a moment to scan for any alternate routes of egress. He pointed towards the right, where a half-open door led further into the temple. Turning towards them, he mouthed exaggeratedly, "Let's look there."

Lucius tiptoed silently along the wall, Hypnocost and Ghdion hot on his tail. He was somehow able to avoid stepping on any of the crunching glass spread across the floor.

"Hurry. One of them is stirring,"

the voice said.

Hypnocost made the mistake of glancing behind him; sure enough, one of the cultists nearby shifted in their sleep. Lucius saw this, as well, and made a split-second decision: he flipped his sword deftly in his hand so it was in a backwards grip, stepped over a pile of broken glass, and slammed the pommel of his blade right against the back of the cultist's head.

The cultist slumped to the side and stopped moving. Lucius hovered silently above them, scanning the other sleeping forms to make sure he hadn't disturbed them. After a tense, solid minute of waiting, he gingerly stepped backwards and around the unconscious form, resuming his spot at the head of the group.

"He should have just killed him,"

the voice said.

"*I agree,*" Hypnocost replied. Why hadn't he?

A light fluttering of panic settled in his chest; at any moment, any number of the cultists could wake up, and who knew what they would do once they spotted the three intruders sneaking about their church? Hypnocost gulped, his throat uncomfortably dry. He wanted to both freeze in place and run right back out of the place. Panic settled around his chest like fluttery tentacles.

His choice was made for him before he had a chance to settle his nerves: Ghdion pushed him gently but forcibly through the cracked open door after Lucius's retreating form.

Stairs let downward into darkness, where a small lit candle flickered near the bottom. It looked to lead into a basement corridor, with rooms branching off each side of the main hallway. Lucius stepped lightly upon each of the steps, which were thankfully made of the same carved stone as the rest of the church; there was no risk of creaky wooden stairs giving away their positions. Once he reached the bottom, he gestured for the two of them to follow, giving them the all clear with a thumbs up.

"Let's check each room," he suggested in a hushed whisper as they huddled together at the bottom of the stairs. "Do a cursory scan, then move on to the next until we finish this corridor."

"What are we looking for exactly?" Ghdion asked softly.

"I dunno, but I have a feeling we'll know it when we see it. Maybe some documents, or books? Maps? Written plans of their next targets, things like that. I'm not exactly sure. Just grab anything you think could be useful."

"I'll check the right side," Ghdion offered, moving towards the first doorway on the right.

"Hypnocost, you're with me," Lucius ordered. "Be ready with any helpful spells or whatever mind magic you use, because we might need it."

It was a testament to how nervous Hypnocost was, because he didn't argue over the semantics of his spellcasting. He just nodded solemnly and followed Lucius as he slowly opened the first door on the left.

It was a small closet, full of trash and remnants of what must have been robes the priests once wore. They were all in tatters, still hanging from hooks along the wall. The smell in the enclosed space was overwhelmingly musty.

Lucius closed that door and moved on to the next one, glancing towards Ghdion, who just shook his head: nothing of value in his first room, either. They both moved on.

The second door was locked. He jiggled the handle a bit to test its strength, to no avail. Turning towards Hypnocost, he raised his eyebrows as if to ask, 'Any way you can open this?'

Hypnocost was about to shake his head when the voice said,

"Place your hand upon the doorknob. I will open it for you."

He tried to school his features to hide his shock but couldn't quite prevent a little shiver from running down his spine. How could a *voice in his head* give him the ability to magically unlock a door? He placed his hand upon the handle, skeptical that anything would actually happen, but when he turned it, he heard the small *click!* from inside the locking mechanism as it unlatched.

Lucius stared at him, shock and delight bringing a crooked smile to his scarred face. "That's pretty damned handy," he whispered as he pushed the door open.

Hypnocost chuffed weakly as a response. *"How did you do that?!"* he demanded.

The voice did not deign to reply, though he sensed smugness in the absence of an answer.

Did the *voice* give him the ability to magically pick locks? Had the voice somehow taken over his body to use his hands, or was it something else? Hypnocost licked his dry lips, more nervous about the voice than he had ever been before. He couldn't ignore it or brush it off as some benign force that simply spoke inside of his head, not anymore. If it could take over his body, could it do the same thing with his mind? Had it been doing that all along?

"Who are *you?"* he asked. Even his thoughts were shaky with alarm.

"Look!"

the voice said, a thin veil of excitement apparent in its tone.

Inside the room, there was a flat sleeping pallet strewn with blankets on the floor next to a floppy backpack and a few candle stubs, one of which was lit. The floor was caked in dirt, and the walls were covered with maps. Some looked hand-drawn, others ancient and tattered, but they all depicted the region of Khamris. A rickety wooden table with only one drawer was propped up in the corner, serving as a makeshift altar to Kax; several candles were placed in a circle on the top, surrounding a Kax holy symbol made of some dull metallic material.

Lucius let out a breath. "I think this might be what we're looking for," he whispered in excitement. He strode over to the altar and began rummaging through the drawer.

"Look in the bag!"

the voice demanded.

Obediently Hypnocost knelt by the sleeping pallet, his hands shaking as he reached for the backpack. There was something inside of it, something round and hard and slightly larger than the size of his hand. He pushed aside the canvas flap and pulled out a dark glass orb. The last time he'd seen it, it was glowing a fierce, horrible red.

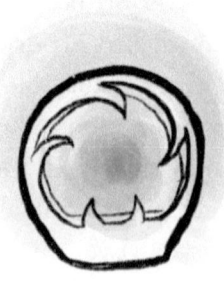

"The blood font,"

the voice said. Even with no apparent inflections of emotion, Hypnocost knew the voice was both awestruck and excited. He could *feel* it's emotions inside his head.

Lucius turned towards Hypnocost, a wad of papers in his hands. "This is perfect," he spoke in low tones, tucking the papers into the waistband of his pants. "I found something called 'The Testaments of Kax,' and ..." His voice trailed off when he saw what Hypnocost held. "Oh shit, is that—?"

"The blood font, yes," Hypnocost finished for him. "I suggest we bring this to Quay. The Church of Vidamae will be very interested in this."

"NO, you ignorant fool!"

the voice hissed.

"Keep it! Do not relinquish that blood font!"

It was too late. Lucius had his hand outstretched, waiting for Hypnocost to give him the glass orb. Reluctantly he handed it over. As soon as it left his grasp, he felt a sharp jolt of pain knife through his mind, no doubt in retaliation for disobeying the voice.

"Hand me that backpack," Lucius whispered. "I'm gonna put everything inside it, then we can get the hells outta here." He pulled a bunch of the maps from the walls as he spoke.

Hypnocost grabbed the backpack, his mind racing as he tried to come up with some excuse to take the blood font back from Lucius. It was so hard to think with that aching pain flaring throughout his mind! "I can carry it," he whispered shakily. "You have your sword, whereas I have no need for a weapon. It makes more sense for me to carry the bag."

Oh gods, was that entirely too obvious? he thought in despair. *There is no way Lucius is going to hand it over that easily!* But Lucius just shrugged and placed the blood font, as well as all the maps and papers he'd scrounged from the drawer, inside of the bag. "Good idea," he whispered back as he buckled the top flap closed. "Now let's go get Ghdion."

He let out a sigh of relief, following Lucius back into the hallway. The pain in his head receded.

Inside the room across the hall, Ghdion knelt before a mirror not unlike the one they liberated from the Kax campsite in Desai. He glanced behind him as they entered, gesturing towards the glass. "There's another of those mirrors here," he murmured. "Should we grab it?"

"No need," Hypnocost answered easily. "We will not be able to use it if it is the same kind as the one we already have. Only Kax worshippers can use these."

They heard a slight scrape just outside the room and froze in place, straining their ears. The silence of the basement thrummed in their ears. Lucius placed his finger atop his lips in a shushing gesture, then, sword in hand, stepped noiselessly into the corridor.

As soon as he exited, a swift blur sped right past him, leaving a sharp breeze in its wake; it headed straight for the mirror. The blur turned out to be an inhumanly quick Kax cultist, wearing gray robes and a gray hood, knives shining in each hand.

The three of them were so taken aback by the cultist's speed they didn't have a chance of stopping them. They reached towards the mirror and spoke a strange word none of them had ever heard before. The mirror immediately lit up a bright red, similar in hue to the blood font when it was activated.

Several things happened all at once. The cultist screamed, "*Intruders!*" then whipped a flurry of small blades towards Ghdion and Hypnocost, one of which stuck into Ghdion's upper thigh. Hypnocost felt one graze his cheek as it flew past his head, only inches from embedding into his eye.

Lucius, now in the doorway, batted three of the knives from the air with his sword; if things weren't so chaotic, Hypnocost would have taken a moment to fully appreciate that amazing feat of swordsmanship.

The mirror, glowing like a bloody beacon, fuzzed a bit on its glassy surface until a face appeared.

The face belonged to a pale skinned man with long black hair pulled back into a bun. He had dark eyes and high cheekbones, and, instead of an expression of shock and outrage, he looked ... amused? He peered from within the mirror, looking directly at the three of them. With a voice both soft and dangerous, he said, "Well, well, what do we have here?"

Chapter 27

What a Shitshow, Huh?

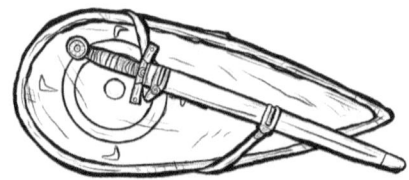

"I call this plenum meeting to order," Chancellor Eldivar spoke in his elegant voice from the head of the table.

Avindea clasped her hands, patiently waiting for the chancellor to call on her. She was bursting with the news of the resurgence of the Kax cultists' vendetta against the Church of Vidamae, and all of her righteous indignation assured her that the plenum would fall all over themselves to help.

What a vast difference a few days could make! Her first plenum meeting, she was so agitated about speaking in front of all of the illustrious nobles that she actively dreaded having her name called. Now she waited restlessly for her turn to speak.

She willed Lord Eglath—he was the bear-like priest of Thulkas, representing his own church on the plenum—to hurry up as he prattled on and on about the new military training regimen he wanted to test with the Praetorian Army. And would the plenum please approve a stipend of 1000 gold coins to cover the cost of the supplies he needed?

Lieutenant Orvessa argued back and forth with Lord Eglath for a few minutes; she didn't feel it appropriate that a religious order get involved with the military. After an unnecessarily long discussion on the matter, they each agreed to compromise: Lord Eglath would take charge of a small cadre of soldiers to test his training methods, and if it worked well, they would adopt the regimen for the whole army.

"Lady Avindea has a matter of some importance to discuss with the plenum," Chancellor Eldivar said with a smile. He gestured towards her to speak. "Lady Avindea?"

She stood up swiftly and cleared her throat. "I have some troubling news to impart upon the plenum today. I'm not sure if any of you have heard of the recent murders in some of our nearby villages, specifically Furow's Ridge and Desai?"

A few of the counselors nodded, including Lady Loresh and Lady Uunar. Loresh was familiar to Avindea, being from the Church of Velthunas; the two temples worked closely together. Lady Uunar, however, was still somewhat mysterious; she was the Headmistress of the Arcane Academy, the school of mages right there in the city. Lady Uunar was tall and dark-skinned and exceedingly beautiful, with her bald head, expressive eyebrows, and heavy golden earrings.

Judge Rodach, cantankerous as ever, scoffed. "Backwater villages, both of them," he muttered under his breath.

Avindea shot him a nasty look. "Backwater villages or no, Judge Rodach, they are still a part of this country, are they not?" She raised an eyebrow in his direction, but he only waved his hand for her to continue. "Well, one of my priestesses, Quay, who has been traveling on behalf of the congregation as part of her training, has recently confirmed that those murders are likely linked, with the Church of Vidamae as their common thread. After she reported another killing in Camfield just last night, we've come to the conclusion that the Kax cultists are at it again and are targeting members of Vidamae's Churches just as they did fifteen years ago."

She awaited the gasps of shock and horror that never came. Confused, she glanced around at the faces of her peers. All she saw was boredom and disinterest. Even Lord Rendevas, usually her ally during these meetings, wouldn't meet her eye as he fiddled absent-mindedly with the lacy cuff of his jacket.

"How, exactly, did you come to the conclusion that Kax is involved?" Lady Uunar asked, crossing her arms.

"The priestess I mentioned witnessed the cultists themselves and was able to procure a holy symbol of Kax from one of the would-be-assassins, who her bodyguards, thankfully, managed to ... ah, dispatch." Her face heated up; it wouldn't be a good look to reveal that Ghdion and Hypnocost, bodyguards of a priestess whose religious order revered *life* above all else, had actually *killed* a couple of the cultists, even if it was in self-defense.

Chancellor Eldivar tented his fingers, elbows resting upon the table. "And what would you like the plenum to do about this?" he asked her, not unkindly.

Avindea sputtered, "Well, I, um ... that is, I wanted to keep the plenum apprised of the situation, and I ..." She trailed off, realizing she really didn't have a sufficient answer. "I guess I thought you should all know."

It sounded limp, even to her own ears. Gods, she looked like an idiot. *Again!*

"Why don't you keep us updated on this? We will consider it a developing situation until you tell us otherwise, hmm?" The chancellor smiled patronizingly at her from the head of the table. "Unless these supposed cultists turn up at our doorstep!" He chuckled at the unlikeliness of that scenario.

The king himself, usually so polite, even looked unimpressed. Nobody there cared. It didn't affect them or any of their interests, so why should they? Avindea clenched her fists in frustration.

Before she could sputter out any other pleas for help, Chancellor Eldivar announced, "Lord Rendevas? I believe you're next up on the agenda."

Yet another plenum meeting; they seemed never-ending sometimes. Rendevas tapped his finger against his thigh, anxious to get this over with. There was so much he needed to get done! From overseeing the endless line at the city gate, to placating angry merchants with promises that yes, soon the restrictions on goods and people trying to get inside the city should be lifted, Rendevas simply didn't have time to waste on another frivolous plenum meeting. And he loved plenum meetings! The play of politics was thrilling and full of interesting tidbits of knowledge. Now, all he wanted was for it to be over with, then maybe, *finally*, he could try to corner the king and speak with him one-on-one ...

It had only been a day since Milford gave him the incriminating documents against Judge Rodach. He was eager to show them to the king, but as plans ramped up for the Uldinvelm diplomat's arrival, his old friend Phil was even harder to pin down than normal. It was nigh impossible to speak with him alone; the monarch was constantly attended by his guards, in meetings with his council or with his daughter, Princess Alandria, who even now sat beside him attentively. Rendevas tried to catch her eye to give her an encouraging look, but she either purposely ignored him, or was not paying enough attention to even notice.

He glanced at Judge Rodach, who sat at the far end of the table. The judge looked bored, which was not unusual. It was no secret the man hated the plenum meetings and only attended because he was forced to. If he'd had his way, he would have sent a more junior judge to attend in his place. *You'd think he would be more engaged,*

Rendevas thought, *as he's making money hand over fist selling his plenum votes, the traitor!*

Just the thought of that arrogant prat made Rendevas's blood boil. He glared daggers down the table, relishing the thought of seeing the judge's stricken face once the king was made aware of his treacheries. Captain Riluk would drag him out of the plenum meeting, in front of all of the other counselors, announcing that the city's highest judge was not as morally upright as he touted himself to be, and he would spend the remainder of his days rotting in a jail cell for his crimes. Rendevas would be applauded as a hero for discovering the vile betrayal, and King Selderin himself would heap honors upon honors on him ...

"Lord Rendevas?" Chancellor Eldivar called loudly. He stared at him expectantly, white eyebrows raised.

Rendevas shook his head to clear it of his daydreams. "Yes, Chancellor?" He smiled, trying to cover up the fact that he hadn't heard a single word that was just said.

"You have an update on Lord Tullie Mason of Uldinvelm, yes?"

"Oh, of course!" He scrambled upright in his seat, shuffling through the stack of papers on the table before him. He didn't have any such thing, not really. In fact, he hadn't heard from the Athessian delegation in days. Just another thing for him to worry about. "If you'll give me but a moment to find the correct papers ..."

Judge Rodach scoffed. "That's typical," he muttered, just loud enough for everyone to hear. "Always showing up unprepared."

Rendevas cleared his throat, his face heating. "Ah, yes, here we are." He pulled out a random paper and pretended to read from it. "Lord Tullie Mason of Uldinvelm sent a reply to my previous letter stating that he still plans to arrive in Praetorius in less than four weeks, just as planned in his original request."

"Is that all?" the chancellor asked, his voice dripping with expectation.

"Ahh, yes, as of right now. Until he arrives, there won't be many updates, I'm afraid. Travel from Uldinvelm and all that. But if we could speak about the situation at the city gates, I—"

A city guard rushed into the council chambers, cutting him off. She looked harried and frantic, her armor clanking loudly as she forced a hasty salute.

"What is the meaning of this?" Captain Riluk cried, standing. He reached for a sword that was not hanging at his belt.

"I apologize, sir, but there's been an incident at the city gate!" The guardswoman panted, her face flushed; had she run the entire way from the gate to the capitol building?

The counselors all watched her with looks ranging from shock to nervousness to amusement. Rendevas, annoyed at the interruption, wondered if it was just another merchant who was out there loudly demanding entrance into the city. That happened three or four times a day lately.

"Well, out with it!" Chancellor Eldivar snapped, his voice tense and annoyed.

The guard gulped a breath before announcing, "It's the Athessian diplomat, sir. He's here, waiting at the gate!"

Ghdion swung his heavy blade in a perfect arc towards the cultist's head, just barely missing as the cloaked person ducked out of the way at the last minute. The fucker was *fast*! If all the Kax people moved as quickly as this one, they were *fucked*.

"We gotta get outta here!" he hissed, shoving into the cultist with his broad shoulder and knocking them askew just as they readied more blades to throw. Their hood fell from their head, revealing their face. It was the same cultist who had murdered the farmer, Chell, in Camfield only the night before.

"*Shhhhhit!*" Ghdion cursed. Hypnocost, clutching a canvas knapsack against his chest, stood rooted to the spot, large eyes wide as he watched the cultist jump back to their feet, smiling at them wickedly.

"C'mon!" Lucius cried from the doorway. "Get back upstairs before we're trapped down here!"

The man in the mirror watched, laughing in delight. "Take them alive, Bennett. I'll be there soon to see what they know."

The cultist, named Bennett apparently, nodded sharply. Knives protruded menacingly from between each of his fingers, and he rushed towards Lucius. With a speed unlike anything Ghdion had ever seen, he threw a set of knives from one hand and lunged at Lucius's midsection with the other. Miraculously, Lucius was able to parry the thrust and bat away all of the knives with his longsword.

Even Lucius looked shocked that he was unscathed. How could one man be *that* lucky? Ghdion couldn't take the time to wonder; he swiped forward with his blade, effectively pushing Bennett back into the room, beyond where he and Hypnocost stood.

"Now!" Lucius roared, and led the way to the stairs with long, running strides. Hypnocost and Ghdion wasted no time in following him.

When they got back upstairs, the entire room of Kax cultists was waiting for them in the nave, awake and with weapons at the ready.

"He's *here*? *Now*?" Rendevas cried, shooting to his feet.

Avindea, from her seat at the far end of the long table, had never seen the diplomat look so frantic. This was obviously not some ploy he had concocted; the look on his face was all the proof she needed that he was not prepared for such an unexpected development. The other plenum members looked smug at his discomfort, but Avin felt sorry for the poor man.

The guardswoman, out of breath from her long run from the city gate, could only nod her answer.

"This is most unusual!" Chancellor Eldivar said, his voice a bit higher than normal. He fairly tittered with anxious annoyance. "Why would he show up so early? Did you have any idea this would happen, Lord Rendevas?"

"I'd be willing to bet our *senior diplomat* screwed up the dates," Judge Rodach sneered.

"Rendevas, with me." Captain Riluk took charge, effectively cutting off any snarky replies from anyone else. "Your Highness, if you'll allow it, I will lead Lord Rendevas and a small group of my soldiers to the gate to greet the diplomat and lead him back here."

Avindea spoke up. "I'd like to join them, Your Highness," she found herself saying. *What am I doing? I've got no authority here! I'm not a soldier or a diplomat. This is beyond my area of expertise for sure!* "I've got military experience, and I can also serve as an ... an official envoy from the Church, to help make the diplomat feel more at ease."

King Selderin nodded, the only sign of his distress a slight raising of his eyebrows. "Yes, that is a smart idea, Lady Avindea. Go with my blessing, captain. The rest of us will await your return. Perhaps after, Lord Rendevas, you can get to the bottom of this mess." He fixed the diplomat with a hard, unreadable stare.

The three headed towards the door, where the guardswoman waited in obvious agitation. King Selderin announced as they left, "Let us take a recess until this situation is resolved, shall we?"

Avindea took long strides to catch up to the diplomat, who walked with the speed of a man running headlong towards disaster. "What in the hells is going on, Rendevas?" she asked, grabbing his arm to get his attention.

He didn't slow at the contact; if anything, he moved even faster. "I have no idea!" he hissed, not looking at her. "The last I heard from Lord Tullie was that it would be weeks until he arrived!"

"Are you sure it wasn't just a miscommunication?" she asked. "Maybe a, I don't know, translation error?"

Rendevas shot her a sidelong glance. "You know as well as I do that isn't the case, Avindea," he spat. "It's not as if they speak a whole different language up there in Athessa."

They moved quickly down the corridor, startling servants out of the way in their haste. "What are you doing here, anyways? Don't think I didn't notice that little show back there about being an 'official church envoy.'"

Avindea flushed. "I couldn't think of a better reason," she admitted. "Trust me. I'm here to help."

After a beat, he gave her a tight smile. "I'm grateful for your support," he finally said. "It would've been much easier for you to stay back and chide my foolish efforts with the rest of those crows."

"Do you suspect something nefarious?" Captain Riluk, ever direct, asked from beside Rendevas. His square jaw clenched tightly, the cords in his neck standing out even from under his armor. He looked wound tight like a bowstring.

They strode determinedly down the marble steps of the capitol building, following as the guardswoman led them on the most direct route to the city gates. Rendevas replied with a shaky, "I don't know," that made Avindea's stomach drop.

Could this be it? Was this how the war started? With a simple *miscommunication?*

"What on Aukera could an Athessian diplomat hope to gain from showing up at his enemy's capital city *four weeks early?*" she wondered aloud. "Is this some kind of ploy?"

Rendevas merely shook his head. "I have no idea. But I have a feeling we're about to find out, one way or another."

Familiar buildings flashed past her as they moved just barely below a flat out run through the streets, the early autumn sun beating down upon them harshly. The streets were blessedly empty of much traffic, as it was just past noon and most citizens were either at home for a lunch break or still working. People mingling outside who saw the harried group of nobles, led by the brisk pace of the city guardswoman, stepped immediately to the side to get out of their way. Avindea nodded towards them as they passed, her well-bred manners at play even in such a stressful situation.

She felt naked without her sword and shield. She could see Captain Riluk's hands twitching towards where his sword would have hung from his belt; he was just as nervous and ill-prepared as she was. If this was some sort of plot, perhaps they should stop for weapons first? Would weapons intimidate the emissary? Would it give him the wrong impression?

Rendevas charged ever onward, picking up speed when the gates came into view. They could see a large crowd of guards clustered on their side, the noon sun glinting brightly off their plate armor and swords.

Captain Riluk shouted orders in his booming, authoritative voice as soon as he was close enough to be heard. The guards immediately stood at attention and rushed to follow directions, some running back towards the capitol building to stand guard along the street, others going back to their posts at the wall or the gate. Another soldier handed Riluk a sword and shield. "I want you all on your best behavior!" he shouted. "No slouching at attention, no nodding off on the job. You're here to show the Athessians just what the Praetorian Guard is made of!"

His soldiers saluted smartly, momentarily inspired. Rendevas, trying to smooth his graying goatee, muttered, "This is a disaster. They caught us looking like ill-prepared, bumbling idiots. I will never live this down!"

"It's not your fault they showed up weeks early," Avindea replied placatingly. She soothed her tone to help ease the poor man's anxiety. They all needed Rendevas, as their top diplomat, at his very best. "If anything, this makes *them* look more desperate. Maybe they are eager to stop the war before it begins and that's why they got here so soon?"

Rendevas gave her a flat stare. "Even you should know it never works out like that, Lady Avindea."

They projected a confidence they didn't feel until the Athessian envoy came into view. It was a much smaller operation than she imagined, consisting of an open-topped carriage pulled by two horses and a squad of six soldiers, four carrying ceremonial blades and the two at the back holding up banners. One was emblazoned with the crest of the Ternian Czars, the three-sibling monarchy of Uldinvelm, depicting the two brothers and their sister in stylized lines and bright colors. The other banner bore the colors of Athessa's flag, red and forest green against a background of black. The soldiers wore armor that was flashier and more intricate than practical, all embossed vines and lamellar colors; Avindea could point out four separate weak points just from where she stood.

Not very practical, she thought. *The armor is more for show than defense. Could be a good sign?*

The carriage was a gilded, atrociously elaborate monstrosity with thin wooden wheels that were hardly appropriate for such a long, rugged journey. A driver sat at the front, wearing a fancy black and gold velveteen ensemble similar to something Rendevas would wear, and a wide brimmed hat pulled low over his eyes to keep out the sun.

The diplomat himself, Lord Tullie Mason, sat alone in the back, nestled against the ivory-colored plush seats. Lord Tullie was a lot younger than she anticipated. As draped in plush robes and fine furs as he was, he looked like a child playing dress up with his parents' fineries. A thin golden circlet lay atop his head of wispy blond hair, and his large ears stuck out prominently from the sides of his head. With his wide eyes and doughy complexion, he would have looked funny if his face wasn't filled with abject terror.

This is weird, Avindea thought. *Something is off about this whole thing.* "Are most diplomats that ... young?" she asked from the side of her mouth.

Rendevas jerked his head no. "They aren't usually that scared looking, either," he told her quietly. "There's a certain amount of ceremony to be expected, but this ... this is unlike anything I have ever witnessed before." His dark eyebrows furrowed.

Once they were within hearing distance, Rendevas stepped forward and proffered a sophisticated bow more fit for royalty than a foreign diplomat, especially one from an enemy country. "Greetings! I am Lord Rendevas, and I bid you welcome to Praetorius. Lord Tullie Mason, I presume?" He held his bow, only his eyes moving as he looked to the Athessian diplomat expectantly.

Lord Tullie shifted uncomfortably in his seat. "Yes, I am he," he mumbled, voice so quiet it could barely be heard even over the hushed, tense silence.

Rendevas stayed bowed for a beat longer and then, when no other words were forthcoming, straightened and smiled, covering his discomfort easily. Avindea cringed inwardly at how awkward the whole meeting was turning out to be. "Well, this is quite the pleasant surprise," he continued, clapping his hands together. "You've regrettably caught us a bit unawares as we were not expecting you so soon, but it's no matter! Shall we escort you to the capitol and get you settled in for your stay?"

Lord Tullie inclined his head, eyes darting this way and that. What was he so nervous about? *I guess I would be just as nervous if I were in his shoes,* Avindea thought. *The poor kid is all alone in a foreign country that's full of people who despise him just because of where he's from.*

She had to stop thinking of him as a kid; he may be young, but he was still an official diplomat, due all the honors and respect that title brought him. As the guards led the envoy through the gates, Avindea walked alongside the carriage. "I wanted to introduce myself, my lord," she said. "My name is Avindea, and I am a paladin of the Church of Vidamae. The Church sent me to officially welcome you into Praetorius." She smiled warmly, doing her best to ease his discomfort.

The diplomat simply gaped at her for a beat before replying,

"That's nice." He then turned away to stare intently at the streets before them.

Well, that was rude. Maybe Athessa doesn't revere the Church as much as we do in Khamris. She scanned the area—an old paladin habit, as they were always on alert for danger—and didn't see anything outwardly threatening or strange that could have drawn his attention. City guards were spaced out along each side of the street, ostensibly to keep any gawkers from getting in the way. There were a few bystanders, mostly old folks and children who didn't have enough manners to know not to stare.

The sun was so high in the sky that the shadows cast by the buildings weren't deep or dark enough to hide much of anything, let alone any would-be assassins. And the Praetorian guards on the roofs of the nearby businesses, hunched over with bows at the ready, were surely there as additional, last-minute security ordered by Captain Riluk.

Avindea did a double-take. *Wait, why are there Praetorian guards on the roofs?* For a moment, her mind didn't register that they weren't actually at the top of the city wall like she'd first assumed. They moved swiftly across the clay tiles, wearing city guard tabards and hoods and masks pulled over their faces. That was not standard issue for any soldier or guard she had ever encountered. What kind of soldier wore a *mask?* She counted at least three on the right side; when she glanced to the left, she could see three more, hurrying across the top of a nearby seamstress shop.

"Captain Riluk," she called out towards the front of the caravan where the man strode side-by-side with Rendevas. "Did you order archers on the roofs?"

Riluk cocked his head, his step faltering. "Archers on the roofs? What are you—"

That's when the first arrows flew, homing directly towards Lord Tullie Mason.

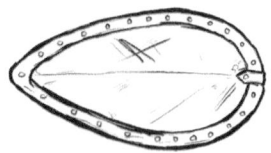

"RUN!" Lucius cried, all hope lost of sneaking back out of the temple.

The Kax cultists rushed towards him as he leapt over a large pile of shattered glass. There were so many of them! Three versus fifteen, no, twenty!? armed and angry Kax worshippers? He did *not* like those odds!

There was also the freakishly fast assassin, Bennett, racing towards them from the basement. It was just his dumb luck that they stumbled upon the killer from Camfield who had managed to escape both Ghdion and Hypnocost; if all the cultists here were as skilled as he was, they were in deep trouble.

A knife-wielding assailant jumped at him; Lucius shoved his sword through his belly without any hesitation. The cultist slumped over, clutching at his midsection; Lucius kicked him backwards, right into the path of another attacker, without slowing his stride.

He risked a glance backwards. Hypnocost was still behind him, clutching the knapsack with the blood font against his chest. Ghdion, at the rear, fended off attacks from two different cultists by swinging his greatsword, lopping clean through one of his attackers' necks and then gouging into the upper thigh of the other one on the downward swing.

The cultists howled in rage at their fallen comrades. The broken doorway was just ahead, but four of the cultists ran in that direction to try to cut them off. If they reached the entryway before Lucius, there was no chance they'd be able to get out.

Ignoring the attackers to focus on escape, Lucius put on a burst of speed and pumped his long legs as fast as they could take him. Wind blew past his face as he nearly flew over the pews, using them as jumping off points in his race to the exit. One of the benches even pushed to the side in his wake, throwing a nearby attacker off balance just enough that they tripped and fell heavily behind him, cursing their ill luck the whole way down.

That cultist's accident caused a jam as three others tripped and fell over the first one; Hypnocost and Ghdion sidestepped the melee in their haste to reach the exit.

Cheerful sunlight streamed through the doorway. *Almost there!* Three flung knives zipped right past his ears, landing with a clatter as they struck the stone wall. Bennett roared in frustration from behind them.

"How many fucking knives does that guy have?!" Ghdion cried, swinging his greatsword erratically behind him to keep Bennett at bay.

Bennett jumped over the greatsword easily and kicked upwards into Ghdion's chin, knocking the blond man into a stumble.

"Hypnocost!" Lucius yelled. He ducked as two more came at him. "Do your mind-thing!"

Hypnocost kept running until he reached Lucius's side, panting and shaking. He squinted his eyes on Bennett, focusing intently … but nothing happened. The assassin didn't even seem to notice, he was so fixed on taking down Ghdion.

"It is not working!" Hypnocost wailed. "Why will you not help me?"

"I'm trying!" Lucius replied. He grabbed one of the fallen daggers at his feet and chucked it wildly at Bennett.

He didn't expect the knife to do anything but possibly buy Ghdion time. The throw was way off, erratic, there was no way it would …

The blade hit its mark, landing with a sickening thump directly in Bennett's neck.

"What the fuck?" Lucius's mouth dropped open in shock.

Bennett clutched at his gushing wound and fell to his knees.

Ghdion sprinted towards them, a trail of blood from his blade flying behind him. "C'mon!" he bellowed. "Let's get the fuck outta here!"

Arrows thudded ominously into the chest, neck, and shoulder of Lord Tullie Mason. They all came from the Praetorian guards perched on the roofs to either side of them.

"NO!" Captain Riluk screamed, drawing his sword and thrusting his shield up, but it was too late. The Athessian diplomat slumped forward in his seat, blood trickling from six different puncture wounds.

"What in the hells?" Avindea cried, taken aback. She was completely out in the open, no sword or shield to protect herself with, so she ducked beside the still-rolling carriage. "Get down!" she cried, trying to push the nearest Athessian soldier down with her, but another hail of arrows rained down from the rooftops.

One of the soldiers went down immediately, three arrows protruding from their chest and neck. Two others on her side of the carriage cried out in pain as they were hit, one in the upper thigh and the other in the back. The three remaining soldiers, on the other side of the carriage, drew their swords and frantically whipped their heads around to determine where the attacks were coming from.

Nearby bystanders cried out in alarm. Within moments, what had started as a staid parade through the city streets turned into nothing short of chaos.

City guards tried to protect both the diplomats and the fleeing citizens. The Athessian soldiers screamed in fear, their sounds mingling with those of the crowd. And over it all, more arrows zipped down from the rooftops with unnerving accuracy.

Two more missiles pierced the neck and chest of the carriage driver, and he fell forward in his seat with a groan. The horses, sensing the lack of control on their reins, slowed to a halt in the middle of the street. Horrified, Avindea crab-walked from beside the carriage until she reached Captain Riluk, who used his shield to cover both Rendevas and himself.

The remaining Athessian soldiers rushed towards the carriage, their shields aloft against another hail of arrows; two slammed into an Athessian's knee, and one grazed another soldier's arm.

"What is going on?" Avindea cried, the sun blinding her as she tried to scan the rooftops for more attacks.

The archers were mere silhouettes against the cloudless sky. They only stood there for a moment, surveying the damage, bows in their hands.

"I have no idea!" Captain Riluk admitted between gritted teeth. "I did not order those archers up there, nor would I have! They aren't even wearing official uniforms!" Sweat beaded across his furrowed brow, but he continued to hold the heavy shield above their heads.

"This is insanity!" Rendevas moaned. "Is Lord Tullie ...?"

Avindea nodded grimly. "He's dead, no question. So are three of his soldiers. But we gotta get out of the open and chase those archers before they get away!" She reached down and pulled a sword from one of the dead Athessian soldiers on the ground, surprised at how lightweight and flimsy the blade felt in her grip. It was poorly made, with multiple scratches and divots along the edge; weren't the blacksmiths of Uldinvelm famed for their excellent bladesmithing? Apparently that particular Athessian soldier wasn't given one of the good weapons.

"Too late for that." Riluk pointed towards the rooftops, where the archers fled the scene, using the tops of the buildings to their advantage. A few of the city guards ran towards them, but they had a hard time tracking the archers from their positions on the ground.

"After them!" Captain Riluk bellowed, waving his sword in the air to get the remaining guards' attention. "Avindea, get into that carriage and take Rendevas back to the capitol. Make sure it's placed in lockdown while we search for the attackers. You," he pointed at a

Faith and Ruin

nearby guardsman, "escort the Athessian soldiers who can walk and follow the carriage to the capitol. And you," he turned towards a different city guard, "grab as many guards as you can and come with me. We're going after them!"

Avindea nodded smartly and grabbed Rendevas by the arm, hauling him into the carriage, where she pushed him next to the body of Lord Tullie Mason. His dejected form offered no resistance. The poor diplomat was in shock. "Up you go," she grunted, eyes constantly scanning the rooftops. "Let's get you to safety."

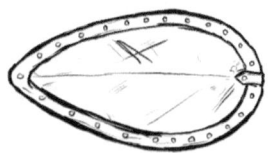

The sun nearly blinded them as Lucius, Hypnocost, and Ghdion emerged from the ruined temple. The horses tied up at the broken-down pillars whinnied nervously, and the scout on the roof hissed, "Shit!" as he saw them appear.

"The horses!" Lucius cried. He had an idea. "Get to the horses and they'll never be able to catch up to us!" He ran towards the pillars and swung his sword down through the rope holding the nearest horse in place.

With an ease from his years of experience riding during his soldiering days, Lucius leapt upon the horse's back. The horse neighed angrily, but he grasped the reins firmly, asserting control over the beast. Flicking its ears in irritation, it followed directions simply enough as he backed it away from the pillar and next to its companion, a white horse with black tipped ears.

"Hypnocost!" he ordered, slicing through the ropes that held the white horse in place. He waved frantically. Cultists emerged from the temple in a flood of dark cloaks and enraged glares. "Hurry!"

Hypnocost pulled himself awkwardly onto the horse's saddle-less back, still holding the backpack against his chest. Beside him, Ghdion had already cut through the ropes of the remaining two horses; he slapped the rear of the farthest one, sending it screaming in fear away from the temple and into the woods.

He swung his leg over the remaining horse, a black and brown spotted stallion that whipped its black mane furiously. With a firm grip and a few muttered words of encouragement, he had the beast under his control just as the cultists raced towards the makeshift hitching posts.

"Go, go, go!" Lucius cried, and the horses didn't need any further urging. They wheeled around the crowd of Kax worshippers, all three horses screaming in confusion and fear as the cultists crowded around them. They seemed reluctant to attack the beasts; Lucius didn't question his good fortune. With a strangled, "Hyah!" he urged them towards the safety of the trees.

Brakten, disguised as Milford, watched from the scant shadows of The Murky Bard's back entrance just as one of the bow-wielding Praetorian guards jumped down from the rooftop.

The archer didn't see him, he was so focused on evading capture. He jumped behind a couple of well-placed barrels in the darkened alleyway to evade two actual guards as they raced past. Letting out a soft breath of relief, he placed his bow onto the harness strapped across his back. Looking quickly from side to side to make sure he was alone, he pulled the tabard off over his head; seen up close, it was an actual Praetorian guard tabard.

Now that was interesting ... He didn't look like any Praetorian guard Brakten had ever seen. The hoods and masks kind of gave that away.

Brakten darted from the corner of the building where he hid. Had anyone else been there to see, it would have looked like he *disappeared* into the shadows momentarily, so lightning fast did he move from one side of the alley to the other.

But since the two were alone in the unnatural quiet, no one was there to witness as he pulled up right behind the archer and brought a dagger to his throat with a flash and a flick of his wrist.

The man gasped as the tip of the blade dug into the soft skin of his throat. "Wh-what!?" he hissed out with garbled consonants. The hand at his side twitched.

"Don't even think about it," Brakten, in his Milford voice, cooed into his ears. "I know you've got a dagger hidden in your waistband. Make one more move and I'll slit your throat all the way through and chase after one of your other 'guard' companions, instead."

"Who are you?!" the archer whispered fearfully, putting his hands up in surrender.

"They call me Brakten," he replied, a smile in his voice.

"The l-leader of The Maelstrom?" asked the man, a true note of fear lacing his already shrill voice.

"Oh, so you've heard of me, have you? Must be a local, then," he answered, flipping the tabard that lay on the ground into the archer's arms with a graceful motion of his booted foot. "Hold onto that for me, will you? I'm gonna need it." He began to pull the archer back into the shadows with him, dagger still held firmly against his throat. "Gods, what a shitshow, huh? You certainly caused quite a mess out there, my friend."

"Are you g-gonna kill me?"

Brakten, his back pressed against the wall behind the Murky Bard's back entrance, reached behind him with his free hand, releasing the catch that opened the hidden entrance to the very secret, very closely guarded center of operations of The Maelstrom, elite and highly sought-after information (and sometimes thieving) guild of Praetorius. "Nah. I've got some questions for you. You and I are about to have a nice little chat."

Chapter 28

Athessian

"This is a catastrophe!"

Chancellor Eldivar's piercing howl of outrage echoed across the plenum chambers. The entire plenum was still gathered inside, anxious and desperate for news. Rendevas, recently returned from the attack at the city gate, flinched, unable and unwilling to interrupt the old man's wrathful tirade.

He stood alongside Captain Riluk and Avindea. The entire capitol building was on lockdown, per the captain's orders. Lord Tullie Mason's body, as well as those of the three soldiers killed in the ambush, had been taken to the morgue nearby. The two wounded Athessian soldiers were being treated next door at the hospital, and the single unharmed soldier was placed in custody for questioning.

Captain Riluk had the unfortunate job of informing Chancellor Eldivar that he had failed to recover a single one of the rooftop assassins. This, immediately after Rendevas and Avindea's grim news regarding the murders of over half of the envoy from Uldinvelm, put the chancellor in a rare fit of hysterics.

He paced back and forth in front of the plenum, his wrinkled face bright red, his hands clenched tightly at his sides. "How could you have allowed this to happen?" he asked the three of them. "The diplomat arrived weeks early and was *murdered* at our doorstep. By our own guards? This ... this is insanity!"

Rendevas didn't bother replying. This day would live on in infamy in Praetorius's history. War was surely inevitable after such a fiasco.

"I agree, sir. I have all my available troops scouring the streets," Captain Riluk spoke evenly. He held his plate helm under one arm, his gaze stony and solemn. His eyes stared straight ahead, and he stood at perfect attention. Rendevas couldn't help but feel bad for him. "Rest assured, we will find the assassins."

"And how do you plan to do that?" Judge Rodach spat, his harsh words echoing across the solemn chamber. "When it was *your own guards* who perpetrated this act of violence?"

"I assure you, those were no guards of mine," Riluk growled.

"We have dozens of witnesses who claim otherwise," Lady Uunar interjected smoothly from her seat at the table. She eyed the captain, her large eyes hooded and mysterious, her dark bald head gleaming in the sunlight that streamed through the windows.

"As soon as the assassins are found, I plan to open an inquest into the—"

"That is not good enough!" Chancellor Eldivar roared. "Don't you realize what this has unleashed? What an *unmitigated disaster* this is? No amount of ... of *inquests* or excuses you come up with will change the fact that Uldinvelm will most certainly declare war upon us now. And they have every right to! Can you imagine if *we* had sent an emissary for peace to their capital, only to find out he had been murdered in cold blood as soon as he arrived?" He took a deep breath, his shoulders shaking with barely contained wrath. "King

Selderin is even now trying to draft a statement to get ahead of this whole thing."

"Please, allow me to assist him." Rendevas perked up, sensing an opportunity. *Bad timing, but this could be the perfect way to get the king alone,* he thought. "I will take full responsibility for my part in this debacle, and—"

"Absolutely not," Captain Riluk interrupted. "The king and the princess are both safe in undisclosed locations, per lockdown protocol." He eyed Rendevas icily from beside him. "No one but the captain of the guard can know of their locations. That includes even other plenum members."

"How convenient," Judge Rodach interjected in his oily voice. "The one man who may be responsible for the attack is the only one who knows the king's location."

The other plenum members looked to Captain Riluk with sudden suspicion. Rendevas opened his mouth to retort, but Avindea beat him to it.

"Don't be ridiculous," she snarled, whirling towards the judge. "Are you casting aspersions upon Captain Riluk's character? What could he possibly have gained by attacking the Athessian diplomat? I was right there with him while it all went down, and it was clear he was just as taken by surprise as the rest of us!"

"Which does not bode well for the people of this city!" the judge spat. "It is *his job* to keep the people of Praetorius safe! He can't even handle keeping *one diplomat* out of harm's way for the short trek from the city gate to the capitol building!"

"Enough!" the chancellor shouted. "It is clear to me that this plenum needs to get their priorities straight. Sniping back and forth at each other is childish and, frankly, shows a level of incompetence never before seen in the history of Praetorian government! Citizens are protesting, merchants are being left at the gates due to the negligence of the gate guards, diplomats are getting murdered in broad daylight! What has this assembly come to? Is this the best that Praetorius has to offer?!"

That shut them all up. No one dared speak.

Chancellor Eldivar continued. "It is clear that we have work to do, and I expect us all to work together to clean up this mess. Is that clear?"

They nodded as one, chagrined.

"Good." He stood a little taller, rubbing both hands against the front of his tailored vest. "Lord Rendevas, find out exactly what happened with Lord Tullie Mason and why he showed up so early. What was the reasoning for it? Was it part of a ploy by Uldinvelm to catch us unawares? Something doesn't add up, and I want you to find out."

He ran a hand through his hair. "Lady Avindea, I want you and Lady Uunar to assist him."

He turned towards the captain next. "Captain Riluk, you will find those assassins, and you will question the remaining Athessian soldiers. Constable Mald will aid in this. He can help at the city gate." He shot a glance towards the constable as if he expected some pushback, but the burly man just nodded.

"Judge Rodach and Lady Loresh, check the defenses of the city. I want a full accounting of the state of the walls and any siege weapons we have. Make sure our supplies can withstand an extended siege, should it come to that."

After a pause, he finished his instructions with, "Commander Rakeld and Lieutenant Orvessa, your job is to make sure our army is in fighting shape when war is inevitably declared. Lord Eglath will help you with training. I will not have Praetorius caught unawares because of this catastrophic blunder."

"We will not fail you, sir," Commander Rakeld replied evenly. Of all the council members, Rakeld and Orvessa looked the most pleased by current events. They tried to look contrite and serious, but Rendevas could see the gleeful glimmers in both of their eyes.

They'd be getting their war. It made him feel sick. This was exactly what they hoped would happen.

Perhaps I need to pay another visit to Milford, see if he can't drag up some dirt on those two, as well, he thought. *Could they have had something to do with all of this ...?*

"This meeting is adjourned," Chancellor Eldivar called out. "You have a lot of work to do. Do not fail me, for if you do, you fail all of Praetorius. Don't forget that."

Rendevas had a feeling none of them would any time soon.

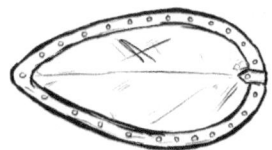

With a crash of branches and trampled leaves, the stolen horses burst from the trees and out into the early afternoon sunlight.

Lucius whipped his horse in a half circle to slow it, bearing down upon the reins with just enough force to calm its panic. The poor creature frothed at the mouth, its eyes large and buggy from the hectic galloping through the thick underbrush.

Hypnocost's mount slid to a clumsy stop beside him, followed closely by Ghdion's. Blinded by the sudden sunlight, all three men shaded their eyes, shocked at how little time had passed since they'd discovered the hidden path to the temple. It felt like an entire day had gone by. Lucius squinted up at the sky; judging by the sun's position, they'd been gone for only two short hours.

He checked behind them but couldn't hear any sounds of pursuit. Either the cultists had given up chasing them, or they'd managed to lose them in their wild rush to get away. "C'mon, we gotta find the wagon and get back to Praetorius."

It didn't take them long to find Mertha, still happily chomping at the sweet grasses near the edge of the forest. An elderly farmer stood nearby; he eyed their wagon, still pulled off to the side of the road, confusion plain on his face. He held a floppy, wide-brimmed straw hat against his chest.

"Ho, there!" he called in a thick backwoods accent, revealing a mouth full of yellowed teeth. "This yer wagon here?"

Lucius cantered up next to the wagon. His nerves screamed at him to go go go, get out of Camfield and back to Praetorius as fast as he could, but he didn't want to spook the old man. That would cause more questions than he was willing to answer and slow them down even more. So he made his features as welcoming as he could, despite the flutter of anxiety inside his chest. "It is. Is there something I can do for you, good sir?"

The old man glanced up, then did a double take as he took in the large scar down half of Lucius's face. "Oh, goodness, ya scared me!" he squeaked.

"I get that a lot."

"I'll bet!" The farmer squashed the hat back on his head. "Sorry, that was awful rude of me. I was just wonderin' why anyone in their right mind would leave a perfectly good wagon sitting right out in the open like this. Just askin' to be stolen, wouldn't ya say?"

"I doubt any would-be burglars would get very far," Lucius answered blandly. "It's very clearly labeled with the Church of Vidamae's symbol." He pointed towards the stylized sun shape that was embroidered upon the fringed flag draped over the side. "Who steals from a church?" He eyed the old man with suspicion. "*You* weren't thinking of running off with it, now, were you?"

The old man jumped a little and took a step backward. "Me? Oh, no, no, I would never!"

Lucius fixed him with what he called his 'scary eye': the milky white one on the scarred side of his face. Back when he'd been a captain in the army, he used it with terrible efficiency on some of the more rambunctious soldiers under his command. They thought he was blind in that eye; he loved using that to his advantage, usually to devastating effect. "You know that stealing from a church is a capital offense, right?"

Ghdion trotted over, scowling darkly at the old man. "Is there a problem here, Lucius? We gotta get going."

"No problem at all, sirs!" the farmer said. He removed his hat again and gave them a shaky little bow. "I'll just be on my way now. Good day to you!" He backed up slowly, bowing over and over, twisting the straw hat between his hands.

Lucius called towards him, "Hey, stay out of those woods! There's bad business happening there. I'd avoid it at all costs if I were you. Make sure everyone else in Camfield knows, too."

"Everybody already knows that," the farmer replied, scoffing. "Don't you know those woods're haunted? Y'all must not be from around here." He shook his head sympathetically. "Anyways, safe travels to ya." As soon as he was far enough away from them, he turned tail and ran flat out in the direction of Camfield, slamming his now-lumpy hat back upon his head.

Ghdion and Lucius exchanged dark looks. "Haunted, eh?" Ghdion huffed. "That's one way of putting it."

"Makes me wonder just how long those cultists have been hanging around here." Lucius eyed the edge of the forest thoughtfully. "Perhaps Midori will tell us when we get back."

Hypnocost stepped up beside them, leading a perfectly calm Mertha by the reins. She trundled along with him easily enough, unaffected by the jumpy horses who eyed her nervously. "I could not spend one more moment upon that horse's back." Hypnocost shuddered, gesturing towards the white spotted mare he'd abandoned. "I prefer to sit in the wagon on the way back to Praetorius instead, if it is all the same to you two."

"Let's get these horses hitched up along with Mertha," Lucius ordered. "We need to get back fast so we can report what we've found. Quay's gonna wanna see that blood font."

Hypnocost held the knapsack against his chest protectively. His eyes had an odd gleam of possessiveness about them, but it cleared after a moment. "Of course," he said, bringing Mertha over to the wagon hitch. "Let us move with all haste."

They made good time on the return journey. There were hardly any other travelers, and the sunny weather was perfect for their short journey. When the fabled walls of Praetorius came into view, their hopes for a quick re-entrance were dashed: a long line of travelers hoping for entrance snaked well past the gates.

Lucius groaned. "What in the hells? This line is even longer than before. We'll be stuck here all night!"

"We've got those papers Avindea gave us," Ghdion said from atop his horse. "Maybe that'll get us in faster?"

A couple guards directed traffic, instructing people to form two lines. They both looked frazzled and overworked.

"Hey," Ghdion called towards the guard nearest to them. "What if we have official papers that allow us re-entry to the city?" He waved the parchment in the air as proof.

The guard hardly looked at him and only pointed towards a shorter line. "Wait over there," he barked. "We'll get to you when we can."

Hypnocost, from the wagon bench, directed the slow-moving Mertha and their new, stolen-from-the-Kax-Temple white spotted horse over into the line. A small caravan of four colorful wagons and a few bored looking mercenaries were in line ahead of them. When Lucius smiled and nodded towards them, they pointedly ignored him.

Then they waited. And waited some more. The gawkers soon grew bored of staring at the scarred man atop the horse, for which Lucius was grateful; he'd spent most of his life dealing with similar rudeness, but that didn't make it any easier to bear. He was just better at hiding how much it affected him.

The mercenaries ahead of them pulled out a pack of cards and settled in for a game of Queens In The Castle. "You want in?" they asked gruffly; Ghdion shrugged and said, "Why not?" Hypnocost declined, saying he had a headache, and Lucius, after a split second of hesitation, swung down from the horse, tied it to the wagon alongside Ghdion's, and ambled over.

The mercenary with the deck of cards was short and stocky, with an agreeable enough face. He had a silver ring pierced through the middle of his nose. As he shuffled the cards expertly, he said, "Figured we may as well do something fun to pass the time. Gonna be a while before the guards get to us."

"Oh yeah?" Lucius replied, resting on his haunches. The other mercenary, a lanky, dark-skinned man with a head full of curly black hair, lounged across from him. An unlit smoking pipe stuck out from his lips. "You guys travel to Praetorius a lot then?"

The first mercenary nodded. "Mmm-hmm, though the leader of this caravan's thinkin' about cutting Praetorius off his route. Just ain't worth it to waste a whole day waiting to get inside, and it's gonna get worse after what just happened."

That caught Lucius's interest. "What happened?"

"You mean you weren't here to see it?"

Lucius and Ghdion both shook their heads. "Nah, we only just got here," Ghdion explained.

The second mercenary, holding up his cards, was the one who spoke next. "Oh yeah, it was the damndest thing. Some bigshot nobleman from Uldinvelm showed up with a bunch of soldiers and a fancy carriage a few hours ago. The guards let him in the city, and next thing you know, he's getting shot with arrows. It was chaos!"

Lucius blanched. An envoy from Uldinvelm was here? And they were *attacked*? What in the hells ...?

"Why do you think there's only a few guards running the checkpoint right now?" the first mercenary piped in. "The whole city's on lockdown, from what I hear. I'd be surprised if they let *anyone* inside today."

"Ah, fuck," Ghdion groaned at the same time Lucius sighed, "Shit."

"Even if we got some official papers from the Church of Vidamae allowing us entry?" Ghdion asked, a thin whining note in his voice. "What the hells good are these then?"

"Shit," Lucius muttered again. He glanced at the cards the mercenary had dealt him—what a terrible hand!—and laid them face down on the ground. "I'm out, keep going without me," he told the group as he sidled over to the wagon.

Hypnocost rested on the bench, eyes closed. "Hey, Hypnocost," he spoke quietly, not wanting to draw the mercenaries' attention. The half-elf cracked open one bright blue eye.

"Can you do a little bit of your ..." Lucius spun a finger around in the air next to his temple, "y'know, mind beams or whatever you call it, to get one of the guards to come over here and let us through so we don't have to wait?"

Hypnocost fixed him with such a fierce glare that he took a step backwards. "No, Lucius, I cannot just—" He mimicked the twirling gesture with his own hands. "It is much more complex than that! The powers I wield are not some ... some *parlor tricks* to be used on a whim!"

"Ahh, I understand," Lucius replied, a look of deep concern on his face. "You can't do it, got it."

"Now wait a moment, that is not what I said!" Hypnocost cried, sitting up.

Lucius held up his hands. "No, no, it's okay, Hypnocost," he continued. "Don't feel bad for not being able to do it. There's lots of things I wish I could do, but I just simply can't, y'know? Like I really can't wear the color red; it clashes too badly with my fucked-up face. So don't feel bad about it."

The half-elf's face turned crimson. "That is not it at all! That is not what I—!"

"Don't be so hard on yourself," he interrupted. "We're in a hurry, of course, but we'll just have to wait in line like everyone else. It's no big deal, really." He made to turn back towards the card game, fighting back a smile.

Hypnocost fully stood up in the wagon, his fists clenched at his sides. "Excuse me, guard!" he called out, his steely eyes glaring forcefully at one of the soldiers currently manning the gate. There were no theatrics, no amazing pyrotechnics that accompanied whatever spell he cast, but it was clear that whatever he had done with his mind was working: the guard's face shot up as he looked directly at him.

The guard shook his head a bit, his face shadowed beneath his plate helm. Hesitating for a moment, he took two slow steps forward until he strode purposefully towards the wagon. "How may I assist you?" he asked.

Hypnocost shot Lucius a triumphant look. Lucius, grinning, held up his hands in surrender and tilted his head ever-so-slightly forward to concede that he was wrong. *That worked better than I thought!*

"Ghdion, please show this guard our papers granting us re-entry. We are in a desperate hurry to reach the Church of Vidamae and thus, we cannot wait in line with the rest of these fine folks."

Ghdion unfolded his long legs from the ground. He thrust the papers Avindea had procured for them into the hands of the waiting guard. He eyed Hypnocost thoughtfully, one eyebrow quirked.

The mercenaries ahead of them grumbled a bit, crossing their arms over their chests to watch what they assumed would be a spectacle. "Dunno what your man just did," the first mercenary spoke as an aside to Lucius, "but this'll never work."

The guard grabbed the papers and removed his helm so he could read through them easier. To Lucius's utter horror, the guard turned out to be none other than Constable Mald, the very same city official who had accosted them the last time they tried to enter the city. The constable's close-set, pig-like eyes and wide, thick-lipped mouth were hard to forget.

Constable Mald glanced up into Lucius's face, and it was very apparent he also recognized him. He smiled darkly and arched one eyebrow. "I remember you," he spoke in hushed tones. "Kinda hard to forget a face like yours, eh?"

Lucius gulped audibly and offered a weak smile. "Heh, yeah, that's true! But this time we have papers." He inclined his head towards the document in Mald's hands. "So there shouldn't be any more problems from us."

Constable Mald looked over the papers for so long that it was apparent he was reading each word with deliberate concentration. *Well, Praetorian constables are nothing if not thorough,* Lucius thought as he stepped over towards his horse.

The second mercenary nudged his companion. "Here it comes," he chuckled softly.

"This all seems to be in order," Mald proclaimed after many minutes of awkward silence.

The mercenaries' mouths both dropped open in surprise.

Lucius, Hypnocost, and Ghdion grinned. "Of course it is," Hypnocost replied in a self-righteous tone. He settled himself more comfortably upon the wagon bench as the others mounted their steeds. "Now, if you will excuse us, we—"

"There's just one thing," Mald said, stopping the half-elf's words with a wry twist of his mouth. "It lists here that one Ghdion Guilphrame, tall, blond, dot tattoos down the entirety of his left arm —" He glanced over at Ghdion, who nodded reluctantly. "And Hypnocost, a half-elf with tattoos upon his bald head—that would be you, I presume," he regarded Hypnocost, who bowed his head, "and a Lady Quay, slender, long dark hair, priestess-in-training of Vidamae, are the three travelers who are allowed access to and from the city gates, along with one wagon and one ox, listed here as named 'Mertha.'"

He lowered the papers and fixed his gaze upon Lucius, who froze in place halfway to mounting his horse. "Am I to assume that *you* are the Lady Quay, Priestess of Vidamae?"

Lucius huffed, panic gripping its fluttery fingers upon his spine. "Obviously not. There must be some mistake. Am I not listed on the papers?"

Mald made a show of reviewing the document. "Nope, doesn't say anything here about a dark-haired man with a huge scar down the left side of his face."

"Lady Avindea must've forgotten to add me to the list, since I'm Quay's new bodyguard, and—"

"I took the time to look into you last time you came through,"

Constable Mald interrupted. His piggy eyes glinted maliciously. "It didn't take me long to find you, due to your 'unforgettable' face." He took a step towards Lucius and grabbed his forearm in a firm grip. "There's only one man by the name of Lucius Trevintor, permanently scarred all down the left side of his body, currently residing in Furow's Ridge. And ..."

Lucius closed his eyes in despair as Constable Mald finished his sentence.

"He is a captain in the Athessian Army." Mald grinned, his face only inches from Lucius's.

Hypnocost and Ghdion's faces both paled as they looked at him in shock. He let out a long, surrendering breath. "*Former* captain," he muttered, but he knew it wouldn't matter. It was too late.

Mald yanked Lucius from his perch halfway in the stirrups. "You're coming with me, *Athessian*."

Chapter 29

A Pain in the Ass

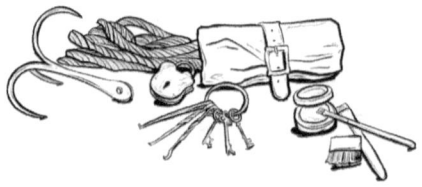

Brakten, dressed as Milford, watched from the shadows as Keegan, the mouthy rabble-rouser and perpetual thorn in Captain Riluk's side, stole hundreds of coins worth of food from the Praetorius storehouses.

I'm not even mad, he thought, crouched behind a stack of old crates in an alley across from the storehouse. *I'm actually impressed. It's like a goblin poking a dragon. The man's got a reckless audacity that I can't help but respect.*

He'd been following the man all afternoon after securing the 'Praetorian guard' following the havoc that took place at the city gates that morning. He hadn't intended on spying on Keegan—the situation with the murdered diplomat was much more important— but when he spotted him taking an unexpected route towards the capitol building, Brakten immediately followed more closely. He had a gut feeling that the man would do something bold this time, and after years of this type of work, his gut feelings were almost always right.

Keegan made a beeline straight for the storehouse, a wide, cylindrical stone building with a round shingled roof where emergency dry goods and foodstuffs were kept. Because of their contentious history with Athessa, the Praetorius government always made it a point to have supplies on hand, should further conflicts—or the threat of another siege—arise. Intrigued, Brakten tucked himself deep within the shadows where he could watch Keegan at work.

Keegan glanced behind his shoulders, checking for spectators. (*Not well enough*, Brakten thought grimly.) He rolled up his sleeves and regarded the stone wall thoughtfully. He then held up his arms, did something with his fingers, and began to *push* at the air around the stone wall.

Brakten's eyes widened as the stone began to *melt*.

The hair on the back of his head stood up as the force of the magic swept out from Keegan's outstretched hands. The atmosphere changed, grew more charged, almost as if lightning was about to strike. Whatever spell he cast was a powerful one; Brakten had never felt the tingle of magic so strongly before, and he was all the way across the street!

A large hole appeared in the side of the storehouse wall. The stone warped and twisted where Keegan directed his magic, until the hole grew just wide enough for an average-sized person to squeeze through. He then dropped his arms with a visible shudder, and the air immediately cleared.

I wonder if Riluk knows the extent of Keegan's magical powers? he wondered, drawing his hood farther down his Milford-disguised face. He itched to get closer as Keegan crawled through the new hole in the wall, desperate to see just what the man was up to. Instead, he hunkered down to wait. It was simply too risky, and for what? To see with his own eyes that Keegan was stealing food from the city? What else could he be doing, tearing magical holes in the storehouse walls?

Sure enough, about ten minutes later, he reappeared, hauling a large, heavy sack behind him. He had to yank it through the hole for it to fit, and he very nearly tumbled to the ground with the effort. Once he was out, he carefully set aside the sack, held out his arms once again, and cast the same spell. The stone firmed up around the melted edges of the hole, closing with a weird slurping sound, almost like a boot squelching through wet mud. He then brushed off his raggedy trousers, grabbed the sack of supplies, and strode away into the rapidly descending gloom of evening.

Brakten scrambled from his hiding place to follow. He stopped at the closed-up hole in the wall, peering at the stones intently. The fact that it had been spelled open at all was only noticeable if one knew where to look; a small rippled edge was all the evidence that anything had changed. Brakten was impressed with the spellwork despite himself.

Keegan headed towards the nearby Temple of Velthunas. It was one of the more populated areas he tended to frequent; the temple catered to the poor and the underprivileged even more so than the Cathedral of Vidamae. Beggars sat outside the temple, holding out their empty bowls, and street children chased each other round and round the little community garden the clerics grew there, doing what children do best: getting underfoot.

Brakten settled on a bench across the garden, where he could easily witness whatever it was Keegan was about to get up to. He grunted and groaned as he made himself more comfortable, just like an elderly man would do while taking a much-needed rest from his daily chores.

Keegan headed towards a rickety old table that was set up just outside the courtyard of the temple, beneath a tattered old awning in front of a closed-up general goods shop. A couple of the beggars perked up when he appeared, but otherwise remained where they sat, watching him intently. He set the sack on the ground beside him, started removing things from inside, and laid them neatly upon the table.

There was a sudden shift in the air, as if the street urchins, beggars, and other indigents that tended to congregate around the temple knew what was about to transpire. The aura of expectation was palpable. The kids ran over to his table, nearly knocking over a few of the beggars who rushed to their feet in their haste to reach

Keegan first. More and more people followed, and soon, a long line had formed there right at his table.

What in Aukera ...? Brakten leaned forward to get a better view.

Keegan was *giving away* what he'd just stolen. Each person waiting patiently in line received either a small box or a cloth sack, though Brakten was too far away to see what they contained. Food of some sort, he assumed.

He had to pretend he was old and weary and in pain as he got to his feet, though every nerve in his body yelled at him to rush over, to get into the line quickly to see what was afoot. He shuffled along slowly instead, grabbing at his lower back as if it ached; two beggar children ran ahead of him, laughing and teasing each other about who would beat the other to the line.

A dozen or so people waited ahead of him. He could hear them thank Keegan for his generosity as he handed over the supplies. "Velthunas bless you, Keegan," the man at the front murmured in appreciation, bowing his head in thanks. "If it weren't for you, my family would starve!"

"Tell everyone you can that it is one of their *own* who is providing for you, not the government," he replied with fervent zeal. "Consider this an act of patriotism, my friend!"

Brakten nearly snorted out loud. *Keegan, you sonuvabitch, you literally stole that food from the very government you hate so much!*

As the line moved, he got a better view of what Keegan was giving away. It was mostly grains and flour in small cloth sacks tied closed with twine, though he also scooped out a measure of dried beans for those who provided their own bags. A few of the sicklier looking citizens got metal cans, labeled 'pickled beets,' 'green beans,' 'asparagus,' and some lucky few were given containers of what looked to be salted beef or pork.

The sack at Keegan's side emptied a lot faster than Brakten anticipated. The line behind him lengthened; it was only a matter of time before he ran out of food. *I should find Captain Riluk*, he thought, glancing at the queue of impoverished people. *Though he's probably busy looking for the Athessian diplomat's murderer ...*

There came a strangled cry from the back of the line, followed by shouts of alarm. Brakten turned around to see a force of three city guards marching towards them, batons held at their sides and their shields up as if preparing for a riot.

"Disperse!" one of the guards cried out in a loud, booming voice. "Citizens are no longer allowed to gather in groups larger than four, per an emergency order given by the Plenum of Praetorius! Anyone who disregards this rule will be thrown into jail for the night!"

The line scattered, the people abandoning their hopes for free food with the threat of arrest. Brakten slipped away with them, but instead of fleeing entirely, he snuck behind one of the garden bushes to watch.

Keegan, enraged, grabbed the remaining boxes and cans and tried to thrust them into the arms of any person who ran past. They were all too frightened to take them. "Do not let them control you with their fearmongering!" he cried, making his voice louder with his magic. "A fearful populace is an easily controlled populace!"

One of the baton-wielding guards stepped towards him. "Keegan. At it again, are you? Captain Riluk won't let you off easy this time, not after the bullshittery at the gates this morning." He pushed his baton right against Keegan's chest, using more force than was strictly necessary. "Give me one reason not to knock you flat on your ass and drag you back to a jail cell."

Keegan sneered. "I've done nothing wrong, and nothing illegal! You cannot take me in for giving food away to the starving peoples of Praetorius!"

Stolen food, Brakten thought, but the guards didn't know that. Not yet at least.

"Sure we can," the soldier spat. "Inciting a riot." He threw his arm behind him to demonstrate the chaos of the dispersing crowds and the other guard who chased them down. "Resisting arrest." He pushed harder with his baton. "And generally being a pain in my ass."

"This is hardly a riot! It's a rout, more like it! Caused by you thugs in armor! And you call yourself protectors of the city? Hah!" Keegan lobbed a giant wad of spit right onto the guard's shiny leather boots.

Ah, shit, Brakten thought. *Do I step in? This is gonna go badly.* He'd seen enough similar situations in his lifetime to know exactly how this one would end up.

"Assaulting an officer of the law," the soldier replied darkly. He swung his baton down onto Keegan's forehead with such force that the crack resounded loudly against the walls of the alley.

Keegan crumpled to the ground, his last box of rations spilling across the cobblestones. The guard's heavy boots stomped all over the food as he wailed on him a second time.

"You brought this on yourself," the guard muttered, the baton held limply in his hand. He crouched down to peer at the unconscious Keegan. "After the morning we've had, the least you could do is stay outta sight, but *nooo*, you had to push your luck. Dumb bastard."

Another guard stepped over and kicked Keegan hard in the side. "This fuckin' guy," he murmured. "Makin' our jobs that much harder. Because of you," he spat, "we had to stop looking for that diplomat's murderer and come deal with your fucking mess!"

The first guard hesitated a moment, then slammed his baton against Keegan's back again. "It's his fault if we don't find that murderer!" he agreed savagely.

Soon the third and last guard joined them after unsuccessfully trying to catch the last few beggars as they sprinted for safety. Brakten winced as all three guards took turns beating Keegan senseless. There was no one around to stop them. He was an easy target. A convenient way for them to let off some steam after the stresses of the morning's pandemonium.

If I don't do something, Brakten wondered, *they could actually beat Keegan to death.* He frowned from his hiding place behind the bush. He couldn't break his disguise and rush out there to stop the guards. That would be the height of foolishness.

He scanned the area, his eyes landing upon the symbol of Velthunas painted upon the temple's front doors. *I can, however,* he realized, *go get help. It's what Milford would do.*

Riluk would have to wait. Brakten, as silent as the night that settled around him, rushed into the temple to find a cleric.

Chapter 30

Are You a Threat to Praetorius?

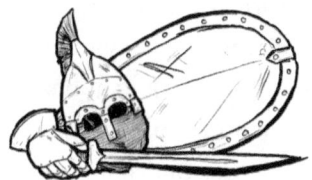

Constable Mald made it a point to hold tightly to Lucius's upper arm as he pulled him into the watchtower stationed just past the Praetorius city gate.

Lucius's heart beat wildly in his chest. This was it. This was where he'd disappear, where the Praetorian government officials would throw him into a jail cell deep underground and toss away the key. Or just execute him on the spot. Back in Uldinvelm, he'd heard of instances of enemy spies getting caught; some of the stories the soldiers would tell around the cookfires at night used to give him chills.

He never thought *he* would be the one living such a harrowing tale.

The constable sat him forcibly onto a hard wooden chair that faced an empty table inside the claustrophobic little room. He glanced around, taking in his sparse surroundings. "This the interrogation room?" he asked, trying hard to keep his tone light and unaffected. His voice wavered on the last word.

Constable Mald didn't reply. He peeked around the door,

muttered some instructions to guards standing outside, then stepped fully inside. "I'd be quiet if I were you," he grumbled. His voice was thick and slow, like his thoughts took longer to form than his words. "Save your breath for Captain Riluk."

Was Captain Riluk the person who would take him out back and slit his throat? He'd heard of captains back home who did such things. It was easier for them to eliminate a potential threat as opposed to trying to gather what information they could. Less paperwork, too.

The silence inside the interrogation room was heavy and awkward. Lucius could hear Mald's heavy breathing from just behind him. The bigger man simply loomed there ominously. When he risked a backwards glance, Mald stared right at him.

He clasped his hands tightly in his lap. His scar itched wildly, but he didn't dare scratch it. For some reason, in his addled, over-stressed mind, if he scratched his scar, Mald would wrap his meaty hands around his throat and squeeze …

The door opened and a broad-shouldered, pale-skinned older man in armor entered. He had short black hair and a square jawline. He looked slightly annoyed at first, but when his eyes landed on Lucius, his eyebrows raised in surprise. "What is this about, Constable Mald?" he asked without preamble. "Selvig told me it was urgent."

Mald crossed his arms and grinned in a decidedly menacing way. "I caught us an Athessian Captain trying to get through the gate." He dipped his chin towards where Lucius sat.

"Former captain," he clarified. He wasn't sure if he should stand or stay sitting. He made to get up, but Captain Riluk walked behind the desk, so he had to try to hastily sit back down mid-stand. He almost fell right on his ass in his haste.

Captain Riluk—that is, Lucius assumed the newcomer was the captain, based on the golden epaulettes decorating his pauldrons—waved him to sit, either not noticing or simply not caring about how uncomfortable the whole situation was. He sat heavily in the chair behind the table and regarded Lucius stonily.

There was nothing but heavy silence for a solid minute. He was well aware of the trick: Captain Riluk stayed silent on purpose as a way to make his captive squirm, to try to force Lucius to spill his secrets without being prompted.

He'd done the same thing to his captives during his time in the Athessian Army. It worked most of the time. He unclasped his fingers and forced his body into a relaxed pose. Even though he was far from relaxed, he could fake it. He simply stared right back at the captain.

Mald was the one who finally broke the silence. "Captain Riluk, he's—"

"I know who he is," Riluk interrupted without breaking his gaze from Lucius. He pulled a folded-up piece of parchment from his belt pouch and smoothed it across the table, then began to read from it. "One Lucius Trevintor of Uldinvelm. Last known to be a captain in the Athessian Army." He glanced up. "Is this true?"

"All but the captain part," Lucius replied. "Like I said. I'm a *former* captain." He leaned forward. "Is this an interrogation? Am I being officially detained?"

Riluk eyed him, his face unreadable. "Not an interrogation. This is an ... interview." He said the last word delicately.

Lucius huffed out a mirthless laugh. "Oh, so I can leave any time I want to then?"

"I wouldn't recommend that."

The constable, from behind him, growled low in his chest. "You get up from that seat, I'll knock your ass out," he warned.

So much for diplomacy. Lucius expected as much. He shrugged and slouched a little in his chair to make it seem like he was at ease. Instead of speaking, he simply regarded Captain Riluk patiently.

"Did you leave the Athessian Army of your own accord?" the captain asked with a directness that caught Lucius off guard.

He hesitated. "... Yes. But not in an, ah ... *sanctioned* manner." No, up and leaving the city of his birth without alerting anyone was definitely not considered a sanctioned removal from the military.

Riluk grunted. "So you left."

"Yes."

"How long ago?"

Lucius pondered the question a moment before answering. "Six years ago."

Constable Mald shuffled uncomfortably from his position guarding the door. "Riluk—"

The captain held up his hand for silence. "Why did you leave?"

Lucius knew he'd be asked that question eventually. He had to be careful how he answered it. This Captain Riluk seemed to be the kind of man who would know if he was lying. "I stopped believing in what the army stood for," he stated. It really was as simple as that, and besides, simple answers in situations like this were best.

Riluk grunted his acknowledgement. "So you left Uldinvelm then."

It was another old captain's trick. He hadn't actually asked a question, but the way he phrased it would prompt anyone unaware of his motives to answer anyways. Lucius knew better than that. He locked eyes with Riluk and quirked his good eyebrow.

A hint of a smile creased Riluk's face. He glanced back down at the paper. "It says here you moved to Furow's Ridge. Why there?"

Taking a deep breath through his nose, Lucius answered honestly, "It was far enough away from Uldinvelm that I wouldn't be bothered by anyone who knew me." He didn't say that he was desperate to get away from the heavily controlled, metropolitan culture of Uldinvelm. That the Ternian Czars, the three siblings who ruled over the capital city of Athessa, were thought to be going slowly insane in their quest to retake Khamris. That the military ruled everything there, that 'might makes right' was the law of the land, if not officially, in every other sense of the word. It had gotten so bad that Lucius, just before he decided to leave, would have daily panic attacks just from leaving the barracks.

"Do you plan to return to Athessa?"

He barked out a surprised laugh. "No." Living in Uldinvelm was not for the likes of him. Not anymore. "You'd have to put me in chains and drag me there to get me to go back."

The slow, sedate pace of the village of Furow's Ridge was just what he needed. And now that peace was under threat. *Maybe I shouldn't have gotten involved with Quay and the church*, he thought with a healthy measure of regret. He clenched his fists and forced himself to remain calm.

Riluk waited a moment, as if expecting him to elaborate. When he did not, he cleared his throat and shifted in his seat. "Where were you today, Lucius Trevintor of Uldinvelm?"

Oh, we're doing the full name bit now, Lucius thought wryly. Luckily, he had a ready answer, one that was both truthful and able to be independently verified. "Traveling from Camfield to Praetorius."

"Why were you in Camfield?"

That answer was a bit trickier. He settled on answering as truthfully as possible without leaving Quay and Lady Avindea out to dry. "Church of Vidamae business. Quay—she's the priestess who hired me—sent Ghdion, Hypnocost, and me there."

"And is there anyone in Camfield who could verify this information?" Riluk lifted his heavy dark brows as he eyed Lucius expectantly.

"Actually, there is. We met a farmer on the road this morning on our way back."

"How convenient." He didn't outright *say* he didn't believe

Lucius, but Riluk's tone of voice was laced with doubt. Would he actually send someone to Camfield to speak with the farmer? If Riluk had been an Athessian captain, he would have already sent a cadre of soldiers out to investigate.

Lucius was beginning to suspect things were done much differently in Praetorius.

"Did you know Lord Tullie Mason?" Riluk asked next. His posture shifted ever-so-slightly, enough so that Lucius had a feeling they were finally getting to the heart of the matter.

He shook his head. "Never heard of him."

"Were you aware that a diplomat from Uldinvelm arrived in Praetorius this very morning?"

"Only recently," Lucius supplied. "A few of the people in line with us at the gate mentioned it. Something about an attack?"

Riluk didn't take the bait. He was good. Very professional. If he hadn't been sitting on the other side of that table, Lucius thought he might even like the man. He certainly respected him.

Riluk met his eyes. His face was grave. "Are you a threat to Praetorius?"

"Not that I know of, no." He sat forward, resting his elbows on his knees. "Why don't you lay it out straight, captain: are you gonna take me out back and shoot me with some arrows or something, or am I about to be thrown in some hidden gulag deep beneath the city?"

Riluk looked startled. "Neither of those things," he responded somewhat tetchily. "I don't know what you've heard about Praetorius, but we don't do things like that here. If anything, you'll be thrown in a jail cell for a few days until we can figure out whether or not you're telling the truth."

Lucius sighed and leaned back in his chair. "Can we skip the whole jail cell business? I'm no threat to you or your city, captain, and I certainly didn't have anything to do with a diplomat's assassination. I—"

"Want me to get a cell ready for him, Riluk?" Mald interrupted eagerly.

"Now wait just a second," Lucius said, sitting upright. "If you could just find Quay, or even the paladin Lady Avindea, both of them can vouch for me!"

Riluk perked up at the mention of Lady Avindea. "I am hesitant to involve anyone outside the city guard in this situation," he said slowly. "Though I suppose it can't hurt to speak with Lady Avindea on the matter." He glanced over at Mald. "Constable Mald, would you please fetch her for me? Tell her it is urgent."

Lucius heard the constable scowl audibly from behind him. "I say we throw him right in jail," he grumbled. "He's obviously an Athessian spy, why else would he show up today of all days?"

"Thank you, Constable Mald, for your suggestion. Please, find Lady Avindea for me. Perhaps she can offer us more information to help with this."

Mald's heavy boots stomped loudly as he left, slamming the door behind him. As soon as he was gone, Riluk sighed and leaned back in his seat. He closed his eyes for a brief moment as if gathering his thoughts. "Allow me to be candid with you, Lucius," he said, his tone more sympathetic and less authoritarian than before. "You picked the worst time to show up to Praetorius."

"I gathered as much," Lucius replied dryly.

"I don't want to lock you in jail," he admitted.

The words surprised him. What kind of captain was he anyway? Who admitted things like that? "But it might be out of my hands, especially since Constable Mald happens to be the one who took you in." He rubbed his prominent chin thoughtfully. "Hopefully Lady Avindea can put in a good word for you, and between the two of us, we can figure out some creative way of keeping you out of sight for the foreseeable future."

Lucius blinked. "What are you saying?" he asked, bewildered. "You mean you're not going to 'take care of me'?"

"Like I said, we don't do things like that here," Riluk told him blandly. "I don't think you had anything to do with the diplomat's death. I think you're just an extremely unlucky sonuvabitch who happened to be in the wrong place at the wrong time."

"You're not wrong," Lucius muttered under his breath.

"But some things are beyond my control. Let's wait to see what Avindea can do. If anyone can bring us a miracle, it's a Paladin of Vidamae."

Chapter 31

A Letter From the High Priestess

Quay paced back and forth in front of the cathedral steps, nervously rubbing at her bare arms. She'd already chewed her thumbnail down to the quick. *Come on, Avin,* she thought heavily. *Please don't let me down!*

Ghdion leaned against a nearby pillar with his arms crossed, watching her quietly. He favored his right leg; she'd already healed and bandaged the knife wound he'd gotten at the Kax Temple, but she could tell it still pained him. "Avin'll come through," he rumbled. "She won't let Lucius rot away in jail. Don't worry."

Quay didn't respond. She watched as the builders contracted to complete the renovations to the cathedral worked outside. She'd gotten so used to hearing their hammering and sawing that the sounds didn't even register to her anymore. A few of them pounded away at a set of scaffolding, and a small group of them took turns hauling large pieces of lumber from the waiting wagons around the back.

She made another circuit around the open marble antechamber that wrapped around the front of the cathedral. Graceful columns held up the roof, and a smoothed balustrade wound up from the grand staircase. Quay sighed, leaning against the railing. She watched as people passed by, wrapped up in their own problems and worries. "I need to be here as soon as she arrives. I just ... what if it doesn't work? What if she doesn't have enough pull in the plenum to get Lucius released?"

"She'll get him out, Priestess," Ghdion replied from behind her. He sounded more confident than she felt about the whole ordeal.

Constable Mald came to the cathedral looking for Avindea only a few hours ago. He'd been sent by Captain Riluk to fetch her, stating that she was needed for 'further testimony' regarding Lucius and what the city guard would ultimately decide to do with him. That word—*testimony*—shook Quay to her core. Were they interrogating him? What would he say? Would they hurt him to get information? Was he being officially detained? Her gut churned with worry for him. The fact that she was essentially helpless made it doubly worse.

All of that excitement overshadowed the news of the Kax Temple and what her three bodyguards discovered there. She refused to discuss it at length, stating that it would have to wait until Avin and Lucius came back. "We gotta discuss as a group," she told them stubbornly. "And Lucius is part of our group!"

She didn't believe for one second that he was some nefarious spy. It was simply a wild coincidence or terrible luck. There was no way he was actually an Athessian spy. Right?

Ghdion shaded his eyes against the setting sun. He settled beside her against the balustrade. "I think I see them coming." He pointed down the street, towards two figures walking side by side.

Quay hiked up her skirts and raced down the steps. Avindea marched up to them, hauling Lucius by the arm.

"Oh, thank Vidamae!" Quay breathed out a sigh of relief. "Is everything—?"

Avindea, her face stormy, cut her off. "Not here. Inside." She eyed Lucius suspiciously. "I don't want all of Praetorius privy to what *this one's* about to tell us."

Lucius looked sufficiently chagrined and very wisely chose to keep his mouth shut. He didn't even struggle as Avindea pulled him around to the back entrance of the church, side-stepping a couple of builders' apprentices as she did so.

"This outta be good," Ghdion grinned wickedly at Lucius.

Lucius shot him a rude gesture as they passed through the doorway into the church.

Quay wrangled her hands as she struggled to keep up with her taller cousin's much longer stride. "What happened?" she pleaded. "I swear I had no idea he was from Uldinvelm, Avin. And besides, I don't believe for one second he's a spy! He's done nothing but help me!"

Avindea didn't respond as she took the steps downstairs two at a time. She waited outside Midori's room for Quay to unlock the door.

Quay's hands shook so badly she nearly dropped the key onto the floor. Gently Ghdion took it from her trembling fingers and undid the lock himself, sweeping his arm in a sarcastic welcoming gesture as he held the door open for them.

"Shut the door," Avindea demanded after they entered.

Midori perched at the side of the bed, and Hypnocost sat on a stool, clutching the canvas knapsack he'd taken from the Kax Temple. They both looked up expectantly at their arrival.

"What—?" Hypnocost started to say, but Avindea cut him off as soon as Ghdion closed the door.

"Speak." She thrust a finger into Lucius's scarred face. "No lies. You owe each person in this room nothing but the truth. I put my ass on the line for you, *Athessian*, so this better be good."

No one in their right mind would have dreamed of disobeying a paladin who spoke to them in that tone of voice. He held up his hands to show he meant no harm and took a step backwards until his back hit the wall. "I'm not a spy," he began, no trace of a tremor in his voice. "I never was, nor will I ever be. I'm just a simple ex-soldier who happens to hail from the capital of your city's most hated enemy."

"Not good enough." Avin reached down to her side where her

longsword was sheathed. "Do you have any idea the amount of shit I'm in after bailing your ass out?"

Quay's mouth dropped open. "Avindea, language!" she whispered. "You're a *paladin*, for Vidamae's sake!"

"Yeah, a very pissed off one at that!" she barked.

Ghdion chuckled, leaning against the wall with his arms crossed. "You didn't think to tell us *before* that you're from Uldinvelm?" he asked.

Quay eyed him sidelong; he seemed to think this whole thing was terribly funny.

"It honestly never came up!" Lucius cried. He ran a hand through his shaggy black hair. "And what was I supposed to say? 'Oh yeah, by the way, I used to be a captain in the Athessian Army, but I left the military a few years ago so I'm no longer a threat to you?' As if you would believe one word of that."

"Well, should we?" Quay asked. Her face was shadowed with his betrayal, her gray eyes large and shining with hurt.

"Yes, you should." He sighed deeply. Rubbing one hand along the blue fabric of shirt sleeves, he continued, "I honestly wanted to leave that part of my life behind. It's why I settled in Furow's Ridge. Seemed as good a place as any to start over. It was small and far enough away from Uldinvelm that nobody there knew who I was, even looking the way I do." He rested his head against the wall and closed his eyes. "The military in Uldinvelm is ... not for the faint of heart. I was good at what I did, but I ... I stopped believing in what my people stood for. I just wanted out. So first chance I got, I left. Haven't looked back since."

"You do realize we have to take your story with a healthy dose of skepticism, given what happened at the city gates this morning, right?" Avindea asked him after a moment of silence.

"Yeah, except I have no idea what happened at the city gates this morning because I *was not there*."

Avindea's face finally showed signs of uncertainty. "There was an ... attack on a diplomat sent from Uldinvelm. It's a long story, but the diplomat, the carriage driver, and three of his soldiers were killed by what appeared to be Praetorian guards."

"That sounds like a massive shit show," Ghdion murmured.

"It definitely was, which is why I'm going to be under some tough scrutiny after convincing Captain Riluk and Constable Mald to release you into my custody. It was bad enough, you being an Uldinvelm native, but to show up at the gate on *today*, of all days? That's some terrible luck."

She eyed Lucius appraisingly. "Constable Mald may not be the smartest man I know, but he's got a keen memory. You're just lucky it was Captain Riluk who questioned you and not him." She shuddered. "The only reason you're free right now is because Captain Riluk and I are on friendly terms, but I'm sure the fact that I managed to release you is gonna bite me in the ass soon. I've no doubt Mald believes you're somehow behind everything that happened with the Athessian diplomat. You'd make a very convenient scapegoat."

Ghdion scowled. "Pretty Boy didn't do anything wrong. He's been with us since we left for Camfield."

"That is true," Hypnocost agreed. "In fact, he has been with us since we left Furow's Ridge. It does not seem feasible he could have masterminded any such plan of attack against the diplomat."

"Nah, soldiers aren't that smart," Lucius said breezily. "Even captains like me. But the city guard's gonna want someone to blame, and I'm an easy target."

"That's why you're under house arrest," Avindea replied smoothly. "Well, *church* arrest, as it is. Since you're technically under my custody while the paper pushers in the city guard look into your history some more, and I can't have you tagging along with me everywhere I go, I'm limiting you to the cathedral until things settle down. No more jaunts out of Praetorius. I don't even want you leaving the building."

Lucius opened his mouth to argue and then, thinking better of it, slammed it shut. "It's the best option I've got, considering the circumstances," he mused aloud. Glancing towards Midori, he said, "Looks like you're stuck with me for a while, Midori."

Midori rolled her eyes. "I've been in worse situations," she replied in her scratchy, still-healing voice.

"Hey, you can talk!" Lucius exclaimed, beaming.

She nodded. "Not well, but yes. Thanks to your priestess here." She nodded at Quay, who smiled brightly at the group.

"Now that that's all handled, tell me what happened in Camfield," Avindea demanded.

Ghdion and Lucius exchanged an uneasy look. "We ran into a bit of a shit show ourselves," Ghdion finally replied, rubbing the back of his neck.

The three of them related the events at the abandoned Kax Temple. They told of finding the hidden path through the woods, discovering the maps and 'Testaments of Kax' and, more importantly, the blood font, and how the same assassin from Camfield, Bennett, was there. They spoke of their desperate flight from the temple and of the mysterious face that appeared in the matching mirror just before the cultists attacked.

Midori, in particular, listened closely as they described the man who spoke to them from the mirror. "What did he look like?" she asked.

She had a look of intensity that gave Quay pause. Did she know him?

"I didn't get a good look at him, but he had dark hair and eyes, shaped sorta like yours," Lucius answered her.

"What did he say to you, exactly?"

"Something about seeing us soon? I can't remember the specifics. Why? Do you know him?"

Midori didn't answer right away. "If he is who I think he is, then yes. His name is Kang." She frowned. "Are you sure you weren't followed? Did you say anything to him? Did he get a good look at you?"

"No to all of those questions, as far as I know," Lucius said. "Is Kang dangerous or something?"

"Very dangerous! You don't want him knowing where you are or anything about you. He is leading the group you came across in the temple, and he is extremely dangerous. If he finds out you are here ..." Her jagged words trailed off. "You do *not* want him to find out you are here."

A fraught tension threaded through the group as they digested her words.

"We do have some good news, at least," Hypnocost broke the tense silence. "We did manage to take this from the cultists." He held up the blood font, which looked small and insignificant in his hands. When it wasn't glowing an evil crimson, it just looked like an unadorned glass ball set in a spiky base of matte gray. "This is fascinating. How does it work? How was it created? Are there more?"

"Gods, I hope not!" Avindea cried in disgust. "Do you have any idea how many people have been killed because of that thing?" She shuddered. "It's evil. We need to destroy it." She reached out her hands to take it.

"No!" Hypnocost shouted, holding the blood font tightly against his chest. "It would be a travesty to destroy such a unique magical artifact." His eyes bugged out of his bald head, making him look a little insane for a split second before he schooled his features back to impassivity. Quay wondered briefly, *Why is he so infatuated with such a horrific magical object?* "At least allow me to examine it. I am curious to discover exactly how such a thing came to be."

"What about you?" Avindea asked Midori with a frown. "Are you planning on stealing it back and using it to finish off what your Kax-worshipping brethren started?"

"Of course not," Midori hoarsely replied, looking affronted. "I've already told you; I'm not a cultist. I've got no interest in killing any Vidamae worshippers or descendants. Haven't I proven how trustworthy I am already?" Her dark eyes flashed. "I told you where that temple would be in Camfield. Without my knowledge, you'd all still be floundering around, trying to figure out what to do next."

"You could be plotting against us," Avindea spat back. "You heard what they said, there were over twenty cultists there in the temple! Did you know that when you sent them there? Were you hoping they'd take care of them so you wouldn't have to? They're lucky they made it out alive!"

"Stop it!" Quay yelled over both of them. She *hated* conflict. It always made her extremely anxious. "We won't get anywhere with you two arguing." She took a deep breath and turned to her cousin. "Avindea, I understand your frustration, and your hesitation to trust Midori. She's done nothing but help us ever since we brought her here. I have no reason to believe she's suddenly changed her mind."

Avindea crossed her arms and pointedly looked away. "You're surrounding yourself with questionable company, Quay," she said. "First Lucius, and now Midori? You're seriously okay with trusting them with your life?"

"Hey, we're both *right here*," Lucius grumped from beside her.

"I am," Quay answered simply. "And you should trust *me*. I know I've made some mistakes in the past, but I truly believe this group here is the best chance we've got of figuring out just what is going on with the Kax cultists and the blood font resurgence."

"Honestly, we're *all* you've got," Lucius cut in.

Avindea rubbed her eyes and let out a long breath. "You're right!" she stated, throwing her arms in the air. "You're right, of course. I don't like it, but it's true."

They eyed each other uneasily. There was a heavy pause, rife with tension, as they waited for the next person to speak up.

"So what happens next?" Lucius broke the silence.

"You just tell me who I gotta hit and I'll do it," Ghdion growled, looking meaningfully at Quay. "As long as you keep paying me, I'm good to go. Everything else is just words, as far as I'm concerned."

"If you can get me out of Praetorius safely, I will continue to help where I can," Midori said, her eyes meeting Avindea's. "I must meet back up with my people. They will be wondering what happened to me, and what we should do next. You may not trust me, paladin, but my word is good."

"I want to investigate this blood font," Hypnocost repeated, unable to tear his eyes from the glass orb.

"For now, I think we all need to rest up while we get things figured out. Today's been way too exciting for my tastes," Avindea told them all. "Lucius, I'll alert the staff here that you'll be with us for an extended stay. Midori, I'll see what I can do about securing you safe passage from the city, but I won't make any promises. The way things have been going, it may take me longer than normal to make it happen."

Midori inclined her head graciously. "I understand."

"Good. Hypnocost, see what you can find out about that blood font, but make sure nobody sees it. Something that dangerous shouldn't be flaunted about. I'd hate to see what happens if somebody finds out we even have one of these inside the cathedral."

The half-elf nodded absently. "Of course."

She stepped towards the door. "And before I leave, Quay, I need to speak with you about some church business. In all this excitement, I almost forgot." She stepped out into the basement hallway and gestured towards the priestess to follow.

"I finally heard from the High Priestess," Avindea related to Quay as soon as they left the room. "She finally decided to tell me just what exactly she is doing, and where she and the other priests are heading." She took a deep breath before saying, "They're on their way to the Altar of Tasuil. They're gonna try another prayer to appeal to Vidamae."

Quay's mouth dropped open. "Again? But why?"

"Because it really is happening again. You were right, Quay. All this Kax stuff you've been discovering? High Priestess Lucina knew about it and just didn't tell anyone." She gritted her teeth, forcing back her anger with difficulty. If she only had some sort of prior warning, she could have better prepared Quay's team. What was the high priestess thinking, keeping everything so hush-hush? "She finally decided to send me a letter explaining it all, and I only just received it today." Avindea reached into her pocket and pulled out a folded piece of parchment that looked like it had been crumpled up and smoothed back out multiple times. "Here. You can read it if you want."

Quay took the letter, her face pale and full of concern. She began to read:

Lady Avindea,
First, I wanted to start this letter by thanking you for

your willingness to step in for me as the interim Church of Vidamae plenum advisor. I know you believe yourself to be a poor choice for the seat, but I would not have asked you if I didn't know you were more than up to the task.

With that being said, I feel it is now necessary to relate to you the reason for my absence, and why I've gathered the highest-ranking priestesses and clergy members of Praetorius to join me. We are currently making the pilgrimage to the Altar of Tasuil, where, after gathering the other ranking members on the way, we will all come together once again to entreat our Goddess Vidamae with another prayer. Why do we need to do this again, you ask? I hate for this to be the vehicle by which you receive this upsetting news, but we have reason to believe Kax and Her ilk are once again attempting to eliminate Vidamae's followers and brethren with the same plot from 15 years ago, and with the same evil doings that preceded The Troubles. There have been troubling reports of murders within our church happening in smaller villages around Khamris. There is enough evidence to suggest this latest plot is just as dangerous as the last, and we, as a group, have decided to take drastic measures to stop it before it gets out of control once again.

We did not want to alarm any of our parishioners, nor panic the younger clergy and paladins, hence the reason for all of the secrecy. Hopefully by the time this letter reaches you in Praetorius, we will be nearing the altar, where preparations will begin immediately for the casting of the spell. I wanted you to know of our plans, but I beg of you, do not reveal the whole truth to the others. I fear it may start a panic. Please forgive me, as I chose to keep this *information closely guarded only to keep our flock safe. I truly hope you understand.*

It goes without saying that, due to the urgency of our quest and the need for the utmost secrecy, you must destroy this letter as soon as you've read it.

Say a prayer for us as we strive to reach our most beloved goddess, and that She, in turn, answers our prayers.

May Vidamae's blessed light blanket you in peace,
High Priestess Lucina Balladoni

Quay was silent after she finished the letter, but her face, always so expressive, showed her roiling emotions clearly. "How ... why ..." she sputtered. "Why would she do this? Why keep something so important a secret?"

"That's exactly what I thought," Avindea replied. "It doesn't seem very smart for her to try to keep such a big piece of news under wraps. It really is just as bad as The Troubles all over again."

"What was it like, Avin?" Quay asked softly. "I hadn't begun my training yet, and besides, I was, what, only thirteen when it all started? Too young to really understand what was happening, anyways. You were already a squire back then, weren't you? Do you remember what happened?"

Avindea stared off into the middle distance as the memories washed over her. She was fifteen when The Troubles started, but already well into her training as a paladin squire. The paladin who sponsored her was named Lord Mithrous de Cullen, a haughty, long-faced minor noble who didn't take the word of Vidamae as seriously as she did. He made all the right motions, spoke all the correct words of their prayers, but he confused her greatly when he brushed aside any part of the church's precepts he didn't particularly agree with.

Faith and Ruin

He was a Paladin of Vidamae! Why did he so flagrantly disregard some of the most important rules?

It wasn't until she grew older and more world-wise that she realized he hadn't joined the paladins out of a sense of righteous duty like she had. He hadn't had a calling to a higher power. For him, it had only been a means to an end: he gave his time and service to the Church, training and crusading as a paladin in exchange for the Priestesses of Vidamae to help him in his bid for his family's succession.

She'd been so furious when she found out! That wasn't what being a paladin was supposed to be about. They were supposed to fight for the greater good, right wrongs, protect the weak. She could remember, fifteen years ago, watching as the more seasoned warriors among them, resplendent in their shining golden armor and atop their powerful steeds, left in a glorious charge to avenge the fallen and take justice against the evil Kax cultists who had done such atrocities against the Church. She'd been so proud! She would be one of them someday, an avenging holy warrior for Vidamae, righting wrongs and slaying the wicked. She may have only been fifteen, but she felt as strongly as the older paladins did. Her religious zeal would lead her to victory against all who strove against Vidamae's Chosen.

Why hadn't Lord Mithrous gone with the rest of the vanguard, she wondered? When she had asked him, he only scoffed and gave lame excuses: he was needed in Praetorius, or he had to remain near the cathedral so she could continue her training. Even then, she thought his reasoning weak, but who was she to question? She was, after all, merely a *squire*. Lord Mithrous knew more about being a paladin and more about the world than she did.

When the paladins returned from their crusade against Kax, however, everything changed. They were victorious, bloodied but not beaten, fresh from the battlefront against the nonbelievers. Avin and the other squires were desperate for stories of valor, but when pressed, the older paladins would only scowl and push the teenagers away and demand they continue with their training.

She finally got her wish when she happened upon Lord Mithrous speaking with another paladin who had been on the front lines.

She didn't mean to eavesdrop, not really. She had been looking for Lord Mithrous's breastplate to polish like he'd asked her to. Did it really matter that, once she overheard them talking, she could have snuck away to give them privacy, but instead had stopped to listen when Lord Mithrous asked, "And just how many women and children did you kill?"

She paused, thinking she must've heard that wrong. But the other paladin answered, "Oh, probably forty or fifty? It was mostly women and children at the camp. There was hardly any resistance!" The other paladin chuckled. "You should've seen their faces, Mithrous. They were crying for Kax even as we cut down their children in front of them! As if that fucking weak excuse for a goddess would do anything to save them. Kax is so feeble She can't even keep Her followers safe from Our Lady Vidamae's shining, righteous light!" They both chuckled after that.

She remembered almost dropping the breastplate from her suddenly cold fingers, nearly revealing herself. She remembered the sick feeling in her stomach, how it did not go away for days, and how she was laid up in the infirmary for almost a week because of it. She remembered not saying a word of it to anyone else, praying fervently that it was all just a fluke, that the paladin Lord Mithrous had spoken to was just an anomaly amidst the ranks. Surely not *all* of the older paladins were like that? Surely they didn't just massacre an entire encampment of innocents, Kax believers or not?

She remembered hearing, in hushed whispers, some of the other paladins speak of a few of their siblings-in-arms disappearing, ostensibly to 'find themselves' on holy journeys of self-discovery, but in actuality they were leaving the church in droves because of their feelings of intense shame. Many of them didn't make it, choosing instead to take their own swords to their bellies rather than live with what they had done.

She knew in her heart that she was telling lies to herself. Not all of the paladins she served with were as vicious, cold-hearted, and cruel as that one from fifteen years ago, but many of them were. She saw it even to this day, in the way some of them delighted in killing, in their desires to go on more crusades, to start fights, to find any excuse to swing their blades, all in Vidamae's name.

And what did that make her? She wasn't cruel and didn't believe in reckless hatred; she truly believed in Vidamae's doctrines and sought only to make the world a better place for having her in it. But the truth was she had remained silent about those atrocities. Was she also complicit in their crimes? Would it have mattered if she'd spoken up?

Avindea blinked, banishing the tough questions from her thoughts. She had to focus on the present, and what she could do now to help mitigate any further damage. "I don't want to talk about it," she finally answered Quay.

Her cousin shot her an inquisitive look, but Avindea pointedly ignored it. "So what do we do?" Quay asked.

Sighing, Avin shrugged. "Honestly? I have no idea, Quay. I'm out of my depth here, and the one person who could possibly help is at least two days away on an arguably futile secret mission for the church. I almost wish she hadn't told me. Ignorance truly is bliss."

"Well, why don't *we* go to *her*?" Quay suggested, brightening considerably. She always operated best when she had a plan in place, when people needed her. "Ghdion, Hypnocost and I can travel to the Altar of Tasuil. We'll just say we are continuing my training, checking out the remaining congregations on the way. We can tell High Priestess Balladoni all that we've discovered about Kax, and she can tell us what we should do next!"

"Maybe," Avindea replied with reluctance. "It's an awfully long journey, and there's no guarantee you'll reach the altar in time. Besides, the trek might be dangerous. Who knows what kind of creatures or bandits or other things might be lurking out there?"

So much was happening all at once. It was overwhelming. "Let's sleep on it, okay? Everything'll look better in the morning. Besides,

I've gotta get back to the capitol anyway. No rest for the wicked, right?"

"Alright." Quay reached out and squeezed her shoulder comfortingly. "It'll be okay, Avin, I just know it. We'll get this all figured out, you'll see!"

She offered her cousin a weak smile. "I hope you're right!"

Chapter 32

A Little R & R

A deep, steaming hot bath was waiting when Ghdion stepped into the luxurious bathing chambers at the Cathedral of Vidamae.

It was one of the many perks of being employed by the church. Aside from the excellent pay, the cathedral boasted the city's best bathhouse, situated on the first floor, right between the main nave and the small hospital. Anyone who worked within the church in any capacity, be it the highest-ranking priestess or a newly hired janitor, was allowed to use the bathing facilities, and Ghdion always made good use of that particular perk every chance he got.

The main room was large and echoey, the floor to ceiling covered in intricately painted tiles. There were metal racks of fluffy towels for bathers to dry with, and spaced evenly along the walls were magically lit, elaborately designed sconces. A giant mosaic depicting Vidamae's sunburst sigil decorated the bottom of the largest public pool, where a few people lounged, wearing loose fitting bathing clothes. Smaller, more private pools branched off on the sides, separated by thick white curtains that could be drawn shut for privacy.

The church employed full-time staff just to keep the giant tubs and shallow pools full of water. The water was not too hot, but just warm enough to relax into after a hard day's work. They claimed it was good for healing; who was he to judge? Ghdion wasn't sure of the specifics on how it all worked, but they used a combination of hot stones and magic to keep the water at the perfect temperature.

He headed immediately to his favorite private pool, all the way at the back. It was the perfect place for him to go when he wished to be alone; no one bothered him while he was there. Grabbing a towel off the closest rack, he strode into the cubby and pulled the curtain closed behind him.

It felt good to get his travel-stained clothes off. He shoved his worn-in leather boots, smallclothes, white(ish—it badly needed a wash) homespun cotton shirt, soft leather breeches, and his socks into a pile in the corner, then stepped, nude, into the calm, dark waters of the pool.

He released a sigh of pure relaxation as he sank beneath the bath's surface. There was nothing quite like a hot bath after a stressful day. Well, stressful *few weeks*, truth be told. In a life full of unexpected twists and turns, and one lived as rough and hard as his, he would take what small pleasures he could get.

The bath water was perfumed with lavender and other herbs he didn't know the names of. The stillness of the surface broke only when he shifted to get more comfortable. A little tray of sponges, oils, shampoos, and soaps sat near the edge; as much as he would rather float there silently in the steamy bath for hours, he decided it would be best to get the scrubbing over with so he could fully relax.

He found he did his best thinking while in the bath. He didn't look it, but he was a man who enjoyed a good soak and a long think. It helped him organize his scattered thoughts, helped bring some semblance of order to an otherwise messy lifestyle. He also *hated* being dirty. It came with the territory, traveling and fighting as much as he did, but it never failed to make him feel supremely perturbed every day that passed between baths. Dirt beneath his fingernails or between his toes? It always made him feel itchy just knowing it was there.

He'd gotten into the habit of daily baths back when he was a fighter in the Pits of Gilden—the prison itself was as hellish as one would expect from a place that housed Aukera's worst criminals, but they certainly knew how to keep their greatest fighters scrubbed and cleaned. It was one of the perks of winning the gladiatorial battles there. And Ghdion won *a lot*. The dot tattoos on his arm—one for each challenge won—proved it.

He sank all the way beneath the water until only his eyes and nose were visible, allowing himself the necessary quiet to ruminate. Foremost in his thoughts was the Kax situation, naturally. He was no strategist or great thinker: he'd let the others figure out how to untangle that mess, but he could kill as many Kax cultists as Quay demanded of him. His strength was in his sword arm: when they told him who to hit with his sword, he would do it, no questions asked. Especially with as much as they were paying him.

He especially trusted that Quay would make the right decision. How could she not? She was goodness and purity personified. He would lay down his life for her if she asked him to, though he suspected she didn't know just how committed to her he actually was.

Since working for her, he'd finally found his *purpose*. He'd had that realization shortly after she hired him. For a man whose past was nothing but a series of tragedies that happened *to* him, it was refreshing to be given some say in the matter, even though Quay was technically his *boss*.

Thinking of Quay made his face flush and his heart beat faster. These feelings were really getting out of hand. He imagined her lovely face, her smooth skin and sparkling gray eyes. How she knew what to say to pull him out of a sour mood. The way she smiled at everything, how she always smelled like plums, which were his favorite. The tiny dimple in her left cheek when she smirked at his stupid jokes.

I'm nothing but a dirty old man, he thought to himself fiercely. *I gotta stop thinking about her like that.*

He couldn't help it, though. He was already intensely attracted to her, and it was all he could do to keep those feelings strictly to himself. It couldn't hurt to daydream about her, though, could it? Just in his imagination, where it was safe for him to act on his impulses. Where she would confess she had feelings for him, too, where he could finally pull her close and bring his lips to hers ...

He dunked his suddenly overheated face beneath the water, so he didn't hear the curtain as someone drew it open. When he brought his head back to the surface, his heart beat wildly at the sight of Quay stepping inside the private cubby.

"Quay!?!" he sputtered, splashing water all over the sides of the pool. "What the hells are you doing here?"

"Sorry, I had to talk to you!" she cried, her eyes wide as she caught sight of him. "I didn't see you in the public baths, so I asked the usher where you were, and he told me you were in here." She peered down at him more closely. He didn't miss the way her eyes traveled from his face all the way down his front. "Are you ... oh my gods, Ghdion, you're naked!"

"Well, yeah, I *am* in the bath."

Her face burned a red as bright as a brand. She slapped her hands over her mouth and whirled around so her back was to him. "I didn't—I mean, I thought you were—ugh, I'm sorry, Ghdion, this is highly inappropriate." She took a hasty step towards the curtain to make a swift escape.

He didn't want her to leave. "Wait a sec, Quay, what was so important you had to talk to me about it in the baths, of all places?" The bath water was dark, steamy, and deep enough that only his neck and head were visible, but he covered his groin with his hands, just in case.

Even in such a compromising position, he desperately wanted her to stay. They had barely exchanged two words since he'd returned from Camfield and, fool that he was, he was eager for more time with her.

"It's nothing," she muttered, drawing the curtain open slightly. "I'm really sorry I disturbed you."

"Quay." Something in his voice made her stop. She shot him a backward glance, arching her eyebrows. "Talk to me."

"But you're in the bath, and—"

He waved her concerns away. "It doesn't matter. You can't see anything past my neck anyways, and besides, you've seen most of me already by now, right? How many times have you had to heal my sorry ass?"

She huffed a laugh. "Do you mean literally? Like the time that demonic pig Princess gored through your left butt cheek and I had to—"

"Yeah, yeah, I remember," he interrupted with a chuckle. *That* particular healing had been both embarrassing and extremely arousing; he had to pull his trousers down—right there in Little Rushford's Church of Vidamae—and she had to put her hands upon his bare ass to heal the deep wound caused by the pig's tusks.

He felt his face flush with the remembrance of it. Shoving those feelings aside, he said, "Tell me what you wanted to tell me."

"Fine." She turned towards him fully but didn't quite meet his eyes. "While you were gone, I did some digging into the old Vidamae history books in the basement."

She stared somewhere upwards and to the left of his eyes, at a spot on the tiled wall behind him, so as not to accidentally lay her eyes upon his nude body. "One of them had lists of all the churchgoers who were killed during The Troubles fifteen years ago."

Ghdion's face fell. He had a feeling he knew where this was going. "Yeah? And?"

"I found a familiar name listed there. Guilphrame. That's your last name, right, Ghdion?"

He could only nod mutely.

"There were four Guilphrames murdered in Camfield during The Troubles. One Sari Guilphrame, and her three daughters Aisling, Ronia, and Bea. They were survived by one Ghdion Guilphrame, their husband and father, respectively."

Just hearing their names made his whole body go cold. Not even the heat of the bath water could thaw the chill that crept up his spine. "Quay, don't," he whispered through trembling lips.

"Ghdion, why didn't you tell me you had a family?"

"Stop," he told her, his words as icy as his cold, dead heart had been on that day. The day his life had ended. "You weren't supposed to know, you shouldn't have found out ..."

He could see their faces so clearly, even now. Sari, her blue eyes forever closed, her lanky blonde hair streaked with blood ... little Bea, fallen behind her sisters Aisling and Ronia as they used their tiny bodies to try to shield their baby sister from harm ...

"Ghdion, I'm so sorry!" Quay breathed, tears welling in her eyes. "Did you know she was a descendant of Vidamae? Did you know that was why she was mur—"

"I said STOP!" he bellowed, his words echoing loudly in the enclosed space. He could no longer keep the stricken look of horror off his face. The memories were closing in, fully freed from the tight confines where he kept them locked away inside of his mind. He couldn't deal with this, not now!

Quay's whole body froze, except for the tears that streamed down her cheeks. "Ghdion, I—"

"Get out."

"Please, let me help—"

"I said get OUT!" He stood to his full, formidable height, water streaming down his body. He didn't even care that he was naked, he was so full of hurt and fear and rage. He trembled uncontrollably, fists clenched tightly at his sides. His chest heaved once in a shuddering breath and he said quietly, "Just go, Quay. Never speak of this again."

She fled, not looking behind her as she ran past the curtain.

He stood there for so long that his whole body erupted in gooseflesh, despite the warmth of the air. That was okay, though. He deserved it after being such an asshole to the one person who had shown him kindness, the one who had begun the long process of thawing his frigid heart.

It would be better to keep to himself, to not let anyone in. Then there would be no risk that it would all happen again, that everything he loved would be taken away. He was broken, and no amount of teasing or laughter or kindness from the priestess would fix him, no matter how hard she tried. No matter how much he wished he could be fixed.

Some things just could not be healed.

"So you're from Uldinvelm," Midori said to Lucius when they were finally alone.

Lucius pulled over a stool and sat next to her bed, a thoughtful look upon his face. "Yep, I'm from Uldinvelm."

"So I'm not the only one with secrets, it seems."

Hypnocost had spent a good hour badgering her with questions about the blood font. Everyone else had left, gone to clean up or rest or do whatever it was they did when they weren't stuck babysitting her in the tiny room she was growing to loathe. She tried to keep the annoyance out of her voice as she answered Hypnocost as best she could: no, she didn't know how the blood font was made, no, she didn't know how it worked, yes, she knew what it did, but that was all.

He assured her it was only scientific curiosity, but something about the half-elf was off to her; she didn't quite trust that he was all that he seemed to be, especially after his disastrous attempt to read her mind. It was the way he would mutter to himself sometimes, when he didn't think anyone was paying attention. And sometimes she saw an odd glint in his eyes, like he wasn't fully listening, wasn't totally *present* or engaged with the people around him. Like he was conversing with himself or perhaps hearing voices inside his head.

She shuddered to think of that. As long as he didn't try to get inside *her* head again.

She could tell Hypnocost wasn't fully satisfied with her answers. When Lucius finally came back, his black hair damp from a bath and wearing clean clothes, Hypnocost headed for the door without a word, focused entirely on the blood font in his hands.

"You'll wanna leave that in here," Lucius had to remind him. "Can't have anyone seeing that out and about." There was a note of warning beneath his good-natured words.

Hypnocost jolted guiltily. He smiled weakly as he placed the blood font back inside the pack, saying, "Yes, yes, of course!" before he left. He seemed strangely reluctant to let go of the thing.

Lucius sighed as he settled in. "I didn't mean for it to be a secret, not really," he answered her earlier question. "It just ... never came up."

She shot him a knowing look. "How convenient for you." Her scratchy voice was dripping with sarcasm.

"Y'know, I liked you better when you couldn't talk." He smiled as he said it, so she knew he was joking. He leaned back against the wall, trying to get comfortable atop the wooden stool, resting one booted foot on the bottom rung. "You doin' alright?"

She nodded. For being stuck inside the same room for days now, she was at least given everything she asked for, like her soft bed, clean clothes, and surprisingly decent meals. Even the doctor who would check up on her each morning was respectful and kind. She had nothing whatsoever to complain about, except for the fact that she desperately wanted to get out of there. Her people were out there still, waiting for her. "Can you get me out of this place? That is the only thing I want."

Lucius gestured towards the door. "Nobody's stopping you from leaving. I wouldn't suggest it, though, given how tense everything is out there with the city guard and, y'know, a *war* starting." He rolled up his white shirt sleeves, revealing one toned forearm and one covered entirely by burn scars. The scars wrapped around his wrist, down his knuckles, and even roughened his palm and the pads of his fingers. "Just say the word and I'll get you whatever you need."

He glanced sidelong at her. "Or you could be patient and wait for Avindea to come through with those papers. It's up to you."

She scowled at how casually he offered her a freedom she knew she couldn't take, not yet. It would be extremely foolish of her to step out of the safety of the cathedral, being who she was and without the protection of the official paperwork Avindea had promised her. "You know I cannot leave," she grumbled, crossing her arms over her chest. "And neither, apparently, can you. Now *you* see what it's like being stuck inside this place!"

He grinned at her then, and she was surprised and a little bit annoyed at how fluttery her chest felt at the boyish charm the smile brought out in his face. He could have been beautiful. He had a straight, proud nose with a rounded tip, full lips, one large, liquid brown eye, the other milky white due to the scars; perhaps it was a blessing that the scar distracted so heavily from his natural beauty. Imagine how radiant, how irresistible he would have been without it!

Looks weren't really what drew her to the man, though. It was his relentlessly upbeat attitude, the deliberate way he spoke, the directness of his gaze when he spoke to her. While the others saw her only as a Kax follower and judged immediately based on that, Lucius saw her for who she actually was. He made her feel *seen* in a way she hadn't for a long time.

"Eh, I think of it as a nice vacation. The cathedral's not so bad. They've got decent food, nice bedding and clothes, and apparently there's even a bathhouse upstairs. We'll have to check it out when we get a chance.

"Besides," he continued, "all the clergy here are *aggressively* nice. It's like they try to outdo each other in who can be the best, most helpful person. It's a little sickening, honestly. Nobody is *that* good, not really."

A snort of laughter burst from her lips. "Except maybe Quay," she admitted. "She's so genuinely sweet she may as well be made of sugar."

"It's disgusting, isn't it?" He laughed along with her. "Ah, well. I can't help but like her, though. She gives off a very eager, very impressionable *little sister* energy. Makes it really hard not to wanna be friends with her. Best boss I've ever had, hands down. And she pays extremely well."

Midori nodded. "I worry about her," she admitted slowly, chewing her lower lip. "And the rest of the priestesses here. They are all so naive and trusting. They have no idea what the real world is like out there. Should anything bad happen, they won't know how to react."

"*You're* worried about the Vidamae Clergy?"

"You know what I mean!" she spat, flushing. "I had no idea their priestesshood was like this. I'd always been told they were close-minded and quick to judge. All beautiful and haughty and arrogant, looking down their noses at everyone else. They are the boogeymen of all Kax followers' childhoods. 'Stay away from the Vidamae Church,' I was always told. 'If they find out you worship Kax, they will stop at nothing to eliminate you!'"

She rubbed her arms to try to rid herself of the sudden gooseflesh that pebbled her skin. "And that was certainly true of my childhood, at least. All of my experiences of the Vidamae religion proved it, right up until this point."

"What happened?" he asked gently. The look of concern in his eyes was so kind that she had to look away for fear of being overwhelmed by it. She didn't want his pity, but that wasn't what he offered, not really. It was sympathy, not pity, that motivated the question. The difference between the two was vast.

"I don't remember it all. I was young when The Decimation happened, eleven or twelve. A great galloping horde of Vidamae's Paladins tore through our village on their horses, burning, killing, and pillaging. My parents tried to fight back, but two of the paladins killed them right in front of us. Just like that, they were dead." She made the motions of a sword stabbing with her hands in the air. "The paladins were about to finish us off when my brother dragged me into the woods, where we hid in the trees until they left. They burned every home. They pulled people from their hiding places and ... and *brutalized* them right there in the street. Then they sliced their throats with their shining swords when they were done with them."

She could still smell the smoke from the fires that burned that day. She recalled scrubbing at her favorite pink skirt, over and over, to try to get the smell out ... "I remember thinking, why us? What did we do to make them so angry? None of the people in my village were a part of the group that started the hunt with the blood fonts. We didn't even know what the blood fonts *were*! We were peaceful! Our mayor even pleaded with the paladins as they tore through the town. He told them we weren't with the other Kax people, that we weren't fanatical cultists at all. But none of them listened. They just lopped off his head and kept right on killing."

Lucius stared at her with a look of horror mixed with pity. "Gods, Midori. No kid should ever have to witness such cruelty. And to think, this was all perpetrated by Paladins of Vidamae?!"

She pursed her lips and nodded. "Most don't believe me when I tell that story. Vidamae is the Goddess of *Life*! Her paladins would *never* act in such a way! That's what they have always believed. Kax has been so demonized that anyone who chooses to follow Her doctrines is automatically labeled a cultist and is not to be trusted. I have heard that Kax followers aren't as hated in other parts of Aukera as in Khamris, but ..."

She sighed. "That was the worst part of Vidamae's crusade

against us, I think. Aside from the killings, Her church spread such hateful lies about us, inflamed the prejudices so much that they've stuck for years. It's almost impossible for any group of Kax followers to live a life of peace here."

"Is that what you're looking for?" he asked softly. "A life of peace?"

"Yes." She closed her eyes. As reluctant as she'd been to speak of her past, it was almost a relief to have it out in the open, if only to Lucius. "My group has been seeking that for years now. We have no home to call our own. We have to travel in secret, scrounge what we can from the land, and we're always afraid of discovery. It is ... not an easy life." She finally turned to look at him, pain and sorrow in her dark eyes. "We hate what the cultists are doing just as much as the rest of you. We've been trying to stop their plans and murders for so long! But we're so small, so weak from life on the run, there is not much we can do. Besides," she sighed heavily, "it's almost too late. The cultists have been infiltrating cities across Khamris for almost a decade now. They are even inside Praetorius, waiting for the right moment to strike."

Lucius gulped audibly. "You know this for certain?"

Midori hesitated before answering. "I do. I do not know who, specifically, is here in the city, but I have it on good authority that someone well-placed in society, perhaps a noble or city official, is one of the Kax cultists. Why do you think I was so concerned when you told me about the face in the mirror at the abandoned Kax Temple in Camfield? If Kang discovers who you are and where you are hiding ..."

She shook her head, her short black hair swinging against her ears. "So please, believe me when I tell you we are on the same side."

"I believe you," he told her gently. "I've always believed you, Midori. You don't have to prove anything to me."

She gazed into his eyes, one dark and one light. It was right then she realized that she did actually trust him. Trust didn't come easily to her, not after her tumultuous life spent running and eking out a wretched existence of simple survival. But somehow this man wormed his way inside her head and laid a claim to a part of her. Maybe it was because she'd been stuck with him for so long, but she didn't think so. Not really. He was simply an easy man to rely on.

She opened her mouth to tell him how she felt when they heard a faint scuffing noise just outside the door.

Lucius was immediately on high alert. He stood in a silent, fluid motion and was next to the door faster than her eyes could track. Reaching out to grasp the handle, he locked eyes with her as she watched mutely. Placing a finger on his lips to indicate she should remain silent, he slowly turned the handle and cracked the door open to peek out into the hallway.

His shoulders slumped with relief a second later. He opened the door fully to reveal Ghdion, a towel draped around his neck and his hair wet and hanging in his eyes.

"Gods, Ghdion, you scared the shit outta me," Lucius breathed, stepping aside so he could come in. "You eavesdropping?"

"Not on purpose," the tall man answered. He looked decidedly glummer than usual, which was saying something. He was always either scowling or swearing. "I was looking for Quay. Did she come down here?"

Lucius shook his head. "Nope. You alright? You look a little, ah ... perturbed."

He waved a hand to brush him off. "I'm fine. I'll leave you to it. Gonna head to bed."

"You heard all that, didn't you," Lucius accused his retreating back.

Ghdion stiffened in the doorway. "Maybe. You aren't gonna hear any arguments from me, though, if that's what you're worried about. For what it's worth, I believe Sunshine over there." He glanced at Midori as he said it; she scowled at the nickname, but made no comment. "The Vidamae Church has never done me any favors, so it's not that big of a stretch for me to believe some of their paladins are bloodthirsty bastards."

Midori acknowledged him with a sharp nod. For some reason, the man's unexpected support brought a lump to her throat.

"You want us to send Quay to find you if she turns up?" Lucius asked.

"Nah." He stepped through the doorway. "I don't think she wants anything to do with me right now." He disappeared around the corner, sounds of his heavy tread retreating up the stairs.

Chapter 33
A Bold Step

Five Years Ago

The Augur's door was unlocked.

He never locked it. Midori knew this as she crept silently across the threshold, pulling the rickety wooden door closed behind her. Everyone called the cozy offshoots from the mining tunnel 'bedrooms,' but they weren't actually rooms, not really; they were more like small caves that could theoretically be served as private sleeping quarters. They even hung ill-fitting doors crafted out of scrap wood and rusted nails for privacy. This was how the vicars attempted to make the mining complex feel more 'homey.'

Midori glanced behind her to double, no, *triple-check* that nobody was watching. It was late—most of the Kax faithful were already fast asleep, though it was hard to tell the exact time deep within the mine. The chances of someone being up and about were slim.

The door latched quietly behind her, and she let out a soft, relieved breath before surveying her surroundings. She'd been inside his room many times before, but she was still surprised by how *sparse* he kept his personal space. For a man so revered, he certainly lived a humble lifestyle. He had only the necessities: a cot large enough for a single person, a squat bedside table cobbled together from uneven wooden planks, a shallow bowl full of clean water, and a few half-melted candles, probably for his scribes, arranged on top of it. His extra clothes were folded neatly on a wooden bench, and a crate that once housed mining tools served as a catch-all storage for his personal effects.

The Augur was asleep in his cot, his frail, bony form covered with a single blanket. Miraculously, he hadn't heard her enter. How had she gotten so lucky? His hearing was impeccable since the loss of his eyesight. But he was old, and constantly weary, always complaining of his sore bones. Perhaps he was so exhausted that a midnight intruder was not enough to stir him awake?

She mouthed a silent prayer to Kax as she tip-toed towards the storage crate. It was filled with papers, extra scraps of cloth he used to cover his horrifically empty eye sockets, broken quills, a clumsily carved symbol of Kax on a string. *The documents must be in here somewhere*, she thought as she crouched down and began to slowly, carefully remove the loose parchments one by one from the crate.

It was hard to see what she was doing in such dim lighting; a feeble band of torchlight shone through the large crack at the bottom of the door, but it wasn't enough to see well by. She squinted as she scanned the scribbled words on the papers, looking for anything related to the crafting of the blood fonts. None of the words were written in The Augur's hand, of course, as he couldn't see to write any longer. He had three scribes assigned to him, their only job to record all his knowledge.

The top sheaf of parchment read: *It is of particular importance that the essence collected be as pure as possible. The only way to achieve that is to construct a—*

This isn't it. She read through a few different sheets, with no luck. It was all instructions that were very dense, very technical, and very much over her head. *It doesn't matter*, she told herself firmly. *These need to be destroyed. We cannot make more blood fonts.*

A few years ago, she realized that it was up to her to stop the vicars' plans of destroying as many Vidamae descendants and followers as possible. Her pleas for peace fell on deaf ears, and none of the vicars would deign to meet with her, including Aunt Solange. Apparently Midori was an outcast simply for entertaining her wild ideas of *letting go* of the grudges of the past and moving on.

Bennett, once one of her closest friends, hardly spoke to her anymore, and Kang was too wrapped up in his vengeance quest and his desperation to prove to the vicars that he was loyal and worthy. The other followers who lived in the compound felt, if not the same, at least sympathetic to the vicars' cause; why should they work against the leaders who provided them safe harbor all these years? They preferred to turn a blind eye to any violence committed. Ignorance was bliss, and most of the people living in the mining compound found it more convenient to believe in *the plan* than to oppose it.

The plan. She scowled to herself in the dark. All things served *the plan*. What even was it? A loose decree to do whatever they could to further the creation of more blood fonts? More blood fonts to be used to hunt down more Vidamae descendants and kill them? But why? Why further the bloodshed? Did that not make them as bad as the Vidamae Paladins who wreaked such havoc on their lives before? Was this really what Kax wanted them to spend their time doing?

Kax never seemed to answer Midori's prayers, but the sick feeling in her stomach every time *the plan* was discussed was enough to spur her to action. She began gently questioning some people who seemed as distraught as she was by the prospect of another phase of The Decimation. It took a while to suss them out—only around a dozen people reluctantly shared her sentiments of peace after gentle and repeated prodding—but it was enough to keep her motivated.

A few of her new friends were wary; Samuel, a man not much older than her, was always asking, "Is this wise? Should we be talking about this?" Midori had to constantly reassure him that, yes, it was well within their rights to form alternate opinions from those of the vicars.

Nobody else was willing to step up. She had to stop this madness from continuing. And the only way she could think of doing that was to destroy the notes about the creation of the blood fonts. If there were no instructions, it stood to reason that no more blood fonts could be crafted.

She tried stealing away their lone blood font to destroy it herself, but it proved harder than anticipated. It was hardly ever unaccounted for. Kang's newly formed band of 'Holy Warriors,' as he liked to call them, had it with them out in the field constantly. When he wasn't using it, the vicars took turns keeping it safe. So the next best thing to destroying it was to steal and eliminate the meticulous notes about it that the scribes had been working on.

The process for creating a single blood font was a complicated one, judging by the copious amounts of notes Midori found inside The Augur's crate. Most of the words on the parchment made absolutely no sense to her. Centrifuge? Slow-building distillation? It sounded like an eldritch ritual. Perhaps it was. *This is what Kax wanted The Augur to do?*

She was just looking over a cryptic passage that stated, 'only the purest will survive,' when The Augur shifted position in his cot. He turned his whole body towards her, his hollowed-out eye sockets seeming to stare right at her. *How does a man with no eyes sleep?* she suddenly wondered with a grim sort of fascination. *He has no eyelids to close ...*

"Midori?" he rasped in a sleep-thickened voice. "What are you doing here, child?"

She froze, the incriminating papers held loosely in her hands. *Shit! Shit!* She could leave. She *should* leave. She should bolt right out the door and leave everything behind, abandon this foolish quest and go back to quietly seething against the asinine *plan* the vicars were so obsessed with ...

She didn't; the answer to her problems clicked into place.

She couldn't destroy the blood font. She couldn't even figure out what notes were what in order to remove all traces of its creation. But there was one thing she could do.

The Augur had to die.

He must have sensed something, the shift in tension, the sudden stilling of the air. He cringed backwards, his hollow eye sockets nothing but dark smudges of shadow in his face. "Midori?" he repeated, a slight warble to his reedy voice. He sounded *scared*.

How does he know it's me? She moved closer. Her breath came out in short little gasps. *Is it my smell, or maybe he can tell by the way I move? By how I breathe?*

"I'm sorry," she whispered into the darkness as she reached towards him.

He only whimpered.

She slid the pillow out from underneath his head.

In the end, death came to The Augur shockingly fast. Midori only had to press the pillow down over his gasping face for a few panic-inducing minutes before his struggles ceased. Her wrists and forearms were covered with deep gouges; a quick death didn't necessarily mean a peaceful one. He fought until the bitter end.

She kept her arms tight at her sides as she strode through the tunnels after. Vaguely she realized her whole body shook with tremors. *Just get back to my room*, she told herself over and over as she walked with stilted motions. *Just get back to my room and I will be safe.*

The tunnels were empty of people. Some of the torches were lit, but not all; supplies were running thin, and the Kax followers had to make do with less and less each day. It made for a harrowing, shadow-filled trek though the mountain. Every dark shape Midori passed seemed to move along with her, like someone tailing her every move. Like the shadows themselves knew of her guilt.

She rounded a bend in the tunnel, her chest fluttery, her breath short and almost-gasping. Then she saw someone up ahead.

It was Kang.

She stopped dead in her tracks. She could turn around. She could
...

Kang glanced up and met her eyes.

It was an effort to control her shaking body and to slow her steps so she could walk more naturally towards him. There was no turning back now.

"What are you doing up so late?" he demanded.

She hid her arms behind her back. "Couldn't sleep," she answered. It wasn't a lie, not really.

He stepped into the middle of the tunnel, blocking the way forward. "What's wrong." He phrased it as a statement rather than a question. How very like Kang to demand answers when he had no business asking for them.

"Nothing is wrong, Kang." She tilted her chin up defiantly. "Can you please move out of the way so I can go to bed?" Her voice wobbled ever-so-slightly on the last word.

His dark eyes darted to her arms, which she clutched tightly behind her, then back to her face. Did he see the scratches? He stared directly into her eyes and said not a word. His suspicion of her was implicit.

Finally, he stepped to the side to allow her the space to just barely squeeze past. As she reached her bedroom door, he murmured, "Midori. You are still committed to the cause, correct?"

Something in his voice told her that he *knew*. He *knew* she wavered, he *knew* she had taken a bold step in the opposite direction from all that he stood for. What would he do about it?

She stopped, held her breath. "Of course I am," she replied evenly. "Why?"

She could hear him shifting from one foot to the other behind her. "I worry about you."

She didn't turn around. If she did, she feared she would burst into tears. Everything had changed between them. It felt insurmountable, especially after what she had just done. Did he suspect how far she had been willing to go? Would he say something? If he ever found out, would he be able to forgive her? Would he even *understand*?

Kang was a stranger to her now. He had been for a long time, she realized. There was no going back to how things were.

"There's nothing to worry about, Kang."

She stepped inside her room and closed the door firmly behind her.

Chapter 34

The Inquisitor

Rendevas was right back at the city gate, processing travelers, checking wagons, verifying papers, and generally hating the bureaucracy of a country on the brink of war, when he noticed a commotion in the second queue beside him.

"What's this?" one of the city guards spat. He stood before a tall, slender man with shiny black hair pulled into a knot at the back of his head. He wore a very eye-catching, fashionably cut outfit in a navy blue velvet so deep as to almost be black, with tall leather boots shined so well the sunlight glinted off them like metal. He held himself with an air of quiet self-respect, but not like someone who felt they had something to prove. No, his influence was self-evident. It was earned. A confidence born from respect.

This man is important, Rendevas thought, lowering the clipboard he'd been reading over. A pompous older man with graying brown hair and a truly horrendous amount of gaudy, brightly gemmed necklaces stood before him, waiting for his cart full of 'expensive' jewelry to be looked over before he was allowed into the city.

Instead, Rendevas watched the well-dressed man across the way with interest. The man smiled, stepped to the side, and that's when he noticed the dog. A *huge* brown mastiff sat patiently at the man's side, its slobbery tongue lolling out of the side of its mouth.

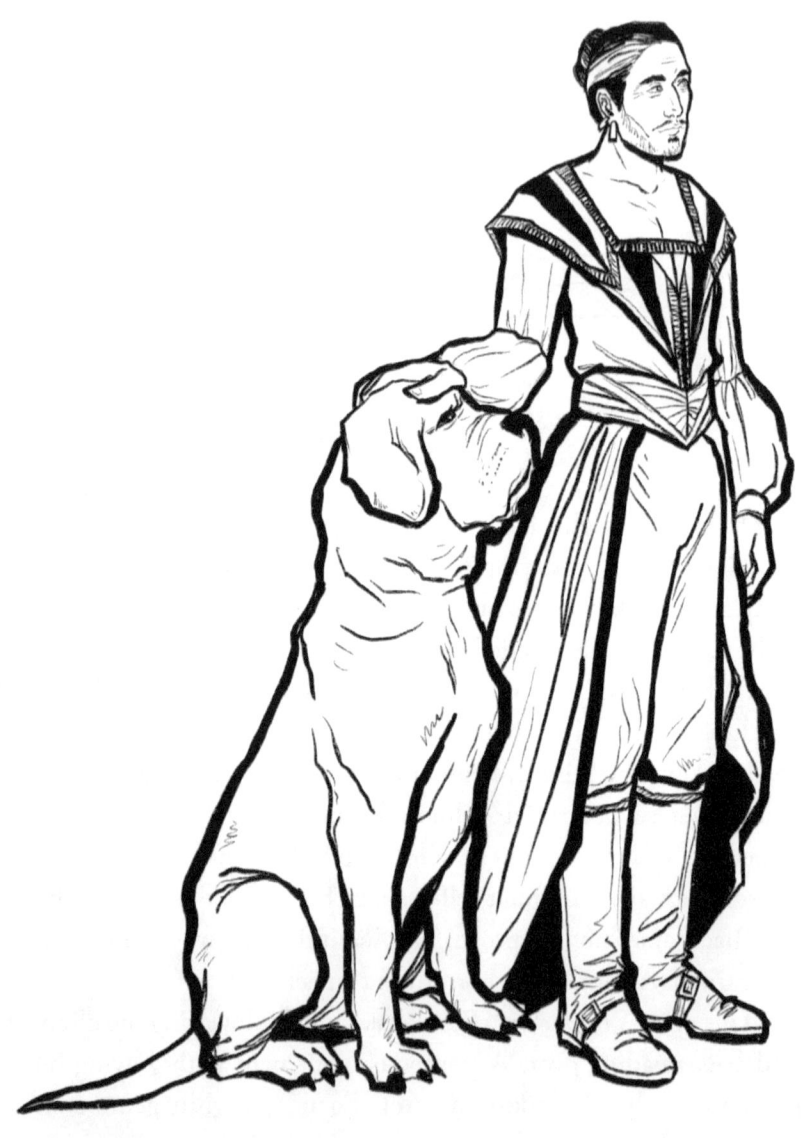

"Am I supposed to know what this means?" the guard speaking

with the well-dressed man continued, looking over a small metallic object held in his gloved hands.

A merchant in line behind the important man and his dog cried, "Hey, you can't cut the line! I've been waiting here all day!"

Rendevas frowned. It was time for him to intervene. "Excuse me," he said to the jewelry merchant, "I must see to this." He strode away, leaving the big-bellied older man to gape after him in sputtering outrage.

The well-dressed man was saying something to the city guard as Rendevas reached them. "—means that I am allowed passage into your city, no questions asked." He shrugged. "You may take the badge from me so you are able to further investigate what it says." He had a thick Vostrum accent.

"Is that so?" The guardsman leaned back and crossed his arms.

"Just so."

Rendevas finally reached the city guard. He smiled politely at the well-dressed man and his gigantic dog. "What seems to be the problem here?" he asked in his best *'I'm a diplomat, therefore I am your friend'* voice.

"This man here claims he can cut the line and get into the city based on this badge alone," the guard answered quickly. He thrust the badge towards the diplomat. "This shiny badge isn't *papers*. If you wanna get inside Praetorius, you need to *present me with your papers*."

"Let me take a look." Rendevas held the small badge up to take a better look. An intricate sigil was stamped upon one side, and the other side read: *By the Order of the Inquisitors of Archaithos, stewards of justice and curators of balance, shall be granted resolute aid and cooperation to the one who holds the Badge of Honor. Attend to them as to those who hold the highest rank in the land, as they will attend to you.*

Rendevas gasped. An Inquisitor? In Praetorius?

He glanced up at the well-dressed man, who smiled beatifically back. "Inquisitor! I apologize, I had no idea you had been summoned. I—"

The Inquisitor inclined his head and took the badge back from Rendevas's shaking fingers. "Think nothing of it. I am Inquisitor Rakeios Burgindore, and I have been summoned here by King Selderin."

Rendevas swallowed dryly. Why on Aukera would his old friend Phil have summoned an Inquisitor of Archaithos, of all people, to come to Praetorius?!

More importantly, why hadn't Rendevas been informed?

The Inquisitors of Archaithos were legendary across Eastern Aukera, for different reasons, depending upon the country. Each region had their own unique stories of the Inquisitors: in Ragházz, they were deemed holy messengers from the gods and their word was as law, but in the deserts of Dorum, they were barely tolerated, regarded with suspicion and a healthy dose of envy. In Khamris, they were welcomed hesitantly, though their authority to act above any and all local laws was thought to be highly suspect. "Just another way for Archaithos to try to insert themselves into other city's interests," people would grumble whenever they were mentioned.

Based in Archaithos—the largest and most powerful city in Eastern Aukera—the Inquisitors were usually employed as a last-ditch effort to root out treachery and deceit within governments, militaries, and sometimes even churches. They wielded their political power like weapons. Some claimed they had the arcane power to force their victims to speak only the truth, and others whispered that their powers came from unspeakable sources, like demons or gods from entirely different realms.

"Welcome to Praetorius," he greeted with a tight bow. "I am Lord Rendevas, Senior Diplomat and member of the Plenum of Praetorius." He hesitated a beat before continuing. "I understand your mission here must be of the utmost importance, but the situation in the city has been ... challenging, as of late, which has led to the need for increased security measures."

Rakeios smiled, tight-lipped. The giant dog at his side sat there calmly, seemingly unbothered by all of the people around. "Rules are rules, of course," he said simply. "What do you suggest?"

Rendevas said to the guard, "Fetch Captain Riluk. He will need to be informed of this development."

The guard nodded and jogged off towards the nearby post, situated at the base of one of the tall towers set on either side of the city gate. The travelers in line behind Rakeios eyed him with looks of wonder, bewilderment, and some even with outright hostility. Whispers of, "An Inquisitor? Really?" could be heard from farther down the queue.

Rumors would spread like wildfire. Rendevas already felt as if he was rapidly losing control of the situation. He hated that more than anything.

"Beautiful weather," the Inquisitor said, shielding his eyes from the bright sun. "I have always loved your country of Khamris, especially during autumn. Your weather is much more pleasant than up north in Archaithos."

Rendevas smiled weakly in response. Small talk? Really? He was anxious to find out why in the hells this Inquisitor was here. He didn't have time to stand around talking about *the weather!*

It didn't take long for the guard to return, followed by Captain Riluk, his square, scowling face stormy, wearing his decorated breastplate. Riluk gestured for the guard to take over in the abandoned queue, then stepped before them. He was a full head shorter than Rakeios, but his much broader shoulders made up for the lack in height.

"Inquisitor Burgindore," the captain stated by way of a welcome. He inclined his head just low enough to offer the precise amount of respect. "I was not informed that you would be visiting Praetorius. What brings you so far from Archaithos?"

Interesting, Rendevas thought. *Riluk didn't know about this, either?*

"I was summoned by your king some weeks hence," the Inquisitor related in his thick accent. "Regarding a matter of dire importance. I apologize for my sudden appearance, but, regrettably, it was a requirement, given the nature of the circumstances."

"I understand your job here isn't something I am privy to, nor would I want it to be, honestly," Riluk replied in his usual direct manner. "If it were up to me, the Inquisitors of Archaithos would stay right there in Archaithos and mind their own business. We don't need any outside help here in Praetorius. As that is not the case," he sighed, "and King Selderin thought it wise to seek your counsel, now I'm stuck dealing with you. No offense."

Oh, Riluk, Rendevas though, suppressing a chuckle. *You are a delight.*

Rakeios grinned. "None taken. You are not the first to feel this way about the people of my order."

"Unfortunately," Riluk carried on doggedly, "we have been dealing with our own delicate situation here, which means the city gate checkpoint has to operate under a much stricter capacity. We cannot allow just anyone into the city. It is a safety precaution."

"Ah, yes, the terrible murder of Lord Tullie Mason yesterday morning," Rakeios said, shaking his head mournfully. "That was grim business, was it not?"

Riluk and Rendevas both blanched. *How in the hells does he know about that?* Rendevas thought, face paling.

"It was," the captain hesitatingly replied, trying to gauge what this newcomer was about.

"And because of this, you must take the time to investigate me, to make sure I am who I say I am," Rakeios continued. "This is all standard protocol, Captain Riluk and Lord Rendevas. I am not troubled."

He lay his hand atop his dog's head, scratching behind his ears. The mastiff's large maw opened, tongue lolling out the side, as he panted happily. "Monty here will keep me company while you do your research. If you could provide me with a tent, or perhaps a large umbrella, so that I am able to sit without the sun getting in my eyes? That would be much appreciated."

Riluk and Rendevas exchanged puzzled glances. "Ah, yes, I am sure we can do that," Riluk answered. He waved over one of the guards standing at attention at the wall, whispered hurried instructions into his ear after he rushed over, and the guard raced off, not before casting a fearful look in the Inquisitor's direction.

"I appreciate your patience, Inquisitor," said the captain. With a curt nod, he stalked back towards the guard tower, leaving Rendevas alone with the well-dressed man.

"Our captain has such a way with words, does he not?" Rendevas chuckled. "It's not just you, Inquisitor Burgindore, I assure you. He is like that with everyone."

"He is a busy man," Rakeios agreed. "I do not begrudge him his responsibilities."

"Nor do I, especially lately." He eyed the taller man surreptitiously, admiring the details on his fanciful velvet jacket. "I wish I could keep you company until the guard returns with your umbrella, but unfortunately, I have a plenum meeting I must prepare for. Once again, I apologize for this delay."

Rakeios opened his mouth to reply, but the guard returned right then, holding a large red-and-white striped umbrella in his arms. He bowed obsequiously after he set it up next to the city wall, just outside of the long line of travelers still awaiting entrance. "Y-your umbrella, sir!"

"Thank you," he smiled softly. Rendevas watched as he set his large pack on the ground and began to rummage inside of it. After a few seconds, he pulled out a large, squishy chair, the kind nobles liked to sit at while lounging out on their patios and drinking fancy alcoholic drinks. The pack was in no way large enough to have been able to physically hold such a huge piece of furniture.

Rendevas cocked an eyebrow. The guard gawked. "How—?"

Rakeios smiled mischievously, then reached his hand back inside the pack. This time, he brought out a pair of dark glasses, which he placed over his eyes with a flourish, effectively blocking out the brightness of the morning sun. "Magic!" He laughed and settled into his chair, Monty the mastiff lowering his muscular form beside him with an affronted huff.

He's a bit of a showboat, then, Rendevas thought, rubbing his goatee. *Could be useful information.* "I bid you good day, Inquisitor Rakeios, and I hope your time awaiting Captain Riluk passes quickly and pleasantly."

Rakeios waved him away breezily.

As Rendevas made his way back into the city, he thought to himself, *So Phil hired an Inquisitor, eh? Secretly, even. I need to speak with him—alone—now more than ever!*

Chapter 35

The Trials of Kax: An Account Following The Troubles

Ghdion never thought he would find himself searching through a library *on purpose*.

Yet there he was, pouring over titles on the spines of the countless books that lined the shelves. He slipped inside the private library a few hours ago, after fruitlessly searching for Quay once again to apologize; clearly, she was avoiding him. He decided to use his free time wisely instead of moping around the cathedral, so, making sure he wasn't followed, he went to the basement and started to poke around.

He found the library by jiggling the handles of all the doors lining the basement corridor; logic dictated that a room with a locked door would be the best way of finding out things the church wanted to keep buried. Sure enough, the first locked door—which he easily picked—turned out to be a dusty room lined with bookshelves and heavy trunks pushed so closely together he hardly had room to maneuver inside.

He hadn't exactly *perfected* the art of lockpicking but had become proficient enough with it to get the job done nine times out of ten. One of his buddies from back when he'd been a mercenary had shown him the trick. Since then, he always kept a spare set of picks in his pocket.

It wasn't long before he had every wooden trunk opened up. They were stuffed with rolled parchments, some so old and fragile he was afraid they would disintegrate just from touching them. He pulled a few out at random, scanning the contents to determine if they were what he was looking for, but no luck. Mostly they were just old proclamations or deeds to lands the church had purchased years ago, nothing he was interested in.

He wanted to find out more about how the Vidamae Church had truly handled The Troubles and their run-ins with the Kax worshippers. Was Midori's story last night really true? Had Vidamae's Paladins *really* decimated whole villages full of Kax followers? He had no love for Vidamae's religion, not since his family had been brutally murdered because of it. But he wasn't truly so jaded as to believe that Her paladins would commit such barbaric atrocities. Sure, the church was full of pompous, self-righteous pricks who thought they were better than everyone else, but what church wasn't?

He gently rolled up the latest parchment, tying it back up as best he could before placing it back into its trunk. He rested back on his heels, frowning. There had to be some sort of system for how the books were organized, but he was either too dumb or too impatient to figure it out.

Ghdion scanned the shelves. There were no signs indicating what each section contained, like in a normal library, so just how in the hells did anyone here know how to find what they were looking for?

Grumbling to himself, he stood with a stretch and began plucking down books at random. Just as he was focusing on determining what the hells the book *The Hierarchy of Hymns Within Vidamae's Religious Orders* was actually about, he heard a soft scuff just outside the door.

He froze in place, his hand upon the thick tome, and watched in silent horror as the doorknob turned, his mind screaming at him to move, to *hide*! If he got caught snooping where he wasn't supposed to be, Quay would have the hells of a time explaining it to her superiors. Not the best way to get back into her good graces ...

But it was too late. The door creaked open, and who was standing there but Hypnocost, peering around the doorway with a very suspicious look on his pointy face.

"Fuck, Baldy, you scared the shit outta me!" Ghdion finally breathed, shoulders slumping with relief. He'd been ready to chuck the book at whoever stepped through that door.

Hypnocost jumped at the sound of his voice. "What are you doing in here?" he hissed, looking harried and more than a little guilty.

"Get in here before someone sees you." Ghdion ignored the question, waving his companion over.

Hypnocost latched the door closed as quietly as he could, then rested his back against it. "How did you manage to get into this room?" he asked again. "And why are you in here anyways? I have been trying to get inside for days, to no avail!"

Ghdion produced the slightly bent lockpick from his pocket. "Picked the lock," he answered casually. Then he narrowed his eyes. "I thought you could magically unlock doors?"

Hypnocost scowled. "It is ... I can only ..." He threw his hands up in the air in disgust. "Apparently it is a skill I am only *sometimes* able to access."

He snorted derisively but magnanimously didn't offer a sarcastic retort. *Mages.* "I'm trying to find out more about the history between the goddesses, but I can't figure out how the hells they organize all this shit."

Hypnocost's face lit up. He walked over, sidestepping one of the unlocked trunks Ghdion had pawed through earlier. "Oh, that is easy!" the half-elf said, smiling. "Most religious texts are organized in the Filonicci Method. They claim it is the easiest and most efficient way to classify texts, but I beg to differ. Personally, I find Altuth's Principles of Organization to be far superior."

At Ghdion's blank look, he clarified, "Alphabetically, first by subject, then by title."

"Riiiight. So, how do I find anything about Kax and how Vidamae's members have treated Her followers in the past?"

Hypnocost tapped his chin thoughtfully. "Well, since we do not have a specific title we are searching for, we should start in the K's for Kax. That should lead us in the right direction."

"Us?" Ghdion cocked an eyebrow. "There is no *us* here, Baldy. You're gonna stand watch while I look through these books."

Hypnocost sniffed haughtily. "Do you not think it would be more prudent for *you* to stand watch while *I* go through the texts? I am much more versed in how libraries work, after all."

Ghdion scowled. He had him there. "Fine. But make it quick. If we get caught, Quay might get in trouble."

"Gods forbid *Quay* should get into trouble," Hypnocost muttered under his breath as he began speedily examining the titles on each of the books' spines. "Why do you need these books in the first place? You have never struck me as a man who enjoys reading. I was not even aware you *could* read."

"Cute." Ghdion rolled his eyes. He stood with his arms crossed beside the door, keeping one ear out for any noises in the hallway. "Just something I overheard. Wanted to check it out for myself, see if there was any truth to it."

"And what did you hear?"

"You're awfully nosy."

He could hear the smile in Hypnocost's voice as he said, "May I remind you that *I* am the one helping *you*?"

He glowered, even though the half-elf couldn't see him from behind all the bookshelves. "Fine. Midori told Lucius about how Vidamae Paladins basically wiped out her entire town when she was little, just because they were Kax worshippers. It sounded far-fetched, so I wanted to find out if there was any truth to it. Happy?"

Hypnocost hummed in response. He was silent for a while, the only sounds his fingers brushing across book spines or flipping through pages. "I am not as well-versed in any of the religious orders of Aukera, as I am not a religious person myself," he finally spoke up in a quiet voice. "But I do not find it hard to believe any of the gods would send their forces on a crusade like the one you describe. Even Vidamae."

"She's the Goddess of *Life*," Ghdion argued half-heartedly. "Why would She condone the killing of innocents?"

"Our gods work in mysterious ways," answered Hypnocost. "You need only look at the histories to see it. Holy crusades, terrible wars, persecutions based on religion ... These are all things that have happened before, and will continue to happen, for as long as mortals populate Aukera."

"That's a pretty grim viewpoint, Baldy," Ghdion muttered. It was one he held himself, but he wasn't about to admit that to know-it-all Hypnocost. He was arguing for argument's sake.

"It is merely logical." Hypnocost turned towards the next tall bookshelf and began scouring through those titles. He let out a thoughtful noise, then called out, "I believe I may have found what you are looking for."

He stepped out from the stacks holding a heavy hardcover book with a faded blue fabric wrapped cover. Gilt foil details scrawled along the top and bottom of the spine. *The Trials of Kax: An Account Following the Troubles*, by Archpriest Dolimeer Dorcus.

"Give it here," Ghdion demanded, taking a step away from the door with his hand outstretched. Hypnocost handed it to him, but his curiosity was piqued, so he stood beside him to read over his shoulder. He had to stand on his tiptoes to be able to see.

Ghdion flipped through the pages, briefly scrutinizing the headers and bold-printed words until he found what he needed. "Ah, here we go," he said, placing his finger upon the top of a page near the middle of the book. "'Khamris and the Surrounding Area.' This is what we need."

> *Various trials were held in Praetorius following the events of The Troubles. As the crimes committed were against the Church itself, the Plenum of Praetorius gave the clergy the option to forego traditional trials by jury; the Church instead opted to gather an assembly of their peers, who would proclaim the guilt or innocence of each Kax worshipper that was brought before them.*
>
> *High Priestess Baraz Segovia, who was the ranking leader of the cathedral in Praetorius at the time, oversaw each of the trials. The jury consisted mostly of clerics, paladins, and some few acolytes of Vidamae's Church, all who had personally suffered from the use of the blood fonts. A total of fifty-nine Kax cultists were brought to trial, and each and every one of the fifty-nine were declared unanimously guilty. In the weeks that followed, a series of public executions took place,*

where the fifty-nine Kax worshippers paid the price for their crimes with their lives. It served as a harsh reminder to the remaining Kax believers that they should think twice about drawing forth the ire of Vidamae and Her holiest servants.

The rest of the text read off the names of the jury members and the Kax cultists that were sentenced to death. Ghdion stopped reading and slammed the book shut. "Well," he muttered, "that answers my question."

"Mmm," was all Hypnocost said.

"There's no way that special jury was impartial."

"I can imagine the spectacle the public executions caused back then," Hypnocost said. "As a show of force to any who would dare attack Vidamae, it would have been very effective."

"So rampaging paladins isn't that far out of the question," surmised Ghdion, frowning. "And if the high priestess was okay with show-trials and death sentences, you can bet your ass she would've turned a blind eye to the war crimes her own paladins were committing."

"It is enough to make one wonder if these things are *still* happening. Would the current high priestess allow a repeat of past mistakes? Are there Paladins of Vidamae using their authority for nefarious purposes, even today?" Hypnocost shrugged. "It is something to keep in mind, for sure."

"Yeah," Ghdion replied slowly. "And how much of this past do the *current* priestesses know about?"

How much did *Quay* know about it was what he really wanted to know. His face darkened as he realized the implications. Was she aware of her beloved church's dark past? If she was, what did that say about his view of her as a person? Was she as good as he thought?

It was something he intended to find out.

Chapter 36

Make It Count

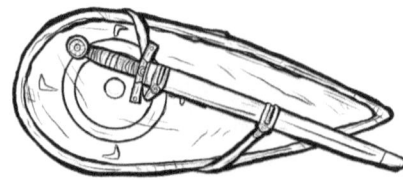

"We have a lot to discuss today, so let's get to it."

Chancellor Eldivar stood at the head of the table in the council chambers, resting both palms against the tabletop and looking more haggard than Avindea had ever seen him. Dark circles ringed beneath his eyes, and his white hair, usually combed and oiled back in a delicate pouf, was a bit lopsided and flyaway. It had been only one day since the murder of Lord Tullie Mason, and it was clear the strain was getting to everyone, the chancellor included.

Neither King Selderin nor Princess Alandria were in attendance; the chancellor, at the very beginning of the plenum meeting, claimed the king was busy drafting a response to send to Uldinvelm. The princess wished to remain in her private quarters for a bit longer as a safety precaution.

Everyone else was present and eager to hear the news: the 'Praetorian guards' who had attacked the Uldinvelm diplomat still hadn't been caught.

"Lord Rendevas, let's begin with you," the chancellor said. "Have you any news as to exactly why Lord Tullie Mason arrived so much earlier than agreed upon?" His voice was short and snide, as if somehow the debacle at the city gate was all the diplomat's fault.

Lord Rendevas, wearing a trim forest-green tunic embroidered with elaborate flowers, shook his head. "I have a missive ready to send off with my swiftest messenger, as well as an accompanying mage and four soldiers, but I am still awaiting the king's response. I certainly cannot begin to make inquiries until I know how, exactly, King Selderin intends to handle this situation." He regarded the chancellor pointedly.

Avindea watched as Chancellor Eldivar's face flushed. "I assure you," he snapped, "King Selderin's response is complete, but as we are still in the midst of this incomplete investigation, we have been unable to send it as quickly as first anticipated."

That sounds like a load of bullshit to me, Avindea thought darkly. Judging by Rendevas's skeptical face, he agreed.

"I believe the king intends to make his announcement regarding the incident as soon as this meeting is adjourned. Now," he nodded sharply, pressing his fingertips to the tabletop, "Let us move on from this. How are the import inspections? Are you able to handle the workload with your team?"

Rendevas stood and regarded the assembly. "To be perfectly honest, no," he answered. "I think we've all seen just how overwhelming the lines at the gate have become. To put it simply, it is impossible for my team and I to keep up."

Naturally, Judge Rodach had something to say about that. "Can't handle inspecting a few crates, Rendevas?" he sneered.

Of all the members present, he looked the least disturbed by the events of the previous few days. His long, wrinkled face was just as twisted with bad temper as ever, and even his relaxed pose as he reclined in his chair screamed how unaffected he was.

Rendevas eyed him contemptuously. "Come now, Judge Rodach, even *you* should know that my job involves much more than just 'inspecting a few crates.'" He turned to the plenum at large. "There's just no possibility that my small team and I are able to keep up with the influx of travelers and merchants trying to enter the city. It's gotten beyond the point where I can handle it. You've all seen the lines! And this is even after we started splitting them into two, one for those with official papers and one for those without."

"What do you suggest?" Chancellor Eldivar inquired.

"A task force," Rendevas answered immediately. "Consisting of members of the city guard, some of my own diplomats, volunteers perhaps. The more people, the better. These lines will only get worse."

"My guards are already overwhelmed with their duties at the gate and patrolling the streets," Captain Riluk said bluntly. "Not to mention the continuing search for those *guards* who went rogue and attacked the Uldinvelm emissary. No, I'm sorry, Rendevas. I cannot help you."

Rendevas scanned the faces of his fellow plenum members, but none offered any assistance. Avindea watched his face fall as all hope of aid was crushed; feeling immensely guilty, she called out, "I could ask some of my fellow paladins at the barracks, see if they would be willing to help out. But honestly, we've all had our hands full at the Church lately."

"Why does this task force have to consist only of city officials?" Lady Uunar asked. She sat, poised and demure as always, her makeup impeccable and her form-fitting dress just this side of too revealing.

Avindea eyed her enviously; Lady Uunar always looked so put together and confident, no matter the circumstances. Perhaps it was the magic she wielded? "Couldn't we appoint civilians?" Lady Uunar continued. "What is stopping us from simply paying some of our merchants to help? They have our same insider knowledge and perhaps know more of the citizens than even we do."

"I hadn't really considered that as a possibility," Rendevas admitted. "We could give them special clearance, or perhaps a temporary status as city officials until the lines are handled."

"I nominate Tobias Wiltwater," Lady Uunar suggested promptly.

"I've worked with him in the past, and he has always been honest and efficient. He has the reach and the manpower we need. Of all known merchants in Praetorius, he has the most contacts. I think he would be a great fit."

Avindea could see the slight wince cross the diplomat's face at the mention of the grumpy borean merchant, infamous across Praetorius for his terrible attitude and bad temper. Tobias Wiltwater had only thrived for so long because of his ability to procure items other merchants could not, earning him a reputation as the most skilled trader in the city.

"I have worked closely with Tobias, as well," Rendevas replied slowly. "I suppose it couldn't hurt to ask if he would be willing to step in ... temporarily, of course."

There were various nods and murmurs of agreement around the plenum table. "All in favor of nominating Tobias Wiltwater to aid Lord Rendevas with gate inspections, temporarily, until the queues have lessened?" Chancellor Eldivar called out in his ringing voice.

Everyone but Judge Rodach and Constable Mald raised their hands.

"Those against?" Mald and Rodach raised their hands, casting smug looks in Rendevas's direction. Even though they had no hope of stopping the motion from passing, they wanted him to know that they despised him so much, they were willing to cast their votes against him every time just out of spite.

How childish! Avindea thought. *And these grown men are in charge of the whole city? Pathetic.*

"Motion is passed. Lord Rendevas, I leave it to you to contact Tobias Wiltwater and explain the situation. We can discuss the pay and other specifics if he accepts. Now, moving on." The chancellor turned towards her. "Lady Avindea, you have an update on the Kax situation regarding the Church of Vidamae?"

"I do." She cleared her suddenly dry throat. It was just like her first plenum meeting, the shaky, anxious feeling of speaking in front of all of those people. She longed for the eagerness she felt at the last meeting. How did High Priestess Lucina do this every day?

"My team has recently returned from Camfield, where they discovered a hidden Temple of Kax that was occupied with a small force of two dozen or so Kax cultists. They confirmed that one of the people they encountered was the very same assassin who murdered an innocent farmer in Camfield the previous night. It is just as we feared: the Kax threat has, indeed, resurfaced."

She waited a moment before continuing. "High Priestess Lucina Balladoni—as you know, I am filling in for her temporarily while she is gone—has just written to tell me that she is meeting with other high-ranking members of the church to address the situation."

Many pairs of expectant eyes watched her. She licked her lips nervously.

"Is that all?" Lieutenant Orvessa spat.

"I confess, your update is a bit underwhelming," said Chancellor Eldivar. He gave her an apologetic look and a little shrug.

"Why is your High Priestess not here now, when her flock needs her the most?" Commander Rakeld asked. It was rare he spoke up during any portions of the plenum meetings that didn't have anything to do with the military.

"Where's the proof?" Lady Uunar interjected. She leaned forward in her seat, narrowing her eyes. "How are you so sure Kax is the one behind these latest attacks?"

"Aside from the fact that my people literally discovered a *hidden* Kax Temple?" Avindea countered hotly.

"That does not make the group inside Kax cultists, necessarily," the judge spoke up. "They could just be a group of bandits using the old church as a base. Probably the Claws of Kharon. They are always causing us no end of headaches."

"That's a stretch, even coming from you." Avindea scowled. "How would they have known to find that old temple? From all accounts, it is well-hidden in the forest." She could feel her face heating up and her temper rising. "Do you just *enjoy* being so *contrary*, Judge? Because it's getting quite tiresome."

"Perhaps Lady Avindea also needs a task force to help her with this problem?" Lord Eglath suggested, smoothly interjecting to try to keep the peace. He folded his giant hands before him on the table, his bare chest flexing with the movement. Did he do that on purpose so everyone would admire his muscles? "I'm sure I could lend some of my clerics. They could act as guardians of your churches, at least until this latest threat is taken care of."

"My church can offer gold to the murder victim's families," Lady Loresh offered. She inclined her head graciously, her earrings clinking softly against the wide golden collar around her neck. "The Church of Velthunas is always willing to give monetary aid to those who suffer, regardless of what deity they worship."

"What I need is help taking down these cultists before they have a chance to kill any more of my parishioners!" Avindea exclaimed. "I don't think anyone else is taking this as seriously as they should be. What if the cultists manage to infiltrate Praetorius again? Vidamae's Cathedral is the largest in the city, and the most popular—hundreds of people visit the church every day. The Kax cultists pose a dire threat!"

"Perhaps you are not equipped to handle this crisis on your own," Chancellor Eldivar supplied gently. "I realize you are still relatively new to the plenum, Lady Avindea, but frankly, your performance leaves much to be desired."

He shook his head with disingenuous sympathy. "We plenum members understand your plight, but there isn't much we can do, given your lack of evidence and baseless accounts from a 'team' we know nothing about."

"For all we know," Judge Rodach cut in, "you could be making this up as some kind of ploy to earn the plenum's pity. No, until I'm shown hard evidence proving the Kax threat is real, I'm not buying it."

Avin opened her mouth to shoot back some hot-tempered, ill-considered remark, but she slammed her lips closed instead. Nothing she could say would sway Judge Rodach or Chancellor Eldivar, so why bother? It appeared she was on her own.

Lord Rendevas threw her a lifeline by saying, "Now, now, Judge Rodach, this isn't a trial, contrary to what you may think. For what it's worth, I believe Lady Avindea. Though I am somewhat overwhelmed by my duties as of late, I would like to offer my assistance, such that it is. Whatever I can do to help the Church of Vidamae, if it is within my power, I will do so. Besides, it's always a good thing to have the most powerful church in Praetorius on your side, hmm?"

Avindea looked towards him gratefully. He winked at her and smiled.

Before she could respond, Lady Uunar piped up. "I, too, will aid her. I can have some of my mages look into her claim. Perhaps this manner needs a more magical touch?" She cocked one elegantly sculpted eyebrow and smiled mysteriously. "The Arcane Academy would be honored to help the Church of Vidamae with this service."

The last thing Avindea wanted was a bunch of mages snooping around the church, especially with Lucius and Midori hidden in the basement. She definitely did not want them discovering they had acquired a blood font, either. But it would be the height of rudeness for her to turn down Lady Uunar's help, so she was forced to nod in thanks. "I appreciate the offer, Lady Uunar. The Church welcomes any help you can provide."

Uunar inclined her head magnanimously; Avindea could only give her a tight-lipped smile in return.

This isn't going at all how I planned.

"That settles that, then" Chancellor Eldivar announced with a sigh. "I won't lie, I'm not very impressed with the attitudes on display here today." He shot the judge a nasty look. "We are all in this together, in case you've forgotten. We must work as a team, especially during times of great strife such as what we are dealing with presently."

He regarded the plenum members with a look of supreme disappointment, not unlike a father disciplining his unruly children. "Now, the king has requested an update on the diplomat situation from Captain Riluk. I will provide an update on that during our meeting tomorrow."

The counselors, sufficiently chagrined, shuffled and stood, effectively dismissed. Avindea sat in her chair for a few moments longer, willing her hot temper to cool before she left. She watched Chancellor Eldivar and Captain Riluk head towards the exit with some haste; Lord Rendevas followed behind them at a more sedate pace. Rendevas called out to Riluk and asked him a question, though she was too far away to hear what they said. Besides, she was too preoccupied with her own worries to bother thinking too much about that; Rendevas was probably up to some secret dealings, as usual. That man had his fingers in all sorts of projects around the city, some of them less than legal. Still, she would rather have him as an ally than not: he knew far too much, especially concerning the Church, than she felt comfortable with.

Captain Riluk, too, was privy to secrets she desperately wished were known only to her, namely Lucius's identity as an Uldinvelm native. She worried he would bring up the fact that a known ex-soldier of the Athessian Army was currently sequestered inside the Cathedral of Vidamae, but so far, he had kept that little nugget of knowledge close to his chest. She was grateful, of course, but worried it could be used against her, should he decide their shaky alliance was no longer viable.

I really hate politics, she thought. *Nobody ever says what they mean.* There were always hidden words laced behind every polite conversation, secret meetings that took place behind closed doors that determined the *real* rules and how they were enforced.

Avindea much preferred the direct route. She'd never had to keep secrets like this before! Never was she required to navigate the murky waters of lies and intrigue, and she was starting to hate herself for getting more proficient at it. Even so, she did not flourish in groups full of two-faced politicians like the plenum.

She hoped she never would.

Lady Uunar sidled up beside her and rested a hip against the table. "I look forward to working more closely with you in the coming days," Uunar smiled smoothly. "We haven't had a chance to work together before. I have a feeling that partnering with a paladin will be a ... refreshing change of pace."

That's certainly one way to put it, Avindea thought. She smiled back as genuinely as she could and replied, "I hope so, Lady Uunar. I appreciate the offer."

"I look forward to getting to the bottom of this distressing situation. I could have some of my students meet with us at the Cathedral of Vidamae today, if you are able. They may prove an invaluable resource for our investigation."

Shit. Too soon! I can't have her mages poking around! "I'm afraid my remaining duties for today take me away from the cathedral," she lied smoothly. "But tomorrow after the next plenum meeting, I would be happy to show them around."

Lady Uunar raised her eyebrows, clearly doubting Avindea's excuse. She was too polite to call her out on it, however. She merely smiled and dipped her head. "Of course. Tomorrow after the meeting, then. I will have my students await us outside the capitol, and we can all travel to the church together."

It was obvious Lady Uunar was not about to let Avindea squirm out of it. Her responding smile was weak. "Perfect. Until tomorrow, then."

"Until tomorrow." Lady Uunar stood smoothly and left in a soft swishing of silken skirts.

Avindea had until tomorrow afternoon to figure out just what in the hells she was going to do about Lucius and Midori, and more importantly, the blood font.

"Captain Riluk, a word, if you please."

Both the chancellor and Riluk stopped and turned towards Rendevas, who forced himself to move at a casual, unbothered pace against his strong desire to rush after the pair.

This was his last chance. If he didn't get Riluk to agree to let him see King Selderin, he would never be able to show him the damning evidence that proved Judge Rodach was committing treason. Nor would he be able to ask just why, exactly, he felt the need to hire an *Inquisitor of Archaithos*.

"What is it, Rendevas?" Riluk asked, strong impatience lacing his voice. "I have an important meeting with the king that I cannot be late to."

"That's just it," Rendevas supplied smoothly. "I've come to beg a private audience with His Majesty." He held up his hands to forestall Riluk's words of protest. "What I have to tell him is very important. I'm willing to submit to whatever safety precautions you deem appropriate. Just ... please, Riluk." He locked eyes with the man, willing all of his formidable charm to win over the stubborn, hard-headed captain of the guard.

Riluk looked him over with a penetrating gaze. "Just what is so important that you must speak about it with the king *alone*?"

Rendevas took a deep breath, hedging his bets on this one last chance. "Treason," he whispered. "That is all I can say right now but know it is of the utmost importance. The king must be made aware of what I know."

Chancellor Eldivar's white eyebrows shot up his forehead in surprise. "Truly?" he asked in hushed tones. "You have proof?"

Rendevas nodded.

"Who is it?" the chancellor asked, his whole demeanor eager for the damning gossip.

"I ... would rather not say just yet, Chancellor," he answered reluctantly. "I prefer if the king has the knowledge first, and he can decide what to do with it."

The chancellor inclined his head, but Rendevas didn't miss first the look of hunger, then supreme disappointment, that flashed across the chancellor's face. "Prudent," he replied. "What do you think, Captain?"

Riluk regarded Rendevas silently. "You know I do not appreciate politics or the secrets and lies that are associated with them," he stated firmly. "King Selderin's safety is my top priority. If what you are saying is true, then he must be made aware of the news. But if this is some sort of ploy ..." He took a step towards Rendevas, until his face was mere inches from the diplomat's. "I won't hesitate to cut you down where you stand."

Rendevas locked eyes with the captain. He didn't dare move, didn't dare take a breath or even blink. The raw intensity emanating from Riluk was intimidating.

"Do we have an accord?"

Rendevas nodded. "We do."

"Good." He turned on his heel and resumed his walk out of the council chambers, Chancellor Eldivar right on his heels. "Then follow me. You will have five minutes, Lord Rendevas. Better make it count."

Chapter 37
Check-Ins

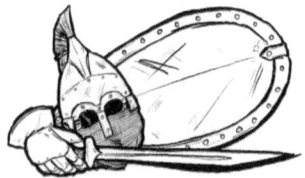

Three guards showed up at the cathedral that morning, asking for Lucius.

He had been scoping out the bathhouse, trying to determine if he could sneak Midori up there while it wasn't busy, when he heard footsteps down the corridor that separated the bathing chambers from the main nave of the church. He was surprised to see Quay walking towards him, followed by three armed and armored city guards.

Quay's face was frantic and stricken, but she bravely tried not to show it. "Lucius, there you are!" she called, her filmy robes fluttering around her ankles. Her voice was much higher than normal. "These guards were looking for you. They have a few questions."

She raised her eyebrows at him in silent worry. His response was a barely perceptible shaking of his head before he stepped forward and offered the guards a little bow. "Good morning, sirs. How can I help you on this fine autumn day?"

The guard in the lead watched Lucius's jovial show with a scowl on his face. "We're here to check up on you. You haven't left the premises, have you?" he asked, eyeing him up and down, particularly the scarring on his face.

"I wouldn't dream of it," Lucius supplied easily. He gave them his most dazzling smile, which was lost on the three taciturn faces. "I'm on house arrest, right? Well, church arrest, actually. Which is pretty funny, if you think about it. How many people have you had to lock up inside an actual cathedral? Probably not many!" He chuckled, the seriousness of the mood ignored with his playful banter.

The lead guard was not amused. "We will know if you take so much as one step outside of this temple. We've got the place under constant watch."

Lucius nodded sagely. "That's smart," he said. "I would do the same thing if I was in your shoes."

The soldiers stared at Lucius, and he stared back, unconcerned with the awkward silence. Quay stood between them, glancing nervously back and forth. She wrangled her hands in worry. "Is there anything I can help you guards with while you're here? Any healing or ... or religious services I could offer? We have the most excellent bathhouse I'm sure you would love to make use of!"

"That won't be necessary," the soldier replied. He glared at Lucius, unmoved by his cheerful mood. It was like he was *personally offended* that Lucius wasn't falling all over himself to impress them. "We will be back soon to check in again. Make sure you are available at any time, or we will assume you are not following your orders and act accordingly."

Lucius nodded, bowing once again, even though such formalities were not required. "I am ever at your service," he said. He couldn't help but inject just a smidgen of sarcasm into his tone.

The lead soldier eyed him disapprovingly before walking away. The two guards with him turned as one and walked in lockstep behind him.

As soon as they rounded the corner and out of sight, Quay let out a breath of relief. "Well, that was nerve-wracking!" she squeaked.

"What in Aukera was that all about? Are they planning on tromping around my church every day to make sure you're still here?"

"Probably," he told her. "Don't worry about it, I can handle them. They're just doing their jobs. Gotta make sure the big scary 'Uldinvelm spy' isn't up to no good, right?"

He peeked inside the bathing chambers. "Hey, Quay, can you help me sneak Midori up here? I think she'd really enjoy having a bath in an actual tub instead of just another sponging down or whatever she's been doing."

Between the two of them, they managed to smuggle Midori upstairs and into one of the private pools. They had her dress in a priestess robe for the short trip, just in case, though they didn't come across anyone else. Quay stood watch outside the curtain, and Lucius, donning a bathing robe from one of the racks, decided to use the time to have a quick soak in the large public bath.

He stripped down to his smallclothes in the changing room and threw the robe across his shoulders to save Quay from having to see his extensively scarred body. The burn marks traveled from his forehead all the way down to his toes, warping his skin in pink whorls around his left arm, leg, and everything in between. He had mostly blocked from his memory the experience of how he had been so horribly burned by his own mother, but every once in a while, he would get phantom pains across that side of his body, as if he were reliving the wrenching, all-encompassing pain all over again. It happened much more frequently when he wasn't wearing all of his clothes, such as right now, as he walked from the changing room and into the public bath.

He didn't remove the thin robe until he was almost all the way in the warm water. He tried to ignore Quay's sharp intake of breath when she saw the full extent of his burn scars.

"Lucius," she blurted, "your scars! I had no idea they—"

"Yeah, I get that a lot," he interrupted her with a mutter and a strained smile, sinking into the bath up to his chin. He had been meaning to visit the bathhouse before now, but every time he checked, the place was full of bathers. The last thing he wanted to do was impose his marked form upon a bunch of strangers. It was bad enough having Quay there to witness, but at least she was a friend.

"You know, we have excellent doctors here." She rubbed her arms and regarded him kindly from beside Midori's private room. "I'm willing to bet there is one who could look over your scars and see if there isn't something they could do to help. Maybe not remove them entirely, but help minimize them, maybe?"

"I appreciate the offer, Quay, but I've had these almost my entire life. They're as much a part of me as … as my hair, or my smile, y'know?" He shrugged, trying to hide the bitterness from his voice. "I try not to let them define me."

Quay nodded. "I understand. If you ever change your mind, please tell me, okay? I want to help."

He sighed and leaned against the tiled ledge of the pool. They sat there in companionable silence, Lucius in the bath, Quay with her arms wrapped around her knees as she sat against the wall. It was peaceful for a time, with the gentle trickle of water echoing across the tiles. Lucius closed his eyes to savor the feeling of relaxation, the scent of lavender soaking into his skin.

Quay shifted her position and sighed heavily, sounding for all the world like she had a lot on her mind. He cracked open an eye to see what was bothering her; her expressive face hid none of her feelings. There *was* something worrying her, most likely all of the issues with the Kax cultists.

But just in case, Lucius paddled over to the side, where he draped his arms across the ledge, not caring that most of his scarred chest was visible outside of the water. "Alright, out with it," he said to her. He spoke quietly, but even so, the sound echoed around the mostly empty chambers. "What's on your mind?"

Quay looked up, her cheeks reddening. "Nothing! It's nothing. Pretend I'm not here so you can enjoy your bath."

"How often do you get asked to spill your guts to someone else?" he asked her, ignoring her request. "As a priestess-in-training or whatever you are, I'm willing to bet people spend all day telling you *their* problems. That's part of the job, right? But who can *you* talk to about *your* worries, hmm?"

She looked away and chewed at her thumbnail. "My purpose is to be a guiding light to my people, to make myself available for all who require spiritual aid." It had the sound of a pre-rehearsed explanation. "It is my sacred duty to—"

"Yeah, yeah, I know all that already," he interrupted her. "But *I'm* asking *you* to unload your problems onto me. C'mon, this isn't an offer I give just anybody!" He grinned at her, his white teeth flashing in the dim light. "I know we haven't talked much since you hired me, but I consider you a friend, Quay. So, as a friend, I am asking you to tell me what's wrong. That's the way you can 'spiritually aid' me." He waggled his eyebrows. "Besides, I'm a great listener."

Lucius rested his chin on his folded arms, his body below the waist floating lazily in the water, and regarded her expectantly. His smile widened in what he hoped was an encouraging way.

She glanced into his mismatched eyes, huffed out a little breath of feigned annoyance, and smiled back. "Fine. You got me. I do have something on my mind, but it's ... it's kinda embarrassing."

"Tell me anyways." He cocked his head to the side. "I'm not gonna judge you."

"So let's just say I have a ... friend. Who I just discovered had a family years ago, a wife—er, a spouse, and three kids, right? And this friend's family was ... was *brutally murdered* during The Troubles."

She paused to gather her thoughts. "Well, this *friend* never told me about their family, and when I asked them about it, they got really mad and told me off." Her shoulders slumped despondently. She wouldn't meet his eyes.

He considered her words. He had an idea just who exactly this 'friend' really was, but he didn't want to embarrass her further, so he kept it to himself. "Maybe your friend is still grieving the loss," he suggested. "Maybe they don't really know how to handle such a terrible tragedy, so they lashed out at you."

"I don't know what to do," she replied softly. "We were close before—before I did that, and now ... now, I'm afraid I've ruined our friendship." Her eyes shone with unshed tears when she finally met his, and she wiped at them fiercely when she saw his matching look of pity. "It's stupid, I know. I need to just get over it."

"It's not stupid at all!" He pondered how best to advise her. "I think you just need to give your friend time to come to terms with what happened. It's pretty normal for one to lash out against their loved ones when they're in mourning. I'm sure they are feeling just as badly as you are."

He could remember how hurt he was, how betrayed, when his mother left him at the orphanage back in Uldinvelm. How the kindly old women who ran the place tried to help him even though he treated them terribly. That lonely feeling never quite went away, not really. That feeling of *abandonment*. Even still, he tended to keep people at arm's length, figuring it was much easier than getting left behind again.

"Y'know, I used to be a bratty little shit who would push people away like that, too," he blurted, as surprised at his admission as Quay was at hearing it. "When I was little, my mom dumped me off at an orphanage. She was the reason for my burn scars—it's a long story, I'll have to tell you sometime—and she just couldn't stand to look at me anymore, so she figured the orphanage was the best place for a disgusting looking boy like me." He chuffed bitterly.

"Oh, Lucius, you're not—"

"Hold on, I'm not after sympathy," he cut her off. "Just listen. When I was at the orphanage, I used to start fights with the other kids. I figured it would be better to make them hate me instead of pitying me for my scars, right? Well, there was this girl there named Marissa. She was adamant about becoming my friend and refused to listen to all the hurtful stuff I used to say to her. She was so stubborn and relentless that I finally gave in and we became friends. She was my closest companion growing up."

He paused, smiling fondly at the memories. The two of them

were quite a pair, raising hells for the poor old ladies who ran the orphanage. She even followed him into the Army, the two of them lying about their ages to gain entry into the ranks. "I promise this is relevant, just bear with me a minute," he continued. "So we grew up together, did everything together. I'd never been as close to someone as I was with Marissa. I'm sure you can guess that we eventually got together romantically."

He eyed Quay sidelong, catching her look of rapt attention, then wiggled his eyebrows to make her laugh. "I loved her, I really did! But it all got to be too much for me, and I started lashing out. I pushed her away because I was an idiot and thought she'd leave me eventually, so wouldn't it be better to just get it over with myself?" He shrugged. "She finally couldn't take it anymore and left me. She was kind about it, at least, which was more than I deserved."

"Lucius, I'm so sorry," Quay murmured. "Is she still—?"

"Around? Oh, yeah. She's a captain in the Army last I knew. A pretty accomplished mage, actually. But I told you all that so you could maybe get some insight into why your 'friend' is acting the same way that I did. Ghdion's just being an asshole, and if he doesn't come around, *I'll* talk some sense into him."

"I-I never said it was Ghdion," Quay blushed even harder.

"Mmm-hmm, you didn't need to." He shot her a knowing look, then stood up from the warm waters to stretch. "Give him a little time. I'll bet it won't be long before he starts talking to you again, tries to make amends. He won't be able to help it. It's obvious how much he cares about you." He winked at her again.

"Ghdion is an idiot," Midori announced as she pulled back the privacy curtain behind Quay, her hair wet and her body covered in a giant fluffy pink robe. On her feet were a matching pair of fluffy slippers. "You can do much better than him, Quay, but if you insist upon pursuing a man like that, who am I to judge?"

She turned from Quay and watched Lucius dry off silently. "I am ready to go back to my room. We should make haste before someone else sees us."

"I ... you ... heard all of that?" Quay sputtered, clambering to her feet. Her face was bright red. "Who said anything about pursuing him?!"

Midori gave her a knowing look. "You two aren't exactly secretive about it." She held the robe around her shoulders with a queenly air about her.

"Yeah, yeah, let's get going," Lucius called, stepping into the changing room to grab his clothes. He wrapped a towel around his waist for modesty before emerging.

"After you, ladies," he bowed them out with a dramatic outstretching of his scarred arm.

Two burly guards stood watch outside King Selderin's private chambers. They both saluted Captain Riluk smartly, then returned their gazes to scan the corridor for any dangers.

Chancellor Eldivar stepped up to the door and looked pointedly towards Riluk. "Well?" he stated, gesturing towards the doorknob. "Are you going to unlock it?"

Riluk slipped his hand inside his pocket. Rendevas watched with growing concern as he patted at his pocket, his face growing pale. "Hmmm. My key ... I swear that it was—"

The chancellor let out a deep sigh of annoyance. "Riluk," he chided, "we've talked about this. You simply cannot lose track of your keys, especially in times of crisis like these!" He pulled out an elaborate metal key, decorated with scrollwork designs along the handle. It was almost as long as his hand. He placed the key into the lock and turned the knob.

"Ahh, there it is," Riluk exclaimed in relief just as the door opened. He held up his own copy of the king's private chamber key, which looked very similar to the chancellor's. "I put it into my pouch instead of my pocket."

The chancellor rolled his eyes. He stepped into the room, gesturing for both Rendevas and Riluk to follow him inside.

Though he had been inside the room many times before, Rendevas never got over just how *plain* the king kept his bedroom. He had only the necessities: a large four-poster bed with richly embroidered maroon tapestries pulled aside, a bedside table with a novel placed face down upon its surface, a long wooden chest of drawers where he kept all of his casual clothes. A window facing Praetorius proper dominated one wall, though the curtains were closed. Several lit sconces lined the walls, casting a warm light for the king to see by. A closet, porcelain washbasin, heavy writing desk, and plush rug completed the space. Overall, it wasn't dissimilar to Rendevas's own apartment, except Rendevas had much finer furnishings. Of the two friends, Rendevas much preferred a life of luxury, whereas Phil was content with the basics.

King Selderin sat at his huge mahogany writing desk, his back to the door as he hunched over various rolls of parchment. He turned towards them as they entered, raising his eyebrows in confusion.

"Chancellor Eldivar, Captain Riluk, and ... Lord Rendevas?" he greeted, unable to keep the question from his voice as he spoke. "I was not expecting you so soon. Is the plenum meeting over already? Is something amiss?"

Riluk shook his head and opened his mouth to reply, but Rendevas stepped forward. "Your Majesty," he interjected with a short bow. "I am sorry to ambush you like this, but I bring you dire news."

The king's eyebrows shot up even farther. Riluk, looming with his arms crossed at the door, grumbled, "You have five minutes, Lord Rendevas."

"What is going on?" the king asked sharply.

Rendevas waited a moment to see if the chancellor and the captain would leave. When neither of them made to go, he sighed deeply, realizing his very important news—news for the *king's ears only*—would have to be shared with the lot of them. He shoved his annoyance down deep, then strode towards the king, pulling out from his jacket the sheaf of papers Milford had provided him.

"Treason," was all he said. He thrust the papers towards the king.

His old friend silently looked them over, his face blank of all emotion. He took his time, reading each line. Rendevas could barely contain himself. He fairly thrummed with anticipation.

"This is troubling indeed," King Selderin finally said, shuffling through the evidence absently. "All this time, Judge Rodach has been lining his pockets at the plenum's expense."

Chancellor Eldivar made a little sound of ... surprise? Excitement? From just behind Rendevas.

"Where did you say you got these?"

"I didn't," Rendevas replied evenly. "And I regret that I cannot. I must protect my sources."

"Mmm," was all he said. He glanced down at the papers again, as if doing so would help him come to terms with what they told him. He looked exhausted. He seemed to have aged since the last time Rendevas had seen him: more gray hairs lined his temples, and fine wrinkles marred the corners of his eyes. Even so, he remained a handsome, if always tired-looking, middle-aged man. Rendevas could still see the familiar face of his old friend, even beneath the strains of leadership. "Well, I thank you for bringing this to me. Your knowledge is immensely appreciated."

"What are you planning to do with it?" Rendevas found himself asking. "Surely you won't let Judge Rodach continue his treasonous activities."

"Two more minutes," Riluk growled from his position at the door.

"No, but I need time. I will handle it." The king sighed and slumped against his chair. "Being the King of Praetorius isn't all power and authority like you might think, Rendevas. You know this. The real power is in the plenum and the laws you all set and enforce. I'm simply a figurehead."

He stared into the distance, brow furrowed thoughtfully. "Though I do have a few tricks left up my sleeve."

Rendevas waited with bated breath for him to elaborate. "Is there anything I can do to help?"

Captain Riluk cleared his throat, causing King Selderin to blink out of his reverie. "No, no, you have done more than enough, Lord Rendevas."

It sounded like a dismissal. Desperately, Rendevas repeated, "Please, count me as someone you can trust implicitly, Your Majesty. I seek only to offer you whatever aid I can. My loyalty is to Praetorius above all else, and whatever you require of me to prove that, I will do so." He bowed deeply.

"I appreciate your candor," the king said softly.

"Your Majesty, one more thing," Rendevas blurted, before he had a chance to dismiss him outright. "Why did you hire an Inquisitor?"

The king opened his mouth to speak, then closed it just as quickly. He eyed Captain Riluk, standing at attention near the doorway.

Rendevas followed his gaze and saw as the captain gave a heavy sigh. "If you deem it wise," he said hesitantly, "I don't see any reason why you cannot tell Lord Rendevas—and Chancellor Eldivar, for that matter—about the Inquisitor. You've all known each other, and worked together, long enough."

Chancellor Eldivar's shocked expression revealed that he, too, had been kept in the dark regarding Inquisitor Burgindore's surprising arrival. *Interesting,* Rendevas thought. *So Phil kept this entirely to himself? That is very much unlike him!*

"An Inquisitor?" the chancellor cried. "Your Majesty, why involve yourself with them?"

Rendevas knew little of the mysterious and powerful guild of magic-using warriors. Rumors abounded that they enjoyed wholesale diplomatic immunity across the land, though how, or why, such a thing was even needed was beyond his knowledge. And why his old friend felt desperate enough to call upon one was a question he greatly wanted answered.

King Selderin pursed his lips, a look of pure contempt crossing his face. "This information does not leave this room, am I understood?" He glared towards the three of them, who all nodded soberly. "It appears," he answered with a sigh, "that someone on the plenum wants me dead. I intend for the Inquisitor to find out who it is."

Chapter 38
Now We Have a Plan

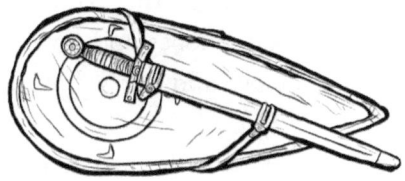

Avindea hurried past a slow clump of parishioners exiting the cathedral after morning sermons, dozens of builders hard at work on the construction of the building's additions, and, strangely enough, a group of three city guards who nodded brusquely in her direction as they left the Church.

Probably here to make sure Lucius hasn't escaped, she thought in annoyance. *Gods, trust Quay of all people to hire an* enemy soldier *as her bodyguard!*

She'd foregone all her other duties to head straight to the church after the disastrous plenum meeting that morning. It was time she hammered out a plan with Quay and her strays, hopefully before Lady Uunar and her pupils showed up the next day.

Her mind raced with possibilities. How could she hide both Lucius and Midori? She had a feeling Lady Uunar would not be daunted by a locked door, though she hoped she could keep the head of the Arcane Academy away from the cathedral's basement. There wasn't any reason she would need to look down there, but just in case …

Avin sighed, rubbing at her throbbing temples as she entered the church. What she wouldn't give to have *simple* problems again! She thought back fondly to when the most pressing matters in her life were whether or not she could trounce Paladin Brocklin in a sword fight, or which squire would be assigned to her when she traveled abroad, or, hells, even what to eat for breakfast!

By some stroke of luck, Avindea spotted Lucius and Quay hurrying down the corridor near the bathhouse, with a figure between them wearing priestess robes and a veil over her face. She flagged them down with a wave and hurried over. "Just the people I was looking for."

Quay's overly bright face was the first sign that something was amiss. "Avin! What're you doing here?"

"We need to talk in private," she added, glancing at the slender veiled person. "Who—?"

"Shh, it's Midori," Lucius hissed, grabbing Midori's arm and leading her towards the basement stairs.

"You brought *her* up here?!" Avindea sputtered. "What were you thinking?"

The four of them rushed down the stairs, slowing to a more casual pace when they ran into a builder's apprentice, his arms full of tools, rolled up blueprints, and a mug of what smelled like strong coffee. He was so frazzled and rushed that he paid them no mind. As soon as they reached the basement room, Avindea slammed the door behind her, locked it, then turned towards the three of them, who stood before her guiltily. "What was *that* all about? She could have been seen!"

"I thought she'd like having a bath," Lucius answered breezily, waving away Avindea's concerns as if she was simply overreacting. "Don't worry, we scoped it out and had the place to ourselves. As you can see, she's dressed like a priestess, so even if someone *did* see her, they'd think she was just another clergy member." He grinned at her proudly. "Don't worry! We've got things under control over here."

Faith and Ruin

Quay, however, wrangled her hands together; Avin could see her nails were chewed to the quick, a bad habit she had since she was a child. It didn't bode well for Avin if Quay was nervous enough to restart *that*. "What else happened?" she asked, eyeing her cousin with raised eyebrows.

"Some soldiers showed up to check on Lucius," Quay admitted. "They wanted to make sure he wasn't leaving the church."

"Yeah, I saw them on my way in here." Avindea frowned and rubbed her face. "This is all getting to be a lot to handle, Quay, not gonna lie."

Their secret knock sounded from the other side of the door; when Avindea opened it a crack, she saw both Hypnocost and Ghdion waiting. "Good, now we're all here," she pronounced after she let them inside. "It's time we discussed our next move."

Ghdion walked stiffly towards the back of the room, not looking at Quay; the tension between the two of them was so obvious that even Avindea noticed. Hypnocost, airy as ever, swooped inside and sat upon a stool with a flourish of blue and orange silken robes, crossing his legs primly and looking at her expectantly. Midori pulled off the delicate priestess robe and veil she'd used as a disguise and thrust them disgustedly on the end of her bed.

"We've got a problem," Avindea told them bluntly. "I just got out of a plenum meeting, where I had to tell them about our Kax issues. Not all of it, mind you, I'm not that stupid," she said, forestalling any enraged exclamations. "They know the cultists are active once again."

She took a deep breath. "They also don't think I'm 'handling the situation well on my own,' so they've assigned me a *task force.*" She spat the words as if they were a curse. "Lady Uunar, the head of the Arcane Academy, is coming here tomorrow after the next plenum meeting to check things, ostensibly to help with the Kax problem, but I really think she wants a chance to snoop around."

"Shit," Ghdion grunted from where he leaned, arms crossed, against the wall in his usual languorous posture. "That can't be good, having a mage poking around here."

"Definitely not," Avindea agreed. "That's why I need you all to clear out. Except for Lucius and Midori, of course, but the three of you," she indicated Quay, Ghdion, and Hypnocost, "need to be outta here by tomorrow morning so she can't use whatever magical powers she has to question you. Who knows what kinda spells she can cast? She might be able to find out about Midori or the blood font just by speaking with you."

"Why don't we go to the Altar of Tasuil?" Quay suggested again, her gray eyes hopeful. "It's the perfect excuse for us to be gone. We can bring the blood font to High Priestess Lucina."

Hypnocost flinched at those words; Avindea, concerned, wondered what, exactly, made him so interested in the blood font. The thing was evil! Was he evil, as well?

She narrowed her eyes at him. It wouldn't surprise her. Quay already had an enemy soldier and a criminal as bodyguards, why not an *evil mage* to round it off? "I'm hesitant to send you so far from Praetorius," she replied. "That's easily a two-day ride, not counting the return journey. A lot can happen in that time."

"We'll have the wagon and Mertha," Quay reminded her.

Ghdion snorted derisively. "I wouldn't count Mertha as an asset," he muttered.

Quay ignored him. "This can work. We can get out of the city, report all we've found out to High Priestess Lucina, and get the blood font into more capable hands all at once."

Avindea wasn't convinced, but she could tell by the excited cast of her cousin's face that Quay would not be swayed. Though mostly easy-going and joyful in demeanor, Quay could be damned stubborn about getting her way, usually to her own detriment.

She could remember when they were both children, growing up there at the cathedral. Quay, aged five or six, discovered an injured rabbit hunkered down just outside the stables. She had been determined to heal the poor creature's broken leg—even as a young child, she'd been a gifted healer—but hadn't yet learned a strong enough spell to do so. She spent days tending to it, trying all sorts of methods to nurse it back to health and stubbornly refusing any assistance or advice from the more learned clerics.

When the rabbit died four days later, Quay had been devastated.

Avindea sighed. Hands on her hips, she regarded her sternly. "I suppose that's what's gotta happen. But for the love of Vidamae, Quay, no more hiring criminals or bodyguards with secret pasts or ... or any problems like that! I've got my hands full enough dealing with everything here!"

Ghdion, Hypnocost, and Lucius shot her dirty looks. Quay just beamed and nodded vigorously. "I promise! No more strays."

"What about us?" asked Lucius, sitting in his customary spot beside Midori's bed. "Neither of us can leave, and it would be a disaster if Lady Uunar found out you were hiding a Kax follower here, of all places."

"Let me handle that," Avindea told him, her eyes flashing with determination. "For now, I want you to stay inside this room. I'll do what I can to keep Lady Uunar away from the basement, but if for some reason she starts snooping around down here tomorrow, we'll have to come up with some reason why you two are here in the first place."

"Why not just tell them the truth?" Midori spoke up in her still-scratchy voice. "Well, not the entire truth. The best lies are those that are comprised of truths, yes?" She leaned forward, warming to her subject. "I am here for medical attention, a special case. I must be kept away from the other patients. Perhaps I am contagious or have such a strange medical malady that it is in the church's best interest to keep me sequestered away from everyone else."

Quay nodded. "We even have Doctor Leonidas seeing her, though he's been paid quite handsomely for his silence. We don't have to worry about him talking."

"She could be some foreign dignitary's daughter, hiding here in the church to keep something secret, like ..." Lucius pondered. "Like a pregnancy! Happens all the time with nobles. A lord's daughter gets caught in a compromising position with, I dunno, the stablehand or something, so she gets whisked away to a church, where the clerics take care of her after receiving a hefty donation from the noble family, of course. The nobles spread the news that their poor daughter is suffering from a debilitating disease and is in the care of the clergy. Then, boom, baby's born and is given to the church, daughter is miraculously cured nine months later, problem solved."

He nodded, ignoring Midori's look of disgust. "Happens so often there's even a name for it, too, at least back home. They call it 'The Bedsheet Disease,' if you can believe that." He snorted. "That way all the rich assholes can talk about it in polite society without ruining anyone's reputation."

"Wow, that's ... oddly specific," Avindea murmured, eyebrows raised.

"Eh, I heard about it a lot from the other soldiers in the army," he answered casually. "You'd be surprised how many wards of the churches in Uldinvelm are actually bastard children of some noble family or another. A lot of them have fathers in the military, too."

"I suspect this happens everywhere, not just in Athessa," Hypnocost supplied helpfully.

"We're getting off topic now," Ghdion grunted. "This might not even come up. Hell, that lady might not actually show up tomorrow."

"Regardless, now we have a plan," Avindea supplied. "You three need to get ready for an extended journey to Tasuil, and Lucius and

Midori, no more risky trips to the bathhouse." She shot them a look as fierce and strict as that of an angry schoolteacher catching her students doing something against the rules. "I'll make sure you all have what you need for the next few days. Are we in agreement?"

They all nodded in unison.

Chapter 39

George

It only took two days for the fake Praetorian guard to reveal everything to Brakten.

That was some kind of record. Usually, the leader of The Maelstrom had to employ more sophisticated methods to pry information from his unwilling guests. This particular man, who called himself George, had only to sit in dark solitude, tied up to a chair inside the hideout underneath The Murky Bard for one full day and night before he started blubbering on about how he would tell Brakten anything, anything at all.

Brakten sat backwards in a chair in front of George, who was still blindfolded with his hands and ankles tied behind his chair. Sweat stains darkened the armpits of his roughspun shirt, and he turned his head to and fro nervously as if trying to see what imaginary horrors awaited him. Brakten almost felt sorry for the guy, until he remembered George was one of the six 'guards' who straight up murdered a visiting diplomat only three days hence.

Arms draped across the chair back, Brakten rested his chin upon his forearms and took a few moments to ponder how best to proceed. This wasn't his first interrogation, not by any stretch of the imagina-

Faith and Ruin

tion. He'd spent a good chunk of his life in situations just like this one, the difference being now he was no longer beholden to the Court of Daggers like he used to be. No, those days were long over, thankfully. He'd done his time and was enjoying his retirement from that bloody business by leading The Maelstrom, a premier information guild and sometimes, if the price was right, best thieving organization in Praetorius.

"So. George, what shall we do with you?" he began, his throaty voice ringing in the cluttered room.

Each wall was covered from floor to ceiling with shelves that held the various accouterments used by members of a thieves guild: one wall contained lockpicks in different shapes and sizes, pitons and pouches full of climbers chalk, heavy-looking practice locks, leather gloves studded with iron spikes—basically anything a thief could use while doing second-story work. A locked door led to Brakten's private chambers, and beside that were seamstress dummies and mannequins displaying all kinds of different outfits, from flowy skirts and robes to a set of armor worn exclusively by the elite guards who protected the richest families in the city. Wigs of all colors and styles hung from hooks on the wall. There was a well-lit vanity and a large mirror. Various jars of makeup and makeup brushes dotted the vanity top, as well as prosthetic noses, ears, chins, and fake eyebrows and beards. Any theater actor would be thrilled with such a setup.

George couldn't see any of that, of course, being as blindfolded as he was. He also couldn't see how different his jailer Brakten looked from Milford, that canny old man who had originally captured him. Brakten's shoulder-length (dyed) brown hair, long, slightly upturned nose, and smiling mouth full of flashing white teeth were the opposite of the wrinkles and crooked nose that Milford sported.

It was a testament to how skilled The Maelstrom's leader was at the art of disguise. Milford, in particular, was a favorite character of his to play when he was out delivering notes or patrolling the streets for information; nobody paid any attention to a little old man. It was almost better than being invisible.

George began to shake uncontrollably. "I-I'll tell you anything you want," he wailed, revealing a mouth of overlarge teeth and an unfortunate overbite. "Just please, let me go!"

"Alright then," Brakten replied amiably. "Tell me why you were on that rooftop, dressed up as a Praetorian guard. Why did you shoot at the Uldinvelm dignitaries?"

George swallowed thickly. "I-I-I was paid to do it!" he whispered. "My family is poor and starving, you see, and—"

"Yeah, you can cut that bullshit right now, I've heard it all." Brakten cut him off before he could really get going on whatever sob story he had concocted. They were hardly ever true, and people always fell on that old standby to try to appeal to whatever goodness they thought Brakten may have had.

Unfortunately for them, all Brakten's goodness had dried up

years ago. It just wasn't worth it to pretend to be good anymore. Didn't make much business sense. "Just stick with the relevant details, please. You know exactly what information I want, so don't waste any more of my time or I'll have to start getting ... creative."

He cracked his knuckles loudly, causing George to jump.

"No, no, yeah, you're right, of course," he stammered. "Can't blame a guy for tryin', right?" He tried to shrug but was prevented from doing so by the tightness of his bonds. "So you gonna take off my blindfold or ...?"

"Nope."

George waited for him to say more, but there was only a tense silence. He cleared his throat nervously. "Could I get some water or something?"

"Tell me what I wanna know and we'll see."

"But my throat is so dry and—"

Brakten's hands were around George's throat in the blink of an eye. He squeaked in surprise and began to thrash frantically. "Enough stalling," Brakten whispered darkly right next to his ear. He was so close he could smell the fear and the sweat that emanated from the killer's oily skin.

"Alright, alright! I'll talk!" George wheezed, releasing a puff of breath so rank-smelling it forced Brakten to lean backwards with a face of disgust. "You can let go of my throat now!"

He wasn't so sure about that. As a little reminder, he squeezed tightly for a moment before releasing his grip, though he remained hovering right above his prisoner. "Talk. Now."

George coughed. "We were paid to dress up like guards," he spoke hoarsely, "and told to wait on the rooftops until we saw the carriage with the Uldinvelm diplomat inside of it. We were given bows and arrows and told to wait until we all had clear shots. Killing the diplomat was the top priority, but we were to try to kill all the Athessians if we were able. Then we were to scatter and remain in hiding until we were told it was safe."

Brakten regarded his prisoner silently, turning the knowledge over inside of his head. "Why dress like Praetorian guards?"

George once again tried to shrug. "I dunno, we were never told. So we could get close enough?"

Brakten had a pretty good guess, but he didn't speak it aloud. He was swiftly coming to conclusions about who was actually behind the plot, but he needed to be absolutely sure. "Alright, how much were you each paid to prance around as pretend guards?"

"Hundred gold apiece," George answered promptly. His voice grew more confident the more he answered the questions. He was bolstered by the hope that he would survive this experience.

"Huh, only one hundred gold to sell out your country," Brakten mused. "Not much of a patriot, are you?"

"I don't care about any of that!" George snarled. "I just needed the gold. Besides, they were just *Athessians*. Why should it matter if a few of them get killed? I'd say killing them is as patriotic as it gets!"

Brakten rolled his eyes. "So who did it, then? Who hired you to kill them?"

At this, he hesitated. "I ... I can't say. They'll kill me if I do!"

In one fluid motion, Brakten pulled a hidden knife from his boot and held it against George's neck. "Oh yeah? I'll kill you if you don't, so looks like we got ourselves a case of 'damned if you do, damned if you don't.'"

He pressed the knife's edge just enough that it drew a single drop of blood from the sharp tip. "So what's it gonna be? Definitely have your throat slit by me, right now, for not talking? Or have a shot at getting the fuck out of Praetorius when I release you for telling me what I wanna know?"

"You-you'll truly release me if I tell you?" George pleaded softly. A thin line of blood trailed down his throat as he swallowed. "The Maelstrom releases those who talk for them?"

"Guess you won't know until you tell me."

He shuddered and gritted his teeth. "He's very powerful. Well-placed in the government, too. If he finds out I squealed ... He said we'd be heroes! He said—"

Brakten tightened his grip on the knife as a reminder of what was at stake. A fresh drop of blood leaked from the cut.

George let out a low whine. Tears ran down his cheeks and wet the blindfold. "It was the Judge! Judge Rodach. He paid us to kill the Athessian diplomat!"

Chapter 40

Unexpected Developments

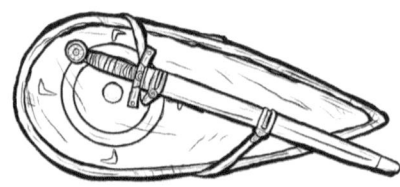

Three new people sat inside the plenum chambers the next morning.

One of them Avindea recognized. Sergeant Ramagos of the city guard was a stocky man with swept back dirty blond hair and a truly outstanding mustache that he obviously kept oiled and groomed—the delicate twists at either end were a testament to that. He was well known by all military-minded folks in Praetorius due to his prowess with a sword and shield; he spent much of his off-duty time dueling with paladins, squires, and other city guards. His jovial attitude made him an ideal sparring partner. Why he was sitting in the council chambers was beyond her, but it was obvious he was nervous. She spied a light sheen of sweat across his forehead.

The second newcomer was a tall, stern-faced man who had the pinched look of someone who was probably much younger than people initially thought. His face was haughty and pale, his cheekbones sharp and his eyes even sharper. He had jet black hair that was aggressively slicked back behind his ears; she had a feeling it would have softened his features greatly had it been left down. He wore a set of unadorned black armor and a pair of wicked black gauntlets on his hands. She understood the appeal of wearing the armor—she felt much more comfortable in armor herself—but the gauntlets were a bit overkill. This was a plenum meeting, not a battle update.

The third newcomer was almost more interesting even than the armored man. His magnetism and charm drew the eye of each counselor as they headed towards their seats. He lounged near the back of the chambers in a plush chair that had obviously been brought in for him, since it didn't match any of the other furniture. He held a small notebook and quill in his lap. His long legs were crossed, and a sleek, fashionable red jacket in a cut she was not familiar with accentuated his broad shoulders and trim waist. His hair, unlike the armored man's, was long and luxuriously loose, falling in dark waves around his shoulders where it wasn't artfully tucked behind his ears. A trim goatee completed the look. He was quite handsome, in a rakish sort of way; he regarded each plenum member with a small nod and a mysterious smile as they passed.

Most surprising was the huge mastiff that lay placidly next to him. Avindea had never seen a dog so large! Even the hunting hounds the church bred weren't as *humongous* as this creature. The mastiff was more akin to a horse or a small pony than an actual dog. In fact, if it had the right disposition, it could probably serve as a mount for one of the shorter-statured boreans. Even so, the dog seemed content to lay with its head between its front paws, its liquid brown eyes watching the proceedings with a sense of polite boredom.

Rendevas slid into his chair beside Avindea, interrupting her gawking. She acknowledged him with a curt nod, then whispered, "Who are those people?" She gestured furtively towards the man in armor and the fancy man with the dog. "I know Sergeant Ramagos, of course, but those other two I've never seen before."

Rendevas glanced towards the three newcomers, his eyebrows

raising. "The one in armor is new to me, but the other one? Fancy lad with the charming smile? That's Rakeios Burgindore." He leaned in closer so he could murmur in her ear, "An Inquisitor from Archaithos."

Avindea's mouth dropped open. "An *Inquisitor*?" she hissed.

"Shh shh, you're not supposed to know yet!"

"What is he doing here?" she whispered harshly, struggling to lower her voice. Lady Loresh and Lord Eglath, both sitting across from her, gave her puzzled looks.

"I think we're about to find out."

King Selderin entered, followed closely by Princess Alandria and Chancellor Eldivar. The king wore his finest clothes, from his polished crown and fine fur cloak all the way down to his shiny black leather boots. The princess wore a much more impressive gown than usual, looking much older than her fifteen years with the mature cut of the bodice and the elegantly draped folds of the heavy fabric skirt. She wore glittering gems at her ears and around her neck.

Both looked more regal than she'd ever seen them; it was a far cry from her first plenum meeting. Even the chancellor, who always dressed to impress, looked prouder than usual, his forest green doublet setting off his white pouf of hair nicely.

The assembly pushed back from their seats and stood, bowing in deference to their monarchs, then sat as one as soon as he indicated it was polite to do so. Chancellor Eldivar remained standing, sweeping his eyes across the council loftily.

"This plenum meeting will be a bit different from our usual affair," he announced. "As you can see, we have three new faces with us today. Allow me to introduce them to you."

He waved a hand first towards Sergeant Ramagos. "Sergeant Ramagos of the Praetorian City Guard. He may be familiar to most of you as he is an accomplished guard in his own right. He has been selected to aid Captain Riluk in the search for the assassins who killed Lord Tullie Mason two days past."

The gathered counselors nodded politely towards the mustached man, who smiled and nodded in return. Avindea caught Captain Riluk's face out of the corner of her eye; he looked tense, his smile forced and his jaw clenched. What was going on there? Was this 'help' for the investigation something he agreed with? Or had it been forced upon him?

"Our next visitor is a newcomer to the city, hailing most recently from a stint as a soldier at the rift in Thalconia. Please welcome Lord Daryér, Knight of Demos, to our meeting."

Avindea couldn't suppress the hiss that escaped her lips. Demos! The God of Power and Control, hated by Vidamae's followers almost as much as Kax was. Where Kax represented pure chaos and thrived on mayhem, Demos extolled strict control and authoritarianism.

It wasn't surprising the knight had worked with the soldiers at the rift in Thalconia; Demos followers were well known for their strict adherence to military codes and rules. They suffered nothing less than the most rigid obedience. They were well-regarded amongst most military orders, welcomed for their strategic minds and martial prowess.

But why in the hells was one of them *there*, inside the plenum chambers?

"Lord Daryér is here to petition us for the building of a new temple within Praetorius," Chancellor Eldivar continued. "He seeks permission to erect a small Church of Demos inside the city walls."

There's no way in hells I'll allow a Temple of Demos inside my city! Avindea thought fiercely. She realized her face was set in a nasty grimace, and it took her a moment to smooth out her features. Lord Eglath and Lady Loresh, both of churches who also had negative views on Demos and his ilk, eyed Lord Daryér with suspicion.

Why are you here now, of all times, to ask us about building a new church? she thought savagely. *We've got enough going on without having to deal with Demos militants scouring through Praetorius.*

Lord Daryér inclined his head at just the correct angle. He met Avindea's eyes for a split second. She felt as if he knew exactly what she was thinking. A shiver ran down her spine, but she refused to look away. She wouldn't give him the satisfaction.

"And finally," the chancellor called, gesturing grandly towards the back of the room, "I give you Inquisitor Rakeios Burgindore, all the way from Archaithos."

He didn't elaborate any further. He didn't need to. Gauging by the gasps of surprise that erupted from the counselors, everyone there knew just exactly what the appearance of an Inquisitor of Archaithos meant.

The inquisitor stood up with a sweep of his long jacket and bowed ostentatiously. "It is truly a pleasure to see you all," Rakeios announced in a thick Vostrum accent. Even with the accent, his voice was smooth and cultured. "Monty and I are looking forward to working closely with you in the coming weeks."

Chancellor Eldivar had to clear his throat three times before the assembly settled down quietly enough for him to continue. "Inquisitor Burgindore is here today to observe the inner workings of our plenum, per his official request. Please, offer him the same courtesy you would of your fellow plenum members."

"Pretend I am not even here!" Rakeios cried out happily, settling himself back into his squishy chair.

Yeah, right! Avindea thought in annoyance. *Everyone's gonna be so nervous with you breathing down our necks, there's no way things are gonna go like they usually do.* This was even worse than when she had to be shadowed by the High Templar, holiest of Vidamae's Paladins, during her last day of training as a squire. She was so nervous then that she fumbled with her sword, despite being so proficient with it that the other paladins joked she had been born with a longsword in hand. She'd nearly dropped it, point first, onto her own toes.

"To celebrate our visitors, and to show them the hospitality of Praetorius, we will be hosting a light luncheon immediately following the plenum meeting," the chancellor announced, beaming. "I expect to see you all there, where you can mingle and get to know our three new arrivals a bit before you go about the rest of your duties.

"Now, we have much to discuss, so let's get right to it," Chancellor Eldivar proclaimed with a clap of his hands and an unctuous smile. "Let's get our updates out of the way first, shall we? Captain Riluk, how goes the investigation?"

The captain looked more diminished than usual, slightly grayer around his mouth and with dark circles under his eyes. He looked as if he hadn't slept in days. "My guards are still searching every crack and crevice of the city, but so far, no luck."

He pursed his lips. "I regret to inform you all that one of the Athessian soldiers succumbed to his wounds earlier this morning, despite the heroic efforts of our doctors and medical staff." He waited for the soft murmurs of pity to die down before continuing. "The other two soldiers are still refusing to speak with me, or any other Praetorian, for that matter, and will remain in custody. They are currently being held within the Arcane Academy. We felt it would be best to keep the Athessians segregated from the Praetorian inmates, to minimize any 'accidents.'"

Nobody would say what they were all thinking: the two soldiers left alive were prisoners, plain and simple. As far as Avindea knew, the king had not yet made any outright overtures towards Uldinvelm, as he was waiting to see what the Athessian soldiers had to say.

This development did not bode well for a peaceful resolution to the conflict. Honestly, how could it? If it had been the other way around, and Praetorius had found out—days after the fact!—that several of their soldiers had been 'taken into custody' in Uldinvelm, there would have been an all-out riot. She hoped King Selderin had some sort of plan, or at least a statement prepared to offer to the public.

Commander Rakeld and Lieutenant Orvessa both sat with smug looks of superiority on their faces. They were getting exactly what they wanted from the beginning: if war wasn't declared within a fortnight, Avindea would renounce her vows as a paladin and go live in the woods as a hermit. (And she *hated* the woods.)

"Perhaps the addition of Sergeant Ramagos will be a boon to your efforts," Chancellor Eldivar said somewhat haughtily. "I expect results from both of you within the week, Captain Riluk. Do not fail me."

Riluk's lips went white, and he merely nodded.

Lord Eglath and Commander Rakeld provided updates on their new training regimen for the soldiers, followed by Lady Loresh and Judge Rodach listing the number of military supplies, siege weapons, and other goods the city had stockpiled in case of a conflict. Strangely, they reported finding small holes burrowed through the stone walls inside some of the supply storehouses; upon further inspections, they discovered a significant number of dry rations and supplies had been taken. Captain Riluk sighed and revealed he had a pretty good idea who was behind the thefts and promised to take care of it promptly.

They then told of the aging city wall and how it desperately needed an upgrade; after a quick vote, the plenum decided to use some of the taxpayer funds to shore up the city's aging defenses.

They next voted on actually *enforcing* the conscription laws they'd earlier brought back into effect; the motion passed with only Avindea and Lady Loresh as the dissenters.

Throughout it all, Inquisitor Burgindore sat quietly in his chair, scribbling voraciously in his notebook. Monty the mastiff lay still beside him, only shifting once or twice to make himself more comfortable.

That dog must be magically trained, Avindea mused distractedly while the rest of the plenum members haggled over what engineer to hire to fix the walls. *There's no way he's that obedient normally*. Even the most well-behaved hounds, in her experience, had their moments of playfulness. Monty, however, seemed content to lie as still as a rather large and intimidating statue.

Lord Rendevas's update was just as disappointing as Captain Riluk's when it was his turn to speak. He still had no idea of the truth behind Lord Tullie Mason's surprisingly early arrival, or why he'd been so brutally murdered. The good news, he related, was that Tobias Wiltwater had agreed to help with the long lines at the city gate, so that problem would be resolved sooner rather than later.

Captain Riluk suggested enforcing a city-wide curfew to keep the streets clearer to help aid in the search; that vote passed unanimously.

When asked for an update on "the Kax situation," as the chancellor named it, Lady Uunar spoke up before Avin even had a chance to open her mouth. "I'll be heading to the cathedral after the luncheon," she explained fluidly. "A few of my students from the Academy will be joining me. Lady Avindea has offered us a tour and a sit down to discuss the best next steps." She shot the paladin a look of pure triumph, dashing any hopes she had of stalling her once again.

I just hope Lucius and Midori are staying well hidden, she thought. *I don't trust Lady Uunar one whit.*

There was something artificial about the head of the Arcane Academy, and Avin's gut told her to keep her at arm's length. Her gut was rarely ever wrong, so she knew to keep her guard up around the headmistress.

"Well, now that we've all been filled in on old business, shall we get down to the new?" Chancellor Eldivar moderated eagerly. "Lord Daryér, you have the floor. Please state your case."

Lord Daryér stood, revealing a powerful frame behind that dark armor. Barrel chested and slightly bow-legged as if he spent more time upon a horse than on his own two feet, he gazed upon the plenum arrogantly. "I thank you all for inviting me within these hallowed walls. I do not take lightly the trust you have placed in me by allowing me here before you."

His voice did not match his build: it was breathy and higher pitched than she expected.

"With that being said, I come to you with a request that I, and the people of this city who follow my deity, be allowed to break ground on a new temple within Praetorius itself: a Temple of Demos. I humbly request that the plenum approves a plan to allow the immediate construction of a small church, to be built on the empty lot where the old Temple of Kax used to stand, so the quickly growing adherents of Demos' faith have a place to worship and call their own."

"What would a Temple of Demos bring to the city?" Lord Eglath asked mildly. His rapidly tapping fingers on his knees proved he was otherwise agitated and barely concealing that fact.

Here, at least, was a man on her side!

"As you know, many of our adherents follow a more martial path in life," Lord Daryér replied. "Armies the world over clamor to have a contingent of knights trained under Demos' edicts within their ranks.

Our superior discipline and military prowess make us ideal soldiers." He eyed Commander Rakeld and Lieutenant Orvessa in particular, who watched him with interest. "No offense to the military officers present, of course, but I do believe having a large assembly of Demos trained knights ready and waiting within the city could prove beneficial, given the escalating aggressions between Khamris and Athessa."

Oh, he's good, Avin scowled. *Of course he'd play the military card!*

Rakeld and Orvessa both nodded approvingly.

"That's all well and good," Avin spoke up, "but how many *actual* Demos followers live here in Praetorius? Does the city have a need for an entirely new temple?"

He turned towards her with his hollow, eerie eyes. She couldn't tell what color they were in the low light, but when he moved, it looked like they flashed crimson. She blinked to clear away the strange sight.

"You would be surprised, Lady Avindea," he answered her simply. "Though we may not have the same number of followers as the Church of Vidamae, for example, there is a large and growing contingent of people who follow the Demos faith both in Praetorius and in her surrounding villages. The hope is that, once the temple is completed, those who live outside of the city would travel here to attend our services and various religious celebrations, bringing more travelers and thus, more monetary and economic value into Praetorius."

A few of the counselors murmured approvingly. More travelers meant more gold, and more gold meant more taxes, more taxes meant higher salaries for the plenum, etc. It was an enticing prospect.

Avindea wasn't ready to give up just yet. "And are you expecting the plenum to pay from their coffers to have this temple built?" she asked, raising her voice somewhat. That ought to grab their attention: the more money promised to public works such as this new temple, the less would line their greedy pockets.

If they couldn't be swayed by their morals, she could always count on them voting with their pocketbooks.

"Of course not." Lord Daryér swept his gaze across the plenum at large, then shot her a sly look. "It was you, Lady Avindea, who gave me the idea to make this petition, actually."

Her breath caught in her throat. "Me?" she blurted, thunderstruck. Just what in Aukera had she, a Paladin of Vidamae, done to inspire a Knight of *Demos*?

"Yes, you. When I heard about your impassioned plea to rewrite the laws that prohibited religious orders to build within the city, I was inspired by your righteous, if misplaced, faith in Vidamae." He inclined his head towards her graciously. "I was even more motivated when you managed to secure the vote. What luck! Because of your efforts to have an addition added to the Cathedral of Vidamae, I was able to legally draw up plans to have my own Temple to Demos erected. My church won't be nearly as grand as your cathedral, of course, but it will be a start. All that stands in my way is the vote of the plenum."

Judge Rodach cackled nastily from his corner of the table. "My, my, how the tables have turned! He's right. He's well within the legal limits to request the construction of a new church."

"But only if he has enough support," called out Lord Rendevas from beside a sputtering Avindea. "Imagine if we let just anyone off the street have the ability to build whatever structures they wanted across the city!" He laughed without mirth. "No, there are steps that must be followed, Lord Daryér. If you do not have the required number of signatures from proven citizens of Praetorius, I am sorry to say your request is doomed from the start."

"Oh, you mean this many signatures?" Lord Daryér produced a long roll of parchment from a black leather bag at his waist. He patiently untied the ribbon that held it closed and unfurled it deliberately, revealing a length of paper that rolled halfway down the table. "May I present exactly five hundred signatures, all witnessed and accounted for, of the citizens of Khamris who desperately seek a new Church of Demos to be built right here in Praetorius."

Lady Loresh, who sat closest to him, grabbed the parchment and scanned its contents quickly. "It looks to be in order," she told them all with much reluctance. "We'll want to verify these are all legitimate, of course, but from what I can tell ..." Her voice trailed off and she glanced at Avindea in despair. Her shoulders moved up in a sad little shrug.

"Of course," Lord Daryér agreed. "I would expect nothing less from the governing body of the city."

There's no way he would supply fake signatures, Avindea thought in despair. *Not being a Knight of Demos. They follow the laws with rigid exactness. Each and every one of those names is an actual person who supports Demos here inside Praetorius. Disgusting!*

No one else spoke up. After a slight pause, Chancellor Eldivar clapped his hands again. "Well, all that awaits now is the vote! If we've heard enough from Lord Daryér ..."

Nobody spoke. Avindea sat there, feeling helpless and appalled, but she had nothing. What could she say? 'Please don't let this man build a Demos Temple because Vidamae Paladins don't like that particular god?' There was nothing left to do but see how the plenum would vote.

"Alright then. All those in favor of allowing Lord Daryér access to the plot of land where the old Temple of Kax used to sit, where he will begin construction on a Church of Demos, raise your hands."

She scanned the sea of raised hands. Judge Rodach and Constable Mald, of course, they were always in lockstep ... Commander Rakeld and Lieutenant Orvessa, naturally—the military might of a contingent of Demos Knights would be too tempting for them to refuse ...

Then Lady Uunar raised her hand.

"I count five yeas," Chancellor Eldivar announced. "The yeas have it. Lord Daryér, your petition has been granted, pending the results of the veracity of your signatures, of course. Congratulations."

Avindea had a moment to reflect on how strange life worked sometimes. Within the space of less than an hour, a man—a complete stranger!—had waltzed into this room and upended her entire existence with his simple request.

He smiled at her triumphantly; *You've made a new nemesis this day*, she thought at him fiercely. *I'll make you rue the day you chose Praetorius for your awful little church!*

It was raining.

Not the clean, fresh rain enjoyed on a spring day, full of hope and renewal. No, those months were long past, and autumn was in full force in Khamris now. This was a cold, relentless drizzle that seeped through one's bones and made a person shiver uncontrollably, no matter how warm the cloak they wore.

It made for an inauspicious beginning to Quay's, Ghdion's, and Hypnocost's journey from Praetorius to the Altar of Tasuil.

They spent most of the morning packing up the wagon. The poor stablehand Hooper, busily rubbing down the three horses that the bodyguards brought back with them from the Kax Temple, took one look at their three faces and sighed, grabbing the set of reins to re-apply to Mertha the ox.

Mertha watched them all dolefully from her stall. "Again?" Hooper muttered. "But you just got back!"

"A priestess-in-training's work is never done," Quay responded with forced cheer, pulling her traveling cloak more tightly over her shoulders.

Hooper sighed and continued his work, fixing a set of wooden stilts to the corners of the wagon so they could drape a waterproof cloth over the back. He loaded the cargo area with the various supplies that had been stacked near the stable entrance.

Faith and Ruin

It was much colder than she'd anticipated. Quay stood beside Lucius beneath the overhang at the back of the cathedral, eyeing the chilly rainfall with resignation. He was there to see them off; he rubbed his arms as he watched the busy proceedings with interest.

She rummaged through her pack to make sure all of her things—most importantly, the blood font!—were safely packed inside. (The little carving of Mertha Ghdion had gifted her was nestled between two spare robes. Her breath hitched in her throat when she saw it.) She debated running back into the cathedral to grab more blankets when Hooper led Mertha, hitched to the wagon, before her.

"Let's go," Ghdion growled as he easily climbed up onto the bench. His own cloak was made of a deep green wool, much warmer than her well-worn gray canvas. The hood was pulled up to keep his face out of the rain. He wouldn't even look at her. "If we don't get movin' now, it'll be a week before we reach our destination with how slow Mertha moves."

Quay *hmphed* at his completely unfair assessment of the gentle ox. She patted Mertha's neck fondly.

"Hey," Lucius muttered at her back. "It'll be okay. He'll come around, I promise." He indicated Ghdion's taciturn face with a waggling of his eyebrows. "And if he doesn't, I'll kick his ass for you, alright?"

Quay smiled sadly at him, then pulled him into a quick hug. "Thanks, Lucius. Tell Midori I said bye, okay? We'll see you soon."

She clambered up next to Ghdion on the bench—she wasn't about to let his recent sulky attitude deter her from taking her place at the front of the wagon. Ghdion offered his hand, but she pointedly ignored it. As she settled beside him, she heard him sigh wearily.

Truth be told, she hated that they hadn't spoken in over a day now. She'd vowed to herself that she would apologize to him for so bluntly revealing she had knowledge of his traumatic past. If that's what it took to get them back to a friendlier, easier coexistence, she was happy to oblige. She owed him that much.

The wagon trundled away from the cathedral. Mertha seemed

unbothered by the cold rain with her thick, shaggy white fur. Quay waved goodbye to Lucius; he watched their departure all the way up until the wagon went over the hill and out of sight.

Within the first hour, it was clear that the vow she'd made was easier said than done. They passed through the city gates, traveling the well-used main road out of the city, and the entire time, Ghdion sat there as stony and silent as a statue.

The ruts in the dirt were deeper and muddier than normal, slowing their progress through the countryside. The cold rain didn't let up, and it wasn't long before she was shivering violently in her seat, completely drenched. Hypnocost, the *devil*, was bundled up, warm and dry, beneath the white canvas covering they had draped over the wooden stilts atop the bed of the wagon. All of their sacks and boxes of supplies were arranged around him, and Quay could see from the corner of her eye that he lounged against the side, happily reading by his little ball of mage light.

Her pack was beside him, and he absently stroked the glassy surface of the blood font every once in a while, as if he were pondering all of its secrets. Secretly, she was glad to be rid of the thing; every time she held it, it made her whole body crawl. That little contraption caused untold suffering. She would be even more thrilled when she could hand it off to High Priestess Lucina, who surely would know what to do with it.

There was nothing stopping her from climbing into the back of the wagon, where it was warm and dry. Nothing but her own mulish stubbornness.

A particularly violent shiver overtook her body, causing her teeth to chatter loudly. She heard a loud, heavy sigh from Ghdion beside her, and seconds later a warm, heavy wad of wool fabric landed with a *fwoomph* on her lap.

"Put that on," he demanded, sounding angrier even than usual.

She glanced over and saw he had pulled off his own cloak. He was already drenched clear through his shirt, which quickly turned translucent from the rain. His blonde hair hung in sopping clumps around his eyes, and rain dripped from the tip of his long, straight nose.

"I'm fine, I—"

"Just gimme yours instead," he cut her off rudely. "Your teeth are chattering so loud they can hear you clear out to Uldinvelm."

He was obviously not in the mood for arguing, so she did as asked and handed him her soaked canvas cloak. He shrugged it on, little ripples of rain cascading down his shoulders with the movement. She spared a thought for how uncomfortable he must be, stuck out in the rain in his bad mood, wearing a too-small cloak that was thin and completely soaked with rainwater.

It didn't stop her from pulling his much thicker and more weather-appropriate cloak over her shoulders. It was warm from his body heat. A little shiver went down her spine, but it wasn't because of the cold. She snuggled against the cloak, feeling shamefully blissful. Gods, but that man always exuded heat! The fabric even *smelled* like him, a mixture of leather, lanolin, grass, (probably from the wool) and light sweat. It was weirdly intoxicating. Why would a sweaty man smell so *good*? Surreptitiously, she brought the extra-large hood closer to her nose and took a whiff.

Of course he spotted her. "Are you sniffing my cloak?" he asked in strained tones. Bright spots of redness appeared high up on his cheeks.

"No!" she squeaked, but her face got so hot that it was obvious she was lying. "I was just bringing the hood closer to stay warm."

"Uh-huh." He looked away, the reins held tightly in his fists.

Vidamae help me, she bemoaned silently.

The silence that followed was so long and thick with tension that Quay desperately searched her mind for something to break it. She realized she hadn't thanked him for sharing his cloak. That was as good a reason as ever to try to get him to talk to her, so she blurted, "Thank you," at the same time he burst out with, "Are you warm enough?"

"What?" they both asked in unison.

He was looking at her, at least! "You first," he mumbled, not quite meeting her eyes.

"Oh, I just said thank you. For the cloak," she clarified.

"Ah. Yep." He turned fully away.

She was losing him! "What did you say? Before, I mean."

"Nothing."

She sighed. It was going to be a long, long, *long* journey.

The luncheon was served in the largest meeting room within the capitol. A rectangular banquet table was set up, sporting a fine tablecloth, artfully arranged flower centerpieces, a large crystal bowl of punch, various plates of fruit, tiny sandwiches, mixed nuts, and other snacks. Servants oversaw the whole event, and they stood stiffly in their uniforms along the wall, beneath the large windows that faced the street.

Avindea was one of the last counselors to enter. She had to collect herself from the shock of the disastrous plenum meeting. She couldn't even run away to rage in the privacy of her own home, either: Lady Uunar and her mage students' impending visit to the cathedral hung over her head like a cloud of doom.

No amount of planning would make the visit any easier, so she had come to the conclusion she'd have to do her best and wing it.

High Priestess Lucina chose poorly with me as her plenum replacement, she thought to herself darkly, not for the first time. *She really believed that I was the best option? When she gets back from Tasuil, she's going to have such a mess to clean up, thanks to me!*

She browsed the little foods absently, placing on her plate a random assortment of delicacies that she had no intention of actually eating. Her appetite had flown from her as soon as that arrogant Lord Daryér's petition had been approved.

The other plenum members glided easily around her as she brooded silently. Even the king and the princess were there, chatting politely with Inquisitor Burgindore in the corner.

Avin kept half an eye on the rest of her fellow counselors. Rendevas tucked into his plate piled high with tiny sandwiches. Rakeld and Orvessa discussed something with Eglath, most likely more troop movements or strategies for a siege. Loresh nodded along politely to Sergeant Ramagos as he prattled on and on about the best practices for implementing the conscription laws, and Judge Rodach stood off with Constable Mald, both looking grumpy and unimpressed.

Rendevas sauntered over, dabbing at the corners of his mouth delicately with a cloth napkin. "So, what do you think of your first plenum luncheon?" he asked airily.

She shrugged, frowning down at her sparse plate. "It's ... eh. Do these happen often?"

"They used to be more frequent," he said. "But with everything that's happening, it would be the height of bad taste to make the taxpayers fund our lavish meals." He peered more closely at her. "That whole business with the new Church of Demos really rattled you, huh?"

"Is it that obvious?" She scowled. "First, the war and the diplomat's murder, then Kax's re-emergence, and now a Church of Demos right here in the city? It's more than I can handle."

"You'll find you can handle much more than you think," he told her gently. "You have to, being on the plenum."

"Yeah, well, luckily for me, this isn't forever." She placed a slice of orange into her mouth and forced her face into a more pleasant expression. "As soon as High Priestess Lucina returns, I'll—"

"Lady Avindea," came the raspy voice of Lord Daryér behind her.

She turned around slowly, willing her hot rage at simply *hearing* his voice to subside. The best she could do was offer him a tight-lipped smile. "Lord Daryér," she mustered by way of a greeting. She gave him a curt nod and turned around dismissively.

"I wanted to tell you that I look forward to working closely with you in the coming weeks," he pressed on, not the least perturbed by her rudeness. "Both Lord Eglath and Lady Loresh have been most welcoming and have agreed to assist me with navigating the inner workings of the religious orders in Praetorius. I trust the Church of Vidamae will be just as helpful?" He worded the last as more of a statement than a question, as if he knew she could only answer in the positive.

She wanted to hiss. Instead, she forced out, "Mmm hmm."

"Excellent. I am especially interested to learn how the Church of Vidamae manages so many public projects and charities. You must have exceedingly generous patrons and a high percentage of tithing from your congregations."

"All of our monetary donations are listed in the public domain." Avindea smiled tightly. It was really more of a grimace. "If you are so interested, you could go to the library and look them up yourself."

He arched a dark eyebrow. "Indeed? That is a relief. So the complaints I heard from some of the citizens about how high tithing is at the Cathedral of Vidamae must be just rumors." He took a sip of punch, eyes never leaving hers. "I was worried that your parishioners were footing a majority of the cost of the cathedral's addition, despite the fact that the building is one of the largest in Praetorius."

Rendevas placed a calming hand upon Avindea's back, as if to remind her where she was. "Surely you are aware of just how popular the Church of Vidamae is all across Khamris." Rendevas smiled. "And for good reason. Vidamae's clergy does good works for a paltry sum, and sometimes for no sum at all! They employ doctors from their own coffers, and don't charge a single gold piece to anyone too poor to afford medical attention. They deliver supplies to the destitute villages around the region. The Church of Vidamae is a bright spot in an otherwise dark world."

"Besides, the addition is well overdue," Avindea snapped, more sharply than she intended. "We don't force anyone to tithe inside our cathedral. It is a purely personal choice that all of our parishioners make." She raised her chin, daring him to contest her.

"Truly, Vidamae's Chosen are passionate in their loyalty to their goddess." He raised his half-full glass of punch before stepping away to darken some other unsuspecting person's space.

As soon as he was far enough away to not hear her, Avindea growled, "I hate that man."

Rendevas patted her consolingly.

Lady Uunar chose that moment to sashay over, looking as pleased as a cat that ate all of the cream that had been set out for the express purpose of its owner's coffee. "Lady Avindea, I trust you are ready to escort my students and I to the cathedral? I can honestly say we've been looking forward to it all morning. I'm bringing my two brightest pupils with me, and they are eagerly awaiting us just outside."

Avin took a large swig of punch to give herself a moment to respond. All of the dancing around the obvious, using pretty words to hide the truth, exhausted her. Nobody would just outright say what they wanted! They had to act as if the whole thing was a stage and the world was their audience. She hated it.

"Of course, Lady Uunar. If you'll allow me to—"

"What is that?" Rendevas blurted, interrupting her. His gaze was directed at the front of the room, where two city guards had just entered, holding a pair of manacles between them. Captain Riluk strode towards them, looking stern and cold, and whispered something to them both.

"Oh, my," Lady Uunar breathed, watching avidly. The guards, led by Riluk, marched towards the corner of the room, where King Selderin stood talking with Judge Rodach. Constable Mald hovered uncomfortably nearby. Inquisitor Burgindore, with his mastiff pressed against his legs, watched closely, a wine glass held in one hand.

"Judge Rodach," Captain Riluk called out in ringing tones.

The rest of the assembly turned as one at his booming voice. Judge Rodach glanced in annoyance at the captain, the deep lines around his mouth more pronounced as he frowned. "What is this?" he cried. Nobody missed the slight note of panic that laced his voice.

"You've been charged with high treason," Captain Riluk announced. He gestured towards the two guards, who stepped forward with the manacles outstretched. "Come with us quietly and you will not be harmed."

"What is the meaning of this?" Rodach screeched, wrinkled eyes beseeching. He turned towards King Selderin. "Your Majesty, this is an outrage! You cannot allow this to happen!"

The king watched the spectacle in silence, his face stoic and unmoved. "That's quite enough, Rodach," he finally said. "You've been selling your plenum votes for years, and I finally have the proof to convict you. It is well past time you were punished for your crimes."

Gasps of shock fluttered around the room. Avindea could hardly believe what she saw.

"This is an outrage!" the judge spat, lips snarling. "What proof? This sounds like a set-up! I deny the authenticity of whatever 'proof' you speak of, and demand to see it! How dare you accuse me of such ... of such cowardly lies!"

The two guards yanked the judge's wrists and clamped the manacles upon them, the loud click of the lock echoing with a note of finality. Captain Riluk placed his hand upon the old man's back and pushed him towards the door. "You will be accorded a trial by your peers in the next few days, though you already know all of that, don't you, *judge*?" He shoved against him ungently. "Your knowledge of the law should serve you well when it comes time for you to explain exactly what you did and why."

"This is a travesty!" Judge Rodach railed.

"Get him out of here," the king snarled. Riluk nodded brusquely and grabbed the judge's arms to maneuver him out the door, the two city guards following closely behind.

Nobody quite knew what to do after that. The other counselors stood there awkwardly, holding their plates and glasses and wondering just where the best place to land their eyes could be.

King Selderin, his shoulders back and his head held proudly, addressed the room. "I am sorry you had to be a part of such a spectacle," his voice rang out. "But it was, sadly, necessary for you all to be witness to the judge's downfall. The depths of his treachery are only just now surfacing. We will have much to discuss in the next meeting."

They stared mutely at their king. Sergeant Ramagos and Lord Daryér looked embarrassed to be there. Inquisitor Burgindore simply smiled mysteriously and jotted down notes energetically. Constable Mald looked enraged, his close-set eyes dotted with hard glints, his meaty fists clenched at his sides. The rest of the plenum looked adrift, unsure what to do next.

Chancellor Eldivar, Avindea was surprised to see, had a look of triumph upon his pale face that caught her off guard. What was he so pleased about? One of the longest-serving members of the plenum was just accused of high treason! What was there to *smile* about?

"Please, avail yourselves of the luncheon," King Selderin called out. "I know you all have questions, and they will be answered at our next meeting. Until tomorrow." He gave them a tight nod, gestured towards his daughter, and they both left, flanked by their guards, leaving a thunderously shocked plenum in their wake.

"Well," Rendevas let out a slow, impressed breath. "That was certainly something!"

"Lady Avindea, may we postpone our tour of the cathedral?" Lady Uunar asked. She looked distracted. "I fear this unexpected development is forcing me to rethink my plans for the day."

Avindea wanted to cheer with relief. Instead, she bowed graciously. "Of course. You may call upon me whenever it is most convenient for you, Lady Uunar."

Uunar smiled tightly and placed her glass upon the table. "Until tomorrow." She gathered her silken black skirts and swished out the door without bothering to say goodbye to anyone else.

Chapter 41

Revelations

It was still raining when it was time for them to stop the wagon for the night.

The route from Praetorius to Tasuil was rugged and barren, surrounded on both sides by thick forests and hilly terrain the closer to the mountains they traveled. Ghdion, Hypnocost, and Quay had long since passed the last village, where they stopped for a quick lunch and a chance to dry off, as well as give to Mertha a much-needed rest. The remainder of the journey would be along the remote path that led up into the mountains of Summuran; there were no other settlements along the route, so they would have to rough it and camp out for the night.

Since the back of the wagon was helpfully covered with the weather-proof fabric, they planned to use that as a makeshift shelter. When the sky darkened past the point that they couldn't see the road ahead of them without the aid of a torch, Ghdion flicked the reins and pulled Mertha off to the side.

"This is as good a place as any to stop," he muttered, stretching. Glancing up at the rainy, starry sky, he added, "Too bad we can't make a campfire."

Hypnocost, spry and good-natured after having spent the entire day warm and dry in the back of the wagon, hopped down from the back. His boots landed with a loud squelch in a shallow puddle, and he sneered at it in disgust.

"Eurgh!" he exclaimed, taking an immediate step backwards. "Must we really stop here, surrounded by all this mud?"

Ghdion gave him a dry look that Hypnocost couldn't see in the dark, but it made him feel better. "Hypnocost. It's been raining all day. There's puddles everywhere."

The half-elf shivered. "Well then, I am going back into the wagon," he announced.

"I don't think so," Ghdion growled, rounding the side so he stood right in front of him. "You've been resting all day back there. After we eat, you're sitting up front and keeping watch so we can get some sleep."

Hypnocost scoffed. "In the *rain*?"

"In the rain. You won't melt."

He let out a heavy, dramatic sigh. "Fine. I suppose I can take first watch."

"Make sure you actually *stay awake* this time," Ghdion grumbled. "The last time you 'kept watch,' you fell asleep halfway through and that ogre almost smashed your brains out, remember?"

Hypnocost didn't deign to respond to that.

Ghdion rummaged through one of their packs until he found the dry rations, which were bundled packs of hardtack, dried fruits and nuts, and some hunks of jerky. It wasn't the most appetizing of meals, but it was better than going hungry. He handed one first to Quay, then to Hypnocost, taking the last for himself; they had enough rations to last them for weeks, just in case they ran into trouble on the road.

The three of them sat huddled in their cloaks beneath the canvas covering, chewing their meager dinners quietly. Ghdion watched Quay out of the corner of his eye; she looked miserable, small and shuddering, encased as she was in his thick woolen cloak. She pushed the large hood down off her face, revealing dark circles under her eyes. She nibbled at her piece of hardtack absently, her face faraway and distracted.

He hated how things had gone back at the cathedral. All of those painful memories rushed in, so he'd been an idiot and lashed out at her. He'd kept that dark part of his life pushed far back into his mind for years, as he was unable (or unwilling) to fully deal with it.

It was easier to simply pretend it never happened. Then he wouldn't have to learn to live with the aching absence of his murdered family.

Now she knew about it. Instead of her playful jibes and good-natured chats, she would have only pity for him and his tragic story. The last thing he wanted from anyone, most of all *her*, was pity! He brooded silently, ignoring his meal as he stared off into the darkness.

Hypnocost munched happily on his fruit and nuts, oblivious to the tension between the two of them. "Quay," he said between bites, "what exactly is to happen at the Altar of Tasuil that is so important? What makes it such an integral place for the Vidamae Church?"

Quay stopped nibbling at her jerky and turned towards him. "Well, from what I know, that area of Tasuil is considered holy by the Church. They claim it is one of the first places the goddess appeared during Her many visitations to Aukera."

She broke a piece off her hardtack and spun it around between her fingers. "They built a huge fortress-like temple there in Her honor. Back during The Troubles, most of the priestesses gathered there to pray together for Vidamae's guidance. The force of their prayers moved Her to act, and She answered the call by casting a light so bright into the eyes of Her enemies that it made them all go blind. I'm assuming they are planning to do something similar."

She glanced up and looked right at Ghdion. "But you should be an expert about that by now, right?"

He started, unsure of what she was getting at. "No," he answered shortly. "How would I?"

"You didn't read about it in the basement library?"

Ghdion and Hypnocost exchanged guilty looks. "How'd you know we were in there?" he asked, suspicion darkening his voice.

Quay rolled her eyes. "I've lived in that cathedral most of my life, Ghdion. I knew you two were in there. I had to make up some story about why the lock was broken when another acolyte discovered it." She sighed. "You're not as sneaky as you think."

He scowled down at his rapidly diminishing dinner. "I'll replace the lock," he mumbled. "Just take it out of my wages if it's that big a deal."

Quay sighed and looked away, her lips bloodless and her face pale. "That's not what I meant," she mumbled.

Hypnocost brushed off his fingertips with a cloth napkin. "We did not read anything about that prayer," he said. "Actually, we read about what happened with your church *after* The Troubles. It was quite enlightening."

Ghdion's head shot up. He shook his head vigorously, trying to silently signal to the half-elf to stop talking, but Hypnocost either didn't understand or didn't care.

He continued, "Did you know that the Church of Vidamae was party to a series of show trials, all against so-called Kax cultists, where they publicly executed every single defendant?"

Ghdion groaned. Hypnocost, unaware, dabbed at his mouth delicately. "I even read that a group of Vidamae's Paladins rode out and massacred an entire village of innocents, all because a few Kax followers lived there. It was quite tragic." He recited the facts with a cold aloofness. "Perhaps you could ask Lady Avindea about it. Maybe she is privy to that little bit of history?"

Quay's face, already waxy to begin with, paled considerably. "What?" she blurted, looking confused and hurt. "What are you talking about? The Vidamae Church would never do something like that!"

"Oh, but they did!" Hypnocost exclaimed, soldiering right on without a thought for the poor priestess's obvious dismay. "It was all there, written in the book, *The Trials of Kax: An Account Following the Troubles*, by Archpriest Dolimeer Dorcus." He leaned back against the wooden side of the wagon, looking pleased with himself. "I even took the time to research this archpriest. It seems he was a leader of the church during The Troubles and was the deciding vote in how the Kax cultists were ultimately dealt with. Fascinating, is it not?"

Quay's stricken face hurt Ghdion more than he would admit. "That's enough, Hypnocost," he growled.

"Oh, but there is more!" Hypnocost breathed, eager to keep lecturing. "That archpriest was also the reason that—"

"I said that's enough." Ghdion's low voice brooked no argument. He glared daggers at Hypnocost, whose mouth dropped open in surprise at how vehemently the statement was delivered.

Quay sat there quietly, shrinking deeper and deeper into his borrowed cloak as the meaning of Hypnocost's words sank in.

"I-I had no idea," she whispered, so softly they could barely hear her over the patter of rain drops. "Is it true? Did my church really do those things?" She locked eyes with Ghdion, her own gray eyes shining with hurt and mute appeal.

He looked away. He was a coward, after all. He didn't want to see that heartbreaking look of betrayal in her eyes. "According to what we read, yeah."

"I see." Her cultured voice was small, as if she was barely able to contain her distress.

If he thought the awkward, fraught silences throughout the day were bad, this awful, worldview-shattering quiet from Quay was so much worse. He felt miserable as he witnessed her faith getting broken into tiny pieces right before his eyes. "Quay, it—"

"I'm going to bed," she declared, wrapping the cloak more tightly around her shoulders. She crawled into the far corner of the wagon bed and curled into a little ball, not bothering with blankets or pillows or any kind of bedding to make her night more comfortable.

Ghdion glowered at Hypnocost. "Nice job, asshole," he hissed softly so she wouldn't overhear him. "You didn't have to be so insensitive about it."

Hypnocost's eyebrows rose. "How is that my fault? I had no idea she was not aware of the atrocities her church committed in the past!"

Ghdion scowled. "Just get outside and keep watch."

"I do not want to take first watch," he whined. "I am always much more tired if I take the first one."

"Fine, then I'll do it." Ghdion stood up as far as the cramped space would allow him and gathered up an armful of blankets and pillows from the wooden crates. He ignored the half-elf as he slunk out of the back of the wagon, grumbling something about having to go 'relieve himself and freshen up.'

Ghdion knelt beside Quay's bunched up form, suddenly self-conscious and hesitant to speak. "Quay?" he whispered. Her back was to him. "I got you some blankets. You'll freeze if you don't use them."

"I'm fine." Her voice was muffled from inside the cloak. "Goodnight, Ghdion."

He sighed, then got to work assembling a bed out of the extra blankets and pillows he'd grabbed. Ignoring her squeak of protest, he gently lifted her head and pushed the softest pillow beneath her neck, then covered her body with a thick flannel blanket.

Outside, the rain continued its incessant pitter-patter on the fabric covering. An owl hooted somewhere in the distance, mournful and lonely. The darkness enveloped everything with a heavy coldness that seeped into Ghdion's bones; despite the long, weary day, he felt jittery and restless.

Hypnocost, back from taking his piss or whatever he was doing, slunk into the back of the wagon, not bothering to acknowledge Ghdion on the way as he got ready for bed.

He sat silently at his sentinel duty, alone with his thoughts.

The Murky Bard was much busier than usual that evening. Poor Jerald had a hard time keeping up with all his orders, slinging mugs of beer this way and that and barely able to give Rendevas a nod of welcome as the diplomat slid into his seat at the bar. "Everyone's getting their drinks much earlier," the barkeep explained at Rendevas's quizzical look. "Because of the curfew they just announced." He sighed heavily as he filled a mug to the brim. "I gotta admit, it's not great for business, Lord Rendevas."

Rendevas smiled weakly and shrugged. There wasn't much he could do about that, given that the law had only just gone into effect. Beside, he was bursting to speak to Milford about the news of Judge Rodach's arrest. All his plans he'd carefully set in motion these long months were finally coming to fruition! He took a sip of his beer, wheels turning inside his head as he pondered more schemes; he was so involved in his own inner thoughts that he didn't hear the old man approach and hop onto the seat next to him.

"'Lo, Milford," Jerald called out, sliding a foamy mug of his favorite spirits across the bar. Milford caught it deftly with one hand and took an immediate swig, jolting Rendevas out of his reveries.

"I'm assuming you've heard the news," Rendevas began, unable to keep a shifty grin from his face.

"Of course," Milford scoffed, wiping his mouth with the back of his hand. "It's all anyone's been talking about. Congrats, my lord, looks like all of your dreams came true."

Rendevas gave a little mock bow from his seat. "It was all thanks to you, my dear. Couldn't have done it without you."

They sat in companionable silence, each drinking their beer and listening to the band play from the stage behind them. Tonight, a full complement of musicians performed for the Murky Bard's patrons: a drummer, lute player, piper, and violinist accompanied an elven singer whose voice was actually quite impressive. The loudness of the music was a boon for them, as it made whatever dealings they decided to discuss much harder for anyone around to overhear.

"So ..." Milford finally spoke up. "You here just to gloat about the judge?"

"Actually, no, though I am always up for a good gloat." He sighed, staring into the depths of his ale. "You know about the Athessian diplomat, yes?"

Milford smirked, eyes twinkling with secrets. "What kind of Maelstrom operative would I be if I didn't?"

He expected that answer. "You don't happen to know anything about the people who killed Lord Tullie, do you? I was there when it happened, Milford. I saw them. There were six archers on the roofs. *Six!* And Captain Riluk *still* hasn't found any of them for questioning. It's been a mess. How could they have gotten away? Where did they go?" He ran his hand through his hair in frustration. "None of it makes any sense, and we aren't any closer to figuring things out."

Milford chuckled. "Well, I might have something that'll cheer you up. If you're willing to travel a bit, I've got some juicy news that I can't divulge here." He shuffled on his seat. "Involving that very incident at the city gate."

Rendevas paused. "Oh really?" Did The Maelstrom actually have information about the Athessian diplomat's demise? This could be huge!

Milford waved over Jerald for a refill on his beer. "Meet me near the statue of King Marius at the docks in a half hour. We can talk there."

Rendevas nodded eagerly. He placed a few coins on the counter before making his way towards the exit.

Faith and Ruin

Brakten, disguised as Milford, brought his refilled mug to his lips when a terrifyingly familiar form slid into Rendevas's recently vacated spot at the bar.

He glanced sidelong at the newcomer and nearly spit out his alcohol in shock.

Niserie ... why was *she* here?!

Niserie was tall and lithe, blonde hair pulled into a high ponytail, red lips quirked in that ever-present half smile that could easily enchant any person who laid eyes on her. Her long, elegant fingers clasped innocently together on the countertop; one wouldn't think they were a pair of the deadliest hands in all of Eastern Aukera. Those hands had ruthlessly killed so many people. Dozens, perhaps *hundreds*.

This woman could make herself the spotlight in any room with a simple brush of lip stain, or make herself forgettable with a deft twist of a head scarf. She almost made Brakten's skills in disguise look like child's play.

Almost. She was *good*, but not *Brakten good*. When it came to her skills at assassination? Now *that* was something he had no trouble admitting she excelled at, well beyond his own impressive talents.

Her presence there was an ill omen to be sure. She was one of the most skilled—and most dangerous—assassins employed by the Court of Daggers. The very same guild Brakten had left years ago.

Jerald hustled over, smiling warmly at the blonde woman. "What can I get you, miss?" he asked, pulling an empty mug from behind the counter.

"Oh, just a shot of something sweet," she requested with a slight smile. Her voice was a husky purr low in her throat. She'd enchanted many men—and women—with that voice alone. She slid a coin across the counter. "Surprise me."

"Comin' right up."

Jerald bustled towards the other end of the bar. Niserie, still with that mysterious smile, lifted a painted nail to her chin and scratched it idly. "Nemboril. Long time, no see."

He blanched from behind his layers of makeup, prosthetic nose, and fake wrinkles. The fact that she used his *real* name was a bad sign. The Court must've sent her to speak with him.

But why? He was retired!

"You must be mistaken, dearie," he responded in his Milford voice. "My name's Milford, and I was just leaving."

Her hand shot out to the side, her nails digging into his forearm painfully. "Not just yet, *Milford*. It's been too long since we've last spoken! Surely you won't deny an old friend a quick drink and a hello."

Jerald reappeared just then, holding a tiny shot glass full of a bright red liquid. "Cherry Jubilee, one of our sweetest concoctions." He presented it to her with a flourish and a wink. "It may be a small drink, but it packs quite the punch."

Niserie's eyes brightened. "Perfect, thank you. And it's even my favorite color, the same shade as my lip stain." She took the small glass between her thumb and forefinger and downed the entire contents in one gulp. Licking her lips in satisfaction, she pronounced it, "Perfect. Just the right amount of sweetness and tartness. You're truly a genius with mixed drinks."

Jerald beamed. "Just holler if you'd like another!" he called before hustling back to his other patrons.

Niserie finally looked him full in the face. She cocked one perfectly sculpted eyebrow. "Milford, your powers with a makeup brush are unparalleled. You know I *almost* believed you were really an old man? That's some talent."

She shook her head, chuffing out a mirthless laugh. "But let's make this quick, shall we? You've got an appointment with Lord Rendevas soon, don't you."

She didn't phrase it as a question. Nemboril (that really was his true name, as, yes, Brakten was yet another layer of his endless disguises) gulped uneasily—she was making it very clear just how much she knew about his work in Praetorius. "What do you want?" he whispered, still using his Milford voice. "I'm retired."

Niserie just chuckled. "Don't play dumb. You know nobody actually retires from the Court, not really." She leaned back from the bar and regarded him coldly. "Why retire? Just to be an information broker in backwater Praetorius? How boring! Your skills are wasted here and you know it."

"Just what exactly do you want?" he asked darkly, controlling his facial features so he wouldn't give away any of his emotions. If she was here on a job, it didn't bode well for anyone in Praetorius. Mostly him. The Court of Daggers hadn't needed to send any of their Blades to this city for as long as he'd been around, so what had changed? And did it have anything to do with what he'd dug up for Rendevas?

"As you may have guessed, I'm here on business." She smiled sweetly. "Just giving you a heads up. You know, as a professional courtesy."

"And what business would that be?"

She gave him a flat look. "Come on, *Milford*. You know I can't answer that." She rested her elbows on the counter. "I'll stay out of your way if you stay out of mine."

"And how am I supposed to do that?"

Niserie laughed, and this time the sound was full of actual merriment. "You're intelligent enough, you'll figure it out." She glanced out the large window at the front of The Murky Bard. "You'd better get a move on, though. It's getting dark, and you'll miss your appointment with Rendevas."

How the fuck does she know all this? he thought. *I shouldn't meet with Rendevas, not with Niserie shadowing me at every turn. Why in the hells is she here? Who is she working for?*

His thoughts were a whirl. He had halfway made up his mind to forgo his appointment with Lord Rendevas entirely when he realized, *Ah, hells, she already knows I'm going to meet with him. If she wanted that information secret, she wouldn't have told me. She could've shanked the both of us in a dark alley without anyone being the wiser. It's really not gonna matter whether or not I go, is it?*

Nemboril stood, gathering his long Milford robes in his hands. "This isn't over," he hissed as he passed behind her, adjusting the shawl more tightly around his be-wigged head.

"I'll be watching," she smiled, voice twinkling.

Rendevas could tell immediately that something was wrong.

He stood as nonchalantly as possible beside the bronze statue of King Marius, situated at the crossroads leading from the center of the city towards the Docks District. The statue was somewhat of a joke to the citizens of Praetorius: King Marius, who served as monarch prior to King Selderin, was a relatively ineffective leader, known more for his penchant for odd artworks than his talents as a leader. He'd had multiple statues of himself erected throughout the city, each one tackier and more extravagant than the last: the bronze one Rendevas stood beneath was the worst of the lot, depicting Marius as some sort of gallivanting hero, wearing a suit of armor and carrying a flag proudly, though he'd not once done either of those things in his lifetime. Local urchins and other young folks loved to graffiti that particular statue; tonight, bronze King Marius sported an elaborately painted giant blue phallus.

Rendevas was just admiring the crude artwork when he heard a couple city guards nearby. "Return to your homes," one of them called out towards some unseen residents. "The curfew is in effect." Rendevas tucked himself more fully within the shadows cast by the statue; it wouldn't do to get caught out past the newly-enforced curfew, especially as a city official.

Milford materialized from the shadows, his hood pulled low over his face. The diplomat could sense from his tense demeanor that somehow, in the short half hour since they'd last met, something had changed, and not for the better.

"Milford," the diplomat called quietly, stepping away from the base of the statue. He glanced behind his shoulder to make sure the city guards still couldn't see him.

The informant strode over. Even his gait was different. Rendevas eyed him curiously, too excited by the prospect of some much-needed news about the diplomat's death to let it worry him overmuch.

"Lord Rendevas, I must be quick. I've got news about Lord Tullie Mason's death that you'll want to hear, but I'll need my entire payment up front this time." He held out a gloved hand. "Trust me, you'll wanna know what I know. It's worth the cost."

His eyebrows shot up, but he pulled a bulging sack of coins from his belt and placed it into his palm. "I must admit, I'm intrigued," he said, watching him secret away the pouch amidst one of the many folds of his robes.

"You will be for sure after hearing this. Brakten managed to capture one of the assassins. He's got the man hidden somewhere safe for now, and he even managed to get the assassin to talk."

Rendevas's mouth dropped open in surprise. "Truly?! What did they say?"

Milford rummaged around in one of his many pockets. "They weren't actually Praetorian guards," he said, pulling out a wad of fabric, "but they somehow managed to get *actual* city guard tabards. They were well-connected." He handed over the fabric.

Rendevas took the folded tabard and let it fall open in his hands. Sure enough, the tabard was real: the Praetorius symbol was expertly embroidered upon the front of the thick cotton fabric. Only someone well-connected indeed could have managed to sneak something like that away.

"This is ... this is incredible," he murmured, awestruck. "How—?"

"That's not all," Milford muttered. He glanced to either side, more nervous than he'd ever seen him. "The fake guard told Brakten who was behind the attack in the first place."

"You have to tell me!" he gasped, heart beating quickly.

"Not here. Too open." Milford frowned thoughtfully. "Follow me. We'll go somewhere more private."

Rendevas eagerly walked beside the old man as he led him deeper into the slums, away from the fishy smells and lapping waves of the docks. He had a brief moment, amidst his building anticipation, that he didn't know Milford all that well, not truly. What was to stop the clever old man from simply leading him into some shadowy spot and murdering him? He worked for The Maelstrom, so it wasn't completely out of the realm of possibility. The guild was known for its ruthlessness. Sure, he'd worked with him for years now, but if he suddenly wanted him dead, what would stop him?

He *had* been acting weird when he first arrived ...

On his guard, he tensed up when he walked to a rusted metal gate set in the stone wall that surrounded the slums district. It wasn't actually called 'the slums district,' of course, as no large city wanted anyone to know they had a slum at all. (Even though they all did, it just wasn't polite to make mention of it.) Officially, this area was labeled as 'The Docks District' since it was the closest part of the city to the ocean and the considerable port Praetorius boasted. Most of the city's poorest citizens lived and worked there, making their meager wages as fishmongers, shipwrights, and sailors. It wasn't exactly the safest of neighborhoods; even the city guard had less of a presence monitoring the streets there, particularly at night, lending the area its dark reputation.

"Where are we going?" Rendevas whispered, perturbed by the eerie silence of the area. The fact that night had well and truly settled all around them didn't ease his anxiety.

"We're almost there," Milford said without looking back at him.

"One might think you are leading me somewhere private for nefarious purposes, Milford," he huffed nervously.

"Nah," he answered matter-of-factly. "You're one of my best paying customers."

Well, it was something, at least. Once they passed through the gate, he brought him over to a heavy metal grate set into the dirty cobblestone street. With surprising ease, he lifted the circular drain cover and slid it aside, revealing an iron ladder that descended into the depths of the sewer. He immediately traversed it downward.

"Must we really go through such theatrics?" the diplomat asked, curling his lip in disgust. "This is one of my favorite vests and I'd hate to ruin it."

"It doesn't actually go into the sewer, Lord Rendevas," the informant called, voice echoing from below. "Now hurry, before someone sees you."

Sighing, he lowered himself into the dark hole, gripping the sides of the ladder for dear life. "If I get anything on this outfit, I'm charging you for the cleaning fee!"

The ladder was shorter than he expected, and he dropped to the stone floor with a *whuff*. Milford hadn't lied: they were not actually inside the sewer itself, but a round, stone-walled chamber. Rendevas assumed the archway led into the sewer proper, gauging from the terrible smells that wafted through it.

Milford stepped into the deeper shadows. Rendevas was just about to call out when he reappeared a moment later, grasping the arm of a blindfolded, tied up man. His wrists were clamped in irons, with a chain that led from the cuffs to a thick iron hook set in the stone wall. Had Milford left the man chained up down here in the sewer?

"Is that—?" he breathed.

The man didn't look like anyone special. It was hard to see with the blindfold covering his eyes, but he just looked ... normal. Darker, shaggier hair, unfortunately large teeth combined with an overbite, a longer than usual neck. He could have been anyone. Perhaps that was what made him such a dangerous assassin?

Milford squeezed the man's upper arm. "Tell him what you told me," he growled.

The man swallowed, his throat bobbing up and down in his long neck. "I—" he croaked, then cleared his throat to try again. "I was hired to kill the Athessian diplomat."

Milford shook him a little. "By?" he prompted impatiently.

"By-by Judge Rodach."

"What?" Rendevas cried, then immediately slapped his hands over his mouth because of the loudness of his exclamation. "This is ... this is ... I am speechless!"

Milford nodded, nonplussed. "Timely, is it not? Finding this out on the day the judge was arrested? It's almost like Rodach *wanted* to get caught."

The assassin seemed to perk up at that. He opened his mouth to say something, but Milford tugged him backwards. Rendevas reached out a hand to stop him.

"Wait! We must bring him before the king!" he pleaded. "This man must be made to testify! It's the only way we—"

"Absolutely not," Milford barked harshly. "It's dangerous enough as it is, bringing him out of hiding like this. You're lucky Brakten trusts you enough to speak with this man, let alone *see* him!" He shook his head. "No, this is the best The Maelstrom can do."

"Please," Rendevas replied. "This could be the breakthrough we need! If he testifies before King Selderin, the judge will be held accountable for his crimes. Hells, he might even be sent to Uldinvelm to answer for his involvement in the plot against Lord Tullie Mason. This would exonerate Praetorius and prevent the war from escalating."

How did he make Milford understand? This was the most important thing he could do to keep the king, and by extension, Princess Alandria, safe.

Milford shook his head stubbornly. "Brakten went out on a limb to let me bring George out here tonight so you could see him," he answered. "He thought that by doing this, you might be able to do something with the knowledge. But that's as far as he's willing to go."

He took a half step closer and fixed Rendevas with a steely glare. "I'm warning you, you're messing about with things you don't fully understand. Dangerous things."

Rendevas reached out and grabbed Milford's wrist in the hopes of getting through to him. His hand wrapped around a much thicker wrist than he anticipated, all corded with tendons and muscles ...

What the hells? Before he had time to think, Milford grabbed Rendevas and pressed his thumb deep into a point in the flesh of his wrist that made his whole arm go numb. Milford twisted the diplomat's arm backwards, forcing his entire body to turn to the side, effectively making him release his grip.

"Ow ow ow!" Rendevas hissed, in shock more than pain. Somehow, the spot the old man dug into with his thumb made his whole body go *rigid*.

"Don't. Touch me." Milford's words had a note of furious finality that sent chills up his spine.

This man was much more dangerous than Rendevas realized. He held up his hands in surrender. "I won't, I won't! I'm sorry, I ..."

He released him, then pulled the tied and blindfolded assassin backwards into the shadows. The chain clinked ominously. "I've gotta bring this guy back now. I suggest you leave," he grated. "I'll give you five minutes to get outta the slums. Don't try to follow us. I'll know if you do." He fixed the diplomat with a dark look. "You'll never see hide nor hair of me nor anyone from The Maelstrom ever again if you do."

Rendevas nodded mutely, rubbing his sore wrist with a grimace. He couldn't fully process what he had just learned. All of his work, the whole investigation into Judge Rodach, all of it—it wasn't for nothing. He had been right all along!

He reached for the bottom rung of the metal ladder to leave. When he turned back towards Milford to thank him and apologize once again, both he and the captive assassin were already gone.

Chapter 42

I Think We Should Answer It

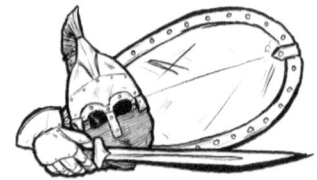

Lucius felt strangely *hopeful*.

Even with the city guard hounding him, his church arrest, and the general state of unease surrounding the whole Kax situation he'd inserted himself into, he had one thing to look forward to: getting to know Midori a bit more. He was drawn to her, regardless of her off-putting, blunt demeanor. Perhaps *because* of it. He genuinely enjoyed spending time with her.

An hour after the others left, Lucius smuggled a tray of breakfast downstairs. The resident cook, a heavyset middle-aged woman named Doloras, was more than happy to supply him with whatever food he desired. She filled two plates with eggs, crusty rolls, savory bacon, sausage links still sizzling from the skillet, orange slices, and bowls of fragrant vanilla yogurt, topping the feast off with two steaming mugs of coffee. Word had gotten around about Quay's 'guests;' she didn't seem fazed at all when Lucius showed up. Instead, she happily handed him a wooden tray bursting with all of the food and sent him on his way with an indulgent smile and a wink.

I wonder if she thinks I'm helping out poor 'pregnant' Midori, he thought as he took the stairs down two at a time. *That would explain the abundance of food.* Had Avin spread the carefully concocted lies about who he and Midori were already? Gods, the paladin was fast!

The resulting small smile on Midori's face when he offered her the bounty was definitely worth the effort. They chatted about mundane things while they ate, swapping stories from their childhoods and regaling each other with tales of their different types of martial training. He told her all about his time with the Athessian Army, where he'd learned how to swing a sword and shield, ride a horse into battle, and lead men in military formations; Uldinvelm prided itself on the might of its army. They were excessively hard on their soldiers almost to the point of cruelty, particularly those who rose the ranks like Lucius had.

In turn, Midori spoke of the unique fighting technique she had learned as a child alongside her brother. They were taught to use their fists and feet in powerful punches and kicks to take out their enemies, though Midori preferred to wield dual daggers as opposed to bare fists. She explained that their martial arts style of fighting was excellent for swift maneuvers and dodging attacks, though it severely lacked when it came to sustaining hits; they didn't wear any armor outside of light leather tunics and breeches.

She even offered to teach him a few of the easier moves, since her wounds were healing up quite nicely and she was restless after so much time spent in bed.

They spent a few hours practicing various grappling techniques and didn't stop until Lucius had successfully managed to flip Midori over his back and onto the soft mattress he'd dragged from the bed onto the floor.

"How do you learn so fast?" she asked him, panting for breath as he helped her back up. "It took me months to perfect that move."

He wiped the sweat from his brow and grinned. "I dunno. I've always taken quickly to stuff like this."

"That's certainly an understatement."

Once they tired of that, they moved on to reading quietly from some of the books Quay had brought them before leaving. Mostly they were dry tomes of church history or treatises on best practices for farming; when Lucius glanced up from a particularly boring text on the seasonal rainfall patterns of the grasslands of Khamris, he saw Midori avidly reading from a battered old paperback. Her entire face was red as her eyes dashed across the pages.

There's no way she's that excited to be reading stuff like what I've got, he thought, curious. When he peered closer, he read the title: *Jewel of the North*, which was written in elaborate, crimson-toned script. The book featured a lushly painted cover with a shirtless knight holding a swooning red-haired human maiden in one arm and a bejeweled sword in the other.

"Hey!" he exclaimed. "Where'd you get *that* book?"

Midori's head jerked up guiltily and she tried to hide the cover under the blanket. "What? Nothing!" she blurted, ears turning as red as the rest of her face. "Wait, what did you say?"

He cocked an eyebrow. "I asked where you got that book, *Jewel of the North*. All I've got over here in my stack is a bunch of history and farming stuff." He glanced at the front of his book and scowled. "*Best Practices in Field and Farming, Volume XIII*. Ugh."

Midori shifted a bit on the bed. "Quay gave it to me," she finally admitted without meeting his eyes.

Lucius closed his book and leaned forward. "Do you have any more?"

They spent the majority of the evening reading romance novels in companionable silence, Midori cross-legged upon the bed, Lucius leaned against the side on the floor with a book balanced on his bent knee. His book was called *The Lady of Laconia* and was about a lovesick noblewoman named Livonia of Laconia (he rolled his eyes every time he saw that ridiculous name) who could not decide between the stoic and uptight but fantastically wealthy Duke Able, (even though Laconia had no dukes, or any gentry, that he could think of) or the rakish and handsome bastard son of a nobleman, Jonethan de Pomfry. Personally, Lucius was rooting for the rake—he had a sense of humor, which had to count for something.

He was just getting to the good bit: "*'Put your hands on the headboard, my dear,' Jonethan instructed her,*" when a strange glow appeared out of the corner of his eye.

He hesitantly lowered his book, but the stricken look he saw on Midori's face alerted him that something was wrong. "What—?" he started to ask, but she just pointed towards the far wall.

There, leaning against the wall, was the Kax mirror Hypnocost had brought back from the cultist camp near Desai. It glowed a faded orange color, pulsing with harsh light.

"What the fuck?" he gasped in shock.

Midori sat frozen in place. "Someone is trying to contact the original owner of the mirror!" she breathed, eyes wide.

"What do we do?" he cried, scrambling backwards, though he had nowhere else to go since he was right up against Midori's bed.

"I don't know!"

"We'll ignore it," he declared promptly.

"Then whoever is calling it will know something is amiss!"

"Well, it's better than them seeing *us*!"

They both stared at the mirror as if it would suddenly grow claws and start attacking them. For all he knew, it could, given the nasty carvings of Kax's claw symbols all around the frame. (Was it supposed to be a claw, or a particularly jagged set of flames? He wasn't exactly sure.) The mirror continued to glow persistently, casting a sickly orange glow across the floor.

Finally, the glow faded, and the mirror resumed its regular, non-luminescent form. They both let out sighs of relief that were promptly cut off when the glow started right back up again. This time it was somehow even *more* insistent.

"Shit," muttered Lucius. "I think we gotta answer it."

He crawled over and placed his hand upon the glass. Nothing happened. The glow kept up its steady, pulsating rhythm.

"It has to be me," Midori reminded him as she slid off the bed. "You cannot answer it because you're not a Kax worshipper, remember?"

She crouched before it, placing her hand upon the surface. That must have been what activated the communication part of the device, for just then, a face materialized on the glass.

A woman peered out at them. She had large, dark eyes, a bald head, and skin the deep brown color of polished sunstone. A pair of shining golden hoops hung from her ears, and her lips were painted an alluring shade of purple.

Lucius didn't recognize her, and neither did Midori, judging by the blank look on her face.

The woman took one look at the pair of them, scowled, and ended the connection. The mirror stopped glowing, and the reflecting surface no longer showed the mystery woman's face. It merely reflected Lucius and Midori's matching looks of surprise.

"Who was *that*?" Lucius asked, turning towards Midori.

"I have no idea," she admitted. "I've never seen her before. She must be a part of the terrorist group of Kax followers if she's got her own mirror."

They regarded the glass silently, anticipating ... something. They didn't know what would happen next, but the air around the mirror felt both apprehensive and vaguely threatening. It was as if they suddenly shared a room with a hissing viper, poised and ready to strike.

After a few minutes of tense silence, they slowly began to let down their guard. Lucius stood up to stretch, stating, "Well, that was a bit of a scare, huh?" when the mirror started glowing once more.

They exchanged tight glances. "I think we should answer it again," Midori murmured, and before Lucius could say otherwise, she placed her hand once more upon the glass.

A different face appeared this time, but Lucius recognized this one. It was the very same man who had shown up in the mirror back at the Kax Temple in Camfield, the pale, dark-haired man with the cold eyes. He smiled wickedly out at them.

"So *you're* the ones interfering with my plans," the man spoke from the mirror. His voice sounded fairly muffled and far away, but they could hear him quite clearly given how silent it was in the room. "I should have known you would involve yourself, Midori."

She scrambled backwards so fast she nearly fell flat on her bottom. Her look of panic-stricken horror put Lucius immediately on edge, so he knelt behind her to help hold her upright.

"And you, scar-faced man. I recognize you." The man's eyes narrowed as he regarded Lucius with a cunning look. "You were one of the men who upset my temple. I bet you think you are so clever, running off with our horses and the blood font, hmm?" He chuckled, his eyes roving around the room as he took in their sparse surroundings. "It will not matter soon. I will find you, and I will kill you. It is only a matter of time." He sounded so sure of himself, as if their murders were a foregone conclusion.

Apparently satisfied with his perusal, the man shot them a sly grin before ending the connection. The mirror's glow faded immediately.

"Who the fuck was *that*?" Lucius repeated emphatically. He ran shaky hands through his hair, spiking it crazily around his ears and forehead. "He knew your name, Midori! Do you know him?"

Her lips were bloodless and white. "I do. That is Kang, leader of the terrorist sect of Kax worshippers." She turned to him, her dark eyes so wide he could see whites all around her pupils. "He is my brother."

Chapter 43

Let's Start a Riot

Nemboril—masquerading as Brakten, masquerading as Milford—knew, once the announcement about the active conscription laws had been made, the people of Praetorius would not take it lightly.

The declaration came via town criers, bellowing the status change from every street corner. It was official: any able-bodied Praetorian citizen between the ages of seventeen and thirty was to report to the barracks to find out whether their name had been pulled for involuntary military service. Stories of young people pulled from their jobs, from taverns, or even from the safety of their own homes reached Nem immediately.

So when he heard rumors of a 'public gathering,' hosted by none other than Keegan, he knew he had to rush over to make sure it didn't get out of hand. It was a pain in the ass re-securing George in the basement of The Murky Bard after the disastrous meeting with Lord Rendevas, but if this gathering turned out like he anticipated, he would be a fool to miss it.

Keegan, only just fully recuperated from his horrific beating by the city guards three days hence, was immediately back on the streets, hollering about the injustice of the plenum and how undemocratic it was for them to require involuntary conscriptions for a war nobody asked for.

This is just great, Nem thought to himself as he made his way to the Docks District, where a massive crowd was already gathering. *Keegan had to start shit right now? As if I don't have enough to worry about with George, and with Niserie in town, breathing down my back!*

He found it darkly amusing that, back when he'd been one of the highest-ranked Blades in the Court of Daggers, Niserie was still just up-and-coming. He never would have imagined she'd turn out to be one of Eastern Aukera's most feared Blades, let alone be there in usually-beneath-the-notice-of-anyone-remotely-well-connected Praetorius, hounding his every move.

He had to push Niserie—and his past with the Court of Daggers finally come to bite him in the ass—to the back of his mind. Keegan's public protest required all of his focus. The new curfew, the scarcity of certain essentials due to the lockdown at the city gate, and now the draft? It was just the thing to push the citizens of Praetorius over the edge.

All of Keegan's activism, public speeches against the government, loud railings against the city guard, handouts of food to the starving and forgotten poor ... it all led to this moment. The people of Praetorius were fed up, no longer content to let their elected leaders trample all over their rights.

It was time to rise up. Whether or not Nemboril agreed with his activism, he had a job to do. Riluk didn't pay him to sit idly by as Keegan stirred up all the shit with the locals.

A much larger crowd than he anticipated gathered in the Docks District, surrounding the defunct fountain, with its graffitied statue of old King Marius. The poor, the desperate, the angry, all of them watched as Keegan, standing beneath the statue, pumped his fist into the air and screamed, *"Down with the plenum! Down with the draft!"*

The crowd chanted it right back. *"Down with the plenum! Down with the draft!"* Dockmasters, shop owners, and whatever random wealthy-looking citizens happened to be there stood back and watched with alarm as the crowd grew.

The worst part of it all? Nem could see a vast majority of the people carried weapons. They weren't the sophisticated swords and shields and maces of the military, but they were deadly, nonetheless. Some held small daggers, others kitchen knives, even a small few wielded blacksmithing hammers.

Keegan held one hand cupped to his mouth, the other grasping the leg of the statue for balance. "Today, the people of Praetorius march! We march to show our displeasure with our elected officials! We march to tell them exactly how we feel! We march ... *for justice! To the capitol!*"

"Ah, shit," Nemboril groaned, breaking character for a moment as he watched events unfold from his hiding place in a nearby alley. Anyone in the immediate area was riveted by the surging crowd as it made its sluggish and inexorable way from the Docks District to the capitol.

The crowd drew more passersby and curious onlookers as they wended their way down the road. They chanted, *"Down with the plenum! Down with the draft!"* as they moved, pumping their fists in the air, the thunderous sounds of their footfalls heard all the way to the city gates. Keegan's face shone with pride as he chanted right along with them, using his magically enhanced voice to make their words heard all across the city.

"Fuck it," Nemboril murmured. Tightening the shawl across the bottom of his face, he sprinted from the alleyway, using well-known shortcuts through the seedy underbelly of the Docks District to reach Captain Riluk, to warn him of the impending disaster.

If anyone saw him as Milford, running as far, as fast, as *silently* as he was, it would be all over for that persona. Nobody was paying attention to the little old man in the shadows, though. Did it even matter if he was disguised as Milford? Could Brakten and The Maelstrom survive such unrest?

The protest grew with each street they passed. A veritable sea of humanity snaked its way towards the capitol.

Luckily, Nemboril was faster. He knew the streets better than anyone in Praetorius, especially since many of the shortcuts he put into place himself. His long robes flapped loudly in his wake, the hood over his dyed-brown hair threatening to blow right off.

He didn't slow as the barracks came into view, the sight of two bored looking city guards at the door filling him with equal parts dread and hope.

"I need to speak with Captain Riluk immediately!" he cried in his wheezy Milford voice, pulling up short right before the two guards.

They startled at his appearance, their hands upon the pommels of their swords. "You can't just barge in and speak with the captain!" one of them answered, scoffing. "He's a busy man, he—"

Nem grabbed the guard's arm tightly. His eyes widened at the strength in what he thought, at first glance, was an elderly man's grip. "An armed mob is heading this way!" he hissed, no longer bothering with the Milford voice. "Get. Riluk. NOW!"

The guard's mouth dropped open. He hesitated a split second before yanking his arm from Nem's grip and whirling inside. The other guard, speechless, watched in dumbfounded silence.

His eyes landed on Nem's deceptively innocent old man disguise, and he fully drew his sword from its sheath. He kept the blade's tip pointed to the ground, though his posture was threatening.

Nem held up his hands. "You'll thank me for this," he murmured, glancing behind him as the sounds of the mob got closer. "Trust me, I'm only here to help."

Captain Riluk emerged from the barracks, followed by a cadre of hastily suiting-up guards. He took one look at Milford and grunted in a manner that suggested he was not wholly surprised at his informant's appearance.

"There's a mob," Nem related, "a big one. Some of them are armed."

"What direction are they coming from?" Riluk asked abruptly, adjusting the straps on his gauntlets.

"Docks District," Nem answered. He used his normal voice. Riluk did a double take. "I think we're even now, captain," he muttered with a jaunty mock salute. "Good luck out there."

With that, he stepped away and blended into the shadows, leaving the two guards confused as to where in the hells he'd so quickly disappeared to. He made his way back to the crowd to watch from the shadows. The sheer size of it took his breath away; it had gotten twice as large in the small amount of time it took him to race to the barracks.

Gods, I hope Riluk can handle this! he thought, struggling to remain on the fringes of the crowd.

It was no use. He was sucked into the swarm of angry humanity, right there at the front. No amount of pushing, shoving, hells, even *stabbing* (with the butt of his hidden dagger) could get him out of it.

It wasn't long before they met the city guard, arranged four lines deep and blocking the path to the capitol building. The guards held their swords at the ready, their shields locked into place to allow no gaps in their defenses. Captain Riluk stood at the forefront, helm perched atop his head and sword in hand.

"Halt, citizens!" came Riluk's gruff voice. "You may go no further, as you endanger the government officials who reside in this district. According to clause nineteen, section four of the Safety and Security Protocols of Praetorius, the city guard has the right to both deny entry and use force, if deemed necessary, to ensure the well-being of our plenum members! We will not hesitate to do so should you continue down this path. Disperse!"

"We don't give a shit about your protocols!" came an angry voice from near the front where Nem had gotten caught. "Down with the plenum! Down with the draft!"

The crowd resumed their chanting more forcefully than ever, fists pumping angrily into the air. *"Down with the plenum! Down with the draft!"* Keegan's cries were as loud and boisterous as the rest.

Nem spotted a couple archers poised on the rooftops, their bows held at the ready, arrows pointed towards the crowd. *Fuuuuuuuck,* he thought, heart dropping. *If they loose arrows on us, it's all over. Gods damn it, Keegan! How could you let things get this far?*

One of the archers spotted Keegan. He pointed his gloved fingers down at him, hollering, "Look, it's Keegan! I can see the bruises from where I kicked his ass real bad even from up here!"

His fellows laughed along with him. Nem groaned and struggled to free himself from the clutches of the crowd, but he was solidly packed in. The people in the lines behind and to his sides began to mutter and swear darkly, brandishing their crude weapons threateningly.

The crowd moved as a singular unit towards the waiting soldiers. Captain Riluk stood his ground at the front. The rooftop guards nocked arrows to their bows, and Riluk growled, "Stand down! Stand *down!* This doesn't have to resort to violence!"

Tensions escalated to a fever pitch. The crowd surged forward, a few people at the front getting right up into the captain's face. The chanting grew louder and more aggressive, calls of *"Fuck the guard!"* screamed violently from behind him. Nem saw Keegan lift something in his hand—was that a rock?—and throw it forcefully at Captain Riluk.

It landed with a metallic thud against the captain's breastplate.

A brief moment of silence followed, fraught with unease. Keegan sneered and lifted his hand into the air. A rock from somewhere nearby zoomed into his waiting fist, pulled by the unseen forces of his magical abilities.

"Hold your fire!" Riluk bellowed.

Three rioters lunged at the captain. *"Fuck the guard!"* they screamed.

Riluk stumbled backwards but didn't quite fall. An arrow shot into the crowd from the rooftop, landing with a sickening thump into one of the protestors' knees. The man screamed and slapped both hands over his leg before falling onto the cobblestones.

Chaos erupted. The crowd roared and pushed forward at the city guards, and the rooftop archers immediately responded by loosing their arrows. They flew gracefully in a downward arc right towards the throng.

Keegan howled with rage and pushed his arms towards the parapet where the archers were, even then, bringing more arrows to their bows. The activist's face purpled with concentration, his fingers curled into claws as he cast a spell so deep and powerful everyone present could feel it rumble at their feet.

Nem braced himself for ... something. He knew not what.

Suddenly, the parapet *snapped* with a resounding CRRRRRACK! The stone supports rippled, cracked, crumbled, and shuddered before falling forward, dropping the archers and several tons of heavy stone onto the cobblestones.

Right into the courtyard where Riluk and the lines of guards stood.

Riluk bellowed for his troops to move back. As one, they followed his orders, but not before one of them near the front was crushed by the weight of the fallen stone.

"Colt!" Captain Riluk cried in a strangled voice. All that was seen of the city guard named Colt was one sad, booted foot, jutting at a weird angle from beneath the rubble.

The crowd, suddenly unsure, hovered anxiously at the fringes. Keegan, however, laughed maniacally, the rock he'd magicked still held in his hand. *"Push forward!"* he screamed. *"Now is our time! Now is our moment!"*

People near the back of the crowd slunk away silently, ignoring Keegan's war cry. More and more followed, until half of the crowd raced from the rapidly reassembling guards, who quickly gave chase.

This was too far. A city guard just *died in front of them.*

Nem, freed from the tightness of the crowd, slunk into the shadows once more. He let out a sigh of relief as the familiar darkness of an alley comforted him; he peered from behind the corner of a building to watch events unfold.

Keegan stood there dumbly with his hands loose at his sides. The rock tumbled from his grip. It rolled away from him until it bounced against Captain Riluk's booted foot.

"*Arrest him!*" Riluk said in a hollow voice, pointing at Keegan with his sword. Four guardsmen rushed forward and tackled him.

Keegan was immediately crushed beneath the combined weight of the four guards and their heavy plate armor. "I can't breathe!" he cried weakly, struggling futilely. "Please, I cannot breathe!"

Nobody heard him. Even if they had, they wouldn't care.

The guards continued to wrestle him to the ground, pushing and scraping his face against the cobblestones and wrenching his arms behind his back painfully. Someone produced a set of manacles, which they clamped viciously tight onto his wrists. They then pulled him upward ungently by his long, scraggly brown hair, nearly tearing a chunk of it out of his scalp.

The crowd had completely dissolved into pandemonium at that point, the people crying out in fear as they attempted to outrun the city guard. Nem sank deeper into the alleyway.

"You've gone too far, Keegan," Riluk spat, removing his helm from his sweaty head and wiping at his brow. His eyes were dark thunderclouds in his craggy face. "It's all over for you now, you know that, don't you?"

Blood dripped from Keegan's nose and split lip. He didn't bother responding. He just stared daggers up into the captain's disappointed face.

"I can't help you any longer, you realize that, right?" Nem watched Riluk shake his head sadly. "If only you'd gone about things differently ..." He sighed heavily. "Bring him to jail. Tell Constable Mald to lock him up for good this time. It'll be death row after this mess."

The guards hauled Keegan's limp form away.

Riluk surveyed the area, face unreadable. The riot was contained ... for now. Other than the ruined parapet, it was as if nothing at all was amiss.

Nem emerged from the alley, not trying to be sneaky. Riluk turned towards him, seemingly unsurprised at his arrival.

He was at a loss for words. What could he say? The situation had gotten so far out of hand as to be laughable to think that a singular man, even one as accomplished as Nem himself, could do anything to mitigate the damage. He pursed his lips, sighed, and offered the captain a tight nod of ... acknowledgement? Approval? Both of those things, or neither? He couldn't tell.

Riluk, looking weary and older than his years, just nodded back. He turned his back on his once-informant and trudged slowly back towards the barracks.

Chapter 44

High Priestess Lucina Balladoni

Quay woke the next morning with a warm, solid bulk pressed against her back.

It took her a moment to recall her surroundings; her sleep had been fitful and plagued with hazy nightmares that disappeared into mist as soon as the sun hit her face. She was in the back of the wagon, covered in Ghdion's cloak and a blanket that she didn't remember grabbing, and when she turned to see what was behind her, she saw it was a sleeping Ghdion, snuggled up close against her back. His tattooed arm draped heavily across her waist, and one bent knee nestled between both of her legs.

Her face burned a hot crimson. Suddenly, it was imperative that she not move one inch, lest she wake him. If he woke up and realized he was basically spooning her ... she bit her bottom lip to stop the effervescent fit of giggles that threatened to erupt from her mouth.

Butterflies swooped low in her belly. She hadn't felt like this in years, not since her last ill-fated infatuation with one of the clerics at the cathedral. (Tove was handsome and charming, but ultimately disappointing; she found out the hard way that he'd only really been interested in getting her into bed. The worst part? He was an obnoxiously *selfish* lover. Ugh.)

She didn't think Ghdion was like that. Her attraction to him grew with each passing day, ever since she hired him as her bodyguard a year ago after posting on the jobs bulletin in Praetorius. She was *pretty sure* he felt the same, but ...

She sighed. She wasn't sure of much of anything anymore, not really.

He was deliciously warm. His body was like a furnace; how could he stay so warm, wearing his typical sleeveless tunic and his arms exposed to the chill mountain air? She could easily stay there like that for the rest of the day, the trip to Tasuil be damned.

He huffed out a sleepy little sigh; gingerly she moved his hand from her waist to prevent him from any embarrassment should he wake.

Immediately he sat up and went for his sword, which lay atop the blankets beside him. "Priestess?" he muttered hoarsely, his face haggard and his hair disheveled. It stuck up in wild spikes in the back. "Is something wrong?"

Quay shook her head and sat up, smoothing the wrinkles from the bodice of her robe surreptitiously. Her cheeks felt hot and red; she glanced away so he couldn't see. "No, nothing's wrong. It's morning," she murmured. "We should get up and get ready for the day."

He didn't seem to realize just how closely he'd slept beside her, thank Vidamae. He stretched and ran a hand through his hair, pushed the blankets from his long legs, and slid off the back of the wagon. "Gotta take a leak," he mumbled, then strode off towards the woods for some privacy.

She shivered at the loss of contact with a heavy sigh. *Well, so much for that romantic moment,* she thought with more than a little disappointment. *Life certainly isn't anything like my romance novels.*

A bright, cold morning greeted them. Luckily the rain passed, leaving them with sparkling wet grass and a slightly muddier road. As long as the weather held, they could make good time that day. Hopefully they would reach Tasuil by nightfall.

Hypnocost tumbled groggily from the wagon bench, looking much the worse for wear after spending part of the night on watch, where he sat alone in the rain. His normally pristine garments looked rumpled and dirty, and even with his ageless elven grace, he had pronounced dark circles beneath his eyes.

"Good morning," Quay greeted him brightly. "How was it on watch last night?"

Hypnocost scowled, trying to wipe the dirt stains from the edges of his robe. "Awful!" he exclaimed hotly. "The rain did not stop until a few hours ago, and it was cold and miserable sitting out here alone.

Ghdion talks in his sleep, and he would not stop crying out about some woman or another, which I found odd, as I thought that you two were linked romantically."

Quay's face burned even hotter. "No, Hypnocost, we are not."

"Well, suffice to say, he must have been having a rather dreadful nightmare, because he would not shut up about someone named 'Sari.'" He sighed, giving up on his efforts to clean his travel-stained clothes. "Whatever it was, his howling kept any pesky nighttime creatures away. Nothing at all happened overnight except for his nightmares."

Quay nodded and bit her lip. "That was his late wife's name," she revealed quietly.

"Late wife? Oh, I had no idea," he answered, his bad mood tempered by the sobering news.

"So he didn't tell you, either." That made her feel a bit better. He wasn't hiding his tragic past from just her, at least. "Maybe don't say anything to him about it, okay? I don't think that would be very tactful."

Ghdion sauntered from the shadows of the trees, adjusting his leather shirt laces. "We should get going," he announced. "We can eat breakfast on the road. If we leave now, we should reach Tasuil just before dark."

Hypnocost eyed the tall blond man with a look of such obvious pity that Ghdion, confused, quirked his eyebrows questioningly at the pair of them. When nobody offered any explanation, he just shrugged, hopped onto the wagon bench, and took up Mertha's reins.

They made good time. Though the path was rugged and sparsely traveled, Quay managed to, with gentle words and more than a few crabapples as treats, convince Mertha to move at a steady pace the whole morning. The shaggy white ox dodged the deepest pits and the largest rocks in the road for a smoother ride. The sky remained unclouded, giving them great visibility once they crested the highest parts of the hilly terrain.

Hypnocost returned to the back of the wagon, where he continued his lazy lounging, reading, and what he proclaimed was 'scientific perusal' of the blood font. Ghdion sat beside Quay on the bench in his customary spot, reins held loosely in hand, his blue eyes clear and constantly scanning the horizon. He never seemed to rest. Was it a bodyguard thing, or a Ghdion thing? She wasn't sure.

It was slightly less awkward to sit in silence, but still Quay felt unnerved and self-conscious. She wanted desperately to speak to him about Sari and his children; the fact that he had been having nightmares about what had happened to them convinced her that he hadn't really had a chance to grieve their deaths. Was it her place to dredge up such terrible memories? What if he lashed out at her again, making the remainder of their long journey even more unbearable?

She tried not to dwell on it. Instead, she humored herself by alternating between reading a romance novel—the one she'd packed, called *The Rogue of Ragházz,* had a scene where, lo and behold, there was only one bed in the room at the inn, which was one of her favorite tropes—and writing letters to the various acquaintances she'd made on her travels for the church. The bumpy road made it hard for her to compose her letters; each jolting movement of the wagon sent splatters of black ink all across her parchment.

She wasn't required to keep a correspondence with the people she met and aided on her path to becoming a full priestess, but she genuinely enjoyed writing to all of her new friends. A surprising amount of them actually wrote her back.

She was in the middle of writing one such missive to Leon of Desai.

I sincerely hope you've received your reparations from the Church,

she penned in her neat, looping handwriting.

Please inform me if you have not, and I will make sure it is done.

Ghdion cleared his throat loudly. She glanced over, her quill hovering over her letter. Another drip of ink splattered the parchment. He stared straight ahead, unable or unwilling to meet her eyes. He looked somewhat flushed and uncomfortable.

"I, um. I met Sari when we were both fifteen," he grunted without preamble.

Quay raised her eyebrows in response. "Oh?"

"We both grew up in Camfield, me on an orchard and her on a farm just outside of town. It was your typical childhood crush, except we got married way too young and then had our first daughter shortly after." He cleared his throat again. "We were happy. Moved into our own house, had an apple orchard of our own. We had two more daughters. It was ... it was peaceful. I was content, y'know?"

Quay nodded quietly, afraid that her words would break whatever spell got him to open up to her.

"I wasn't there when they ... when the ... when it happened." He swallowed dryly; his throat bobbed up and down. "I found 'em, though. Afterwards. It was ... it's not something I wanna talk about."

She reached out and gripped his hand. He squeezed it back.

"I still have nightmares about it. I overheard Hypnocost talking about it this morning. Sorry if I kept you awake."

"You didn't," she said softly.

And that was it. He gave her an odd look, nodded sharply, then turned back towards the road.

It was enough. Things were much easier between them afterwards.

For the last few hours of the journey, they navigated by moonlight. Ghdion was hellsbent on sleeping in an actual bed that night. He pushed Mertha harder than he ever had, and the ox, bless her grumpy soul, actually complied. Perhaps she understood the time constraints they were under, or maybe she just wanted to taste the sweeter mountain grasses that lay ahead. Either way, they made it to the altar just as the moon was rising.

"There it is!" Quay pointed excitedly. "The Altar of Tasuil!"

When their wagon finally trundled around the final bend in the road, the famous Altar of Tasuil stretched before them in all its glory. It was more of a fortress than an actual temple, set within the rocky mountains of Summuran, the country to the west of Khamris. Constructed of a shimmery white stone, castle-like towers stood at each corner. High crenelated walls were built between them, with a grand staircase, not dissimilar to the cathedral in Praetorius, that led inside. Marble sculptures of angelic winged creatures decorated the tops of the walls, giving the fortress an air of classical beauty.

The actual altar itself was just outside the main doors to the fortress; from far away, it looked like a circular, flat open section ringed with unlit firepits, a short wall of the same white stone surrounding it.

The entire front lawn was covered with large tents and temporary hitching posts for the many pilgrims who made the journey there. Near the fortress, there was a barn and a stables, both of which teemed with activity. Stablehands led the horses and oxen into the stalls or unhooked the other wagons and carriages that still needed to be parked.

"Well, this is certainly something," Ghdion proclaimed as they headed towards the stables.

He wheeled their simple little wagon past rows and rows of exquisite, expensive-looking carriages. Nearly all of the stalls were occupied with fine stallions and well-bred mares who chuffed haughtily at the humble Mertha as she passed them. The ox didn't seem to mind; they led her into a smaller stall near the back, where a trough full of sweet grasses and hay awaited her.

Quay went to look for someone official to alert them to their presence. Hypnocost took care of the wagon while Ghdion finished unhooking all of Mertha's gear. He patted the ox fondly on her soft nose, murmuring so no one could hear, "You did good, Mertha. I'm proud of you."

She nosed him gently, then licked his fingers until he was covered with sticky slobber. He huffed out a surprised chuckle; perhaps Mertha was finally coming around to befriending him.

A young man paused outside the stall. He looked to be about seventeen, face full of acne scars and a mop of ashy blonde hair on his head. He had an air of self-importance that immediately set Ghdion off.

The boy eyed Mertha in obvious disdain. "Um, sir, the stalls are only to be used for the *clergy's* mounts," he said in a snooty tone. He straightened his starched white tabard as if to draw attention to the brilliant yellow embroidered Vidamae symbol on the front.

"Mertha *is* a clergy's mount," Ghdion answered back mildly. He turned around to regard the boy. He wasn't impressed by the altar boy's, or whatever he was, tone of voice. "*Priestess* Quay Hallandor of Praetorius. Is there a problem?"

(Quay wasn't actually a priestess yet. If she had been there, she would have been quick to correct him, like she always was. But Quay wasn't there, and the boy certainly didn't know whether or not she was a full-fledged priestess, so ...)

The boy sniffed. "I wasn't aware there would be a priestess arriving so late in the night." He eyed Ghdion up and down. "And I had no idea she'd bring her own *stablehand* with her. I'll leave you to it, then. My apologies." He whirled on his heel and flounced off.

Stablehand? "What a prick," he murmured.

Mertha let out a soft chuff of agreement.

He left the stables to go look for Hypnocost and Quay. He found the half-elf, carrying the pack with the blood font hidden inside. "Oh, good, you are finished with Mertha," Hypnocost said as Ghdion strode towards him. "Can you gather the rest of our supplies? Alas, I am only able to carry this." Patting it fondly, he leaned closer and said in a stage whisper, "We do not want to disturb the item that is inside of it, of course!"

Ghdion gave him a flat look that the half-elf promptly ignored. Instead of arguing—it had been a long day, and he wasn't in the mood—he jogged back to the wagon to grab the rest of their bags.

Hypnocost waited for him near the bottom of the staircase. As Ghdion made his way over, burdened as he was with Quay's three bags, Hypnocost's two rolled packs, and his own single backpack, Quay rushed down the stairs, looking both frazzled and excited.

"Hurry!" she called to them both, hitching up her robes to run faster. She was nearly out of breath when she finally reached them. "We're lucky we arrived when we did; the prayer is happening tomorrow morning. We didn't miss it!" She beamed up at him.

"Great," he responded hesitantly, hefting one of the bags higher up onto his shoulder.

Being around the fancy carriages and horses made him feel nervous, like he didn't belong. That asshole's *stablehand* comment certainly didn't help. Everyone he saw mingling around the temple was dressed in fine fabrics and sporting ludicrous amounts of jewelry, as if they were visiting dignitaries or wealthy nobles. Even the hired help, servants and *actual* stablehands dressed nicer than Ghdion ever had. Granted, he just spent two long days on the road, so he had somewhat of an excuse. But the riches on display were extremely off-putting.

He glanced along the grassy, sloping lawn that spread in front of the temple. The people hunkering down in tents and lean-tos looked more like what he was used to: workers, farmers, people of the land. None of them wore yards and yards of silk fabric or tiny gemstones in their hair.

"Who are all those people?" He nodded towards the rows of tents.

"Pilgrims," Quay answered promptly. "They traveled here with their congregations to witness the prayer tomorrow. I think some of the disciples who run the smaller churches are out there as well." She squinted at them in the deepening night. "Hmmm, that's strange. Why aren't they inside the temple with the rest of the clergy?"

"What do we do now?" asked Hypnocost, interrupting Quay's musings. "Are we meant to sleep in tents like they are?" His lip curled in disgust.

"Oh! No, we have a room inside. High Priestess Lucina made sure of it. She isn't ready to speak with us yet, but her archpriestess is waiting to show us to our room." She peered up at Ghdion and all of the bags he carried. "Do you need some help with those, Ghdion?"

"Nah, just lead the way, Priestess."

Casting a doubtful look over her shoulder, she led them both up the staircase and into the temple proper. *How would any parishioners who are old or lame be able to make it up all of these steps?* Ghdion wondered. The setup was similar to the cathedral in Praetorius, with the main nave at the entrance, lined with wooden pews and dominated by a raised pulpit in the middle. Wings along each side housed bedrooms, offices, and other spaces; it was probably too much to hope for a bathhouse, just like in Praetorius, but Ghdion checked as they walked down the corridor, just in case.

Quay veered to the right, stepping around the other priestesses mingling in the hallway; some of them gave them downright distrusting looks. It made him feel extremely self-conscious. He wasn't used to that.

He hurried up to walk beside Quay. "You're sure these are all clergy?" he muttered, leaning down to speak close to her ear. "They look more like royalty. Do you see how that woman is dressed?" He jerked his chin to the side, where a priestess in elegant white robes of shimmering silk passed. Her ears, neck, and wrists were laden with glittering golden baubles, and it even appeared she had tiny diamond chips interwoven through her hair. She looked upon the trio as if their humble appearances personally offended her.

Quay glanced at the well-dressed men and women; most were pointedly ignoring them as they walked past. "I guess some of the churches are more well-off than others." She sounded unsure.

Finally, they stopped in front of an open door at the end of the long hallway. "Here's our room," Quay announced. It was small and windowless, with only two cots and a ceramic wash basin as furniture. There wasn't even a mirror above the wash basin, it was so sparse. A threadbare rug that looked about fifty years old covered the stone floor, and only one of the cots had a ratty looking blanket. The other cot was completely bare of any bedding at all.

Ghdion scowled in annoyance. "Seriously? They can't even get us the correct amount of beds? Or even blankets?"

"I'm sure they tried their best," Quay exclaimed placatingly. "It's so busy here, and they have to accommodate so many people ... besides, we can bring some of our blankets in from the wagon. It's not so bad."

He could tell that even she didn't believe what she said. She was trying to make the best of what was quickly turning into an extremely disappointing situation.

Hypnocost immediately claimed one of the beds by plopping

right onto the one with the blanket. "This will have to suffice. If we are lucky, it will only be for one night. How long do you believe this prayer will take tomorrow?" He began unpacking his bag, careful to keep the blood font tucked away and hidden.

Ghdion sighed. *So much for sleeping in a bed tonight.* "You take the other bed, Priestess," he gestured towards the naked cot. "I'll run back outside and grab some bedding."

Before he got two steps towards the door, a thin, sour-faced older woman stepped in his way. She was draped in the fine white silken robes and a heavy gilt holy symbol that denoted her title as an Archpriestess of Vidamae. She had short, spiky gray hair and a long nose with which she very obviously looked down upon all three of them.

"Quay?" the archpriestess called in a nasally, prim and proper voice. "Who are these *men*?" She spat the last word out as if describing a slimy, disgusting creature.

"Archriestess Elna! I didn't expect you back so quickly!" Quay hopped up from the cot so quickly it was like she sat on hot coals. She immediately began to brush off the front of her dress and smiled forcefully. "These are my bodyguards, Ghdion and Hypnocost. They accompanied me on my journey here and have been with me every step of the way since I began my training."

Elna took a good long look at each of the bodyguards and sniffed haughtily. She obviously found them both lacking. "I was not aware you would be bringing companions." She let an awkward silence hang in the air, expecting an apology from Quay for daring to buck her strict expectations.

Quay stood before her, wrangling her fingers in her robes, and said nothing at first. "I, ah ... I have some important news for High Priestess Lucina Balladoni. Do you know when she will be available to see me?"

"That is precisely why I am here," Elna huffed. "Come along and I will bring you to her." She whirled around without a backward glance and strode off, forcing the three of them to abandon their unpacking and scramble after her.

The other people in the corridor hastily stepped out of the way when Elna passed. The woman obviously commanded, if not respect, at least an amount of authority that gave most people pause. She moved so swiftly and so purposely that it was hard even for Ghdion, with his long legs, to keep up; he had to grab Quay's hand to keep her from falling far behind. Hypnocost was forced to jog just to keep the pace.

"Archpriestess Elna," Quay huffed from behind her, "is it true the prayer is tomorrow morning? That's what I overheard when we first arrived."

Elna didn't bother turning around. She simply nodded. "At dawn's first light, when Vidamae's powers are at Her strongest."

Her voice was so persnickety, it got on Ghdion's nerves. She sounded like she had something stuck far up her ... well. It wouldn't be appropriate to have such thoughts, especially about an *archpriestess*.

"Some of us have been called upon to assist the high priestesses with the ritual. Those clergy who have been graced with a space inside the temple will be allowed to witness it all from the steps. You're lucky," she added, eyeing Quay sidelong from around her shoulder. "You will have one of the best seats in the temple."

"What about the rest of the pilgrims?" Ghdion asked hotly.

At his voice, she glanced behind her and gave him a withering look. "They will watch from the lawn. The witnessing of such a grand and glorious occasion is standing room only, out of necessity. There is simply not enough room."

Ghdion held her gaze. He refused to look away out of principle. "Interesting. You'd think a church that values its parishioners would at least allow *some* of the pilgrims a spot up front. They came all this way, didn't they? But what do I know?" He shrugged. "I'm just a simple-minded man who can swing a sword."

Quay shot him a quelling look, then turned towards Elna, smiling uncomfortably. "What Ghdion means is that surely there will be room for *some* of the pilgrims to watch up close, right? Like he said, they traveled all this way."

"And so have the higher-ranked clergy," Elna cut in smoothly. "I realize you are still learning, Quay, but there is a system in place for a reason. You will learn that firsthand once your training is complete."

They passed the nave and headed down the hallway on the other side of the temple. Less people lined this hallway, but what few they did see were extravagantly dressed. Ghdion even saw a servant walk past, carrying a silver tray with empty wine glasses and plates of barely touched delicacies.

He grew uneasy about what was going on behind the scenes of the Church of Vidamae. He'd been traveling so long with Quay, who never spent any of the church's funds on nice things for herself, that he had begun to believe that all the Vidamae clergy were like her. Even with the ample coinage the church provided for her training, she never spent any of it on fine wines, fancy inn rooms, or servants. She used it all up on supplies for the poor and downtrodden and was always worrying that it wasn't enough.

Apparently, she was somewhat of an anomaly. It only served to ramp up his admiration for her even more.

Elna brought them all the way to the end of the hallway, where she knocked briskly upon the ornate door at the end. Two paladins, covered head to toe in shiny golden armor, stood guard on either side of the door.

Really? Paladin guards? he thought with a scowl. That seemed a bit much.

A muffled voice answered, "Enter," from within, so Elna pushed the door open and stepped aside.

The room put the rest of the temple to shame. It was the most richly appointed, elegant room Ghdion had ever seen. A large four-poster bed dominated the center, its gauzy white drapes pulled aside to reveal a bed so large it could easily fit two whole families onto it. There were piles of white pillows and soft blankets draped casually across the fluffy mattress. Beneath the bed was a plush rug that covered the entire expanse of the floor, woven with rich colors that depicted scenes from legends that involved Vidamae's many exploits on Aukera. A heavy wooden trunk sat at the foot of the bed, bursting with garments of all the colors of the rainbow, and a gilt full-length mirror stood in the corner near the bedside table. There was even a private bath chamber off to the side.

So this is how the high priestess lives, Ghdion thought bitterly. *Quay sleeps on church floors during her pilgrimage while her beloved High Priestess enjoys a life of luxury, huh? I see where all the tithing goes. Looks like my suspicions about the church were right. I wonder if Quay even realizes?*

The high priestess stood up graciously from her perch on the side of the bed. Lucina Balladoni was an elegant, middle-aged woman of beauty, one of those who aged so slowly and gracefully that she probably attracted much younger admirers. If he had to guess, he would say she was in her fifties, but only because of the slight wrinkles at her eyes and around her mouth. She had curly gray-streaked dark hair that hung to the nape of her neck. Her brown arms were covered with bangles at the wrists, her fingers long and glittering with gemstones. A simple golden holy symbol lay against her breast. She wore a dress similar in cut to Quay's, floor-length and tightened under the bust with golden trim. Her kohl-lined dark eyes regarded them thoughtfully.

"High Priestess." Quay immediately curtseyed low in eager deference. Hypnocost and Ghdion followed suit with a set of low bows.

"I bring you Quay, priestess-in-training of Praetorius, and her two bodyguards," announced Elna with a flourish. The archpriestess took a spot to the side of the closed door and clasped her hands in front of her, waiting and watching.

"Thank you, Elna." Lucina smiled, bringing out the wrinkles around her eyes. Instead of making her look older, they only enhanced her ageless beauty. "I will call upon you should I need you." She dismissed the archpriestess with a flick of her wrist.

Elna looked briefly put out but swiftly covered it up with a mask of pure obedience. Bowing, she slipped out of the room and shut the door behind her.

"Now, Quay, I hear you have news for me?" Lucina's voice changed timbre from an awe-inspiring, breathy rhythm into something much more practical. She bustled over to stand right before Quay, looking both earnest and less ... ethereal, that was the only word Ghdion could come up with. His eyebrows raised at how swiftly the woman switched from untouchable High Priestess (with capital letters) to an old friend of Quay's from back home in Praetorius.

It was obvious the two women knew each other well. Lucina gave Quay a quick hug, eyeing her up and down in a motherly fashion. "Wait, before you tell me the important news, you must tell me how your training is going. Well, I hope?"

Lucina was quite tall for a woman, so Quay's petite form made her look like an overeager child standing in front of her mother. Quay nodded. "I've visited about half of the churches in Khamris so far, but things have stalled a bit lately," she admitted nervously. "That's the reason I came all this way. We stumbled upon a few victims of the newest Kax cultist plot, and we found proof that they are behind multiple murders near Praetorius! Ghdion, Hypnocost, and Lucius—he's not here, he's stuck back in Praetorius, long story—found a hidden Kax Temple in the woods near Camfield, and—"

"Oh, child, don't tell me you came all this way just to tell me *that*?" Lucina gently chided. "We know about the Kax plot, the hidden temples, the extremist groups of Kax worshippers who have been gathering to try their hand at weakening Vidamae again with their silly plans. All of it. That's why we are all going to pray tomorrow." She shook her head. "Quay, you always were impulsive, but I am honestly surprised. Why on Aukera would you think that news worthy enough to justify traveling all the way here? And you on the cusp of full priesthood?"

"It's more than that," Quay mumbled, chagrined. Her body stiffened, and though Ghdion couldn't see her face from where he stood, he knew she was blushing profusely. "Nobody knows what to do, and people keep getting killed, and we can't seem to pin down the killers ..."

Lucina patted Quay's shoulder fondly. "Don't you worry about a thing, my dear. Once we pray tomorrow, all will be made clear. Vidamae will answer our prayers once again, and the Kax cultists will be punished for their crimes. The best thing you can do is return to Praetorius tomorrow to spread the news of our success and ease the fears of our congregations."

Ghdion shifted from one foot to the other. He didn't appreciate the patronizing tone that Lucina spoke to Quay with. Why wasn't she taking them seriously? She kept brushing off Quay's concerns without truly listening to what she said.

"Now, the most important thing for *you* to do, Quay, is to continue with your training," Lucina continued sternly. "Praetorius could really use a fresh, eager new priestess to take the helm. You're just beautiful enough to bring in new parishioners, but not so much so that you come across as intimidating or untouchable. Hmm." She held Quay at arm's length and looked her up and down thoughtfully. "Yes, you have a certain 'girl-next-door' innocence about you that lends itself nicely to our next phase of outreach. We can just get you some makeup to make you look a little more alluring, and—"

"We found a blood font," Quay blurted.

A rapt, pressure-filled silence enveloped the room. Hypnocost shot Ghdion a panicked look, which he responded to with a curt shake of his head. His eyes said, *let's wait and see how this pans out.*

"You what?" Lucina whispered.

"A blood font," Quay repeated. "We found one, at the abandoned Kax Temple in Camfield. Lucius, Ghdion, and Hypnocost risked their lives to bring it back to me in Praetorius."

"That's not possible," Lucina stated. "We destroyed them all fifteen years ago."

"Well, one of them survived somehow." Quay rubbed her arm

nervously. "Ghdion and Hypnocost even witnessed one of the cultists using it."

"There is simply no way." Lucina shook her head vehemently. "You must be mistaken. What did it look like? Describe it to me."

Quay glanced behind her at Ghdion for reassurance; he nodded and spoke up to give her a chance to regroup. "It's smallish ... about this big," he gestured with his hands in an approximation of its size. "When it's inert, it looks like a regular crystal ball kind of thing. But when it's being used, it glows an angry red and shoots these thin beams of reddish light out. I'm assuming it's to guide the user to whoever has Vidamae blood nearby or something."

Lucina's face took on an ashy cast, and she flopped back down onto her bed in distress. "How ... how is this possible? You have an actual blood font?"

Now *you take us seriously?* Ghdion thought in annoyance.

"If they have one, there could be others! This could be The Troubles all over again!"

"This is why we came here with such haste, High Priestess. We need to know what to do next!" Quay exclaimed.

"Do you have it with you?" Lucina demanded. Her voice was rough and slightly unbalanced. "I must have it, Quay. Give it to me."

Quay hesitated for a split second before answering, "No, High Priestess. We left it back at the cathedral in Praetorius. It seemed safer to leave it there."

Well, well, that's interesting... Ghdion thought in surprise. *Quay's lying to her?*

Lucina scowled. "Damn," she cursed, causing Quay's eyebrows to shoot far up her forehead. Ghdion thought with some dark amusement, *Now maybe she won't give me such a hard time about swearing.*

"Tell me everything about it. Leave no detail out. I need to know *everything*," Lucina demanded.

So they told her, beginning with where they found it, what it was stashed with, who used it and what he looked like, where it was used, *how* it was used ... Lucina was relentless in her questioning. By the time she finished grilling them, they were all exhausted.

Quay finished repeating an answer to a question Lucina asked earlier when Ghdion finally stepped in. "With all due respect, High Priestess," he cut in, "it has been a long and weary day for all of us. Perhaps we can continue this tomorrow after your big prayer?"

Lucina glanced out the window. It was full dark outside, the sky lit only with a smattering of glittering stars. "Of course. Forgive me, I wasn't aware it had gotten so late already." She brought a shaky hand to her lined forehead. "Please, go get some rest. We will speak more on the morrow."

Hypnocost yawned as he stepped through the doorway; Ghdion hesitated on the threshold, waiting for Quay.

"Go on ahead, I will be right there," she said with a tired smile.

He raised his eyebrows at her in a silent question. She only shook her head and waved him off before turning back towards the High Priestess.

As soon as Ghdion and Hypnocost left, Quay steeled herself as if for battle. She wasn't leaving until she had some answers.

"High Priestess," she uttered after a deep breath, "before I go, I have some questions."

Lucina stifled a yawn with the back of her hand. "Of course, child, but please make it quick. I have a big day to prepare for."

Quay didn't even know where to begin, so she simply blurted out what was foremost on her mind. "Did the Church of Vidamae really kill a bunch of innocents after The Troubles?"

Lucina started, whipping her face around so she stared directly at her. "Wherever did you hear such a thing?"

Quay licked her lips. "I ... may or may not have gotten access to the private library in the basement of the cathedral," she admitted, not wanting to reveal her bodyguards had actually done the snooping. "I was looking for more information about Kax, and there were books there that talked about show trials and villages that were decimated and ... and Vidamae's Paladins rampaging through women and children ..."

Lucina took both of Quay's hands in hers. She gazed directly into the younger woman's eyes and smiled reassuringly. "Quay, what you have to understand is just how frightening and dangerous a time it was back then," she spoke in gentle tones. "The church had just been dealt a terribly grievous blow, and we had no idea how to tell friend from foe. Much of the upper clergy had been killed by the Kax cultists, and the leadership was in disarray. Nobody knew what to do next."

"But how does that justify killing entire villages of people just because they worshipped Kax?" she questioned. "Not all the Kax followers are terrorists. Some of them are just normal people who happen to follow the same goddess."

She thought of Midori, whose entire life had been upended because of her religion. How was that fair? How could anyone in the Church of Vidamae explain that away?

"Yes, just as most of us in Vidamae's grace are normal people just trying to make our way. That didn't stop the cultists from killing hundreds of 'normal' people during The Troubles, now did it?"

She sighed and brushed a stray lock of brown hair out of Quay's face. "Your concern truly does you credit, Quay. It is well within your rights as a priestess-in-training to question how things were done back then, but you did not live through it, so you cannot fully comprehend just how terrifying an ordeal it was."

"But High Priestess," she soldiered on bravely, despite her deepening unease. "Wouldn't punishing killing with more killing, righteous or not, just serve to further Kax's own goals against us? Wouldn't that create the next generation of cultists to be raised to hate us and want revenge?"

"The punishment must always fit the crime, Quay, you know this," Lucina scolded. "Just because our benevolent Goddess values life above all things does not mean She is not willing to dole out harsh sentences for those who do Her wrong." She shook her head sadly. "It is late, Quay. I know you question. I can see the fire in your eyes! But now is not the time for your faith to falter. We need every priest and priestess we can to make the prayer tomorrow a success."

Quay knew a dismissal when she heard one. Disappointed, she

Faith and Ruin

nodded mutely and pulled away from Lucina's grip. "I understand, High Priestess. I will pray upon this."

She left, feeling troubled. Elna waited right outside the door and looked extremely annoyed that Quay had dared to take up so much of the high priestess's time. She slipped past her to head right back inside Lucina's room. *No doubt they will be discussing the blood font and everything that I told her*, she thought glumly.

I thought coming here was a good idea. High Priestess Lucina was supposed to help me! Now I feel more confused than ever.

She didn't come across anyone else on her way back to her room. Quietly she slipped inside, not wanting to disturb Hypnocost or Ghdion's rest. Hypnocost was already fast asleep, snoring lightly from beneath the blankets on his cot. Ghdion, however, was still awake, lounging on a single blanket he'd spread on the floor beside the other cot.

"How'd it go, Priestess?" he asked quietly as she shuffled over.

She plopped onto the cot with a heavy sigh. "I don't know, Ghdion. This isn't going at all like I thought it would."

He rested an elbow on the edge of the cot and gazed up at her seriously. "You lied about the blood font," he stated, so quietly she could barely hear him. "Why is that?"

"I don't know!" she moaned, hiding her face in her hands. "I just ... had a feeling that giving it to her wouldn't be the best option, y'know?" She peeked one eyeball from between two fingers. "I feel awful."

"But not awful enough to go back in there and tell her we actually have it?"

She shook her head.

"Good. You made the right choice."

"Really?" she breathed, hopeful. She lowered her hands from her face and stared at him intently.

"Mmm-hmm. I don't trust anyone not already in this room, Quay. The best place for that cursed object is with us." He glanced over at the sleeping Hypnocost. "As much as I hate to admit it, Hypnocost is probably the best person we know to figure that thing out. I vote he keeps it—hidden, of course—for the time being."

"I agree," she stated emphatically. "I just don't know what to do now. I dragged us all the way out here, thinking High Priestess Lucina would actually *help*. But so far all I've gotten is ... is *little head pats* and condescending words, as if I'm some sort of *wayward child*."

"Well, you kinda are now." He eyed her mischievously. "Lying and hiding magical artifacts. You're a regular bad apple." He shoved her playfully with his shoulder.

She shot him a quelling look. "You know what I mean! I'm just concerned that we're gonna be stuck figuring this out ourselves."

"Oh, Priestess," he chuckled fondly, "we already are."

Chapter 45

A Tribunal

Four Years Ago

Her bag was packed. Her weapons were secured at her belt—two wicked daggers, recently sharpened, as well as a set of tiny throwing daggers strapped to her wrist for easy access. She wore her most comfortable set of black leathers and the best pair of boots she owned, the only pair, really, but at least they had no holes or visible rips.

All that was left for Midori to do was to leave.

She couldn't help but sift through the bag one last time to make sure *it* was still there. Nestled beneath her spare set of clothes, looking innocuous and benign with its clear glass surface: the blood font.

Every time she laid eyes upon it, her breath caught in her throat. It was finally in her grasp. She had, after almost a year of careful planning and avoiding any suspicion in regard to The Augur's untimely death, managed to snatch it out from under the vicars' noses.

After a ruthless and frantic investigation into how The Augur died, the vicars still had no idea he had actually been murdered.

They determined he had simply died of old age in his sleep, despite Kang's particularly loud insistence that his death was far from natural. Miraculously, her murder of the old man remained undiscovered.

It must mean Kax is with me, Midori thought. *Kax approves of my choices thus far!*

She eyed her reflection in the orb's surface. Her pale face was determined, her eyes shadowed beneath the dark hood she pulled over her cropped black hair. She waited long enough. Her luck would end eventually, and either Kang, Bennett, or the vicars themselves would find out about her crimes. It was time to go.

Just as she was hiding the blood font deeper into her pack, someone walked into her room.

"Are you going somewhere, Midori?" came Kang's clipped voice behind her. There was an undertone of danger to his words. Before she even had time to respond, he was beside her, his gaze fixed upon the contents of her bag.

"I am going on a hunt," she said, impressed that her voice was so even as she lied. She snapped the pack's flap closed before he could get a good look at the inside.

"Alone?" He crossed his arms. His belt was laden with weapons he carried on his person at all times now; Midori wondered how many attacks he expected from within the safety of the abandoned mine. It seemed silly to be armed with four different daggers and a set of matching shortswords, not to mention the hidden knives he kept tucked up his sleeves and inside his boots.

"No, not alone," she answered. "Not that it's any of your business." She grabbed her bag, swung it over her shoulder, and turned to leave.

His hand shot out and clamped onto her arm like a vise before she was able to take more than one step. "Midori," he growled, but said nothing more.

The air in the room grew charged with tension. Midori met his eyes.

She tried to wrench away. "Kang, stop it, you're hurting me," she hissed.

"What's in the bag?"

He knew. *He knew!* Her breath came out in short, uncontrollable bursts; frantically she tried to school her features into indifference. "It's only some supplies in case the hunt takes longer than anticipated."

Before she could react, he yanked the bag from her shoulder and tossed it upside-down onto her bed. All the contents spilled out: neatly wrapped dry rations, flint and tinder, a whetstone, an extra pair of trousers and socks, and the most damning item of all, the blood font. It rolled away from the rest of the contents, as if trying to distance itself from her guilt-ridden countenance.

Kang didn't say a word as he picked up the blood font in one hand. He didn't look at her. He merely gazed into its glassy depths, his other hand still clamped firmly around her upper arm.

Without a word, he started to drag her out of her room. "Kang, what—!" She tried to explain, but he just pulled her along even harder. She dug her heels into the stony ground, but it was no use. His pull was as inexorable as the tides.

"Kang, stop!" she pleaded as he dragged her down the tunnels and deeper into the mountain. She knew without a doubt where he was taking her. They were headed towards the vicars' private meeting chamber. The one she used to eavesdrop on as a child.

"Kang, please! Let me explain! I was going to hunt for Vidamae descendants. I want to help contribute to the cause!"

He ignored her, not before shooting her a look of pure disbelief from over his shoulder. Deeper through the tunnels they went, Kang striding purposely forward, Midori trying desperately to free herself from his grip. But instead of turning left, where the intersection led to the vicars' private rooms, Kang towed her towards the right and into the large cavern they used as a public meeting space.

The torches lining the meeting cavern were all lit. The space, usually echoing and empty, was full of people: everyone who lived there was gathered, and all eyes were upon the pair as they entered. The four vicars—Jebedaiya, Jessica, Baylus, and of course, Aunt Solange—were lined up at the front, wearing their long ceremonial robes of blood red trimmed in orange.

Those were the robes they wore only during a tribunal, and even then, only for the most serious cases. The fact that they were all arrayed in their formal attire did not bode well for her. Not at all.

Midori's heart sank. *He set me up*, she thought in despair. *My own brother set me up for ... for ...* She had no idea what was about to happen to her.

Kang still held tightly to her to prevent her from escaping. He lifted the blood font high into the air, giving everyone there a good look at it before handing it off to Aunt Solange. "We have been betrayed, my brothers and sisters in Kax! As I suspected, Midori took the blood font."

His eyes focused solely on the four vicars, as if he was engaged in a private conversation only with them. His booming voice suggested otherwise. He *wanted* everyone to hear what he had to say. "When I asked her where she was going, she told me she was going on a *hunt*."

He turned towards someone in the crowd. "Thank you for your timely warning, Samuel," he said with a slight nod of acknowledgement. "It was as you said: she was sneaking the blood font in her bag as soon as I entered her room."

Midori's eyes widened in horror as she turned towards Samuel. He was supposed to be her *friend*. He was supposed to be sympathetic! He had privately spoken to her of his disagreements with the vicars and their insane plan ...

It was all just a front. He sold her out. His eyes shifted from hers in shame, and she saw him shuffle on his feet nervously. He wouldn't meet her eyes.

"Niece," Aunt Solange called out, scattering Midori's spiraling thoughts of betrayal. "What were you planning to do with the blood font?"

This was a tribunal, plain and simple. She took a deep breath, remembering the plan she had concocted with her little group of like-minded dissidents: Midori would steal the blood font, meet the dozen Kax followers who had joined her cause against the vicars, and they would run away from the abandoned mine. Afterwards, they would dispose of the blood font using any means necessary. It had taken almost a year for her to gather the courage for her task, as well as find the right moment when the blood font was not in use. And now it was all going up in flames.

She took a deep, centering breath. "I was going to destroy it," she answered in a clear, ringing voice.

A hush descended upon those gathered to witness. The vicars regarded her stonily, none more so than her aunt. Solange's dark eyes bored into hers fiercely.

"And why," Solange continued after a beat, "would you want to do a thing like that?"

"Because it is the only way to steer us from this path of madness!"

Midori scanned the crowd, looking for anyone sympathetic, any of the few people who, up until this point, had been so committed to helping her. All she saw were angry glares and accusing faces. The only thing keeping the assembly from lashing out at her in violence were the four robed vicars blocking their path.

"We cannot continue like this," Midori bravely cried out. "We will only further the cycle of death and destruction. Vengeance serves nobody! If we continue to hunt the Vidamae clergy, we are no better than they were when they ran us all down almost ten years ago!" How could she make them see? How could they fail to understand that her words had merit? "If the plan is what Kax truly wanted from us, wouldn't it have worked the first time?"

"Blasphemy!" Kang hissed, and in an eyeblink, he had a dagger held tightly against her throat. Midori couldn't even swallow for fear of slicing her own skin on the frighteningly sharp edge of his blade. He pinned her arms ruthlessly against her back with his other hand.

"Hold, Kang," Aunt Solange instructed blandly. She lifted her hand, palm out, in a placating gesture. "You would really condemn your own sister to death for what she has done?"

He hesitated just a fraction, loosening his grip on the dagger. Midori felt a tear slip unheeded down her cheek. "Kang," she whispered, "don't do this. Please. You know I'm right!"

"If the vicars demand it," he answered hotly, jutting out his chin.

"Since you discovered your sister's treachery," Jebedaiya called out, "perhaps you should be the one to judge her punishment."

Midori stilled in Kang's arms. This was surely it. He would kill her for what she had done. He already suspected her involvement in The Augur's death, though he had no proof, and had, as of yet, said nothing of it. And now? After discovering her in the act of stealing the world's last blood font, the only tool they had left with which to hunt down the hated Vidamae's beloved followers?

He would kill her for sure.

She closed her eyes and waited for the end. The dagger's edge was cold against her trembling neck.

As suddenly as it appeared, it was gone, leaving only a thin line of blood from where the blade had sliced into her skin. "Banishment," Kang cried out. "I move that we banish Midori from this place forever."

Her eyes flew open. He wasn't going to kill her? He wasn't going to slit her throat in front of all of their people as an act of loyalty to his beloved vicars?

The four vicars watched the siblings with matching faces of shock and anger. It appeared they, like Midori, had not expected mercy. "As you wish," Jebedaiya responded tightly, slashing into the air with his hand, his scarlet robes rippling.

Feeling bolder, Midori took a half step forward. "Those of you who feel as I do," she exclaimed, seeking out her friends in the crowd, "come with me! Come live your lives away from the spectre of revenge and death! That is all that the vicars offer you, and you know it as well as I do!"

"Enough with your sacrilege," Kang breathed into her ear. Though he loosened his tight grip on her arms, he still held her close and began to yank her bodily out of the cavern. She wrenched herself away from him, desperately searching the faces of those assembled for anything other than pure hatred.

"There are none here who wish to follow you into folly," the vicar Jessica spoke. "Take her away, Kang."

"You have swayed no one!" Kang choked out in triumph. "Surely this is proof enough that your plan was nothing but—"

"I will go with you!" a wavering voice rang out from the crowd. A short, dark-haired woman named Arellia stepped forward; Midori befriended her months ago. She was one of the dozen she had managed to recruit. Arellia's dark-skinned face looked wan in the dim light of the cavern, but her mouth was set in a determined line nonetheless.

"I will as well!" a young man named Daniel cried out next, followed by three others Midori called friends. Soon, the voices of ten of her friends cried out in her defense, all save Samuel, who remained silent and fuming near the front of the crowd.

The vicars eyed each other apprehensively. "Then begone with you," Solange growled, swatting at the air in disgust, "and may Kax have mercy on all your souls for your treachery!"

The dissidents walked with stilted steps towards Midori, who Kang still held before him near the entrance to the cavern. The rest of those gathered eyed them with distrust and open rancor.

"Take them away," Solange repeated Jessica's demand. "You should be ashamed of yourself, Midori. Thank Kax your mother and father are not alive to witness such blasphemy from their own child!" She offered Midori one last pitying look before turning her back on them all in an act of clear dismissal.

And just like that, Midori and her comrades-in-arms found themselves at the entrance of the mine. They were not allowed back to their rooms to gather any supplies. They were expected to leave their home with nothing. It was more than Midori had expected; she was lucky she at least had her weapons still attached to her belt. The others had nothing but the clothes on their backs.

Kang shoved her roughly across the threshold where the mining tunnels and the outside world met. The others walked away immediately; Midori, instead, paused and turned towards her brother.

"I know you killed him," he spoke in a low tone, eyes locked onto hers. "I know you killed The Augur."

She pursed her lips. "I know."

"And still I thought you would come around, that you would come to see the error of your ways. I was a fool," he snarled, whether angrier with himself or with her, she had no idea.

"You are the fool for believing your plans of vengeance will bear fruit," Midori responded calmly. "Please, Kang, see reason!"

"I do see reason!" he spat, his eyes wild with fervor. "I will not stop until Vidamae and Her priestesses all pay for what they did to us! The church must be reduced to rubble and the high priestess must die, Midori. Perhaps once I kill her, you will see. Perhaps you will finally understand ..."

She shook her head. "We will never be in accord on this, Kang. *Never*." She searched his face, hoping for some flash of sanity, some hesitation or at least an openness to hear her out. But there was nothing there. Nothing but pure hatred.

The Kang she had known and loved was gone.

She started to walk away, but his voice stopped her.

"If I ever see you again," he whispered, "I will kill you."

Midori's steps faltered. She didn't bother turning around.

"I know."

Chapter 46

Prayer

The morning of the prayer or the ritual or whatever it was all the priestesses wanted to do dawned cold and clear. The entire temple was frantic with activity and last-minute preparations. Ghdion, having hardly gotten more than two hours of sleep on the cold stone floor, was kept awake by the dull sounds of booted feet walking back and forth in front of their room all morning.

He tried his hardest not to be in a grumpy mood, mostly for Quay's sake. She looked downright exhausted when he shook her awake shortly after dawn; it was clear from her withdrawn expression that she hadn't gotten much more sleep than he had.

They each took turns getting ready in the tiny, cramped bathroom included in their suite. Quay went first, and while she washed up, Hypnocost swanned around the room, trying to decide what color silk robes he should wear. He made Ghdion hold up a little handheld mirror (did Hypnocost really deem *a mirror* as a necessity to pack?!) as he held up first a violet hued jacket, and then a teal blue, against his bare chest.

"Which is more appropriate for a religious ceremony?" he

wondered aloud. "Is the teal too bold? Or perhaps the purple too regal? I simply cannot decide. Hmmm."

"They're both fine," Ghdion responded without looking. He had long since learned to live with Hypnocost's many eccentricities.

"Perhaps I should stick with my usual gold? That might make me look like I am trying too hard, though ..."

Quay stepped out of the lavatory in a fresh dress of pale pink with flowing skirts that reached the floor, cinched tightly under her bust by a decorative gold cord. As ever, her holy symbol sat prominently against her collarbone; hers was made of simple brass, unlike the elaborate golden and jewel-encrusted things the higher-ranking clergy sported. She was in the middle of trying to wrap her long brown hair, still damp from her washing, around her head in a braided crown.

"Why ... won't ... this ... stay?" she muttered in frustration. She jabbed a few pins into her hair, but the braid kept sliding off to the side.

"Here, let me help." Ghdion shoved the mirror into Hypnocost's hands and ambled over. He took the hair pins from her hand.

She eyed him in surprise. "You ... know how to do hair?"

"I had three daughters," he reminded her, swallowing the lump that suddenly formed in his throat. That always happened whenever he thought of them. "Of course I can do hair."

He deftly twisted her braid so that it sat above her ears, then pushed a couple of strategically placed pins to keep it from falling down again. "Aisling, my oldest, had long hair like this, and she always wanted it in two pigtail braids. I got really good at doing those."

He patted her back to signal that he was done. Hypnocost offered her his mirror; Quay glanced at it to examine his handiwork. "Wow, okay, we can add 'excellent hair braider' to your list of many talents." She beamed at his reflection behind her. "Thank you. That was really sweet."

His face started to heat up, so he turned away. "Yep," he croaked, then cleared his throat. "So. You ready for the big prayer?" he asked as a way to change the subject.

Her shoulders visibly slumped. "I'm not sure if I'll actually be a part of it, to be honest. They had everything assigned before we got here."

"Their loss." He shrugged, pulling off his dirty leather shirt and shoving it into his bag. He badly needed a long, hot bath to wash the road dust from his skin. *Too bad this temple doesn't have a bathhouse like the cathedral,* he ruminated. *I could go have a soak in there instead of watching this farce. What a waste.*

Hypnocost spent so long getting ready that Ghdion only had time to splash some water on his face, brush his teeth, and run a comb through his hair before it was time to go. Quickly he changed into a clean shirt and trousers and buckled his sword across his back.

"Are you really going to need that?" Hypnocost asked, gesturing towards the greatsword. "We are inside a *temple*. I doubt we will run across any bandits or ne'er-do-wells here."

"Don't go anywhere without it if I can help it," was his curt response. That sword had been his constant companion for years. He took it with him everywhere. "Let's go."

The overall atmosphere at the next plenum meeting could only be described as 'weird.'

Avindea strode into the chambers after spending a fitful night not actually sleeping; eventually, she gave it up as fruitless and headed to the training yard outside the barracks to get in some early morning swordwork instead. She was really out of practice since joining the plenum. Before, she used to spend at least two hours a day going over the various sword thrusts and parries and shield maneuvers that were the bread and butter of all paladins' training. Nowadays, she was lucky to get in an hour a week, and it showed; her muscles screamed at her mistreatment and lack of good rest.

The other counselors were already gathered near their assigned spots, all except for the judge, of course.

That was all anyone talked about. Who would replace Judge Rodach? What had he actually done to warrant an arrest? Was he really a traitor? The room was abuzz with rumors and gossip. The Athessian diplomat debacle was nearly forgotten because of it.

Inquisitor Burgindore was there again, sitting lazily in the same spot as before. His huge mastiff was ever at his side. When he caught her eye, he gave her a mock salute and a mysterious smile.

Rendevas was seated when she joined him at the table. He jiggled his leg up and down vociferously, his eyes darting all around the room. "What's got you so agitated?" she asked by way of a greeting.

"What? Oh, hello, Lady Avindea," he said absently. Instead of answering, he kept up his ceaseless scanning of the room.

What's gotten into him? She waved her hand in front of his face to try to grab his attention. "Hello? Are you in there, Rendevas?"

"Yes, yes, sorry," he relented, smiling weakly. "I'm just distracted, is all. I tried to visit the king this morning to talk about Judge Rodach, but the guards turned me away." He sighed. "I think Chancellor Eldivar will reprimand me for this since I didn't go through the proper channels. I know I'm supposed to request through him if I wish to speak with the king, but ..."

"But what?" Avindea asked. She leaned towards him, her curiosity piqued.

"I have some important information that the king should be concerned about," he told her after a split second's pause. "Information Milford provided me."

Avindea scoffed. "You're still working with him?" Her eyes darkened in disappointment as she regarded him. "Rendevas, you're gonna get yourself in trouble if you keep conspiring with these ... these *spies*." She spat the last word out as if it was a curse.

Rendevas kept quiet, his gaze going cloudy as he stared off into the distance.

Uncomfortable with his uncharacteristic solemnity, she asked, "I wonder who Judge Rodach's replacement's gonna be? You think they're gonna be worse than he was?" She scowled, remembering Rodach's acid tongue and extreme rudeness.

"Don't say that!" Rendevas replied. "That's inviting bad fortune!"

"Can't get much worse than him." She rested her elbows on the table and watched the rest of the plenum.

Constable Mald looked diminished without his pal the judge next to him. His large frame was almost too big for his chair, and he looked extremely uncomfortable sitting there alone. With the judge out of the picture, what would Mald's contributions to the plenum look like? It was obvious to everyone that, of the pair of them, the judge was the one with all the brains. Mald was simply the brawn.

Lady Loresh and Lord Eglath sat beside each other, chatting animatedly. Being the representative from the only other church in the city, Avindea felt a certain kinship with them both, though her status as a temporary plenum member prevented her from reaching out.

Commander Rakeld and Lieutenant Orvessa waited silently for the meeting to begin. Both looked tense—well, tenser than usual. Impending war would be enough to make any military leaders anxious, not to mention the toll the conscription announcement had on the general public. It was certainly not a popular ruling by any stretch of the imagination, and they were both to blame for that.

Captain Riluk made his way to his seat, with Lady Uunar close behind him. Avindea overheard some of what they said. "—has a large burn scar down the entire left side of his face," Lady Uunar was in the middle of saying to Riluk. "Does that ring a bell?"

Avin's heart lurched in her chest.

Burn scar? Was Uunar asking about *Lucius*?

"Actually, yes, it does," Riluk told her as he took his seat. "His name is Lucius Trevintor. He's staying at the Cathedral of Vidamae for the time being. Why do you ask?"

Shit shit shit! Why does Uunar wanna know about Lucius?

Lady Uunar's smile was full of wicked glee. "I was just wondering. Don't you find it a bit concerning that there is a known *Athessian* inside the city? I am surprised you aren't more worried."

Riluk replied flatly, "He's been interviewed extensively. I have no reason to suspect him of any wrongdoing, though you are certainly more than welcome to speak with him yourself, if you wish."

"I do have a few questions for him, actually," Uunar said smoothly. "I should be able to speak with him today when I meet with Lady Avindea at the cathedral."

Avin hid her face behind her hand to cover her look of panic. How did Lady Uunar find out about Lucius? What in the hells could she want to question him about?

"Fuck," she murmured under her breath.

"Hmm?" came Rendevas's reply. *Now* he was listening?

"It's nothing."

Chancellor Eldivar finally sailed into the room, looking just as suave and ready for the day as ever. He smiled generously at the assembly as he stepped up to his seat. "Good morning. Hopefully you are all well-rested and ready for this meeting, for we have much to discuss."

He turned towards Riluk. "I'm sure we all heard of the little riot that was quelled yesterday. Do you have any news on that, Captain Riluk?"

The captain scowled. "It's all been taken care of. The instigator is well-known to the guard, a man by the name of Keegan." He glanced over at Lady Uunar. "He's currently in custody at the Arcane Academy. Since he is a dangerous spellcaster himself, we deemed it prudent he remains under Lady Uunar's care."

Lady Uunar inclined her head graciously. "I will make sure he is well-attended to," she said. The wicked grin on her face sent chills down Avindea's spine.

Chancellor Eldivar nodded, then glanced towards the empty seat where the king was supposed to be. Frowning, he said, "King Selderin is not here? That is odd. He is usually so punctual."

The counselors shuffled nervously in their seats. A wiggle of unease burrowed itself into Avindea's mind and took up residence there with the rest of her worries: where was the king? She hadn't been a plenum member for long, but in every meeting she had attended, the monarch and his daughter were always on time, even if they were usually the last to arrive.

She gave a sidelong glance to Rendevas, who wasn't paying attention. He was staring off into space, his thumbnail between his teeth.

"Captain Riluk, would you mind checking on King Selderin for us before we begin?" the chancellor requested. "I would hate for him to miss such an important conference."

"Of course." Riluk stood up and left the room swiftly, his back stiff and straight.

Of course Lucina would give a speech. She never could let a public event go off without a bit of grandstanding.

Quay, Ghdion, and Hypnocost stood with the rest of the crowd. Those poor souls traveled so far to the Altar of Tasuil, for what had been promised to be a life-changing prayer to their beloved Goddess Vidamae, only to be relegated to the outside lawn to watch. Nobody who wasn't already inside the temple or on the grand staircase could see much of anything at all due to the sheer number of bodies, and the only reason they could hear what was said was because of a sound-enhancing spell the clerics cast on the area.

Throngs of pilgrims and acolytes from smaller churches crowded closely together, standing on tiptoes to try to get a better look at the altar. Quay, flanked by Ghdion on one side and Hypnocost on the other, stood on one of the bottommost steps; apparently, it was the closest Lucina's aides could get them after they arrived unexpectedly overnight. They acted as if she should have been grateful for it, too, and she was, but at the same time, she couldn't help but be filled with a supreme sense of disappointment.

This wasn't what the Church of Vidamae was supposed to be about! She'd always been taught that Vidamae was welcoming of all, regardless of social status. Why, then, was her own high priestess acting so arrogantly?

Normally, a grand spectacle such as this would have excited her. Instead, she wished to get it over with it, if only to be on her way back to Praetorius. At least there, she could discuss her next steps with all of her friends present. Maybe Avin would have some ideas ...

She sighed, turning her attention back to the altar. All she could see were the backs of the heads of everyone around her. It was one of the many drawbacks of being so petite. People blocked every which way she tried to look, no matter the angle or how hard she stretched on her tiptoes.

Ghdion, noticing her plight, kneeled down in front of her, holding out his clasped together hands like a makeshift stirrup. "Here," he offered gruffly, meeting her eyes. "Let me boost you up so you can see. You can sit on my shoulders."

"Oh, no, that's fine," she started to refuse, but he just shook his head.

"Don't argue, Priestess. Don't tell me you're more interested in seeing all of these strangers' asses than Lucina's grand speech?" His lip quirked. He mimed holding something on one shoulder and against his neck, as if he was hauling a sack.

Was he teasing her? The terrible/wonderful thing about it was that it worked. No longer daunted at the prospect, she backed up against him until she met the warm, solid expanse of his chest. Kneeling as he was, she could look down behind her right into his startlingly blue eyes. Her breath caught in her throat; she could see his throat bob up and down as he swallowed.

"Ready?" he asked, and without awaiting her response, he swiftly boosted her up onto his right shoulder. She squeaked out a little "oh!" of surprise. Once she was seated, he wrapped his arm around her knees to hold her firmly in place.

She panicked and wrapped her arms around his head; she felt like she was going to tip over backwards! Her flailing arms effectively blinded him.

"Sorry!" she squawked in embarrassment. She'd basically just squashed her not inconsiderable chest right into his face. She patted his head awkwardly as she shifted her weight to keep her balance.

He settled her more comfortably atop his shoulder. Glancing down, she could see he blushed furiously.

"How's that?" he asked. "Can you see better?"

She grinned down at him. "Yes! This is amazing!"

Hypnocost rolled his eyes from beside them. "Can you lift me onto your other shoulder, Ghdion?" he asked in a singsong voice, "or is that spot only reserved for pretty priestesses?"

"I'm not a priestess yet, Hypnocost."

Quay gazed across the sea of people, all eagerly awaiting the start of the ritual. She could see the altar itself, there at the front of the temple. Lucina and Elna and a couple other archpriests she didn't know were gathered there, all wearing simple white robes to denote the purity of their faith. They swapped out their expensive holy symbols for simpler brass ones, similar to what Quay wore around her neck, to symbolize their eschewing of material desires. And lastly, all of them had Vidamae's holy symbol chalked upon their foreheads, to symbolize their undying loyalty to the goddess.

Lucina glided forward. A hush descended over the crowd closest to the altar.

"I think it's starting," Quay informed them.

High Priestess Lucina Balladoni, head of the Cathedral of Vidamae in Praetorius, gazed out at the gathered multitudes and smiled down upon them as a mother would a favorite child. The rest of the crowd quieted as she raised her hands into the air and cried out in her magically enhanced voice, "Good people of Vidamae! I, High Priestess Lucina Balladoni of Praetorius, bid you welcome and well met on this glorious day!"

The crowd cheered, the sound of it rumbling against the marble temple and echoing across the stone walls. Those on the lawn stomped their feet and clapped riotously. It sounded like thunder, loud and deep.

"What is she doing up there?" Hypnocost asked, trying unsuccessfully to get a better look. He was only a few inches taller than Quay, so he had a hard time seeing much of anything.

"Elna and the archpriests are arranging the ritual components," Quay narrated from her perch. "Looks like small bowls of some liquid —probably holy water—sticks of incense, that sort of thing."

Two of the archpriests strode purposefully towards Lucina and stopped a few paces behind her. They each wafted tightly bundled sticks of incense into the air all around her, then stooped to the floor to light a ring of candles around them.

"Many years ago," Lucina continued in her strong voice, "a woman by the name of Tasuil built a symbolic temple, the very same one we gather around today. This momentous event came as a great beacon of light and hope to millions of those who sought a way to connect with Vidamae. As they were seared and slaughtered in the flames of withering injustice, it came as a joyous prayer to end the brutal attacks and murders by the followers of Kax."

"What is this, a history lesson?" Ghdion grumbled. "Just get on with it already."

"Shh!" Quay chided, putting a hand over his mouth to quiet him.

One of the archpriests handed his bowl to Lucina, who took it, held it aloft for all to see, and poured it slowly across the marble dais at her feet. The archpriest backed away with a bowed head.

"Here we gather, we are still not free from harm," Lucina boomed. "Here we gather, the life of the devout still sadly threatened by Kax. Here we gather, exiled from our homes and lands in the hope to find an end to this dreadful situation."

The other archpriest took his turn, handing over the bowl and standing aside as Lucina poured that liquid onto the dais. It wasn't water, but something dark and deep purple, probably a red wine. Elna then took her place behind Lucina, holding a bundle of incense in one hand and a small lit torch in the other.

"But we refuse to believe that the grace of Vidamae has forsaken us." Lucina paused, scanning the assembled masses. "We refuse to believe that there are no longer any rays of hope shining down upon us. And so, we've come to gather at the Temple of Tasuil to ask for the grace and hope of Vidamae, that She will grant us freedom."

Elna stepped directly behind Lucina.

"That she will grant us serenity."

Quay watched Elna shift the bundle of incense in her hands.

"That she will—"

Elna thrust forward against the middle of Lucina's back, cutting off the high priestess's words.

Quay gasped in alarm.

"What happened? Why did she stop?" whispered Hypnocost.

"Oh, fuck," Ghdion groaned, eyes wide.

The crowd witnessed in confusion as the high priestess stumbled forward, clutched her belly, and coughed weakly. The sound echoed loudly and wildly around the temple grounds. A slow stream of red leaked from Lucina's open mouth, a matching blossom of crimson spreading across the middle of her white robes.

"Oh, gods, no!" Quay moaned, bringing a trembling hand to her mouth. "Lucina's been *stabbed!*"

It was many minutes of tense, impatient waiting before Captain Riluk finally returned to the plenum chambers. He strode directly to Chancellor Eldivar, his face stony and impassive, his gait somewhat stilted; Avindea went immediately on high alert. No soldier walked like that unless something was seriously wrong.

He stepped beside the chancellor and leaned down to whisper into the older man's ear. Chancellor Eldivar's face paled considerably. "You're certain?" he muttered behind bloodless lips.

Riluk nodded, then stepped behind him, snapping to attention. "Your orders, sir?" he asked, his voice low and schooled to sound impassive, but Avindea wasn't fooled. That was the voice of a man whose whole world had changed in an instant. He hid his true emotions out of a strict sense of duty.

Chancellor Eldivar cleared his throat once, stood up, and regarded the plenum solemnly. He tried to speak, but no sound came out. He looked bereft, adrift, at a loss for the right words.

Avindea's heart pounded furiously in her chest.

"I have just been informed of some truly terrible news," Chancellor Eldivar finally rasped.

The plenum members awaited the announcement with bated breath.

"King Selderin is dead."

"What the fuck?" Ghdion cried, tightening his grip upon Quay's legs protectively.

"Ghdion!" Quay whispered harshly. The crowd had yet to fully realize what just happened. *Elna just stabbed Lucina!*

"What? Why?" Hypnocost hissed, shifting his pack on his shoulder. The blood font was safely packed inside; he'd agreed with them both when they told him to bring it with him during the ritual casting, as it was too dangerous to leave in their room unattended.

Elna thrust her hand forward into Lucina's back once more, causing another angry red blood stain to appear on the high priestess's belly. The archpriestess threw the stack of incense down onto the dais in disgust, stepping to the side as Lucina stumbled onto one knee. The incense had been hiding the small dagger she clutched in her hand.

The hidden dagger flashed as Elna lifted it to the sky, Lucina's blood dripping from its sharp edge. The torch in her other hand began to flicker and spark before the flames burst upward in a huge rush of power.

"This is the day of our reckoning. I dedicate this death to OUR LADY KAX!" Elna screamed.

Faith and Ruin

Chapter 47

Too Late

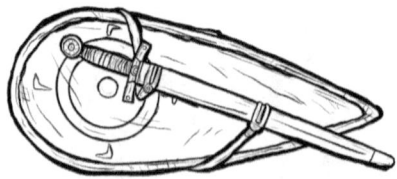

"He's ... dead?" Rendevas blurted uncomprehendingly.

"Yes," Chancellor Eldivar replied in a shaky voice. He burst from his seat, his eyes flashing, and rushed towards the double doors. "I must see this for myself!"

Riluk scrambled after him. Avindea, after a quick internal debate, decided to follow; perhaps King Selderin could be healed? Maybe he wasn't so far gone that a strong healing prayer would be able to save him? She ran out of the chambers, ignoring the shocked looks on the faces of the other counselors.

Down a long hallway and around the corner, Riluk and the chancellor headed into the open door to the king's private chambers. Two guards stood watch outside, looking unsure of what to do.

The three plenum members hurried inside. Avindea had never been inside the king's bedroom; it was less extravagant than she imagined. It looked like any typical nobleman's room ...

Except for all the blood.

It was ... a mess. The king's body was on its side, as if he had tried to get out of the bed after he was attacked. Blood soaked the blankets beneath him and dripped into a spreading pool on the rug. Was there a struggle? Had it taken him long to die, or was it quick? Avindea winced and turned away, trying to will away those dark thoughts.

Chancellor Eldivar rushed over, Avin right behind him. He placed his hands gently upon the king's neck and checked for a pulse; Avindea called forth the golden glow of her healing, a gift from Vidamae Herself for Her paladins.

"Do something!" the chancellor hissed, his voice cracking. "You're a paladin, heal him!"

She knew it would be futile just from looking at the body. There was so much blood ... A deep, gory gash sliced from one side of his neck to the other. Whoever did this had been thorough. "It's too late," she whispered, her glowing hands hovering over the wound. "He's been dead too long for me to do anything, Chancellor. I'm sorry."

Riluk stood silently near the doorway. Chancellor Eldivar leaned back on his heels and rubbed his hands across his thighs. "Riluk!" he snapped, "did you not check for vitals when you discovered him like this?!"

Riluk's dark eyebrows raised, wrinkling his forehead. "No, Chancellor, I wanted to alert you to the situation immediately."

The chancellor's mouth dropped open. "What is wrong with you?!" he gasped. "You could have saved him! You could have—"

"It wouldn't have mattered," Avindea cut in softly. "He's been dead for hours, chancellor. No amount of ... of healing or medical attention will make a difference."

Avindea could see the two guards who had been stationed at the door surreptitiously peek inside. Three other people crowded the open doorway: Lord Eglath, Lady Loresh, and Lady Uunar. They must've left the plenum chambers to come investigate. All looked on in horror.

Chancellor Eldivar glanced up, caught them watching, and scowled deeply. "Don't just stand there gawping!" he berated them. "Captain Riluk, secure the city gate and the capitol immediately. Lord Eglath, take the two guards there so they can be questioned."

Lord Eglath's mouth dropped open and his bearded face paled, but he didn't argue. He just did as he was told.

"One of you there, Lady Loresh, fetch a doctor. We will need an autopsy immediately."

Lady Loresh nodded sharply before she strode away.

"The rest of you, quit loitering and go back to the plenum chambers! We will discuss this in an emergency meeting as soon as possible!"

Captain Riluk rushed back to the council chambers, ostensibly to summon both Commander Rakeld and Lieutenant Orvessa to help secure the city. Avindea, glancing once more upon King Selderin's unmoving form, felt an overwhelming sense of dread mixed with unreality. Was this really happening? King Selderin was *actually dead?*

Who murdered him? And why?

Faith and Ruin

She didn't look back as she left. Instead, she took deep, steadying breaths as she strode purposely down the corridor and back into the council chambers. Panic settled in her chest. If she wasn't careful, it could overwhelm her. She used an old soldier's trick to settle her nerves: take stock of the surroundings, take three deep breaths, count to ten, and refocus.

She looked at each of the plenum members still there in the chambers. Constable Mald stood up and began to pace, his face emotionless but his body language broadcasting his agitation. He stalked over to Rakeld, Orvessa, and Riluk as they finished their mini conference; they quietly discussed heated plans to close the gate, secure the walls with soldiers, institute martial law ... it was all very serious.

Lady Uunar, recently returned herself, silently watched them all, her eyes narrowed, her face more brooding than sorrowful.

The inquisitor remained seated next to his dog Monty, taking it all in with a cool serenity Avindea couldn't help but envy. He scribbled copious notes upon the parchment held in his lap as Monty panted quietly beside him.

Okay, three deep breaths, she told herself. *One ... two ... three breaths... and refocus.*

It helped. She felt much calmer, less jumpy and overwhelmed. She turned to Rendevas, who she had forgotten to check out during the first part of her little ritual. He sat stock still next to her, his face wan and mouth rigid with shock.

"Rendevas, are you okay?" she murmured, placing a hand on his forearm. He was so tense, she could feel his tendons through his shirtsleeves.

He didn't answer her. His teeth were clenched, and his eyes were fixed upon some unseen point far away.

The king's death must have rattled him more than she realized. She patted his arm sympathetically. "It's gonna be okay, Rendevas," she murmured.

She realized as she spoke the words just how empty they were. Did she really believe that? Would they be okay? Would anyone?

Rendevas didn't acknowledge her. She was left with her own dark thoughts, wondering, as she walked away, just what this latest catastrophe would mean for Praetorius's future.

Epilogue

Rendevas allowed himself five minutes of mourning. He let the waves of pain and sorrow and overwhelming anxiety wash over him, the ebbs and flows of grief taking his breath away.

He was only vaguely aware of Avindea patting his arm in sympathy. After a moment of quiet, she stood up and walked away, leaving him alone at the plenum table.

He closed his eyes and took a deep breath through his nose. *King Selderin, one of my oldest friends ... dead.*

A lifetime of memories threatened to overwhelm him, glimpses of their time together before his ascension, when King Selderin was just plain Philemon Selderin, known as Phil to his friends. Back when Phil was the chancellor and Rendevas a simple scribe. Their late nights at The Murky Bard, sharing drinks and swapping gossip. When Phil met Brina and became completely enamored with her, and their marriage not long after. The sharp pang of jealousy and regret each time he thought of Brina and Phil, together ...

That's enough, he told himself. *That is all the time I can allow myself for grief. Now it's time to get to work.*

He stood up, adjusted the lapel of his immaculate black brocade doublet, and strode out of the room.

He went to the king's private chambers first, where servants and guards hurried about in a flurry of activity in the corridor. Chancellor Eldivar oversaw it all, barking out instructions like a drill sergeant.

Rendevas caught the eye of one of the servants, a willowy, dark-haired woman by the name of Verochka; she hustled over, holding a bundle of soiled linens in her arms. Was that Selderin's blood he spied on the edge of the fabric?

He leaned in towards her and whispered, "I have a favor to ask you," and then, more loudly, "When you are finished here, could you send someone to the plenum chambers? Constable Mald has requested refreshments."

The other servants shot Rendevas nasty glares; he just shrugged, trying to make himself look contrite. Constable Mald had asked no such thing, of course, but he couldn't have the other servants overhearing him. Once he was sure they were sufficiently annoyed and not paying attention, he hurriedly murmured his request to Verochka, who nodded sharply and walked briskly past him.

He stepped up to Chancellor Eldivar next. "Has anyone seen to the princess?" he asked.

The chancellor wouldn't even look at him. He was too busy watching the servants intently as they cleaned King Selderin's room. "Not yet, no," he answered distractedly. "She has her personal guard, of course. Why don't you check on her, Rendevas? As you can see, I have my hands full here." He waved Rendevas away as if he were nothing more than a fly buzzing about his head.

Excellent. The diplomat nodded, even though the chancellor couldn't see. He turned on his heel and walked purposefully across the corridor to Princess Alandria's private chambers.

Her door was open, her personal guard standing at attention just outside. He glimpsed her within, sitting at her desk; her hands gripped the edges so tightly, he could see the whites of her knuckles. She stared unblinking into nothingness.

Oh, you poor child, he thought. He wanted nothing more than to wrap her into an embrace, but that would be highly inappropriate. Being the princess meant that, even though she was suddenly and violently now an orphan, she was not allowed any comfort.

The guard did not stop him from entering, so he strode right over to her and knelt at her side.

The princess glanced towards him. "Lord Rendevas," she greeted with a slight waver to her voice. "Have you come with more news from the plenum?" Her face was drawn, though her eyes remained clear. No tears had been shed, not yet. Those would come later.

"No," Rendevas answered her. "I came to check on you."

She looked at him then, *really* looked at him. He could read slight shock in her eyes, as well as sorrow and a glint of rage that took him aback. She looked so much like her mother in that moment that it made his breath catch in his throat.

"Why did this happen?" she whispered hesitantly, as if she feared the answer. "Who could do something so heinous?"

He took a beat before responding. "I ... I do not know, Your Highness," he admitted. "Rest assured, the plenum will do whatever it can to get to the bottom of this." He itched to take her hand in his. "Your safety is our top priority. We will make sure nothing happens to you while we investigate your father's death. We will find who did this."

She nodded. A coldness crossed her features, visible in the set of her shoulders, in the bright glints of anger in her eyes. "We will find them," she repeated. "And I will make them pay."

Rendevas blinked. That was ... certainly not what he was expecting her to say. A chill ran down his spine.

She watched him silently. That rage he spotted solidified into determination. She brought her hands down from where they clutched at the edge of the table and clasped them tightly in her lap. "My father, he ... he is—*was*—always so busy, always so worried about the ruling of this place."

She wrangled her hands in her lap, as if grappling with how to get her point across. She spun the golden signet ring on her left pointer finger back and forth, back and forth with her thumb. "He didn't spend much time with me, not as I got older. There was always something, meetings he had to attend, my lessons, tutoring ..."

She paused. Instead of hurrying to fill the silence, he remained quiet to allow her a moment to gather her thoughts.

Finally, she met his gaze. "What was my mother like?" she blurted. "He never spoke of her," she rushed, as if afraid he would deny her the information. "And none of my servants were around when she was alive. You knew her, right, Lord Rendevas? Can you tell me what she was like?"

There was a need in her voice that nearly broke his heart. "I knew her very well," he replied softly. He knew her maybe even better than her own husband had. "You remind me a lot of her, you know. She had a fire about her, one that drew people to her like moths to the flame." His eyes took on a faraway cast. "She was magnetic. Spunky. Self-assured. She—"

He stopped, seeing a look of confusion cross the princess's face. *Careful*, he thought. *You are starting to wax poetic.*

"Ah, well, she was beloved by all who knew her," he finished lamely. "As I am sure you will be, as well, Your Highness."

"So I will be queen then?" she asked, her gaze sharpening.

Rendevas blinked. "I ... I confess, I do not actually know." He shrugged. "As you are not yet of age, I would assume leadership will pass to Chancellor Eldivar. I'm sure it's all written into our laws." He eyed her with concern. "I would imagine it will be the topic of discussion at our next plenum meeting."

Princess Alandria sat up straighter. "I will need you to find out." Her lips pursed and her brow furrowed. It was a look Brina had when she had made her mind up about something, one Rendevas remembered well. His heart lurched; he had to swallow the sudden lump in his throat.

"Thank you for checking on me," she inclined her head graciously. "It was kind of you to think of me, Lord Rendevas."

It was a clear dismissal. The last thing he wanted to do was leave her alone after such a traumatic shock, but it was clear she no longer wished for his presence. He stood up, bowed low at the waist, but hesitated before leaving.

"Your Highness," he began, struggling to find the right words. "I ... you can ... I hope you know, that ... should you have need of anything, anything at all," he spoke earnestly, "you can come to me."

She watched him solemnly. "Thank you, Lord Rendevas, I appreciate that."

How could he make her understand without words? He offered her a weak smile. "Good day, Princess." Without another word, he turned on his heel and walked stiltedly out of her room.

Surely the turmoil of his emotions must be evident on his face! The guilt he felt, the wretchedness ... But the guard barely gave him a second glance as he passed. It was business as usual for him.

But for Rendevas, and by extension, the rest of the plenum, and all of Praetorius? Things were about to drastically change. Whether for good or ill remained to be seen.

End of Book One of Faith and Ruin

Thank you so much for reading!

If you at all enjoyed this book, we would love if you left a review! Reviews help indie authors get seen, and the more people who see and read our books, the more we are able to write them for you. More traction equals more sales, and more sales equals more ability for us to continue doing what we love.

Reviews are absolutely the best thing you can do for your favorite indie authors. If this book made you feel something—anything!—please consider reviewing on sites like Goodreads, Storygraph, Fable, and of course, Amazon.

We appreciate you so much!

Acknowledgements, written mostly by Amanda because she yaps a lot:

You've made it this far? Oh my gosh, I love you. You are my people. I can't believe there are people—strangers, even!—who took the time to actually *read our book*. This is insane to me. Thank you so much for being here. I hope you'll stick around to see what else we have planned for these characters who we love and also torture a little bit, all in the name of good storytelling.

This whole story wouldn't even be here if it wasn't for the original DnD group who played through the—admittedly much changed for the sake of the novel—original campaign all those years ago. Colin,

Trav, and Casey, thanks for sharing your time and your characters with us at our table, complete with pizza, pop, chips and salsa. And dice. Soooo many dice. DnD has been so much fun with you guys, and we wouldn't have it any other way. We can't forget Bret, either, who was a part of the first part of this campaign. Between the six of us, we made something fun and exciting together.

(Except for when I forgot to add my proficiency bonus to my attack rolls *for months*. I never said I was *good* at DnD.)

(And Colin, I *super* hope you are chill with how I handled Hypnocost and Rendevas. Just little tweaks, right? It's a testament to your excellent character creation skills that we loved them both enough to keep them in this iteration of the story.)

To the beta readers who got all the way through this absolute chonk of a book: we cannot thank you enough. Your comments were insightful and helpful and so appreciated. So thank you to Courtney "Beefy" Karkkainen, Calli Arena, Adam "Mr. Beef" Karkkainen, and Aiden Blumberg. It's nice knowing you're in our corner.

To our editor, Anna P, this from Amanda specifically: I love you so much. You're stuck with me forever. I mean that as an affectionate threat. This book would suck so much without your encouragement, guidance, sass, and eyebrow wiggle gifs.

Also from Amanda: to my biggest online cheerleaders and some of the coolest, best friends I've ever had the pleasure of meeting: Fox Emm, Joy Peregrine, KH Anastasia, and Mo Luchessi. I love you so much. I don't think I could have gotten as far as I have without your encouragement and willingness to listen to me whine all the time. (And Fox, specifically, you cheerfully becoming my official Patreon manager is a delight. Here's hoping we can actually go to that Sleep Token concert together soon.) You four know the unique challenges that come with writing books and trying to market as indies on social media, and it's life-saving to have people to talk to about the stress of it all. You make me feel less alone.

And of course, thank you, readers, for taking a chance on us newbie authors! Here's hoping for many more acknowledgements pages in the future. We have *plans*. We hope you'll stick around; it's gonna be a wild and bumpy but ultimately satisfying ride!

About the Authors

Rory and Amanda Webb are the husband and wife team behind Faith and Ruin. Married since 2006, they both graduated from Grand Valley State University, Rory with a Bachelor of Arts in Film and Video Production, and Amanda with a Bachelor of Arts in Art and Design. They reside in Grand Rapids Michigan with their three kids, lazy rescue dog, and basement full of old action figures, eccentric movie props, and vintage video games.

Also by Amanda and Rory Webb

Faith and Ruin: Eye of the Maelstrom (Book 2 of Faith and Ruin)

The Problem With Pigs

In the Shade of the Elderwood Tree (Novelette published as part of She Was Monstress Volume 2)

www.ingramcontent.com/pod-product-compliance
Lightning Source LLC
LaVergne TN
LVHW040034080526
838202LV00045B/3340